THE
SECRETS
OF
BRIDGEWATER
BAY

THE
SECRETS
OF
BRIDGEWATER
BAY

JULIE BROOKS

REVIEW

First published in 2021
by HEADLINE REVIEW
An imprint of HEADLINE PUBLISHING GROUP

1

Cataloguing in Publication Data is available from the British Library

ISBN Hardback 978 1 4722 7913 2
ISBN Trade Paperback 978 1 4722 7914 9

Typeset in Minion Pro by Avon DataSet Ltd, Arden Court,
Alcester, Warwickshire

Printed and bound in Great Britain by Clays Ltd, Elcograf S.p.A.

HEADLINE PUBLISHING GROUP
An Hachette UK Company
Carmelite House
50 Victoria Embankment
London EC4Y 0DZ

www.headline.co.uk
www.hachette.co.uk

For my grandmothers,
Rose and Ivy

Prologue

Rose scrambled down the bank in a storm of sand, arms flailing and legs protesting. Funny how her legs didn't work as well as they had once. Inside she still felt like the girl who had landed on these shores forty years ago, yet her body resembled an old woman's more each year. Sometimes, catching a flicker reflected in a window, she didn't recognise herself.

Reaching level ground, she shook the sand from her shoes, before settling the canvas hold-all on her shoulder and looking up to see the bay spread before her like a half-moon of glittering blue, Cape Bridgewater jutting into the ocean to the west with rugged Cape Nelson and its lighthouse rising to the east. The bay was fringed with two and a half miles of white beach, the surf rolling in long easy lines to the shore. Yet beneath those lazy breakers strong currents swirled, while sudden waves could trap unwary swimmers.

Keeping to the firmer sand to conserve energy, she set out for Cape Nelson. The further she trudged the less likely she would be spotted by a farmer herding sheep on the grassy headland or the occasional motorist exploring this wild strip of coast. But the sand was hard going, sucking at her feet so that she felt each of her sixty-four years. After half an hour, she reached a point in

1

the shadow of Cape Nelson where rocks invaded the beach and dense scrub defended the foreshore. Here was as good a place as any. She didn't need to take a moment to reconsider for she'd had more than forty years to think about this.

Traipsing to the high-tide line, she placed her bag upon the sand before turning to the sea. Then, without removing her brown loafers, she braced herself for the cold waters of the Southern Ocean in midwinter. The water was icy, filling her shoes and needling her skin through her stockings. As she waded deeper, the wet wool of her pleated skirt belled around her, water creeping up her torso and soaking her twinset. She sucked in her breath, cold piercing her lungs. When the breakers hit she held her ground, letting the first waves wash over her, foaming to her chin. Then, abandoning her shoes, she struck out in a slow crawl, the way Jim had taught her all those years ago, shocked that his new bride couldn't swim. She wore almost as many clothes then as she did now, the woollen swimming costume they had purchased in Portland weighing her down even as the saltwater bore her aloft.

Not far enough yet.

She continued swimming, arms crawling feebly through the water, legs barely kicking. Each breath became more laboured than the last. The cold tightened her chest in its vicelike grip. Soon she could no longer feel her fingers and her clothes were dragging her beneath the waves.

Never mind. It wouldn't be long now.

1

Port Fairy, Victoria

2016

It's easy to forget the good things, but the bad have a way of staying with you forever. Molly eyed the roll-top desk waiting patiently in one corner, wondering if she could leave it until tomorrow. As a child she had often sat there, creating crayon masterpieces for her grandmother, yet here she was ruthlessly sorting through Nan's life. It was only months since she had last seen her and already she barely recalled her laugh. She could picture her soft powdery face, the coral lipstick bleeding into the fine lines frilling her mouth, but she couldn't hear her. Nan's voice had faded into eternity.

Running her hands through a thicket of sticky chestnut hair, she rolled her neck, inhaled deeply, and blinked to clear her eyes. Dust motes stirred up by the unaccustomed activity floated in the last rays of sunlight and the air was thick with memories. The desk was the last remaining item in the room to be cleared, but it had been a long day immersed in a jumble of cartons brimming with newspaper-shrouded knick-knacks, and she was exhausted.

'Do you want me to make a start on the desk?' she said, turning to her mother.

'Thanks, sweetie, I'll finish up with the bookcase and we can call it a day.'

Picking her way through boxes, she crossed to the desk, her eyes drawn to a hand-tinted photograph stuck to one of the pigeonholes. She had never seen it before. A studio portrait of two boys wearing crisp cotton shirts, hair slicked to their scalps, with a small girl in a smocked dress and patent-leather shoes posed on a chair between them. The boys had laid protective hands upon the girl's shoulders, making Molly momentarily wish she had brothers.

'Is this Nan? With Great-Uncles Ted and Harry?' she asked, prising the photograph from the desk and waving it in her mother's direction.

'I wondered what happened to that,' said Wendy. 'It used to be mounted in a perfectly hideous frame on the mantlepiece at Wuurnong.'

'Can I keep it?' She liked the idea of seeing her grandmother in a new light, a reminder that she had once been young enough to have big brothers.

'Sure. I have others. Remember that one of her on a bicycle? She was about sixteen, with a boy and a picnic basket . . . and the boy wasn't your grandfather. It's hard to believe.'

'What – the bicycle, the boy or the basket?'

'I think they came as a package.'

'I wonder if Pop was jealous.' Molly couldn't imagine her grandmother with anyone other than her grandfather, but if you had asked her twelve-year-old self to imagine her mother with anyone other than her father she would have laughed in your face. Yet Wendy and Leo had been married for ten years now.

'It's all ancient history, isn't it?' Wendy mused.

'Not so ancient.'

'I suppose you just have to get on with it.'

Placing the photograph in her to-keep box, Molly rifled through sheaves of paper stowed in various pigeonholes, discarding fliers for discount toiletries and window-cleaning services, before spying the yellow-and-white gridded cover of a Spirax sketchbook. She slid the dog-eared book from its shelf, placing it on the desk to flip through the first pages. To her surprise, rather than drawings, she found pages filled with yellowed newspaper clippings, the brown stains of ancient glue seeping through the headlines.

MISSING PRESUMED DROWNED
LOCAL WOMAN FEARED DROWNED
SURF TAKES ANOTHER LIFE
SEARCH CONTINUES FOR MISSING WOMAN . . .

Intrigued, she flicked back to the beginning, scanning the text of the first clipping, where a notation '5 August 1963' had been written alongside in a younger, neater version of her grand-mother's shaky handwriting.

A woman is missing, feared drowned, after her car was found abandoned at Bridgewater Bay by a local farmer about noon yesterday. The car, a late model green Holden belonged to Bessiebelle local, Rose Turner . . .

'Granny Rose,' she whispered, surprised to see the name of the great-grandmother who had died long before she was born.

'What about Granny Rose?' asked Wendy, looking up from a box of books that were destined for the local charity store.

'Nan's got all these clippings about Granny Rose. Did you know about this?'

'What? No.' Wendy levered herself up from the floor with a groan and came to stand at her daughter's shoulder.

'Look at this.' Molly flipped through pages, the news articles becoming shorter and shorter until they shrivelled to the size of a postage stamp. 'Not just news clippings but personal notices from all over Australia.'

MISSING PERSONS
TURNER, ROSE – Would any person claiming to be, or knowing the whereabouts of, Rose Turner, wife of Jim Turner of Wuurnong, via Bessiebelle, please contact Brown Day Solicitors of Collins Street, Melbourne. Reward.

Personal notices, dozens of them, all annotated with the names of regional and major newspapers, with dates ranging from the 1960s to the 1980s. In some cases, names and phone numbers had been written alongside, mostly struck out.

She heard a soft intake of breath and her mother's voice at her shoulder saying, 'I had no idea. All these years . . . I had no idea she was searching. I had no idea she thought Rose might still be alive.'

Molly took a step back, turning to face Wendy, whose eyes unexpectedly welled with tears.

'I thought she'd accepted Rose's disappearance like everyone else,' her mother continued.

'You told me Granny Rose drowned.' After years of practice she could finally utter the word without a wobble.

'She did. At least that's what we thought. Her car was found out near Cape Bridgewater, and some of her clothing washed ashore later. But the body was never recovered.'

'Didn't the police investigate?' Molly pictured sombre police, armed with notepads, and armies of volunteers combing the deserted sands of distant beaches.

'I remember a lot of hushed voices. And once, a police car appeared at Wuurnong while Mum and I were there. She tended to shoo your uncle and me out when the talk got maudlin.'

Wendy studied the newspaper clipping as if it might reveal something unexpected.

'There would have been a coroner's report surely?'

'Apparently, she often took herself off to the beach so it wasn't out of character. I suppose if the police weren't suspicious, the coroner simply declared her missing, presumed drowned.'

'Poor Nan, she must have felt bereft. She obviously felt she couldn't talk about it,' said Molly.

'Dad would have known. She wouldn't have kept a secret like that from him.'

'But then Pop always went along with her. About everything,' said Molly. She bit her lip, hesitating a moment before adding, 'Do you think it might have been suicide?'

'I don't know. The story they gave your uncle and me was that she went swimming alone in the sea and . . .' Wendy shrugged. 'Anyway, after a while I didn't give it much thought. Everyone seemed to accept that she was gone, so your Uncle Craig and I followed suit.'

But it seemed that one person at least had never stopped looking. One person believed that, for whatever reason, Granny Rose might be leading another life altogether, somewhere far from home.

'Oh, Mum, all that grief and you never said a word.' Wendy shook her head, frowning at the tiny notice clipped from a newspaper fifty years before, somewhere on the other side of the country.

That was the thing, though; words didn't help so much with pain, as Molly knew from experience. Maybe the only way Nan could deal with her mother's suicide was by pretending that it hadn't happened. If Rose was merely missing, there was always a chance she might return.

'Here, you take a look,' she said, suddenly worn out by the sad, flimsy book and everything it didn't say. She picked up the tattered Spirax from the desk, but as she passed it to her mother, an envelope fluttered to the floor. They both stood looking down, surprised to see Molly's name scrawled on the envelope in Nan's shaky block letters.

'It's not going to levitate.'

'I know that, Mum.'

'Don't you want to know what's inside?'

'Not really.' Molly wasn't fond of surprises. But she retrieved the envelope, sliding from it a sheet of lavender notepaper folded around what appeared to be another old photograph. 'Is this Granny Rose?' she asked, handing the picture to her mother.

Wendy squinted, holding it as far from her face as her arm allowed. 'I'm not sure. It's a bit blurred.'

'It's your vision that's blurred. I don't know why you don't wear your glasses. You can't see your dinner properly without them.'

'I know what's on my plate because I usually cooked it.'

'You're just vain, Mum, admit it.'

She peered over her mother's shoulder at the photograph.

Two young women stood shoulder-to-shoulder, arms linked at the elbow. One girl had stowed her hand in the pocket of her long white apron and the other girl's hand had snuck into the pocket alongside it. Both wore old-fashioned nursing uniforms: long sleeves with elbow-length protective covers, high-necked dresses with stiff white collars, full-length aprons with large crosses appliquéd on to the chest. White cloths tied at the nape covered their hair, a few curls escaping at the foreheads. Molly recognised the First World War uniforms, probably British VAD nurses.

Her mother was right. One girl's face was slightly blurred, as if she had lifted her chin at the last moment, her eyes shifting slightly to the right of the camera. Her eyes were light coloured, blue or perhaps green. Her complexion was fair, her lips small and neat, parted as if in surprise. The other girl stared straight out, her face arranged primly except for her mouth, which was curved in a half-smile. She shared her friend's fair complexion but her face was less open, her mouth tilted. As if she had a secret. Her apron was also crumpled and Molly detected the smudges of stains, as if she hadn't been able to wash out the sad reminders of her work even when making a special trip to the photographer's studio with its painted backdrop and potted palm.

Wendy turned the photograph over to read aloud the words penned in faded blue on the rear, 'Rose and Ivy 1917', and beneath them a photographer's stamp, 'Catford Brothers, Ilfracombe. Copies may be had any time.' Below that, scrawled in a more haphazard hand, were the words 'Together forever'.

What could the words signify? Those captured hands, entwined forever? And what had caught the first girl's attention so unexpectedly that she had turned her head away from the camera.

'We didn't talk about her much after she disappeared,' Wendy mused. 'But your nan told me once that she'd sailed from England to be married not long after the end of the First World War.'

'She was a war bride?' Molly wondered what else no one had mentioned about her great-grandmother. And she thought she knew all the family stories, had researched the hell out of them in high school.

'Not exactly. According to your nan, she didn't meet Granddad Jim until she arrived here. It was a love affair by correspondence.'

Why would Rose have left everything she knew for a life so far from home, with a man she could only imagine from words inscribed on paper? What if everything had gone horribly wrong and she was stranded alone, six weeks away by sea? Molly was still reeling since her own relationship had ended, struggling to sleep without Matt hogging the quilt beside her, neglecting to forward his mail just so she could see his name on the envelope leaning against the fruit bowl. What if she had sailed to the other side of the world and been abandoned?

'Perhaps they were sisters,' she mused, thinking for a moment of her sister Daisy, half a world away yet barely a day going by without some form of communication pinging between them.

'I don't think she had any sisters,' said Wendy. 'I've never actually seen a picture of her before.'

'Not even a wedding photo?'

'Nothing. Mum didn't know much about her childhood either. It seems odd now, doesn't it? I mean, we take photographs of our brunch.'

It was almost as if Rose hadn't existed before she came to Wuurnong, or hadn't wanted to be reminded of her former existence. She had survived a world war and a pandemic. Maybe she was burdened with too much sadness to lug it all the way from England. Molly held on to her own memories with a death grip, but some people would do anything to forget. And yet . . . Rose couldn't quite let go of her memories. She had kept this one photograph.

'Any time someone took a family photo, Granny Rose would wriggle out of it. She was a tough old bird, your great-grandmother.'

'I wish I'd known her. Maybe she could have taught me a thing or two.'

'Oh, I think you inherited that gene already,' said Wendy. 'Even as a two year old you had a will of steel. You used to stand on your chair when we tried to get you to eat your vegetables. Your little legs were so stiff there was no way we could get you to sit down without hurting you.'

Molly might not remember standing on chairs but she remembered how strong willed she had been. 'I remember.'

Wendy reached out a hand towards her daughter that Molly

avoided by deciding to read her grandmother's note. 'Let's see what Nan has to say,' she said, scanning her grandmother's handwriting silently.

My dearest Molly,

I've debated asking this of you because I know you've never recovered from your father's death and I don't want to burden you with my ancient losses. But I would like to know before I go, what happened to my mother Rose. The trail is long cold but you're the historian of the family and you might have more success now with the Internet and everything. I've never been able to accept that she drowned herself. She was too strong, too stubborn. And she wasn't a woman to take chances with the ocean either. If she left us deliberately, she would have had her reasons.

I enclose a photograph I found recently, hidden behind a portrait of my brothers and me. Perhaps it will offer a clue. I know it's a great deal to ask. An impossible task, but if you could only find out what happened to her, where she went, well . . . it would set my mind at rest.

The letter ended there. Perhaps Nan had second thoughts about her request. Or perhaps she simply ran out of time. Anyway, it made no difference now. Looking for a woman who disappeared more than fifty years ago was a pointless exercise – and Molly wasn't a professional historian, she was a teacher. She had made that choice years ago, opting for a career of fifteen-year-old boys fizzing with testosterone and bored thirteen-year-olds glued to their mobile phones instead of the more uncertain path into research and academia.

Refolding the letter, she stuffed it into her jeans pocket before glancing across at her mother who was still staring at the photograph. She seemed as if she were searching for something she had lost.

'What are you looking for?'

'I was just wondering how she got there.'

'Australia?'

'No, there . . . at the end of her life in that lonely car park by the beach. Here she is with her face unlined, her life untravelled. Yet when I knew her she was a cranky old woman before her time. How did she get there? How do any of us get there?'

'Stop being so maudlin,' Molly said, giving her mother a hug. She had never thought of her as old, but clearly Nan's death had jolted her.

'She was the same age as I am now, when she disappeared.'

'You've got a lot of life left in you. Besides, you know what they say: "Fifty is the new forty, and sixty is the new fifty".'

'Tell that to the doctor next time she nags me about my cholesterol.'

'Well, you should listen to her.'

'Never mind. What did Nan's note say?'

Molly glanced at the photograph in her mother's hand. There was so much strength in those linked arms. The girls didn't know it then but there was a century of massive change coming. Yet together they looked like they could face whatever the world had in store. What could have driven a young woman like Rose to erase her entire past? Except for this one photograph.

She recognised her grandmother's urge to cling to her clippings and her keepsakes.

To save a voice message long after the person who left it has gone. To continue searching when everyone else has given up. So you don't have to relinquish that last fragile connection, no matter how much it hurts. For pain has to be better than nothing.

'She wants me to find out what happened to Rose.'

2

North Devon

1906

According to Rose, the south lawn was so named because it was on the south side of the house, but Ivy called it the sunny lawn because the house's long shadow never crossed it. Not like the other side, where tall shadows shuttered the yard and giant walls locked people out. She was waiting for Rose near the lake at the bottom of the south lawn. They were going fishing with the butterfly net Master Robert had given his sister for her eighth birthday. Actually, Ivy wasn't supposed to be playing by the lake; she was supposed to be walking straight home from school, not dawdling for a moment. She wasn't supposed to be playing with Rose either, except when the big house had a party for everyone on the estate. Then it was all right, Ma said, because the Luscombes had a duty. But Rose was her best friend and she was Rose's best friend and nothing could come between them. They had spat on it.

Rose wasn't allowed to play by the lake either. She was supposed to be in the nursery learning her times tables but Miss Sarah always rested at three o'clock, asleep in her chair by the nursery fire, and Mrs Luscombe would be in her boudoir having her first cocktail of the day. Rose didn't have a father but she did have a pony with long eyelashes that snorted into your hand and snuffled at your apron pocket for apples. She had a dress for each day of the week, three pairs of good shoes and two pairs of boots. Once she had snuck Ivy into the big house to play in her room, where the walls were papered with stripes, lace curtains hung at the windows and dozens of ribbons lay wound into neat rolls in a box on the dresser.

Soon enough Rose appeared, skipping across the lawn in full view of the house, dipping and twirling the butterfly net about her head. Ivy hoped no one was watching, for the house had rows of windows like eyes. Behind the heavy curtains there were so many possibilities for betrayal: housemaids in frilly white caps, a footman in knife-edged trousers and Greep, the butler, who spoke with a voice like gravel. Worst of all, if word got back to her da, she would soon find out about it.

'Look what I caught!' called Rose, holding the net under Ivy's nose so that she peered into it, expecting to see one of the orange butterflies that sunned themselves in the park.

'I can't see anything.'

'Look closer.'

She bent further so that her face almost disappeared into the net. 'Maybe it flew away.' She was about to raise her head skywards, searching for the elusive butterfly, when Rose jerked the net up and over, capturing her so that only her plait escaped.

'You! I caught you!' she laughed.

Ivy joined in the laughter. It was true. She had been caught by Rose's trick, as surely as she was always caught up in her antics. Her friend's pranks were like her, full of fun and mischief and easy to forgive. Rose released the net's handle and Ivy straightened, the net covering her face so that she saw the world through a gauzy haze, thin white bars criss-crossing her view of the wide green lawn, like a fence to keep her out.

'If I set you free will you fly away?'

'Not without you,' she laughed.

'Come on then, let's see who can catch the first fish.' Rose released her and they swooped towards the lake.

The lake was Ivy's favourite place in the whole world. It had its own jetty, where a rowing boat bobbed, and a bridge with five arches. A gravel path wound around the shore, snaking between a jumble of rocks called 'the ruin' at one end and circling 'the folly' at the other. The Luscombe's lake was bigger than the village duck pond but smaller than the angry sea where Ma once took her for a picnic. Lilies floated on the water, their leaves as large as dinner plates. Sometimes she and Rose played tea parties, piling the leaves with rosehips and acorns, chestnuts and flower buds.

Yesterday they had sat on the jetty with a fishing pole fashioned from a length of bamboo, pilfered from the potting shed, and a ball of yarn from the housekeeper's mending basket. They had baited it with poached haddock from Rose's breakfast and sat on the jetty until the sun was almost touching the treetops. Rose was certain she felt a nibble, but when they pulled up the soggy grey yarn the haddock was gone – and so was their catch. That was when she had the brilliant idea of turning her butterfly net into a fishing net. After all, the fish wouldn't know the difference.

Rose sat on a flat rock at the water's edge, unbuttoning her boots and rolling down her stockings.

'Come along, take off your boots,' she said. Then she stood up, staring with dismay at her dress. Long bell-shaped sleeves ended in tight cuffs at her wrists. A white satin sash belted yards of material at her hips so that the skirt gathered into a huge flounce below her knees, and an enormous collar flapped on her shoulders. Ivy thought her friend might fly away if the wind caught the collar just right.

'I can't go fishing like this.'

Ivy longed for a dress like that but conceded it wouldn't do for fishing. Miss Sarah would know they had been up to no good as soon as she spied its wet skirts.

'You could tie it up at the sides, that's what Ma does when she scrubs floors.'

'Or tuck it into my drawers,' Rose giggled. 'There's so much skirt I shall look like a ball.'

'Here, let me.' Ivy knelt on the ground next to her friend and gathered bunches of fabric at the tops of her legs. Then she tried to knot it in place, but there was too much material for her to manage.

'Use my ribbon.' Rose pulled the length of yellow ribbon from her golden hair and handed it to Ivy.

'What if you lose it?'

'I'll get another one.'

As she knotted the folds in place Ivy thought how nice it would be to live in a house where ribbons were obtained so easily.

'Now you,' said Rose, standing over her expectantly.

Ivy hadn't considered this. Kneeling at the water's edge, her eyes were level with Rose's bare knees, where fine golden hairs speckled skin as satiny as her friend's sash. The legs were as pale and unblemished as the discarded stockings. She thought of her own legs and stood up.

'I'll wait here.'

'Nonsense!' Rose wrinkled her brow. *Nonsense* was a favourite expression of Miss Sarah's.

'Da will know I've been in the lake.'

'How will he know if you don't go home wet?'

'Someone will see us.'

'The lake is hidden from downstairs, and everyone upstairs is sleeping.'

'What if the bottom is muddy?'

'Well, if you don't come fishing I shan't either.'

Rose had a knack for getting her way. She never bullied or

threatened. She didn't throw tantrums, wheedle or cry, but sooner or later everyone came around to her way of thinking. Ivy knew she was lucky to be her friend, for surely she could have her choice of friends amongst all the girls in the world, yet she had chosen Ivy. So Ivy didn't want to disappoint her, but she didn't want to give her reason to feel sorry for her either. She wanted Rose to think she was worthy of being her friend.

'Come on, hurry up, the fish won't wait all day.'

Perhaps she wouldn't notice, if Ivy was very quick.

'All right.' She sat on the grass, bending forward, fumbling to unlace the boots that no amount of blacking could make new. She rolled down the grey woollen stockings that were held together by darns, curling her bare legs beneath her to stand in one brisk movement. Like Rose, her legs were winter pale and speckled with fine golden hairs. Except where Rose's were satiny smooth, angry red welts criss-crossed Ivy's.

She hadn't been fast enough to evade her friend's notice. Rose opened her mouth in a little 'O' of surprise.

'What happened to your legs? They're covered in red marks.'

Ivy looked away to stare at a blade of grass. How could she explain what it was like to be her? And live in her house? Rose would never understand.

'Nothing,' she said with a shrug.

'Ivy, what happened?'

'I don't think my da likes me very much. He's always angry with me.' Her father's anger was like another person living in the Toms' house – a person to steer clear of, if you could.

'At least you have a father,' Rose said with a sigh, and Ivy almost wished she could take back her words. Sometimes she forgot that her friend didn't have a father, but perhaps she could do without one too if she had everything Rose had.

'I'd rather have a pony and some ribbons,' she ventured, a mutinous pout to her mouth.

'Ribbons aren't everything.'

Perhaps not, except when Da was shouting at her for being a 'stupid, wretched maid' she thought they might at least be something. And when Ma was stirring the copper with a big paddle or scrubbing sheets in steaming soapy water, she thought drinking cocktails in the afternoon might be easier than laundering miles of linen. But Rose was staring at her with a puzzled frown and she wondered whether she should say sorry. Losing your father *was* a terrible thing; Rose was practically an orphan, after all. Maybe Da was right . . . she was a stupid, wretched maid . . . and Rose wouldn't want to play with her any more.

'I didn't mean it,' she said, lurching forward to wrap her arms about her friend's bare legs, crushing them as if she would never let them go. Being friends with Rose was the best thing that had ever happened to her. She couldn't lose that. She couldn't lose Rose.

'That's all right, Ivy. You can have my ribbon once we're done fishing. I don't need it.' Rose squatted next to her, ignoring the billowing fabric drooping into the lake, and touched her forehead to her friend's. 'Friends forever, remember? We spat on it.'

Ivy wasn't quite sure what the word 'forever' meant. But Rose was smiling, so she supposed it must be something good.

3

Port Fairy, Victoria

2016

She didn't need shoes for the short sprint through the dunes to the ocean, not when the day was set to be a scorcher and the breakers rolled in, small and perfectly formed, on a jewelled sea. At the water's edge she paused to check the beach; rocks footed cliffs at both ends and a shallow river flowed lazily into the sea in the middle of the bay. A woman was walking a dog to the right and a man fished to the left. Yesterday the beach had been crammed with holidaymakers jostling for a patch of sand, but this early in the morning it was almost deserted. The sea appeared placid and she remembered exactly where the flags had been yesterday.

She waded out, skipping over waves that dawdled shoreward, enjoying the sensation of her toes sinking into wet sand. When the waves grew taller she jumped through or dived beneath, over and under, just as Dad had taught her, lost in the pleasure of the cold salty water. Then she jumped and when the wave passed, her feet no longer touched bottom, her legs bicycled through the water. But she didn't panic, not yet, for she and her sister were excellent swimmers. Not even when she noticed that she had drifted away from the clubhouse towards the rocky end of the beach where the woman had been walking her dog. Except the woman was gone now, and so was the fisherman. She was the only person in the water, the only person visible in the little cove.

Treading water, she turned back towards the clubhouse, breathing in gasps from her effort and trying to calm the first quivers of alarm. The shore was so far away and the current was pulling her further out to sea. Despite her strongest strokes, she couldn't make headway. In fact, she realised that the water had lost its glassiness and was churning with ripples, murky where underwater currents stirred the sand. She realised that she was caught in a rip and the current was dragging her out to sea, out into the wide waters of Bass Strait. Out where the whales swam . . .

Molly woke breathless, struggling to escape the undertow of her dream. Plunging her face into the pillow, she tried to vanquish the lingering images. Yet in the blackness her father was there, along with the ghostly form of the long-dead Rose, drifting before her eyes. They were both fighting the sea that sought to swallow them. And there was Matt too, surfboard beneath his arm, wet hair clinging to his cheeks, hovering on the periphery, between sleeping and waking.

Lately, all her ghosts were infiltrating her life again.

She sighed, turning her head from the pillow to see a pale watery light leaking through the curtains of Nan's back bedroom. A brisk walk was what she needed. Dressing quickly, she let herself out the back door to wade through dew-soaked grass towards the wharf. The river flowed silver in the early morning light, the street lights on the opposite bank haloed by mist. Several cormorants perched on a jetty, wings outstretched, as a great egret swooped over the water like a white arrow, long black legs stretched behind. Old sailboats, million-dollar catamarans and crayfish boats all elbowed each other for berths along the wharf. She listened to the water lapping at the pylons and fancied it beckoning softly to all those who would venture out into unknown seas.

After following the wharf towards the river mouth, she headed out along the causeway to Griffith Island. The shearwaters would be digging out their burrows ready for mating. Each year, tens of thousands of shearwaters migrated 15,000 kilometres from the Aleutian Islands to nest in the same burrow with the same partner. The first Europeans called them 'mutton birds' for their fatty flesh and abundant oil, and hunted them in the millions. She felt sorry for those long-dead birds, travelling so far, showing such faith and resilience yet being slaughtered as their reward.

The last time she walked this island, Matt had been with her, striding ahead and then slowing to wait for her when he realised she hadn't kept pace. 'Come on, slowcoach,' he'd said, his hair drying into salty curls from the surf. There was no beach break near the island, merely a jumble of black boulders speckled with orange lichen, the swell surging straight on to rocks, dragging a curtain of kelp with it. But danger gave the ride an edge.

'I'm looking for mutton-birds,' she had said, though truthfully she hadn't been looking for anything, only thinking about the island and how it might have been to live in the lightkeeper's house, one hundred and fifty years ago. The bluestone lighthouse still functioned on the tip of the island, although these days it operated on wind and batteries, rather than oil, and all that remained of the houses were their scattered foundations and the recalcitrant jonquils. But she hadn't said this, for Matt didn't understand her preoccupation with the past. From the moment she met him, during her practice teaching rounds, she had been attracted by his ability to focus on the present. He called it screening out negative energy. She called it blind confidence in the world bending to his will.

So she had dragged her attention back to the present, slipping her hand into his, large and tanned and sprinkled with fine blond hairs. Her hand had felt warm and safe, just as her body felt warm

21

and safe nestled next to him at night. They had walked in silence for several minutes before Matt cleared his throat and said, 'You know the trip to WA we talked about?' She had the sense he'd been rehearsing his words, waiting for the right moment.

'Ye-ah.' She was looking forward to a leisurely week sampling the spectacular coastline and wines of Margaret River – scenic walks, a bit of sun and a great deal of Sauvignon Blanc – her kind of holiday.

'Maybe we could do something different this year. It's always me surfing and you lying on the beach with your nose in a book. Why don't we do something together?'

'You mean like both-of-us-lying-on-a-beach-with-our-noses-in-a-book kind of together?' she laughed, knowing that wasn't what he meant at all. But sometimes you have to go through the motions of a conversation even when you really don't want to get to the end.

'I was thinking about something less sedentary.'

'Uh-huh.' She hoped he wasn't trying to persuade her to para-glide again. Simply thinking about all that empty space beneath her made her want to vomit. There was no way she was getting her feet further off the ground than could be accomplished with a skipping rope.

'What about going scuba-diving in Fiji? We've always talked about going to Fiji.'

He had talked about going to Fiji. She had liked the sound of the beach and the people, but the scuba-diving . . . not so much.

'You could do your PADI certificate,' he continued, his brows lifted hopefully. Matt was always encouraging her to step outside her comfort zone. He'd managed to get her to Thailand once, where she had promptly come down with food poisoning. They had done a bicycle tour in New Zealand, which had gone fine apart from some chafing in places she didn't want to remember. He had even encouraged her to try snorkelling once, when the water was shallow and the coral a few steps from the shore. But scuba-diving, with her only air coming from a tiny tube connected to a fragile tank? The water deep and dark, with no way to tell which way was up, and sharks prowling nearby?

'I don't think I can. Sorry, babe.' She willed him to understand.

He had looked at her then, as if searching for some clue, some hint that she might change her mind, but he hadn't pushed her. Perhaps he couldn't be bothered.

'You could go diving and I could snorkel from the shore.'

'Yeah, okay, if that's what you want,' was all he'd said.

She had thought no more about it, had pretended not to notice the disappointed tone of his voice. But thinking back, she realised *that* must have been the moment when he started leaving. Maybe if she had suited up and taken the plunge, he would still be by her side, his long legs propelling him past the whitewashed stone of the lighthouse and the immigrant pines, to where foaming pearly sea, overcast sky and grey sand merged into one. Propelling them both into the future.

Wendy was cooking breakfast when she returned, the smell of frying bacon drifting out the back door. She had made a pot of tea and dressed it in Nan's tea cosy with the little woollen bobbles.

'You're using Nan's cosy.'

'The old brown pot looked lonely without it. I might have to take them both home with me.'

Molly tried to picture Nan's knitted cosy presiding over her mother's sleek modern kitchen, like an incongruous relic from someone else's past.

'Leo keeps saying we should jettison the teabags and go back to a pot,' Wendy said brightly, but Molly caught the shine in her eyes. She slid an arm around her mother's waist and leaned her head on her shoulder, sniffing back a tear of her own.

'I'm glad you've got Leo.'

'So am I. But I'm going to miss Mum. You know, I really thought we'd have her forever.'

'So did I.'

'I mean you know someone can't live forever. But your brain tricks you into not thinking about it.'

'Well, there's a little bit of Nan inside all of us. I can see her in the colour of your eyes, in the shape of my hands, in Daisy's curls. And we've got our memories too. So in a way we'll always have her with us,' Molly said, trying to convince herself as much as her mother.

And now she had the scrapbook to haunt her too.

'By the way, I rescued something else of your nan's.'

'What?' Molly asked, half dreading the thought of more ghosts, half excited at the thought of another puzzle.

Wendy led the way into Nan's bedroom, hugging a smile like a lucky-dip prize.

'This had better be good. You're making such a production of it.'

'Ha! You'll see.'

She crossed to the tallboy leaning against the wall next to the window. Crouching, she wrenched open the bottom drawer, timber grating against timber. There were no neat plastic rollers on this ancient Victorian chest, just wormy old mahogany that had swelled after decades of humid riverside air. She reached into the drawer and withdrew a dark grey box from underneath layers of neatly folded garments.

The box was a rectangle about the size of a hardback book. Probably made from thin ply, it was covered in time-scuffed paper, mottled to resemble leather. The thin brass clasp that secured the lid was shaped like a three-leaf clover and engraved with flowers and leaves so fine that at first glance they went unnoticed. She unclipped it and opened the box. The lining was navy-blue velvet, speckled here and there with mildew, and inset with a heart-shaped hollow of royal-blue satin. Cradled in the heart rested an elaborate confection: two long strands of pearls, bordered by fine silver chains, meeting in a fan-shaped mother-of-pearl pendant from which dangled strings of round and teardrop pearls.

'It's a sautoir . . . a tassel necklace,' said Molly. In the 1920s they were often worn draped over the shoulders to show off a low-backed evening dress, but this was probably Edwardian and definitely imitation. She reached into the box to drape the necklace over one hand. Some of the silver plate had rubbed off the clasp and the pearl had peeled, revealing the glass underneath.

'The pearl is flaking but it's still pretty.'

'I need my glasses in this light.'

'You need your glasses in every light.'

'I don't remember seeing Mum wearing it.'

Molly handed the necklace to her mother in order to focus on the box itself. Maybe she could find a clue. The velvet panel looked like it should be sitting lower in the box. 'I think there's something under it,' she said. She tried wedging a finger through the heart to lever open the panel, but it was stuck like glue. 'Damn, I wish I didn't bite my nails.'

'I'll get a knife from the kitchen.'

While her mother was gone, she closed the box and turned it upside down looking for clues, but there was nothing on the bottom except a gold embossed rectangle and a few more rusty brown spots. Wendy returned with a bone-handled bread and butter knife, and Molly set to work gently prising the knife under the heart, trying not to pierce the satin. After wiggling it around for a few seconds she managed to loosen the glue, and the velvet panel popped free of the box. What had been a sumptuous velvet nest was revealed on its underside as a rough bit of ply glued with a scrap of blue satin. And beneath that deceptive cover was a bundle of yellowing envelopes bound with ribbon.

'Wow.'

The top envelope bore the faded red profile of George V and was addressed to 'Miss Rose Luscombe' in a sprawling hand. Perhaps these were the very letters Wendy's grandfather had written to his prospective wife.

'Rose must have given Mum the box.'

'Either that or she found it after Rose disappeared. But clearly she didn't find the letters.'

What other secrets had Rose hidden? Could Nan's search be more than wishful thinking?

Wendy placed the sautoir back in its shiny blue nest. 'Well, we'd better get on with the packing. There's still a lot more to sort,' she said with a sigh.

'Sure, I'll leave the letters for later.'

With a reluctant glance at the bundle of envelopes, Molly set them aside. They reminded her of all she had given up when she abandoned research to take the safe road into teaching. She had finished her master's degree on a high, her passion for old documents ignited. But when she looked ahead to the prospect of years of study, with little hope of a secure job at the end, she had given up. She had dropped the idea of pursuing a PhD and began a Diploma of Education instead. She hadn't the stamina to follow her heart.

Was Rose offering her a second chance?

4

North Devon

1909

The stables were Rose's favourite place in the world. No matter how often they were swept clean they always smelled of hay, horse and dung. Up at the house, Mrs Tucker had banned the smell of anything resembling an animal, including the human kind. Once, Ivy had accused Rose of being haughty because she suggested that the stable lad was in urgent need of a bath, but Mrs Tucker would have approved heartily.

The stables were quiet when she arrived, except for soft whickering and the gentle swish of tails. She peered around the arched doorway that opened on to the gravelled yard, looking for signs of human life, but the cobbled passage was empty, the long row of stalls closed with no sounds from above. Hay was stored in the loft, the ceiling plastered to prevent dust falling into the horses' eyes. Horses were treated well at Luscombe Park.

She turned towards her pony's stall. She had outgrown her first pony – Mrs Tucker complained that as soon as her skirts were let down, her knees were peeking out again – so last month Robert had brought home Buttons, a large white pony of twelve hands, splattered with black spots. Rose loved Buttons and rode her as often as she could cajole someone into riding out with her, which wasn't nearly often enough for her liking, or Buttons' either. She didn't see why she shouldn't be allowed to ride alone. She was already 'quite proficient'; Robert had said so.

'Buttons!' There was a clatter of hooves and Buttons' speckled white face peered optimistically through the slats. She didn't fool herself that the pony's love was all for her; she had come armed with a suitable bribe. Reaching into the pocket of her pinafore, she brought forth an apple saved from luncheon, offering it palm up while stroking Buttons' nose with her other hand.

Still no one appeared, so sliding the bolt she opened the stall door, the horse butting at her hopefully as she closed it behind her. Perrin must be out exercising the hunters. The groom exercised all the horses for two hours a day, and the stable boy, who should have been grooming horses or shovelling dung, was likely to be found larking about with the gardener's lad, something he did at every opportunity. Last month she had come upon him wrestling with the hall boy behind the stables and was impressed with the way he knew how to go about it. She wondered whether all boys had lessons in such things, but Ivy had said no, that wrestling wasn't difficult with practice – and she should know, since she got plenty of practice with her brother Samuel. Ivy was a year older and several inches taller, but that didn't deter him in the least. Rose found their squabbles puzzling – for who would have imagined that brothers and sisters pulled each other's hair or hid frogs in school satchels? Robert was seven years older than her, and such pranks were far beneath his dignity.

One of the things she liked about Ivy was listening to stories about Ma, Samuel and little brother Danny, who could be counted upon to eat dirt and snails and pull the cat's tail. And there was always the threat of what Ivy's da might do to send shivers up her spine. Rose's house was bustling with people but no one ever did anything interesting. The other thing she liked about being friends with Ivy was the adventure of sneaking out of the house without any of those busybodies finding out about it. Miss Sarah didn't think Ivy a suitable friend, and neither did Mrs Tucker. Rose's mother rarely paid attention to anything she did, but even she scolded if the Toms name was breathed within her hearing.

Buttons' bridle hung neatly on its hook, beckoning her. It couldn't hurt to take her pony out for a quiet walk about the stable yard. Why else had Robert taught her how to attach the bridle? Unhooking it, she looped the reins over the pony's head, carefully holding the straps out of the way as she introduced the bit into her mouth. Then she slipped the headpiece over her ears before buckling it, nice and neat, at nose and throat.

'There you go, girl,' she said, receiving a nudge for her efforts. She leaned her face against Buttons' silky cheek. 'Fancy a walk?'

Ivy was waiting at the folly when she rode up, an impatient expression on her face. Lately she had grown snippy if Rose was late and gloomy when she had to rush home to tea. 'Rose, where's your saddle?'

'Perrin hasn't taught me that part yet, and Buttons begged for an outing, didn't you, girl?'

'But I can see your drawers.'

She shrugged. It was true that her hitched-up skirt revealed the scalloped edge of her drawers, but who was there to see except Ivy? She wasn't wearing her riding habit, because she hadn't *planned* to ride. Buttons had beseeched her.

'Climb aboard,' she said with a grin. 'The folly is as good as a mounting block.'

'But I don't know how to ride.'

'I'll do the riding, you only have to sit still.' She didn't mention that sitting still was harder than it looked; Ivy would find out soon enough.

'Are you sure?'

'Uh-huh,' she said, stifling a giggle.

'You won't go far? Da will kill me if he finds out.'

'No, I won't go far.'

Some while later, Ivy was moaning and groaning in her ear. 'You said you wouldn't go far!' She had clamped her arms around Rose's waist, her body jolting about as Buttons rolled through the park and out the front gate on to the lane that led to the village.

'Don't grip with your knees. You're confusing her. Keep your legs long.'

'She's trying to get rid of me.'

'Nonsense. She's a very good-natured pony.'

'To you maybe . . . and there's a trail of flies following us . . . ow!' Ivy squealed, rubbing at her cheek. 'A horsefly bit me.'

Miss Sarah's cousin twice removed had died from a horsefly bite, his tongue so swollen that he couldn't breathe. Ever since, Miss Sarah was loath to venture out for fear of being bitten and dropping dead. Rose supposed that was as good a reason as any for staying indoors.

'Can we go back now, please?'

Rose ignored her pleas. The only way Ivy would learn to ride was by riding, Perrin would surely concur. Besides, she didn't feel like turning around yet.

'Look, isn't that your brother?' she said a few minutes later, spotting a sandy-haired boy with dirty knees dawdling towards them. He was kicking a stone along as he walked and bashing any encroaching shrubbery with a stick.

'Quick, turn around before he sees me.'

'It's only Samuel.'

'You don't understand.'

She debated turning Buttons towards home, but it wasn't much of an adventure if they had barely escaped Luscombe Park.

And she wanted to find out what Ivy was worried about. Samuel didn't look very dangerous to her.

'I don't think Buttons wants to go home yet.'

They had drawn close enough now for Samuel to spy exactly who was clinging like a limpet to Luscombe Park's Miss Rose, her unruly chestnut hair flapping about her head.

'You're going to get it now, Ivy Toms,' he called, a devious gleam to his eyes. 'I'm going to tell Da. You're not to go to big house.'

'Go and tell him! I don't care!' Ivy shouted as her brother scrambled up and over the hedgerow and sprinted across the fields in the direction of the Toms' cottage.

But Rose knew that Ivy did indeed care. She always cared what her da would do, because he had a history of doing unpleasant things. Rose couldn't remember her own father, but she couldn't imagine him taking to her with a willow stick or shutting her in the coal box for an afternoon. Maman said she lost her husband in a hunting accident when Rose was still in the nursery, and that was why she was always sad. Rose thought that her mother might be less sad if she left her room more often and didn't drink so many cocktails. But adults were even more peculiar than the Toms family, and there was no point suggesting anything sensible, for they never listened to anyone shorter than them.

'Perhaps Buttons is ready to turn back now,' Rose finally conceded ten minutes later, aware that Ivy was in danger of falling off.

'Get 'ee here, you stupid, wretched maid!' bellowed a voice behind them.

Both girls turned to see Walter Toms loping towards them, Samuel following in his footsteps, grinning widely.

'Go faster!'

'If we go faster you'll fall off.' Besides, they both knew that going faster would only delay the inevitable. 'Perhaps we should stop,' Rose suggested, nervous about what might happen if they didn't. It wasn't only Mr Toms who had alarmed her; it was his daughter. At the first sound of his voice, Ivy's hands had hooked into claws, digging at her waist. And when she swivelled around to watch Mr Toms, she caught a glimpse of naked fury on her friend's face.

'Don't worry, Rose, he won't hurt *you*,' Ivy whispered in a flat voice.

She urged Buttons to a halt, holding one rein to bring the pony around. Then, in her best imitation of Miss Sarah, she said, 'Mr Toms, how nice to see you. Ivy was on her way home, right this minute.'

'She be going home all right. She's no business being on a horse. I be teaching her to disobey me!'

'I think there's been a misunderstanding. I—'

'Begging your pardon, miss, but I know my own daughter and she's a right baggage. Always stirring up trouble.'

Walter Toms had caught up with them now, his powerful body looming over pony and riders. She could feel her heart galloping in her chest and even Buttons was edging away, raising her head, ears pinned back. 'Please, Mr Toms,' she said, 'Ivy didn't mean any harm.'

Toms had the same sandy colouring as his son, but Samuel's freckled boyishness had grown ruddy and coarse in his father and the boy's whippet-like grace had turned to the muscled meanness of a mastiff.

'Mean no harm? Happen she brings nought but harm. Happen she knows not to come to big house. There's nought but trouble there.'

Rose wondered why he considered Luscombe such a fearful place. It was boring, to be sure, but not dangerous. And there was always plenty of cake.

'Her ma knows, there's nought at big house for a maid like her. Now get on with 'ee!'

Rose nudged Ivy in the ribs with her elbow but her friend didn't move. She sat there, stubborn as a mule, breathing in shallow gasps. Toms grabbed his daughter by the arm, hauling her from the pony so that she landed in the dusty lane with a thud. Then dragging her to her feet, unresisting, he towed her back the way he had come, she following like a sleepwalker, with Samuel trotting in his shadow.

Rose watched them go, a frown lining her forehead. She knew that the Toms house wasn't peaceful, but she had thought that the fun to be had might make up for that. At least with two brothers, a father and a mother there was bound to be someone to talk to, someone to play with, to care about you. But perhaps she was wrong. Perhaps being left to your own devices had much to recommend it, after all.

5

Western District, Victoria

2016

Looking to the south, where a long hummock of grass-covered dunes concealed the sea, Molly thought the scene had probably changed little in the last century except for the row of soaring turbines rising above the dunes like a garden of Jack's giant beanstalks. Their car cruised the rolling plain, lush with spring rain, past a brimming dam where black swans foraged for breakfast. Beyond the dam a bluestone homestead squatted, square and solid, date palms standing sentinel at each flank. Cypress windbreaks, like ragged green walls, criss-crossed paddocks and everywhere eucalypts gathered in their tattered grey cloaks.

They turned off the main road soon after, heading for the house where Rose had once lived and where Nan and her brothers had been born. As the Volvo clattered over the second cattle grid, Molly glimpsed the homestead peeping between two century-old bunya pines. Then the track rounded a gentle rise and Wuurnong came into full view, its dark stone facade rising from the volcanic plain, with the ancient crater – named Budj Bim by the Gunditjmara people and Mount Eccles by her ancestors – crouched in the distance. Two Blue Heelers greeted their arrival, nipping at the wheels as Wendy manoeuvred the station wagon to one side of the circular drive.

'Get out of it, Sukie! Get down, Bob!' Wendy's cousin Brian shouted to the dogs as he appeared around the side of the house.

'Hi, Brian,' Molly said as she opened the car door, trying to avoid being knocked down by the dogs, who were enthusiastically frisking her legs. 'They're very friendly.'

'You're not wrong there. When you've got friends like these two you don't need enemies. Get out of it, Sukie!' he growled at the bitch, who had corralled Wendy between door and car. The two dogs, realising he meant business, slunk away to settle themselves on the veranda.

'Are they Minna's pups?' asked Wendy.

'Poor old Minna, I reckon she's been gone three years. These two scamps are from her last litter.'

'Is that how long since I've been here?'

'About that. Anyway, how are you, Wendy? Joanie was so pleased you called.' Brian enfolded his cousin in a bear hug, a huge grin splitting his face.

'We missed you at the funeral.'

'Yeah, I was sorry to miss it, love, but we had a bit of an emergency with the flood warning. I would have liked to say farewell to Aunt Queenie, though. And look at you, young Molly, the fellas must be beating down your door.'

'You always were an optimist,' Molly laughed.

'And I hear you've found some letters amongst Queenie's things?'

'Love letters. Great-grandfather Jim's letters to Rose,' said Molly.

'Well, that's a surprise. Love letters, eh? Wasn't much love lost between those two, you ask your Uncle Ted.'

Those love letters had kept Molly awake reading half the night, so much so that she had suggested this detour to Wuurnong to speak to Nan's brother Uncle Ted.

'According to the letters, Granny Rose nursed Jim's younger brother, Henry, during the war,' she said.

'Did Henry introduce them?' asked Brian.

'No, apparently Henry died from his wounds and they began corresponding after his death.' Rose had fallen so hard for the man behind the words that she sailed across the world. For a second Molly felt a flicker of shame that her love had been too meagre to get her to Fiji. 'I think Rose was the last thread that connected Jim to his brother,' she said. 'He seemed to feel a lot of guilt about letting Henry go to war without him.'

Wendy flicked a glance at her daughter, saying, 'Perhaps Rose helped him to forgive himself.'

I carry your letter in my pocket, worrying that tomorrow I'll wake and realise I've been spun a yarn and you're not coming, after all, Jim had written in his last letter to Rose. *Mum says a rough chap like me doesn't deserve a fine girl like Miss Rose Luscombe, but knowing you're to be my wife is the one thing that keeps me going. You helped me climb out from my trench of despair and take my gruel like a man.*

'Maybe,' said Molly.

'Anyhow, let's get on in, or Joanie will be wondering where we've got to.'

As they climbed the stairs to the veranda, Molly noticed that the boards were splintering at the edges, with patches where the decking had rotted altogether.

'The old girl needs a bit of work,' Brian nodded, 'but she's held up these past hundred and sixty years so she's got a few good years left in her, I reckon.'

'She's beautiful.'

'She's a money pit! You'd keel over if you knew what the architect quoted me to do her up properly. You can't replace a downpipe without getting the National Trust involved.'

'Did I hear my name mentioned?' asked Joan, wiping her

hands on her apron as she emerged from the house, a shorter, cuddlier version of her husband. She had the same shaggy salt-and-pepper hair and sun-worn face, but in Joan the wrinkles were softened to a mesh of fine lines. She kissed both women on the cheek, then threw her arm around Wendy's waist. 'It's so good to see you! You'll need a cup of tea after dealing with Aunt Queenie's place.'

The dogs escorted Brian and Molly across the paddocks to inspect the bluestone woolshed in all its utilitarian grandeur, barking at a couple of wood ducks on the dam, before the little party headed back to the homestead for the promised afternoon tea. Brian guided Molly across the gravel yard at the rear of the house and in through the kitchen door. They had already toured the interior of the house, Molly admiring the lofty ceilings and marble fireplaces that contrasted sharply with the slope-roofed bedrooms in the older Georgian farmhouse. The front section of the house had been built from Victorian basalt in the 1870s, in the Italianate style, while the rear dated from the 1850s and was built from local freestone rubble. She had always found the rear, with its jumble of small, whitewashed rooms, more homely, as if formed from the soil.

'Thanks for giving me the tour.' Molly smiled as Brian opened the door for her. 'It's so long since I was here, I'd forgotten a lot of the detail. Reading Jim's letters made me curious, I suppose.'

Brian ushered her through to the parlour, where Joan and Wendy lounged on a sagging Victorian sofa catching up on family news over a second cup of tea. Uncle Ted appeared to be snoozing in his favourite recliner. The room was a time capsule of furniture styles from the previous two centuries. Molly loved the nineteenth-century landscapes painted with varying degrees of talent and the early sepia photographs of Wuurnong that Joanie had enlarged. Her favourite showed the house in the

1850s, with the family posed in a line out front, the little girls with their centre-parted hair and the father with his mutton-chop whiskers. She found it incongruous that the first settlers brought their Georgian architecture with them all the way from Britain, with not an eave or veranda in sight to protect pale skin from the ravages of the Australian summers. The house and its occupants could have stepped straight from the pages of a Brontë novel, except they were in western Victoria and not the moors of northern England.

Accepting a cup of tea from Joanie, she sat back in an old leather squatter's chair. 'Brian, what did you mean earlier when you said that there wasn't much love lost between Jim and Rose?' she asked.

'Well, I was ten when Gran died, and the way I remember it is she and Granddad hadn't spoken for a year. They lived in the same house, slept in the same bed but only spoke through intermediaries. Rose would say, "Ted, ask your father if he wants mashed potatoes for tea," and Jim would grunt or say, "Tell your mother I'll leave it up to her." Don't know how they got on in the bedroom. Beggars belief really.'

'Do you know what went wrong between them?'

'Not a clue, and Dad doesn't know either. One day they were talking and the next they weren't. Apparently it had happened before, but they eventually got tired of it. I suppose Rose disappeared before they could start talking again.'

Wasn't that the truth of any long relationship? If you caught it at any given moment the protagonists might be lovers or fighters. 'We found a scrapbook Nan kept about Rose's disappearance,' Molly said.

'A scrapbook?' Brian repeated with a frown.

'Apparently Mum didn't believe that Rose drowned,' Wendy explained with a shake of the head. 'She searched for twenty years, hoping that her mother might one day return.'

'Poor Aunt Queenie, not much chance of that, I reckon. One way or another, Rose was gone for good. But it's hard to let a parent go, no matter how old you are,' Brian said, with a sideways glance at Uncle Ted who appeared to be sound asleep in his recliner.

Molly bit back her own memories. 'Do you think Jim and Rose's spat had anything to do with her disappearance?' she asked.

'I wouldn't like to say, love,' said Brian. 'She was a strange one, your great-grandmother. She could get in these moods where she'd go off on her own. She had an old EJ Holden, though I suppose it was new then, and she'd drive down to the coast alone. These days the doctors would probably diagnose depression and medicate her, but I reckon she just got sad sometimes and went away to lick her wounds. And then one day she never came back.'

'My gran would have recommended a Bex and a lie-down,' said Joan. 'Bex was her remedy for everything.'

'Anyway, before you knew it, Granddad's friends were leaving casseroles and cakes at the front door and no one would mention her name.'

Nobody spoke for a few moments, as if Rose was finally getting her two minutes of silence, fifty years after the fact. And then Ted's cracked old voice croaked from the comfort of his La-Z-Boy.

'He turned up, you know, a few days after Mum disappeared.'

'Who turned up, Dad?'

'All the way from England, with never a word of him coming.'

'Who, Dad?' Brian repeated with a lift of one eyebrow in Joan and Wendy's direction. Ted was becoming known for his mental meanderings. When you'd lived as long as he had, the past was a many-branched road map, whereas the future didn't lead very far at all.

'Rolled down the drive in his big black car. Chauffeur in a peaked cap.'

'Who rolled up, Dad?' Brian asked, with good-humoured patience.

'The brother. Never heard a peep out of him, all those years. And he turns up when she's gone.'

'Whose brother?'

'Mum's brother. Uncle Robert Luscombe.'

6

North Devon

1910

Rose led the way up the narrow stairs at the rear of the house, hushing Ivy with a soft hiss whenever she stepped too heavily on a creaking floorboard. They had timed Ivy's arrival to coincide with Miss Sarah's afternoon nap. Rose's mother was rarely seen beyond her boudoir before dinner, while the servants were busy cleaning silver, sewing on buttons and ironing Mrs Luscombe's intricate blouses and petticoats. It was the quiet hour upstairs.

'You'd better take off your boots or Greep will hear you. He has better hearing than a bat.'

'He looks like one too,' Ivy giggled, for the butler did have rather large ears and beady black eyes. But she dutifully removed her boots, hoping Rose wouldn't notice the hole in her stockings that was yet to be mended.

She followed Rose along the corridor, hurrying past the grand central staircase, while trying to avoid the accusing stares from a wall of Luscombe ancestors. Her friend's bedchamber was situated at the rear of the house, overlooking the park, its walls papered in candy-striped green with billowing lace curtains draping the windows. Rose wanted to show her the doll's house that her brother had ordered to celebrate her twelfth birthday, and Ivy was a willing collaborator. In the few times she had been invited to visit, she'd been mesmerised by the wonder of Rose's room, like the tower of a fairy-tale princess.

She noticed the doll's house as soon as Rose opened the door, for it took pride of place in the centre of the room, perched upon an ebony stand on the rug. She saw at a glance that the doll's house had more rooms than the Toms cottage. There was a proper bathroom with a claw-foot tub and copper geezer. There was a kitchen, a dining room, a morning room and a drawing room. Why, there was even a billiard room with a rack of cues the size of toothpicks. And at the top of the little house, complete with a fireplace, a four-poster bed and a rocking horse, was a room with exactly the same wallpaper as Rose's bedchamber.

She stepped closer so that her eyes were on the same level as the miniature room, peering inside to find that it also had the same curtains at the window. She felt something stir inside her, like a pain or a burning that had not been there a moment before.

'Robert sent a drawing and samples to London and they copied the wallpaper and curtains,' said Rose, clapping her hands with pleasure. 'Look, Ivy, it even has my rug upon the floor.'

Ivy looked down to find that, indeed, the rug was the exact shade of gold splashed with pink peonies as the one upon which they now stood. 'It's very pretty,' she said in a small voice.

'And there are dolls to go in every room.'

The doll occupying Rose's room had curling gold locks and painted blue eyes and wore a familiar blue floral dress. There was a grown-up lady doll with tightly cinched waist and feathers in her hair; a young man in a hunting costume; a pipe-smoking older gentleman; a little boy in short pants; plus a footman, a cook, a butler in a black suit, and a maid in a smart black dress with frilled white apron and cap.

'Let's play "Getting ready for dinner",' said Rose, plucking her twin from the doll's house. 'I'll be me and you will be . . .'

'Maman!' said Ivy, reaching for the grown-up doll dressed in a lilac silk evening gown with silvery feathers in her nest of faded blond hair – the doll that resembled Rose's mother in all her finery.

'But Ivy, if you're Maman,' said Rose, her pale forehead marred by an unaccustomed frown, 'who will help me dress for dinner?'

'Can't we help each other?'

'Ladies don't help each other dress. Well, perhaps they may if they're sisters, but certainly not Maman and I. Ladies have a maid to dress them,' explained Rose in the voice she used for speaking to the gardener's lad.

'Then who shall I be?'

'You shall be my maid.'

Ivy wasn't sure that she wanted to be the maid, for although the maid's black skirt and neat white apron were prettier than her own – which had been cut down from one of her mother's worn and faded garments – the Rose doll wore a dress cut from pink silk and tied with a white satin bow. 'Well, if I can't be Maman, I shall be you,' she said, challenging her friend with a determined look.

Rose prised the grown-up doll from her hand, saying, 'But you don't know a thing about living in a big house. I bet you don't even dress for dinner at your house.'

In truth, Ivy's mother struggled to get her father and brothers to wash their hands and faces before meals. And how could they dress for dinner when they had but two sets of ordinary clothes and one set for Sunday best? But she wasn't about to admit this fact to Rose, who was the original owner of her single Sunday dress, worn but twice and bequeathed to Ivy for being too itchy. The more she thought about it, the more Ivy was determined to wear that silk dress, even if only as a doll.

'Of course we dress for dinner,' she said, punctuating her statement with a jutting chin.

'Why Ivy Toms, I do believe you are a fibber!'

'I am not!' said Ivy, snatching the Maman doll back so swiftly that Rose did not have time to release it. They both looked on in horror as the silvery feathers were torn from the little doll's head and fluttered to the floor.

'Now look what you've done,' said Rose, her voice rising in pitch and volume until it was almost, but not quite, a screech. Rose never screeched. Not even the time a wasp got stuck in her hair and Ivy had to fetch the groom to extract it. So Ivy knew that she had ruffled her friend's usual composure. 'You've ruined her!'

'I didn't do nothing!' spat Ivy.

'What *is* all this noise, Rose?' said a tinkling voice behind them.

Startled from her indignation, Ivy turned towards the doorway where Rose's mother leaned against the door jamb, a horrified expression upon her face. She had the same blond hair as her daughter, but Rose once divulged that her mother's fading locks were aided by a secret recipe from France, known only to the most talented of maids. And although it was long past noon, Mrs Luscombe's hair hung loose about her shoulders and she wore a robe of silver velvet lined with pink satin, wrapped about her thin frame.

'And *who* is that?' The words were spoken softly and tinged with a faint sniff of disgust.

A cat seemed to have caught Ivy's tongue but Rose had no trouble answering. 'This is my friend, Ivy, who lives in the village,' she said, as Ivy backed towards the window, her path to the door blocked by Mrs Luscombe. In the terror of the moment she forgot that she was on the second floor.

'And what is she doing here?'

'She has come to play with my new doll's house that Robert gave me for my birthday.'

'Has she now? And has she also come to ruin my floors with her dirty boots?'

Ivy's back nudged the windowsill as her eyes followed Mrs Luscombe's gaze to where she had left the dirty boots at the top of the stairs. Without her mother to remind her, she had forgotten to wipe her boots before entering the house. She felt her cheeks flush at the thought of her trail of muddy prints tramping across the gleaming floors of Luscombe Park, like the spoor of a fox or a rabbit.

'What have you to say for yourself, girl?'

Ivy opened her mouth to speak but no sound emerged. Not a squeak or a bark in her own defence.

'Oh, Maman, it's only a little mud,' said Rose, flashing a kindly smile in her friend's direction, now that Ivy had been put in her place. Only a moment before, she had forgotten herself enough to screech her displeasure.

'What's "only a little mud"?'

A man appeared at Mrs Luscombe's side, resting his chin momentarily upon her shoulder before pecking her on the cheek. Ivy's eyes widened at this surprising familiarity. Had Mrs Luscombe got herself a new husband? Yet the man looked significantly younger than Rose's mother, with a full head of dark blond hair, an unlined forehead, and no hint of a paunch beneath his waistcoat. He too smiled kindly at Ivy, his blue eyes dancing with good humour.

'We didn't expect you down from Eton until tomorrow,' said Mrs Luscombe, her expression of disgust giving way to pleasure. She took one of his hands in hers and raised it to her lips. 'And looking so handsome too.'

'You've grown whiskers,' said Rose, in mild approval, and Ivy realised that the man was in fact a boy, most probably Rose's brother, Robert. She had not seen him at close quarters for at least a year and he had changed beyond all recognition. He was almost a man now.

'Hello. Who's this?'

Ivy looked away, not wanting him to witness her distress, giving her time to school her face to blankness.

'This is Rose's little friend Ivy, from the village, who has tramped mud all through the house. Really, these village children have no idea how to behave like civilised beings.' Mrs Luscombe waved a hand in Ivy's direction as if to shoo her from the room.

'She looks civilised enough to me. And it is only a little mud, Mother. Muriel will have it cleaned up in a trice,' said Robert, 'while I see Ivy safely home.'

'But Robert, it's almost teatime,' said Rose.

'Don't worry, Chicken, I'll run all the way home.'

With that he crossed to the window, crooking his elbow in invitation. In the face of her son's blithe disregard for propriety, Mrs Luscombe could do little but stand aside as he marched Ivy towards the door, arm in arm. No one noticed that she still clutched the silk-clad doll in one sweaty palm.

7

Western District, Victoria

2016

Joan set the table in the dining room, in honour of her guests, and they ate watched by ancestors in ornate golden frames staring from the walls. The room glowed in the dying light that filtered in through west-facing windows, catching the crystal wine glasses and glinting off the family silver. Nothing was kept for best at Wuurnong, and in the soft light, no one noticed the fraying silk cords tying the curtains or the water stains marring the faded Victorian wallpaper.

'I love the salad,' Molly said appreciatively, wiping her mouth with the damask napkin. 'Niçoise is one of my favourites, and everything's home-grown.'

'Well, I can't take credit for the tuna,' said Joan.

'Maybe we could look into that,' said Brian with a twinkle in his eye. 'I've been thinking about what we could do with the lower dam.'

'Yabbies,' mused Ted, 'used to be a ton of yabbies in that dam when I was a kid. You ask your nan.'

No one ventured to correct Ted. He didn't need reminding that his sister was gone.

'We used to sit down there with a string, a piece of meat and a bucket and wait for them to take the bait.'

'Did you catch many, Uncle Ted?' asked Wendy.

'Nah, the yabbies were too smart for us. Your grandfather had the knack, though, knew just when to pull in the string with the yabby holding on to that meat for dear life.'

'I remember him taking us yabbying once,' Brian commented.

'Mum hated yabbies. Wouldn't eat them. And rabbits. During the Depression, Dad and Harry and me would go out shooting and come back with a brace of rabbits and Mum would refuse to cook them. Said we weren't so poor that we had to eat coney and bottom feeders.'

'Was Rose a bit posh, then?' asked Molly.

'Not that I recall, no, she would roll up her sleeves and get on with it, but she did get a bee in her bonnet about some things. She wouldn't let us get away with coming to dinner in our work clothes. She'd meet us at the back door, hands on hips and us boys all towering over her. Oh no, it was faces washed, hair combed and a clean shirt or we didn't get fed. Didn't matter if we'd been down at the shearing shed all day and too tired to lift a saltshaker, or fighting a grass fire or digging out stumps, we had to change for dinner. That was Mum, a stickler for manners,' Uncle Ted said, looking through Molly to a lost country somewhere in his past.

'We have something to show you. Two things actually,' Molly said, pushing back her chair to fetch a plastic bag she had left on the sideboard.

'What is it, love?' asked Ted.

She slipped back into her seat beside Ted and slid the battered grey box from the bag. Opening the box, she placed a photograph on the table and picked up the necklace nestled beneath. Holding it high, she slipped the pearl strands over her head so that the necklace rested against her body, the long pearl tassels dangling almost to her waist.

'Do you recognise it?'

48

'Mum used to wear it on her birthday. The rest of the year she only ever wore her wedding ring. I haven't seen it since she was alive. Where did you find it?' he asked, reaching out an age-spotted hand to touch the flaking pearls.

'At Nan's place.'

'Oh, I didn't know she had it. Mum must have given it to her sometime before she disappeared. A bit too grand for our Queenie.'

'She would have rattled like a train in that thing,' said Wendy.

'There's something else. A photograph.' Molly turned the photo face up and passed it to her great-uncle, who studied it with a look of deep concentration. She watched him for a minute or two, giving him time to take himself back to that other country, the country of his childhood.

'I've never seen a photo of Mum as a young woman. If you tried to take one she'd say, "Why would anyone want a picture of an old chook like me?"'

'It reads "Rose and Ivy" on the back, with the words "Together forever". Do you know who Ivy was?' Molly prompted.

Brian and Joan had come to stand behind Ted's chair, looking over his shoulder. He sighed and wiped his eyes with the back of his free hand. Molly didn't know whether he was wiping away a tear, a memory or merely clearing his vision.

'I don't even know which of these girls is Mum. It's been a long time since she died, and these girls are so young. I could pick Dad out of a line-up because we've got photos of him, but Mum . . .'

'What colour was her hair, Dad? I can only remember it being grey.'

'A light colour, and wavy, but all the women had perms then. Ah, it could be either of them. You wait until you're my age and you'll have trouble recognising yourself in a school photo.' Ted sighed again and held out the photo towards Molly.

'You keep it, Uncle Ted. Molly and I took copies,' said Wendy.

'Sorry, love, I don't remember any Ivy. We didn't find out about the brother until he turned up after she died. But Uncle Robert didn't mention anyone named Ivy. He . . .'

'Yes, Dad?'

'He just seemed . . . sort of lost when he found out she'd drowned. As if he didn't know what he was doing here. He stayed for the afternoon, more out of politeness than anything, I think, and then he was gone. Could Ivy have been another sister?' asked Ted, his eyes glued to the photograph.

'I don't think so,' said Molly, pushing a stray lock of hair behind her ear. 'I did a bit of online digging last night after reading the letters. I found Rose listed in the parish records in Devon, along with her brother Robert, and I cross-checked with the Registry of Births, Deaths and Marriages and the UK census for 1911, but as far as I can see she didn't have a sister.'

'She might have been a friend,' suggested Wendy.

'They're both in uniform, so she was probably local if they volunteered together,' Brian added.

'Yes, I thought so too. I checked the parish records for any Ivy of a similar age, and I found two. One was born two years before Rose and the other a year after. Ivy Jones and Ivy Toms. Then I followed up their parents' occupations in the 1911 census and Ivy Jones was listed as the daughter of a doctor – her father was a widower – and Ivy Toms' father was an agricultural labourer, her mother a laundress.'

'If Granny Rose came from a well-to-do family, it's more likely she was friends with the doctor's daughter,' said Wendy.

'Mum didn't have a lot of friends,' Ted mused. 'She wasn't an easy person to get close to.'

'Well, Ivy was definitely close. Jim mentions her in his letters, and apparently she intended to accompany Rose to Australia.'

Yet Ivy disappeared from Rose's life once they arrived. 'Forever' hadn't lasted very long.

'I scoured the passenger lists for ships arriving in Melbourne in 1919,' said Molly, 'and I found Rose listed as an incoming passenger on the SS *Oracle*.'

'And Ivy?' asked Ted.

'There was no mention of Ivy at all.'

8

Melbourne, Victoria

2016

Molly stood across the road from the beachfront apartment block, yellow plastic carrier bag clutched in her hand. For six weeks the bag had sat on the coffee table in her flat, mocking her with its cheerfulness. Her grandfather's ancient football jumper lay inside, wreathed in the smell of mothballs and oily old wool. She had discovered it while cleaning out Nan's house. Pop had worn that jumper for twenty years, huddled under a raincoat and wrapped in a scarf, cheering for his footy team, the mighty Cats. It boasted the faded remnants of Gary Ablett Senior's signature scrawled across its blue and white bands and a vague smudge of tomato sauce that Nan never managed to remove.

The beach road was logjammed with beachgoers at this time of the day, the sun shimmering on car rooftops in a long line along the bay, the avenue of palms giving little shade. People came from all over the city to find a place on the sand here, from teenagers in boardies and bikinis to African mothers in hijab, giggling children in tow. The sand stretched in a wide ribbon from St Kilda to Port Melbourne, seething with sunbathers, castle builders and volleyball players.

She spotted Matt's battered Land Cruiser parked across the road, separated from her by four lanes of traffic and a grassy plantation dotted with wind-sculpted ti trees. Through its tinted windows she noticed that the rear was piled high with bundles. Pressing her body up against the side of her car, she waited for a break in the traffic. Then, clutching the yellow bag, she took a deep breath and waded out into the traffic, making it to the centre plantation with a quick jog over the last few metres. She had only been out of her car's air-conditioned interior for a couple of minutes and already the afternoon heat prickled the back of her neck. The grass was mere metres wide, a small oasis in the middle of the shimmering, heat-soaked tarmac.

Taking a moment to steady herself, she tried not to think about her motives in coming here. She was delivering a memento, that's all, something Nan would have wanted Matt to have. He would likely put it behind glass with his other sporting memorabilia but she liked to imagine him squeezing his broad shoulders into it when he watched the big men fly. Any other ideas were merely trying to sabotage her peace of mind.

A gap appeared in the traffic and she willed herself forward, fuelled by a seductive cocktail of hope and self-deception. Her sandal was a whisker away from stepping on to the tar when a familiar figure appeared at the entry of the apartment block, surfboard under his arm. She stayed where she was, watching him for a moment, drinking in the sight of him, the lanky grace of him. She hadn't seen him in the flesh since Nan's funeral but she knew every inch: his hair slightly longer than when she had seen him last, curling at the nape of his neck; his limbs strong, tanned and furred in a light covering of golden hair.

He turned his head for a moment, looking back towards the glass door to the apartment block and she could tell that he was laughing at someone. In her mind she could hear his light, easy chuckle. She followed his gaze to see another figure trying to manoeuvre a surfboard through the doorway with one arm while keeping the door open with the other. He walked back towards the entry, covering the hot expanse of concrete in a few long strides, and held the door for the laughing girl who appeared in his wake – the girl who wasn't Molly.

She stepped backwards on to the grass and out of his life. Who was she kidding? He didn't miss her. The small space she had once occupied in his heart had been well and truly colonised by a long-limbed girl with a sunny laugh who juggled her surfboard as lightly as his affections. There was no room there for a quiet teacher of history with an aversion to risk and an eye firmly turned towards the past. Perhaps there never had been. Perhaps she had merely been minding that spot for the right girl to come along.

She closed her eyes, shutting out the vision of the girl. But she couldn't shut out the memories. She thought back to the night a year ago, when she had arrived home from Year 9 camp, exhausted and smelling of mud, stale socks and campfire smoke. Matt had been sitting at the kitchen table, several empty beer bottles lined up in front of him.

'What's up, babe?' she'd said.

Later, she was to wonder whether she might have been more compelling if she hadn't been so tired. But at the time she was so exhausted that she wasn't quite human. She dropped her sleeping bag and pack on the floor next to the door and walked over to the table, taking a chair opposite him. She didn't notice that the autographed picture of Kelly Slater was missing from its spot on the wall by the window.

'Do you want a drink?' he asked.

'Do I need one?'

He shrugged and got up to open the fridge, taking out a bottle of her favourite Chardonnay and pouring her a generous glass. He had obviously been to the bottle shop to prepare. She took a gulp and waited. What was the point in hurrying bad news? He still hadn't looked at her, running his hand through his hair and speaking into his beer.

'I can't do this any more,' he said.

People don't say this and mean the washing up, but she went along with the charade. Fatalistic. Too weak to fight for their love.

'Can't do what?'

'You . . . me . . . our life together, it's not real.'

'It feels pretty real to me,' she said, tears threatening.

'Come on, you know it's not working. We're just going through the motions. It's habit.'

'It's not habit to me.'

He looked at her then for the first time since she'd opened the door, and she saw that his eyes were puffy. She wondered how long he had been sitting there waiting for her, nursing his beer and rehearsing his words.

'You don't surprise me any more. I know that as soon as you walk in the door after school you'll make yourself a cup of tea, sit on the couch and scroll through your phone. I know that every Saturday morning you'll get up at eight, put on your runners and go for a jog by the beach. That on Sunday you'll visit your mum and on Thursday night you'll catch up with your friends. I can predict exactly where you'll be and what you'll be doing at any time.'

'Just because I like a routine, that doesn't mean I don't like to do different things. I like to visit new places as much as anyone.' Wherever they travelled, she couldn't wait to find the local museum.

'I need more adventure in my life.'

'I'm not stopping you.'

'No, but you're not sharing it with me.'

Her sister appeared on the screen, pyjama-clad and bleary-eyed, her hair as snarled and knotted as a tangled fishing line. Behind her, Molly noted the usual incursion of coffee cups, rumpled bed linen and a bombardment of clothing flung over every available surface. The only order was the workbench, neatly arranged with camera equipment.

'What happened to you?' Molly asked by way of greeting. 'Out all night again?'

'It's six a.m. You'd better have a good reason for waking me.' Daisy scowled from the screen and Molly wondered how her sister managed to look cute at six in the morning.

'And what happened to your hair? It looks like a family of rodents is nesting in it.'

'I slept on it wet.'

'You *sooo* need some serious attention to personal grooming. And a cleaner.'

'Not going to happen. Do you have any idea how much it costs to live in London? I'm surviving on two-minute noodles and bananas.' Paying £1,000 a month for a cramped semi-basement studio in Shoreditch, the money Daisy scraped together as a freelance photographer didn't go far.

'You could come home, you know. I've had no one to fight with for so long I'm losing my touch. Even Mum can win an argument with me.'

'You really have lost your touch, then. And I miss you too, by the way.'

'Anytime, hon, no need to thank me.' She felt her younger sister's absence like a missing handbag. Without her, she always had a vague sense of disquiet. Of course, Daisy might not appreciate being compared to a handbag.

'Maybe I'll come home later this year. My visa's running out anyway so the Home Office will be on my back. Nan's money will come in handy for the ticket—' She broke off, looking sheepish. 'Sorry, that was thoughtless.'

Her sister had a tendency to say exactly what she was thinking, but Molly knew she felt Nan's death as much as she did. They had both adored their grandmother. 'True, though,' she said. 'Uncle Craig says he should have the estate settled soon.'

'It seems like forever since I saw her,' Daisy sighed.

Molly caught a glint of tears in those bleary blue eyes. Her younger sister had never been a sook, even when Molly stomped on her sandcastles or let the air out of her netball. She would get a sneaky look in her eyes and Molly knew to expect revenge. Daisy had the same strong nose and bone structure they'd both inherited from their father, except whereas Molly's eyes were green, she had inherited his eyes, the colour of a summer sky. They suited her sunny nature, her determination not to dwell on the past, her carefree attitude.

'You know she used to email me every week? Just to keep me up to date with all the goings-on in Port Fairy. I've still got her last email on my phone,' said Daisy. 'And then there were all her Facebook posts.'

'She was such a sweetie.'

'I really miss her.' There was a moment's silence before Daisy said, 'So, what's up?'

'Oh nothing, just wanted to chat. Can't I call my sister for a chat?'

'At this hour? Spin me another one.'

'Sorry, I needed to talk.'

'About he whose name shall not be mentioned?'

'Yeah . . . no.'

Daisy rolled her eyes and Molly shrugged.

'You were doing so well too.'

'I think I was fooling myself into believing I was over him.' Or fooling herself into thinking he might realise his mistake and come back.

'You didn't go over to his place, did you? I warned you. Love is a sickness. The only way to recover is to take the medicine. And the medicine is *not seeing him*.'

Two years alone in London had given Daisy an air of authority; she had grown an extra layer of armour.

'I know. I didn't see him for ages and then school finished for the year and I had too much time to think and I was missing Nan, and I had Pop's old footy jumper to give him and it didn't seem right to post it so I . . .' Molly took a deep breath.

'You decided to deliver it personally?'

She nodded.

'And what happened? Did he offer you tea like an unexpected, not entirely welcome guest? Did he ask you what you'd been up to and then keep glancing at his phone while you talked?'

She watched her sister's mouth move, her stern expression, and felt even worse than she had before she called. When had she become so pitiful? And how could she have been deluded enough to think that Matt might have had a change of heart?

'Did he make you feel like those five years you were together never happened?' her sister asked, with far less sympathy than Molly thought she deserved.

'I didn't actually speak to him.'

'Okay, you'd better tell me exactly what happened. I'm not going to prise it out of you, humiliation by humiliation. I haven't had my morning coffee yet.'

'Couldn't you just give me a hug?' It was remarkable how she regressed when she talked to her sister. It could have been high school and the incident with David Lee and the infamous deb ball rejection all over again.

'Apart from the fact that I'm talking to a computer screen? No, you've had all the sympathy you're getting.'

'He had a girl with him, a girl with a ponytail and a surfboard. Her name's Jordana.'

'How do you know her name?'

'I saw it on Instagram.'

'So you've been stalking him on social media too?' Daisy

shook her head. Rolling her eyes, she added, 'Why do I always feel like I'm older? Sometimes I think you *want* me to yell at you.'

'Because you're the only person who tells it like it is.' Her friends were still treading on eggshells or avoiding her so they didn't have to hear Matt's name one more time. She suspected she was beginning to sound like Carrie from *Sex and the City*: one long whine about Big that lasted six seasons. 'I'm pathetic. I need a pep talk.'

'You need more than a pep talk, hon, you need a lobotomy.'

'Remember when you wanted to follow that guitar-playing Argentinean to South America after you'd known him three days? I had to be the big sister then and yell at you. That's what sisters do, they take it in turns shouting at each other.'

This time it was Daisy's turn to heave a sigh and run her hand through her hair. 'You know what, you have to make a decision. Ever since Dad died, you've been lugging around all this regret. You've got to let it go. And you've got to let Matt go too. It's time.'

'I know.'

'I liked Matt as much as anyone, but enough is enough. I knew you when we were kids, remember . . . and you were different then. You were the risk taker, the ringleader, the one who always found the best places to hide, the tallest tree to climb. What happened to that girl?'

In the top right-hand corner of the screen Molly saw her image reflected. Even the crappy camera on her computer caught the sadness in her eyes. Daisy was right, that girl had gone into hiding so long ago now that it was hard to believe she had ever existed. The only relics were photos. Yet however cautious she had become, until now she had always retained some remnant of her younger self, some core of resilience and optimism that had kept her moving forward in her own prudent, sensible way.

But this year had been a low point, sucking the last vestiges of courage from her bones.

Daisy ran a hand through the melee of her hair, considering her sister sternly. 'This is going to sound harsh, but you can't blame Matt for wanting more adventure in his life. Hell, *you* need more adventure in your life. You need to find that girl again and reclaim the best parts of her.'

'I kinda think she's gone forever.' That girl was sunk so deep that she was part of a previous civilisation. Hidden under layers of silt and sand, in the same place where she had buried her father and her childhood.

'You're the historian,' Daisy said gently. 'Track her down. Dig her up.'

After the call ended, Molly lay sprawled on the sofa scrolling randomly through her laptop, looking at photographs – of Wendy and Leo, pictures Daisy had sent from London, a few shots of her Year 8 students' re-enactment of the Eureka Stockade (the boys all wanted to be troopers) – searching for that missing girl. She finally found her in a rather fuzzy shot Wendy had taken years ago, looking down at the camera from the saddle of a giant Clydesdale. She must have been about ten. Daisy would have been eight. She remembered the horses picking their way through scrubby eucalypts, skirting koalas napping in the manna gum, and her sister poking out her tongue at them.

Daisy, as the youngest, had been given the shaggy pony. Dad, as the most experienced rider, rode a temperamental bay. Mum, who was allergic to horsehair, opted to stay behind, and Molly was propped up high on her magnificent Clydesdale. She even remembered his name – Minty. She had felt like a queen on Minty, the largest, most handsome horse with his feathery fetlocks and imposing physique. She had been so fearless then. Even when Minty deviated from the main trail and took what she thought would be a step over one log, which turned out to be a giant leap over two, unseating her, she wasn't worried. She just picked herself up off the ground, brushed off her dad's concern and clambered back on. Studying the photo eighteen years later, she saw that the Clydesdale wore its brown and white patches with a proud nonchalance and the ten-year-old girl sitting on his back had absorbed some of that attitude, heedless that she had ridden a horse only two or three times before Minty.

She had lost that girl the day her father died. The sound of a helicopter beating overhead could still fill her with dread, the roar of the surf induce panic. The story of a long-dead great-grandmother disappearing into the surf could still incite night-mares. She had lost her fearlessness at the same time as she lost her father, dragged out to sea along with his lifeless body. Her life since had been tamer. But that girl would have plunged into life. She would have pursued her doctorate instead of taking the safer road into teaching. She would have been first on the dive boat with Matt, or sharing a flat in Shoreditch with Daisy.

She continued scrolling through photos. There she was, a laughing child hanging upside down from the bough of a peppercorn tree, and here a skinny-legged girl in a checked bikini balancing wildly on a surfboard imagining she was Layne Beachley. And there *they* were in the portrait she had uploaded to her phone. Rose and Ivy. One girl carefree, the other staring earnestly into the lens. It was as if those two girls represented the two Mollies – the younger, braver girl and the older, fearful woman she had become. She didn't want to be that second girl any more. She wanted to take a leap without worrying about what lay ahead. If she didn't, she might be stuck in her cosy flat with her books and her plants, marking student essays and pining for people she had lost.

Forever.

9

North Devon

1913

'But I don't want to go to finishing school in Switzerland.' Rose turned to her brother with a forlorn expression. He was focused on the road ahead, his gloved hands gripping the steering wheel of the Silver Ghost with relaxed confidence. 'I want to go to The Priory, like Patty in *The Nicest Girl in the School* and play hockey and be in the popular set.'

'Don't be absurd. Girls like you don't play hockey,' Robert snorted, tearing his eyes away from the road. 'Girls like you learn where to place the second son of a duke at dinner and how to address the wife of an earl.'

'But at The Priory all the girls play hockey and have jolly nice teas.' Much more fun than a stuffy old duke's son. She knew there was a whole world waiting to be explored if she could only escape Luscombe Park, but she doubted she would find it locked up at Mont-Choisi, exhausted from behaving properly. All she would find there was a posse of American bankers' daughters, a lot of nonsense about manners and not a hockey stick in sight.

'The Priory is a figment of that woman Brazil's imagination. I wish I'd never bought the silly book for you!'

'Well, I know The Priory isn't real,' Rose replied, rolling her eyes, 'only I meant a school like The Priory . . . Ellerslie or somewhere. You went to Eton.'

Rose had read all of Angela Brazil's books and thought that boarding school was a grand adventure where girls spent their time playing cricket and tennis. If they had to learn something useful they had pretty *mademoiselles* or frightfully clever misses to teach them, not dreary old spinsters like Rose's governess Miss Sarah. Sometimes Rose felt so stifled at Luscombe that she could barely breathe.

'Public school is fine for a man but you need a different kind of education, Chicken. If you don't want to go to Mont-Choisi you can stay at Luscombe. We can engage a new governess. Old Sarah is getting on, I know.'

'I adore Sarah, I do, Robert, but she's so . . . so dull.'

'We can find someone else to get you ready for your first Season. Then, in a year or two, we can engage a maid. And in the meantime, Mother might be persuaded to take you to Paris.'

Rose swallowed a lump in her throat at the mention of her mother. Other girls had mothers to guide them in life, to be their staunchest allies, but not her. Sometimes she wished she had a mother who took her on shopping trips to London and summers with family friends in Scotland, even if it did mean accounting for every moment of her day. Still, there was no use crying over a bottle of spilled Sydenham's; a girl simply had to get on with her life the best she could.

'Maman has to be persuaded to take me to Cissy's house and she only lives ten miles away!' She congratulated herself on this argument. Robert could have no answer, since it was true that their mother rarely went anywhere. She had become almost in-distinguishable from the furniture: dusted daily, polished weekly, kept out of harsh sunlight and moved irregularly. Her maid, Gibbons, fed her a daily diet of gossip and interpreted her wishes to the rest of the household, but Elsie Luscombe herself was rarely sighted beyond the confines of the dining room.

She was about to continue her argument when Robert slowed the Ghost to walking pace to overtake a young woman on the road a hundred yards ahead. The woods closed in on the country lane at this point, leaving little room for people and vehicles to coexist. The girl's hair was escaping from its plaits, her shoulders hunched as she wove unevenly along the road, too overcome to be aware of where she stepped. She paid no heed to the overgrown grass on the narrow verge, which brushed her skirts with those tricky grass seeds that once attached would not let go. Rose realised that she knew that skirt – that faded blue, patterned with delicate white flowers. It was one of her outgrown garments that had been handed on, wrapped in a bundle along with a pair of little-worn boots and a much-thumbed copy of *The Children's Magazine*, the page on 'How to keep a hedgehog as a pet' dog-eared for reference.

'Stop! It's Ivy,' she said, leaning over to grasp her brother's arm on the steering wheel.

'Who?'

'Ivy Toms, the daughter of one of our tenant farmers, she looks upset.' She wondered what could have happened to send Ivy so far from home without even a hat or shawl. Miss Sarah would have a fit if Rose took off into the countryside without her gloves, never mind her hat (not to mention pony adventures with one's drawers showing).

'Walter Toms' daughter? No surprise she's upset. But I think we should stay out of it. No point getting involved in another man's business.'

Surely Ivy's feelings were her own business not her father's? That was typical of men, always knowing what was best for other people. There was far too much of that going on, in Rose's opinion. She was tired of people telling her what time to go to bed and when to have breakfast. She longed for the day when she could talk to whoever she wanted, and no one would glare at her if she told a joke in public. One way or another, she was determined to tread her own path in life, not one ordered by someone whose main claim to authority was a pair of trousers.

'Robert, you must stop.' She put a little hiccup of tears in her voice. Tears were quite a useful commodity, she had found, especially when applied sparingly, and could usually be relied upon to produce the desired results.

Robert brought the great white and silver beast to a halt a few paces behind the girl. Ivy was so deep in thought that she either didn't hear the car's approach or simply paid it no heed.

'Ivy! It's me, Rose!' she called, struggling with the door, unable to wait for her brother to walk around and open it. The door open, she broke into a trot to catch up with Ivy who, hearing her name called, quickened her pace. 'Wait!' she demanded, reaching out to grasp the other girl's sleeve. Ivy turned, blinking in surprise as if she didn't recognise her friend.

'It's me,' Rose repeated, wondering if Ivy really was so lost in thought that she didn't recognise her, or if this was a silent rebuke. She hadn't been a very attentive friend recently, she had to admit, but she couldn't help it if she had outgrown their small make-believe world. At fifteen, she was rattling at the schoolroom door, chafing to escape, put up her hair and enter the drawing room, even if it meant changing her clothes three times a day and struggling with old-lady bustles in crowded ballrooms. And if she must go off to school, she was more inclined towards gossip and games than books. She couldn't wait to grow up, while Ivy didn't want to let go of her little-girl games. She would probably like nothing more than to return to her one-roomed village schoolhouse. Except her da had made her leave school, and now that Robert was down from Oxford and gadding about with Rose, she didn't even have their friendship to escape to.

Rose allowed that she might become a little deaf in Ivy's place too.

In truth, they had been growing apart for years. Her mother, in one of her rare lucid moments, had made it clear Ivy wasn't welcome at Luscombe Park. Miss Sarah had also turned up her nose if Rose suggested inviting Ivy to tea with Cissy or one of her other friends. She had argued the point with her governess but their friendship had simply become too hard. She felt a small prickle of guilt – but after all, what could she do? The gap between the Toms' cottage and Luscombe Park was wider than the acres of park that lay between them. It was as wide as the distance from social invisibility to Buckingham Palace.

But for all that, Rose suspected they would have remained friends if only Ivy had been more . . . adventurous. Stubbornness wasn't the same thing at all.

'Ivy, what is it? What's wrong?' She tugged lightly at her erstwhile friend's arm.

Forced to respond, Ivy lifted her head but her gaze was directed over Rose's shoulder towards Robert. Rose had never seen her cry – she was more inclined to sullenness than tears – but today she had been surprised, like an injured animal come upon in its den. The remnants of tears made her eyes shine, her lashes dark. Her hair hung dishevelled about her face and one cheek glowed red. She looked small and vulnerable, not like the girl Rose knew at all. That girl was feisty and fearless – and even a little frightening, when roused to anger.

'Miss Toms,' Robert murmured, and a certain tone in his voice prompted Rose to turn and look behind her, catching a flicker of interest in his gaze. He was looking at Ivy as if she were the most fascinating creature he had ever seen. Ivy, a girl with skinned knees and darned stockings and a father who was all too fond of his willow stick. Rose wondered whether she was seeing the kind of sexual interest that was hinted at in Maman's novels. Although pretty in her country girl way, with large green eyes and abundant hair, Ivy was only fourteen.

'Miss Toms, let me help you.' He led the dazed girl in the direction of the Ghost's open passenger door and urged her to sit.

'What happened?' Rose asked, standing slightly behind her brother, who was crouching down in front of the seated girl, almost as if he were kneeling at her feet. The dusty road would certainly ruin his trousers, newly purchased from Henry Poole of Savile Row and unaccustomed to such careless treatment.

'I'm to go to the factory. Da says he can't have me lazing about eating him out of house and home,' she said, her voice dull with misery.

'But you don't laze about, you're always helping your mother with the laundry, and working in the garden.' Rose was indignant on her friend's behalf. 'And you would still be at school if there were one nearby.'

'Da says he has Sam and Danny to feed and it's time I was bringing home more than "too many big ideas". He says he should have sent me to the factory when I turned twelve but he let me waste time lagging about. Now I'm to go to Bristol and stay in lodgings.'

Rose rather thought it might be quite jolly staying in lodgings, almost like boarding school but without teachers telling you what to do. Ivy could be like one of the bachelor girls in Miss Una Silberrad's novels, learning to type by day and going home to a cosy set of rooms and an agreeable landlady putting up supper for her. And at least it would get her away from her father. Rose wouldn't mind being a bachelor girl herself, promenading arm in arm with her best friend along Regent Street or shopping for a new hat in Selfridges. There would surely be more possibility for adventure than stuck here at Luscombe.

For a moment she was almost envious. Then she broke off her reverie, realising that her brother was still staring at Ivy, as if searching for something useful to say.

'Surely another arrangement can be found?' he said, finally finding the words.

Ivy felt her shoulders quiver despite her efforts to remain calm. She didn't want these folk from the big house feeling sorry for her. It was bad enough accepting Rose's offhand gifts. She didn't want her offhand sympathy as well. There'd been little enough friendship between them this last year and Ivy was beginning to suspect that Rose was only available when she had nothing better to do. Her ma said she was foolish to think that she and Rose could remain friends – that sooner or later they would grow up and then she would be left behind like an outgrown doll. For the best part of a year she had made excuses for her friend's absence, her endless parade of 'engagements', but eventually she had to admit that Ma was right.

And now, here was Rose with her lord-of-the-manor brother when Ivy was at her most wretched. One minute she was walking off her anger and fear, the next she was sitting in this expensive leather seat with the master of Luscombe Park kneeling at her feet. She snuck a look at him from under her lashes. She hadn't been in such close proximity to him for several years, not since the day he rescued her from his mother. He was seven years older than Rose and not in the habit of befriending village girls, at least none that he made public. And in latter years he had been away at university. Up close, she was surprised at how smooth his skin was, so different from the ruddy complexions of the boys she knew. His dark blond hair was trimmed neatly and his chin had been closely shaved that morning. The hand resting on the car's open door had nails buffed to a soft sheen and there wasn't a single spot of gravy on his crisp white shirt. There was something attractive yet at the same time subtly repellent about his smooth shininess.

He frowned at her as if he were truly concerned, while Rose stared at him with a small frown pinching her forehead. Well, perhaps he was worried about her, in his master-of-the-manor way, but didn't he understand that there weren't any other arrangements to be had?

'My da has already made arrangements, Mr Robert. I'm to leave on Saturday.'

'Saturday. Well, there's plenty of time before Saturday to make other arrangements,' he said, as if he hadn't heard her the first time.

She supposed when you had as much money as he had, inherited from his dead father's cotton business, you only heard what you wished. Whereas Ivy was obliged to hear everything, even words like 'lazy' and 'stupid' and 'good for nought'.

'Da has promised me to Packer's chocolate factory,' she sniffed, more emphatically this time, wiping her sleeve across her face.

She noticed his perfect fingernails begin a little drumming movement on the perfectly upholstered door of his perfect car and wondered whether his concern was already running thin, replaced by impatience. It was to be expected, of course, for what interest would a young man like Mister Robert have in a village girl?

'Perhaps it won't be so bad,' Rose was saying. 'You'll have money and rooms of your own. And there's a cinema in Bristol. Robert took me to see *Dr Jekyll and Mr Hyde* at the Picturedome in Barnstaple, just last week, and it was smashingly scary,' she added with a shiver. 'You could go to the cinema with the other factory girls.'

Ivy looked up, puzzling at her words.

'But I don't want to go to the factory, Ro . . . Miss Rose,' she added hastily, remembering where she was. 'I don't want to leave Luscombe.'

Rose didn't seem to understand that there would be no cinema for her. No 'rooms' or kindly landlady providing her meals. Her room would be a dormitory bed in a common lodging house for fourpence a night. And at six o'clock, when she returned from her ten-hour day at the chocolate factory, her meals would be bought from the teashop around the corner and anything left over from her meagre five-shilling wage would go straight home to Da to help keep her two brothers.

Rose seemed to have the same hearing problem as her brother. 'I'll miss you, of course,' she sighed, smiling ruefully, 'we've seen so little of each other lately. Robert has monopolised my time since he came down from Oxford so we'll have to make up for that before you go. Perhaps we could have tea tomorrow . . . at Luscombe. Robert . . . ?' she trailed off, possibly expecting some kind of assent from her brother. After all, she could scarcely invite *Ivy* to tea without permission.

Once upon a time, they had simply been two young girls with scraped knees looking for mischief. But there was no room in Ivy's life for mischief any more, not at Luscombe and certainly not at Packer's chocolate factory. Perhaps they had never been friends. Perhaps she had only ever been one of Rose's playthings, like her skipping rope or her pony. With that thought she felt another knot of anger tighten around her gut.

'Robert?'

Mister Robert didn't answer his sister. He appeared to be mired in some important thought from which he couldn't be roused. The fingers were still drumming on the door of the automobile and he was looking at Ivy as if she were a conundrum to be solved.

'Ivy shall come to tea tomorrow, shan't she?'

'What did you say?' Robert muttered, looking back at his

sister for the first time since he had ushered Ivy to her seat.

'I think that we should have Ivy to tea tomorrow. Before she leaves for Bristol.'

'No. I don't think so,' he said, returning his gaze to Ivy's face.

Ivy should have expected this, of course. She didn't belong in the drawing room of a grand house like Luscombe Park. How incongruous that tableau would be: the handsome, aristocratic Luscombe siblings and little Ivy Toms. Still, for a moment . . .

'But you don't understand. Ivy is my friend.'

'I do understand,' he said, the frown returning to his face. 'But I hardly think "tea" will solve her problem. As I see it, she doesn't want to go to Bristol, work in a factory, and live all alone in common lodgings with no one to look out for her. I've heard about such places.'

Yes, that's exactly how she felt. She wanted to stay here in the village, have Ma within whistling distance and her little brother Danny pestering her to show him how to cat's-cradle. She wanted to live close enough to hear the village church bells and catch old Mrs Tolly's titbits of gossip. How could she do that in Bristol? But how did Mr Robert, with his smooth shininess and brilliantined hair, know how she felt?

'Yet her father insists she must earn a wage. And not wishing to malign your father,' he continued, turning back to her once more, 'but you might be happier out from under his roof.'

Until now, she hadn't considered this aspect of her situation for she had been too disturbed at the idea of leaving Luscombe. Now the idea penetrated, and with it came a rush of possibility. Did she wish to be out from under her father's roof? Out from under his constant scolding and harsh words. Out of range of his swift backhand and twitchy belt. Away from her brother Samuel's whining and troublemaking. Away from the sad and resigned expression that had worn furrows into her once pretty mother's face. Did she want to escape the need to be ever vigilant? Of course she did. What girl with more than a tuppence of sense wouldn't?

But even if she went to Bristol and the chocolate factory, she wouldn't escape her da. He would take any pennies she saved; he would have it calculated down to the last farthing. She would have no chance to better herself – to have a life different from her mother's – she would just exchange the drudgery of the farm for the drudgery of the factory. Education might have been her path to a different life but there would be no more education for her. Any learning she got from now on she would have to fight for.

'We will just have to think of another way,' said Mr Robert.

Ivy tried to suppress the rush of hope his words excited.

10

North Devon

2017

Molly set out from Ilfracombe hoping for a more amiable relationship with her satnav than the journey from London. She had travelled so far that she could hardly believe she was here. Soon Luscombe Park would be more than a mere red blip on a map, more than an Internet image of a gracious, somewhat shabby, Gothic Revival mansion. It would be stone and mortar, park and trees. When she first considered travelling ten thousand miles to investigate the puzzle that had been her great-grandmother's life, she wasn't sure the house would still exist. So many of Britain's great country homes had been lost. Since 1900, more than fifteen hundred country houses had been demolished. There was no reason to believe that Rose's ancestral home hadn't also been a casualty.

A search confirmed that it had indeed survived, but if it was once the centre of a large estate, now it sat on a few acres. British Listed Buildings described it as a 'country house in an emparked landscape' and gave it a Grade II listing. Although parts of its fabric were certainly Tudor, the major sections of the house had been designed in 1859 in Victorian Tudor-Gothic style. Photographs showed a significant mansion of dressed stone, with steep gables, mullioned windows, a tiled roof and walled forecourt.

Somehow Luscombe Park had survived and Molly was on her way to see it. She had taken six months' leave of absence from her teaching job, let her apartment, and boarded a plane for London and her sister Daisy. And now she was hot on Rose's trail. She didn't know what she expected to find. Hopefully, something about the woman her great-grandmother had once been – and a clue to what may have become of her if, as Nan suspected, she had escaped to another life.

Coast soon gave way to pasture and woodland, the landscape becoming a patchwork of small paddocks stitched together with fields of vibrant yellow rapeseed and waving green spears of wheat and oats. She passed through several small villages lined with storybook cottages, her heart beating loudly enough to keep time to the music on the car radio. According to her navigation screen Luscombe Park should be just ahead. But perhaps she was becoming overconfident, or perhaps satnav lady had begun playing tricks again. Despite the instruction to turn right in 50 metres, Molly hesitated, staring down a narrow gravel lane that headed into the midst of a wood. Surely this couldn't be the entrance to Luscombe Park? She found it hard to believe that this track had ever been the drive of a large country home. Nevertheless, she heeded satnav lady's command to 'Turn right. Turn right.'

'Okay, okay, I'm turning right. But you'd better not lead me astray again or I'll . . . I'll . . .' Well, she didn't know exactly what she would do but it was bound to involve electronic failure of some kind.

She turned on to a rutted lane, unfenced woodland crowding close. The high canopy was made up of ancient-looking oaks, with here and there stands of beech. She was surprised at how bare the understorey was, being accustomed to the forests of south-east Australia with their soaring eucalypts and thick understorey of smaller trees, coarse bracken and native shrubs.

Here the groundcover was sparse, with scatterings of spindly, stick-like trees she didn't recognise and bluebells peeping through the leaf litter. She couldn't imagine getting lost here. At home, only the foolish or the brave ventured from the forest path. She might not be lost in the woods but this certainly didn't look like the entrance to a once stately home. Even satnav lady was having second thoughts, the screen showing Molly's vehicle veering off into the blankness of uncharted territory.

'Now the cat's got your tongue!'

She followed the track, curving to the right and down a steep incline, watching her car's path on the screen as it ventured further and further into no-man's-land.

'When safe, do a U-turn,' satnav lady suggested.

'Yeah right, good suggestion.'

'When safe, do a U-turn,' the voice repeated, just in case Molly hadn't heard the first time.

She rounded a bend, cursing as a branch scraped the side of her car, and was brought to a sudden halt facing a barrier constructed from two rough wooden poles supporting a single crossbar. A sign fixed to the bar read 'Nevermind Wood' and a narrow walking path straggled towards a stream trickling through the gully beyond.

'Well, this can't be Luscombe Park,' she muttered as she opened the door and stepped out to survey her surroundings.

'Not quite,' croaked a voice to her right.

She jumped, startled by the sight of an elderly man resting on a shooting stick under a broad oak. In his stillness, and his brown tweed jacket and cap, he was barely distinguishable from the trees.

'Oh hi, you gave me a fright. I didn't see you there.'

'That would be my "old man" camouflage. If I was wearing my purple velvet smoking jacket it would be a different story.'

'I'm sure I'd notice someone out bushwalking in a purple velvet smoking jacket,' she agreed.

'You're Australian?'

'How did you guess? I usually wear my cork hat,' she said with a laugh.

'That would be your use of the term "bushwalking". Here one would call it walking.'

'Even cross country?'

'Must be our habit of understatement. So, you're looking for Luscombe Park?' He pushed his tweed cap back on his head, a wad of white hair escaping from under the brim, so that he could get an unfettered view of her. He considered her with evident curiosity, his faded blue eyes squinting in a friendly smile.

She liked him, she decided. She could tell already that he had a twinkle in his eyes.

'Satnav lady led me astray. Told me to turn right, and I ended up here at the end of the road. I think it's going to take at least a nine-point turn to escape.'

'I think satnav lady may have been a little premature. The turn-off to Luscombe Park is just up the road. But these woods once belonged to the estate, so she could be forgiven.'

'Really?' She stared at the offending woods as if they were to blame for misleading her.

'However, that was a long time ago . . .' He paused for a moment, as if coming to a sudden decision. 'I can guide you to Luscombe if you like,' he offered, levering himself from his seat with the aid of the oak's trunk. 'I might be rather old-fashioned technology but I'm quite reliable.'

'That's very kind of you.'

'Are you visiting the Luscombes?' he asked as they walked back to the car.

Molly was startled for the second time in their meeting, the name jumping out at her in ambush. She hadn't really considered whether any of the Luscombe family might still be living at the house. But of course, that would have been a reasonable assumption. Just because Rose Luscombe had made her home in Australia, it didn't mean there weren't Luscombes left in Devon. There had been her brother Robert, for one thing, and he could have a whole cavalcade of descendants.

'No, not really,' she said, 'just stickybeaking. But I wouldn't want to take you out of your way.'

'Only busy people have that problem. And I think I miscalculated my energy this morning, so you'd be doing an old man a favour. Luscombe Park is much closer to home.'

'That's very kind of you, Mr . . . ?'

'Richard. Call me Richard, dear.'

'Nice to meet you, Richard, I'm Molly . . . Molly Wilson,' she said, reaching out to take his age-spotted hand in hers.

'I'm surprised you're here to see Luscombe Park. It's not on the usual stately homes itinerary, doesn't open to the public and so forth. No one much turns up looking for it, certainly not all the way from Australia.'

'I'm surprised to find myself here too. I feel like a bit of a cliché actually. You know, the whole searching for my roots thing. But I think my great-grandmother used to live there. A long time ago.'

'Really, what was her name?'

'Rose. Rose Luscombe.'

'Ah well, you most certainly deserve a guide then, Rose Luscombe's great-granddaughter.'

Is that who she was? Molly wondered. Rose Luscombe's great-granddaughter? It was funny that, in all her thinking and planning for this trip, it had been about discovering the truth of *her* great-grandmother. Not the other way around.

She had never thought of herself as belonging to Rose.

11

'Nearly there,' said Richard as they arrived at a pair of lopsided wrought-iron gates, propped open to show a long drive bordered by grass straggling on to gravel.

'Maybe we should stop here,' she suggested, a little alarmed at the private nature of the gates.

'The Luscombes won't mind. They know me. And I can slip home the back way. It would save my legs.'

'Well, if you're sure.'

She edged the car slowly forward, taking in her surroundings: the mature oaks and cedars shading the grounds; the chimneys and steep tiled roof peeping through trees at the end of the drive.

'That drive leads to the stables,' Richard explained, pointing out a path to their left. 'There's another entrance further up the road. The stables were subdivided and sold off several years ago now. Turned into a lovely home. Wouldn't mind living there myself.'

'You've been inside?'

'Yes, quite lovely, excellent architect, kept all the historical detail intact – some of the stonework in the stables is fourteenth-century so you wouldn't want to mess with it.'

'No, I should think not,' she said, contemplating the idea of living with so much past. Would you revel in it or drown under its weight? 'I imagine maintaining an estate of this size is costly.'

'Not so much of an estate any more. The farms and most of the park were sold off over the years. There's just the house and a few acres left. Now, follow the drive into the yard –' he said, indicating a gap in the wall that enclosed a rear yard and circular drive – 'and park just there by the entry.'

Molly followed his instructions, pulling up in front of an imposing Gothic arched door of dark wood. She stared up at the regiment of windows. Perhaps if she had grown up in Britain she would have been accustomed to grand manors sprawling across acres of lawn, pitched roofs rising like mountain ranges with their forests of chimneys. But she had been raised in the suburbs of Melbourne, where a grand home meant twelve rooms, four bathrooms, a tennis court and a swimming pool.

'It's huge!'

'It's not Buckingham Palace – but too large to keep the cobwebs at bay, all the same,' said Richard, before adding, 'well, come inside now you're here. They rarely bother locking it. Nothing worth stealing except the house itself.'

He was out of the car and marching towards the door before she could reply. She was beginning to get a sense that perhaps all was not right with Richard. He'd seemed perfectly affable and quick-witted ten minutes ago, but first impressions could be deceptive. After all, she told herself, she *had* found him wandering alone in the woods. And he was quite elderly.

'Richard, wait!' she called as she stepped from the car to give chase. But he prodded open the front door with his shooting stick and was shuffling through an oak-lined vestibule towards a further door by the time she caught up with him. 'Richard, perhaps we should ring the doorbell.'

'Oh, there's no one home, dear. The housekeeper only comes

on Mondays and Thursdays, and the owner is rarely home in the mornings,' he answered, waving at her airily and opening the inner door.

She followed him into a great hall, the size of her entire apartment, a vast expanse of scuffed floorboards with faded rugs dotted like islands in its midst and acres of linen-fold panelling lining the walls. An enormous pale stone fireplace, looking like it belonged in one of those Tudor TV series, dominated the far wall and ranks of windows illuminated the space. The ceiling soared above on oak rafters, but Richard had been right about the cobwebs. They festooned the chandelier and draped the curtain rails like dusty pelmets.

'I don't think we should be here without the owners' permission,' she ventured, conscious that someone might appear at any moment to find a perfect stranger and a strange old man taking a grand tour of their home. Yet she was reluctant to leave him here alone. She had found him in the woods, loitering like Puck, and felt responsible for him, despite the fact that he most probably was about to cause her considerable embarrassment.

'Not to worry, you might as well take a look now you're here,' he whispered conspiratorially. 'And you can always blame the crazy old man if we're caught.'

'I think you're about to get me into a lot of trouble.'

'Oh, I'm always up for a spot of trouble.' He winked, linking his free arm through hers and guiding her towards a foyer on their left where a sombre-looking staircase led upstairs. Several stone archways divided the foyer from a corridor that presumably led to service rooms in one direction and more reception rooms in the other.

'I really think we should go,' she reiterated, gazing wistfully towards the entry just as footsteps sounded a knell above. She tugged firmly on his linked arm, urging him towards the door, but he was surprisingly solid for a wood sprite. 'We really have to go now!' she hissed.

'Lucas!' Richard chimed as the footsteps resolved themselves into a large, thirty-something man wearing old jeans and a damp T-shirt, towelling his wet hair as he rounded the corner of the stairs. He came to a halt on the landing, looking down at them. Obviously they had interrupted his shower. It's a wonder he wasn't armed with a cricket bat (or worse) to head off intruders. She gave up her tugging and relinquished Richard's arm, bracing herself for, at best, a stern rebuke and, at worst, the imminent arrival of the police. At least Richard appeared to know the owner, so that was some consolation.

'Richard!' the man exclaimed. But he was looking straight at her, an expression of bemusement on his face. 'You've got someone with you.'

'Oh yes, this is Molly, she . . .'

'Mr . . . Lucas . . . I'm so s-sorry,' she stammered, 'we were just leaving. I didn't realise Richard was coming inside. I thought we were just going to have a look at the house from the outside. Really . . .' She couldn't resist glaring at Richard and flicking her head in the direction of the door, hoping he would take the hint and they could make their escape before any more trouble came stomping down the stairs.

'She's a bit flighty. Seems to be under the impression that we're intruding. We're not intruding, are we?' Richard pronounced shamelessly.

'No, I just finished fixing the shower.'

'Good man, that thing's been plaguing me for weeks.'

Molly stared at the side of Richard's head – he was studiously avoiding her gaze – then back at the imposing figure of Lucas, who had descended the stairs and was holding out his hand, the towel now roped casually about his neck. She couldn't help noticing the way his cotton T-shirt clung to his broad chest and how his longish hair glistened inkily, drips of water poised to dribble down the back of his neck. She took his hand, returning his firm grip, and wishing she had a plumber this gorgeous back in Australia. It would make blocked drains so much more compelling. Then she turned accusingly to the old man who stood grinning wickedly at her side.

'*You're* the owner. You're Richard . . . Luscombe?'

'Guilty as charged, dear.'

She let out the breath she realised she had been holding. 'You had me worried for a minute. I thought you were—'

'Demented?' asked Lucas. 'Loopy? Decrepit?'

'There's no need to exaggerate, old man.'

'All of the above, actually.'

'Richard does like to play his little games,' Lucas said with a sympathetic smile. 'Obviously he doesn't have enough to keep him occupied.'

'She found me in the woods like a sprite. I quite like being taken for a sprite.'

'More like a goblin,' Molly muttered with a glare.

'And I couldn't resist a prank. I hope I haven't offended,' he added, so contritely that she found it difficult to maintain her indignation.

'You're quite wicked, but I suppose I'll have to forgive you, especially since you've led me into your remarkable home, though it was under false pretences.'

'Well, to make up for it, what say you follow me to the kitchen for a nice cup of tea? There's no point looking around for the butler,' he added, when she seemed surprised that he should make the tea himself. 'I'm my own cook, valet and butler. You'll join us, won't you, Lucas?'

'Wouldn't miss it for the world,' Lucas said with an engaging grin.

Was she imagining things? She had the distinct impression

that there was more than an invitation to tea in his smile. The sliver of attention gave her a fledgling glow. It was pathetic really, being charmed by a man's smile. 'You're only here for a few days,' she reminded herself, 'and your heart is still taped together with Band-Aids, so don't get any ideas.' Besides, a man as attractive as Lucas probably had his own Jordana somewhere nearby.

Lucas relieved Richard of his shooting stick, placing it in an umbrella stand before taking the older man's free arm and turning towards the corridor. At that moment she noticed a photograph amongst a group arranged on the wall opposite. It caught her eye, not for its elaborate golden frame or the proud military bearing of the uniformed man staring back at her, but for the bright-eyed young girl posing next to him, her hair contained by a white veil, her plain dress protected by the long white apron and sleeves of a VAD nurse.

'I know her,' she gasped softly, realising that the question she had posed Uncle Ted in Wuurnong's dining room was being answered here in the faded glory of Luscombe Park.

'Who?' asked Richard, searching the gallery of long-dead ancestors.

'That's Rose, isn't it? That girl in the nurse's uniform?' she asked, studying the face of the young nurse with her arm linked through that of the handsome young man in uniform. 'And who's that standing next to her?'

Richard glanced at the portrait she indicated, his eyes losing their twinkle for a moment. 'That's Robert Luscombe,' he sighed. 'My father . . . Rose's brother.'

Rose's brother, who according to Uncle Ted had waited forty years to travel the ten thousand miles to visit his only sister, arriving mere days after she had disappeared. She stepped closer to the wall to examine the Luscombe siblings. You could tell they were related. You could see it in the tilt of their eyes and something about the shape of their chins – a little haughty, a touch arrogant. Or was she making judgements based more on the size of their house than the contours of their faces?

'You know who she was?' Lucas asked. He was staring at her in some surprise.

'Yes. Yes, I do. That's why I'm here.'

'I detect a mystery,' he said, looking at her as if she were the mystery, not Rose.

Richard glanced from Lucas to Molly as if weighing which words might make the greatest impression. She could tell already that Richard Luscombe was an old showman at heart. 'Well, Lucas,' he answered for her. 'I believe Molly may be my long-lost cousin from Australia . . . twice removed. That would make Rose her great-grandmother, my father her great-great-uncle and Molly my only living relative.'

She laughed. 'Oh, Richard, that's where you're wrong. There are a lot more like me where I come from.'

12

Before setting out for lunch at Luscombe Park the following day, Molly wandered down to Ilfracombe harbour where a flotilla of small white yachts elbowed for space against fishing boats with red buoys braiding their sides like pompoms. The tide was ebbing, leaving those boats moored at the harbour's edge stranded like beached whales. She took a deep breath, inhaling the familiar scent of the ocean with its undertones of fish and seaweed – the smells of her childhood. What was she doing here? She had come so far and yet here she was, back in the same place, walking by the sea feeling sorry for herself.

'You're here for Nan. So just get on with it,' she told herself sternly, not realising how she echoed her mother. 'Just live your life,' she scolded silently as she walked the shore, all the time conscious of the massive promontory hulking over the town, the salty tang in the air and the unpredictable swell of the sea whispering to her of grief and regret.

Twenty minutes later she returned to her hotel, surprised to see an Audi parked outside with a familiar figure standing by the kerb scanning the road in the opposite direction. He was dressed in a pair of tailored grey trousers and a navy shirt – obviously not planning on unclogging any drains that day.

'Lucas!' She hailed him with a wave.

'Molly! You're back,' he said, turning towards her. 'Richard sent me to save you getting lost. But you weren't in when he called the hotel and he forgot to get your number so . . . here I am,' he shrugged.

She couldn't help noticing the breadth of those shoulders beneath his slim-fitting shirt. 'Thanks but I think I have satnav lady's number now. She's being very meek at the moment.'

'It's no trouble.'

She smiled, hoping her cheeks weren't too red from her walk. 'So you're Richard's chauffeur as well as his plumber?'

He threw back his head and laughed. 'You thought I was the plumber?'

'You're not?' Oh dear, he was probably a family friend, or relative, or something equally mortifying.

'I impressed you that much with my wrench?' Reaching into his pocket for his wallet, he withdrew a business card.

'Lucas *Toms*,' she read aloud. 'Architect.'

'You sound surprised.'

'You're a Toms.'

'That I am.'

'You didn't by any chance have a relative by the name of Ivy Toms, did you? Whose father was an agricultural labourer and mother a laundress?'

'Now you're beginning to sound like the constabulary. Should I be worried?'

'No, nothing like that,' she laughed.

'Then don't tell me you're *my* long-lost cousin twice removed too?'

'I doubt it. My great-grandmother sailed to Australia with someone called Ivy and I found an Ivy Toms on the parish register so I was just wondering whether—' She broke off, not

86

quite sure how to explain herself. Whether to mention those words 'Together forever'.

He looked at her speculatively for a moment as if considering what to say. 'You were wondering whether Ivy Toms was the Ivy who sailed with Rose.'

'Uh-huh.'

'Ivy Toms was my great-aunt. And yes, she did set out for Australia with Rose.'

'She did?' Molly smiled, pleased that one of the puzzle pieces was falling into place. 'But she didn't arrive with Rose. And as far as we know, they had no further contact. Do you know what happened to her?'

'Ivy came down with Spanish flu and died en route, in Colombo,' Lucas said with a small shake of his head.

'Spanish flu?'

For months she had imagined that Ivy, like Rose, had migrated to Australia and begun a new life. She had envisaged her as the matriarch of a clan with a long, fruitful life. For whatever reason, Rose's life had turned sour; she hoped that her friend's had worked out happier. Now the disappointment of discovering that Ivy's life had been cut short was a blow. And to discover that she had died of Spanish flu was even worse. That pandemic had killed more than fifty million people in the wake of the First World War. Poor Ivy would have died in a delirium of fever, her lungs drowning in her own bodily fluids.

It was just so sad.

'That would explain it then,' she sighed.

'What?'

'Why I only found Rose's name when I searched the passenger arrivals for 1919 at the Public Records Office back home.'

'You look heartbroken.'

'You must think I'm ridiculous.'

'No, but it was a long time ago. A lot of people died . . .'

Lucas's words were a bleak reminder of that first great war and its aftermath.

'I know.' Ivy was an important part of Rose's story, she was sure, and now her trail ended somewhere in the Indian Ocean.

Nan might have set Molly upon this journey, but for some reason it had become a mission. Instinct told her that if she could find the answers to her questions about Rose and Ivy, she might know what questions to ask about her own life. Having discovered that Ivy died en route, she would have to reorient her thinking altogether.

To distract her on the drive to Luscombe Park, Lucas told her about his work as a heritage architect and more about his family. The Toms, it turned out, had lived in the area for at least two hundred years, initially working as agricultural labourers for the Luscombes. Until recently, they had occupied a cottage that had once been part of the estate. Lucas's grandfather, Daniel, had purchased Ashcott from the Luscombes in the 1950s. His parents had also lived there until a few years ago when they retired, selling the cottage and moving to Exeter.

'So you're an only child, then?'

'I have an older sister who lives in London. Luckily. I say luckily because if she lived here she'd drive me crazy. Caroline likes to boss me around – she says someone needs to sort my life out.'

Molly wondered what it was about him that needed sorting out. 'I have a sister like that, only she's younger. That's probably worse.'

'Maybe we should get them together,' he said with a grin.

It turned out that Lucas was the 'excellent' architect who had converted the Luscombe stables to a home, where he now lived. He had planned the subdivision for Richard and, once it was approved, purchased the property and redeveloped it in an agonising five-year process. The purchase money had allowed Richard to make running repairs to Luscombe and keep his head above water . . . just.

'The work would have gone a lot faster if I hadn't done so much myself. But I didn't have the money for a builder to do it all. And before you ask, no I didn't do the plumbing.'

'I'm sure you'd make an excellent plumber.'

'I'd probably make more money.'

'But your work will last for centuries.'

'So will PVC pipes.'

Lucas had to concentrate as he turned the car on to a narrow road, more of a lane than a proper road. It gave her the chance to return her thoughts to Ivy and Rose. Two friends bound for a great adventure on the far side of the world, yet only one had made it. She wondered how Rose had fared in Colombo, watching as Ivy sickened and died. Or had she abandoned her? What a terrible decision it would have been: whether to stay and risk her own life, or go on alone. If she had stayed, she might have caught the flu and died too. But if she abandoned her friend to save herself, she would have had to live with the guilt for the rest of her life. Molly wasn't sure which choice was worse.

'You look thoughtful,' Lucas ventured, flicking her a side-ways glance as the road widened once more. 'Not still thinking about Ivy and Rose, are you?'

'I was wondering how Rose coped, alone in Colombo, with her friend dying from the Spanish flu.'

Lucas shrugged, saying, 'Oh, but Ivy wasn't Rose's friend. I thought you realised . . . Ivy was Rose Luscombe's maid.'

Molly remembered the two hands sharing one pocket of an apron. The gesture was so intimate, as if they shared a secret. They looked like best friends. And the notation on the photograph suggested the same. 'Together forever' – or at least someone had thought so once.

Rose and Ivy's secrets were becoming more intriguing at every turn.

13

Port Said, Egypt
1919

She wasn't built for adventure, Ivy decided, fanning herself against the hot offshore wind that seemed to carry with it half the sand of the Sahara. The Toms were landlubbers; born to grub in the dirt or scrub sheets, not face the uncertainties of the ocean. She and Rose had been at sea two weeks already and Ivy was yet to become accustomed to the pitch and roll of the ship in rough weather – or the pitch of her stomach. On this day the entire complement of passengers lined the decks to bid farewell to the Mediterranean as the SS *Osprey* entered the Suez Canal, laughing and chatting as they planned quick excursions to the pyramids, or camel rides into the desert. Meanwhile Ivy's heart beat a tattoo against her ribs at the thought of leaving Europe and the world she knew behind.

Rising from the flat sandy coastline, a long white building, resplendent with green domes, greeted the ship as she steamed towards the canal entrance. A large bronze gentleman some thirty feet tall pointed the way from a jetty while on the other side of the canal a lighthouse warned of dangerous waters. The waterway had been opened to great fanfare forty years earlier, according to the purser; and here in Port Said, East and West mingled in this cosmopolitan port city. Wide-bottomed boats, with twin triangular sails like butterfly wings, jostled for space with the steamers and rowing boats in the crowded port. The laden sailboats sat so low in the water that Ivy wondered how they were not swamped by the larger ships. She flinched each time she spotted one veering close to the *Osprey*'s hull.

The town spread out along the shore in a tidy arrangement of timber and iron buildings, sprinkled with the dusty green of date palms, while the waterfront was crowded with beached rowing boats, men in long pale robes or billowing dark trousers, even the occasional camel bearing sacks and baskets. Ivy watched it all, mesmerised and appalled at the same time by its strangeness. What if Australia turned out to be just as alien? How would she get on then?

On the promenade deck, the first-class passengers had donned their finery at the dressing bugle in preparation for venturing ashore. The men wore lightweight suits and panama hats, while the women wafted about the deck like a sea of poppies in floaty dresses and fine silk blouses tucked into linen skirts. Ivy was looking her best too, in a cream linen frock of Rose's from two summers ago that she had remodelled, narrowing the silhouette, shortening the hem and adding a design of black embroidery running the length of the front panel. With it she wore a sweet black hat of woven braid and cream shoes that buckled at the ankle. The mirror in the first-class suite she shared with Rose had told her that she looked *très élégante*, with her hair parted on the side, ironed into neat waves around her face, and knotted low on her neck.

Rose had returned to the cabin after breakfast to freshen up for the day ashore so Ivy was free to lean on the railings, day-dreaming as she observed the other passengers. Amongst the waiting crowd on deck, one man in particular caught her eye, threading his way through the milling passengers, with a smile for the ladies, a pat on the back for the younger gentlemen and a firm handshake for the older gents. Although they were yet to be introduced, she knew the ship's surgeon by sight. The purser had allotted Rose and Ivy places at the opposite end of the dining saloon from the good doctor, but once or twice their gazes had brushed each other's across the long expanse of white damask and gleaming silver. Sandy-haired with a high forehead, slightly crooked nose and a firm jaw, Dr Sullivan had the air of a man who knew he was good-looking but affected not to notice. Much like Mr Robert and his friends before the war came along.

Before she could quite banish the thought, she felt a moment-ary grabbing pain and she clutched at her chest. She had promised herself she would not think about any of that.

'Are you quite all right, miss?' said the doctor, appearing at her side.

'Quite all right,' she answered, taking a restorative breath before she turned to smile at him. 'I suspect breakfast did not agree with me this morning.'

'Perhaps if you sat for a few moments before the tender arrives,' he said, taking her by the elbow and leading her towards an empty deckchair.

'Thank you, Doctor.'

'You have the advantage of me, Miss . . . ?'

'Toms. Ivy Toms. I'm travelling with Miss Rose Luscombe to meet her fiancé in Melbourne.'

'I've met Miss Luscombe. The redoubtable Mrs Brigham introduced us,' he said with conspiratorial smile.

Ivy acknowledged his smile with a nod. She had already dis-covered that the redoubtable Mrs Brigham made it her business to meet everyone on the first-class deck. She and her husband, the Colonel, travelled from Colombo to London so frequently that she considered herself an old hand at the crossing and liked nothing better than to share her knowledge with anyone she could prevail upon to listen. She also seemed to have a finely tuned antenna for anything of note that occurred aboard ship, and delighted in sharing that too. Even now Ivy could feel the woman's attention burning the back of her neck. Somewhere behind her Mrs Brigham was watching with interest this innocent conversation between the ship's surgeon and Miss Luscombe's companion.

'Will you be going ashore this morning, Miss Toms?'

'I expect so, I'm waiting for Miss Luscombe to join me,' she said, aware that her careful pronunciation mimicked Rose's speech. After two weeks in this company she was learning to soften her West Country accent. Any 'ee's and 'be's had been eradicated years earlier.

'Perhaps I could escort you, if you and Miss Luscombe haven't already arranged a shore party?'

His words caught her off guard. Invitations had been rare in her life thus far.

'I beg pardon if I've offended in some fashion, Miss Toms,' he added when she responded with a frown.

'Not at all. We'd be delighted to join you.'

'Excellent . . .' He paused, and she followed his gaze towards the deckhouse where a familiar figure stepped gracefully on to the deck. 'And here is Miss Luscombe now, if I am not mistaken.'

Who could mistake Rose when she was determined to be noticed? At the breakfast bugle she had been pale and pretty in blue silk chiffon, but clearly she had returned to their staterooms to change, for now she emerged into the bright morning air a vision in red and white stripes. Ivy knew the dress, as she knew all Rose's garments intimately – from her fine lawn drawers to her sanitary apron – but only last week Rose had declared she looked like a red and white humbug in the despised dress and had relegated it to the back of the wardrobe. Now it had been resurrected, skimming over her long slim frame, and tied with a sash at the side of her waist like a gift. With her narrow shawl collar, cuffs of red, and ruby drop earrings that accentuated her fine bone structure, every eye on the promenade deck was drawn to her.

'Miss Luscombe.' The ship's surgeon hailed her with a wave.

'Dr Sullivan,' she said, drifting towards them.

'I've just prevailed upon Miss Toms to let me escort you ashore. It looks to be a warm day,' he said, glancing at the cloche hat by the fashionable Miss Reboux that crowned Rose's head.

'Oh, I left my parasol on the bed. Ivy, would you mind fetching it for me? You're so much quicker than me, and we don't want to keep Dr Sullivan waiting.'

Ivy looked to the doctor for a response but he appeared not to have heard. All his attention was reserved for Rose's wide blue eyes and the sweet blond pin-curls decorating her cheeks, which Ivy had taken such pains with that morning. Swallowing the defiant words that sprang to her tongue, she returned to their suite, rueing the day so long ago that she had agreed to work at Luscombe Park.

'You could come and work at Luscombe,' Robert had said, that day by the road with her at her wits' end and the threat of Packer's chocolate factory hanging over her head. 'That would give you a wage and get you away from Toms . . . I mean your father.'

'I see.' She had imagined all too clearly long days of toiling in the kitchen or laundry of the big house, just as her mother had done before she married Ivy's da. A girl like her, like her mother before her, inherited her life as much as the colour of her hair or the shape of her face.

'Thank you, sir, but I doubt Da would let me,' she had said through tight lips.

'Robert, I don't think being a kitchen maid at Luscombe would suit Ivy at all,' Rose had interrupted.

'Not as a kitchen maid, no, I was thinking that it won't be

long before you'll be needing your own maid – and who could be better than someone you've known your whole life? Someone who knows and understands us . . . Luscombe.'

'But Ivy doesn't know a thing about being a lady's maid,' Rose had protested, her voice rising half an octave at least. 'What would Gibbons say?'

'She has time to learn. She can start as housemaid and Gibbons can train her up.'

'I don't know what Gibbons will say about that.' Rose had rolled her eyes before adding, 'And what about Toms?'

'Don't worry about him. He'll come around with the right inducement.'

Ivy had been forgotten. The discussion had bounced between the two, a matter to be decided between them as if it weren't her life they were discussing. Her future. Not so different to her da, really.

'So what do you say? Would you like to come to Luscombe and train as a lady's maid?' Mr Robert had beamed, as if expecting congratulations on a job well done, while Rose hovered behind him with her arms crossed, looking decidedly put out.

He was so shiny and handsome. Was it this that had convinced her, even then? Gleaming like something expensive and unattainable from the high street shop window. It wasn't as if she had choices. She could go to Bristol and work in the factory, giving any spare coins to her father, or she could go to Luscombe, work as a housemaid and give her coins to her father. But at Luscombe she would be close to her ma, and the future Robert dangled before her offered a way out if she were clever, if she worked hard, if she were lucky. At least she had thought so then. Lady's maid, companion, perhaps in time wife to a respectable tradesman . . . she had flirted with the dream of finding a different life.

She remembered looking at her once-upon-a-time friend:

the charming arrangement of her golden curls, the lustre of her pearls, the hip-length linen motoring jacket, the perfectly laundered blouse and wondering – did Rose want her as a maid? It certainly had not looked that way, for she stood with her arms crossed defiantly and a distinct pout to her mouth. In a way, Ivy sympathised with her. Robert had stolen her choices as much as Ivy's father had robbed her of hers. But then again, why should it have mattered what Rose wanted? She always got what she wanted in the end.

'Yes, Mr Robert,' she had said, feeling her habitual knot of anger loosening a touch. 'I should like that very much.'

But that had been six years ago, when she thought fate might have a different life in store for her. So much had happened in between and yet, here she was . . . still fetching Rose's parasol and no doubt playing chaperone on the good doctor's excursion ashore.

Snatching up the offending object, she hurried back on deck just in time to see Rose flattering the doctor with her most enchanting smile and hear her saying, 'Oh, but Ivy isn't my cousin or companion, Dr Sullivan. Ivy is my maid.'

She had travelled thousands of miles, survived a myriad of woes, worked a lifetime in her meagre years, and yet it appeared that she had not gone anywhere at all.

14

North Devon

2017

'We lost the baronetcy at the beginning of the nineteenth century,' Richard commented as if it were an event that had occurred last week.

'That was a bit of bad luck.' Molly was unsure what the correct response should be. Did you commiserate about family misfortunes that were two centuries old? Lost titles weren't a regular topic of discussion in her social circle. Her friends were more likely to complain about lost rental bonds.

'Yes, the estate passed through the female line. Though it wasn't entailed, so that was fortunate. Plus the heiress, Lady Prudence Traherne, married Alfred Luscombe, a wealthy cotton merchant, so there was also an injection of funds.' Richard paused on the first-floor landing to catch his breath. She stood at his side, her arm linked through his, Lucas trailing behind.

He was taking her on a tour of the house after a delightful lunch on the terrace, spent discussing her background in history and Richard's continual battle to stop the house from falling apart. Now they peered into a phalanx of sad, empty bedrooms opening from the upstairs gallery. Although elegant at first glance, the rooms were uninhabited except for spiders and the ghosts of Luscombes long since departed. Dustsheets shrouded furniture, decades of grime smeared windows, and the air had the fusty smell of a seldom-worn coat.

'Which room belonged to Rose?' she asked. Now that she was here in this once grand home in its stately park, she was having even more trouble understanding why Rose had left it all behind to marry a stranger on the other side of the world. How could she have given up the heft and security of centuries for the mere idea of a man? For Jim Turner was a man made of words. It was his letters she had married. How could she have known the feel of the real man? It would have been like building your house out of paper.

'She had Father's room while he was away at the war, the corner room on the south-east side. When she left for Australia, Father moved back in. Then after my grandmother died, he and my mother moved into the master bedroom next door. Rose's old room is right along here.' He indicated the door to a large room in the south-west corner of the house.

As they followed him towards Rose's room, Molly was conscious of Lucas at her side. He knew the house well and added his own comments about its architecture as Richard expounded on the history. He was clearly attached to it, and she wondered how he might feel seeing a stranger occupying its vast spaces once Richard was gone. A hotelier perhaps, since Richard had no heirs, or a tech mogul with a yen for tradition.

They reached Rose's room and Richard stood back to let her enter. She pushed the door open partway and poked her head around, half expecting to get shivers up her spine. But there was nothing like that. It was only a room, a large airy room papered in a faded green stripe, with a worn oak floor and windows overlooking the park. There was little furniture except for a bed covered by a dustsheet, an old dresser and a couple of simple wooden chairs.

'It must have been very handsome once,' she said.

'It has great proportions and beautiful light,' said Lucas.

'My father always loved this room.'

But his sister, perhaps not so much. Why else had he let forty years pass before seeking her out? Molly didn't know why she felt so disappointed. Had she hoped to feel some trace of Rose in the room? Find something that belonged to her? Or had she hoped for a more personal revelation. Silly, really. She sighed and Lucas looked at her.

'What's up?' he asked.

'Nothing,' she answered with a shake of the head. 'Expecting ghosts.'

'Oh, we don't have any ghosts,' Richard said, 'not in the house at any rate. No, our ghosts are all in here,' he added, placing a hand over his heart.

'I think, in her own way, my nan was haunted by Rose,' she said. Richard was so affable and sympathetic, so interested in her quest, that she suddenly found herself telling him every-thing about Rose's disappearance, the scrapbook, and her grandmother's long search that she had made her own. 'I feel like Nan bequeathed me Rose, as much as any money I inherited.'

'We all have our ghosts, dear. Some take human form, while others are as ephemeral as regrets.' Richard patted her arm while Lucas stood alongside, at home with his past and its secrets.

She had made this pilgrimage for Nan; for all that she had been, and all she had done for her. She had also intended to research Rose and Ivy's story, as a springboard to further study, perhaps even a future thesis on unmarried female emigrants. Except there was more to it than that. Somehow, she was convinced that if she could get to the essence of those two young girls in the photograph, she might rediscover that other young girl who had gone missing with her father's death seven-teen years before. If she could understand why Rose and Ivy had taken the risks they had, she might be able to get her own courage back.

Well, she knew now that Ivy's story had ended abruptly in the Indian Ocean at the age of twenty, but she didn't know why Ivy had followed her employer in the first place. Surely other arrangements could have been made for Ivy? Other young aristocratic Englishwomen needed maids. What had bound her so tightly to Rose that she expected it to hold forever? Or would the real risk for Ivy have been staying behind?

Maybe that's what she was doing in her own life. Plodding along behind. Was that the real danger, being unwilling to deviate from the past?

'The servants used to inhabit the attic rooms,' Richard said, dragging her away from her thoughts. He halted his tour at the foot of a narrow staircase leading to the attics. 'Your own Ivy would have slept up there.'

She wasn't sure whether he meant to assign Ivy to Lucas or to her. Since his discovery of her family connection she seemed to have acquired ownership of Rose and all her history in his mind, including Ivy. It was as if he had latched on to her as tangible proof that the Luscombe line wouldn't end with him in this brooding old house. Lunch had included a long discussion of Jim's letters, the sautoir she had found, and her idea for a book about unmarried women's immigration to Australia: all those governesses, servants, farmworkers and brides who travelled ten thousand miles to make new lives.

Then Richard had reminisced about his early years growing up at Luscombe Park, while he accompanied his tour of the house with a potted history of all the Luscombes and their forbears, back to medieval times when the family settled there. During the nineteenth century some of those first rubble-filled walls had been incorporated into the stable buildings where Lucas now lived. It was almost as if, through Molly, Richard was trying to join the dots of the past with the future.

'I wonder how Ivy came to be Rose's maid,' Molly mused.

'Ivy grew up on the estate, so they'd known each other since childhood,' said Richard.

'My grandfather told me that Ivy used to sneak off to play with Rose when they were little girls. She got into trouble for it with her father. Apparently he had quite a temper, old Walter Toms,' said Lucas.

'There's probably a photograph of Ivy somewhere in the attic rooms. We have photographs of family and staff dating from the 1860s. I'll take a look for you, dear, if I find the energy. But there are so *many* boxes – and it's worse than the Sahara in a sandstorm up there with all that dust.'

'I have a photograph of Ivy on my phone – of Rose and Ivy, actually. Would you like to see it?' She took her phone from her pocket and flicked through her gallery to find the portrait of two young women in their VAD gear.

'It must have been taken the same day as the one of Rose and Father,' said Richard.

'It was enclosed with Nan's letter to me. Their names and the date 1917 were written on the back, along with the words "Together forever". Only, until I spotted that photo downstairs, we weren't sure which of the two was my great-grandmother Rose and which was Ivy. Apparently my great-grandmother hated having her photo taken so we had nothing to compare it with.'

Richard sighed, leaning a little more heavily on his walking stick. 'The VAD. Awful business that. My father always regretted letting Rose join, and he regretted asking Ivy to accompany her to Australia even more bitterly. Together forever indeed.'

'Robert asked Ivy?'

'Yes. Apparently he was concerned that Rose was too flighty. He thought Ivy would be a steadying influence.'

'It's ancient history now, you don't want to upset yourself,' Lucas chided, placing a hand on Richard's shoulder.

'History is the reason we are what we are. We can't simply bury it and forget,' Richard faltered.

'You're talking to a historian, so . . .' Molly was eager to hear what he might say – and yet, like Lucas, she didn't want to upset him.

'Father blamed himself. He said that he had set in train a series of events that led to Ivy's death. That if Rose hadn't nursed Henry Turner at the hospital, then she wouldn't have corresponded with his brother Jim, and neither girl would ever have left England.'

'No one can know that,' Lucas said, 'least of all a century later. And Ivy could have just as easily caught the Spanish flu here in Devon.'

'And if Rose hadn't met Henry . . . I for one wouldn't exist. So it did someone some good,' said Molly. And if Nan hadn't bequeathed her the scrapbook, she wouldn't be here at Luscombe Park searching the past for answers to her future.

They finished the tour downstairs in the study, which Richard also used as his bedroom. She was surprised to find that it resembled a shrine of sorts, with photographs of Richard and another man covering every available surface.

'Dev was an opera singer. We travelled everywhere together,' he said, resting an affectionate hand upon a photograph taken in front of the Taj Mahal. 'He passed away ten years ago now.'

'I'm so sorry. You obviously miss him a great deal, but I see what you mean about touring everywhere,' she said, raising one eyebrow, for the photos pictured Richard and his partner all over the world, posing in front of enough famous monuments to fill a coffee table book.

'Lucas put Dev's picture on my phone for me. See . . .' He

showed her the wallpaper of his phone, a photograph of an attractive young man with soulful brown eyes and well-groomed brows. 'So now I carry him with me always.'

'He's very handsome.'

'All these photos are very clichéd, I know. Dev made terrible fun of me, but now that he's gone at least I have them. They're like our babies. Oh, and you of course, Princess,' he added as a Siamese cat rubbed impatiently against his legs. 'It must be suppertime. She never turns up until then.'

'I think it's time I left you in peace,' Molly suggested, looking enquiringly at Lucas, who nodded his agreement. 'I've taken up so much of your time and you've been very patient.'

'Not at all, dear, it's refreshing having a young and enthusiastic visitor, and I do think you should pursue your calling. If history shouts, you must listen, for it has so much to tell us.'

'I think you're probably right. I should have listened years ago, but I let my fears drown it out. Teaching has been good for me, though. I've learned some very useful negotiating skills from my students.' She had met Matt for another thing: PE teacher, surfer, man of action. So unlike her. Perhaps they were never meant to be together forever.

'Well, I'm pleased you're listening now and . . . I think I may have a proposition for you,' he said, bending to pick up Princess, who had begun using his right leg as a scratching post.

As Richard unfurled his tall, frail body, cat enfolded in his arms, Lucas steadied him, all the while watching her, a puzzled expression on his face. He pantomimed enquiry over Richard's shoulder. 'A proposition, that sounds intimidating.'

She gave Lucas a tiny shrug of ignorance. It was the first she'd heard of it.

'The truth is that both the estate and the family have dwindled over the last hundred years, until the house and I are all that's left. There hasn't been money for a conservator or historian, and

I devoted too much time to travelling to attempt the job myself. I've been worried about what will happen to the family archives. And now you've arrived on my doorstep like manna from heaven.'

'I'm not sure what you're suggesting.'

'I thought you might like to be my archivist.'

She thought at first that he was joking. She had already discovered he was something of a trickster. But he was in earnest, offering food and lodgings in exchange for help sorting two centuries of documents that had been consigned to oblivion in the attics where the servants once slept. She could stay as long as she felt inclined and was welcome to copy any documents that shed light on her great-grandmother's life.

'It's an intriguing offer,' she said, once she realised he was serious.

'Some would call it slave labour.'

'I'm not sure how long I'm planning to stay. I only have six months' leave. Conserving and cataloguing the archive of an estate like Luscombe is a big job, and I'm not really an archivist.'

But he dangled the offer before her like a promise. There might be a treasure trove of documents in this attic that she could happily bury herself in for weeks, if not months. And who knew what she might find? Not least, further clues to the mystery of Rose and Ivy, clues that might lead her to some semblance of truth about Rose's disappearance. Yet a nagging voice held her back. The same voice that always held her back, whispering to her of deceit and deservedness, of guilt and atonement.

She would be doing it for Nan. The fact that she might enjoy the search was irrelevant. Except why should she be happy when her father was dead?

Richard must have sensed her hesitation, for he added, 'Stay as long as you can spare. You'd be doing me a great favour.'

'I'm not a professional historian.'

'Ah, but you have a master's degree. You told me,' he replied smugly. 'This could be an opportunity to begin your professional career.'

He was right. As well as being an opportunity to pursue Nan's quest and discover more about Rose and Ivy, cataloguing the Luscombe archive would look good on her résumé.

'I'd be most appreciative, dear. And the company would be lovely.'

It was the last comment that decided her. Richard was such a nice man and was obviously lonely. She might not deserve such an opportunity, but he did.

'Okay. If you're sure, I'd love to help out.'

'Excellent. And you never know what you might find buried amongst all those relics.'

At least she could make someone happy.

As Lucas walked Molly to the car she couldn't resist one last glance at the house looming grandly behind her. Now that she had arrived, it was difficult to leave those centuries of stories behind. She would like time to delve into her family's history in more detail.

'It's imposing, isn't it?' said Lucas. 'So long as you don't look too closely.'

'Mmm . . . sad, though.'

'What?'

'That the Luscombe family thread is about to be broken. That whoever inherits won't be related. There aren't any cousins or anything?'

'Only you and your family.'

'I'd hardly call that related. The connection is so distant.'

'Well, it's lucky you turned up before it's too late.'

'Yes. Yes, it is. At least I got to meet Richard.'

'And Richard got to meet you,' Lucas added with an enigmatic smile.

And she had seen where Rose and Ivy grew up, one girl in her elegant sunny room looking out over the park, the other in her tiny attic closet under the eaves.

15

North Devon

1913

Rose woke to the tread of heavy feet somewhere in her vicinity. She opened her eyes to see early morning light peeking around the curtains. Accustomed to the light-stepping Muriel first thing in the morning, she froze at the sound of unfamiliar boots clomping around her room. A sharp smell wafted to her nose and she heard the swish of skirts as someone bent to pick up her chamber pot. Ivy was emptying the contents and there was nothing she could do about it. She knew what she would like to do with the pot's contents – but Robert in his wisdom had chosen to employ the girl, and now Rose had to live with his decision. It was all too embarrassing. Her childhood friend was dealing with her urine and washing out her small clothes, and she had to pretend she was fine with it. How could she explain all this to her brother?

She closed her eyes for a moment, drifting into a world where her maid was named Odette and answered '*Oui, mademoiselle*' so prettily, as she anticipated Rose's every whim. Odette would soon discover all the village gossip and tell naughty stories to make Rose laugh. She would know how to style her hair in the latest fashion and agree knowledgeably with all Rose's selections. Odette would travel with her to London, perhaps even Paris and . . .

There was a bang and a crash and the sound of breaking china.

'Oh. Oh no . . .' The words hiccupped into a sob.

Rose turned over, pulling the blanket over her ears to block out the sound of her new maid crying, and the stench of her own urine puddling on the floor.

'Odette, where are you?' she muttered to herself.

After two weeks at Luscombe Park, Ivy concluded that the higher you climbed up the service ladder, the further you were removed from the dirt. The scullery maid and hall boy were closest to the dirt: the scullery maid up to her elbows in pig grease and offal, and the hall boy drowning in the other servants' chamber pots. While on the highest rung, the housekeeper merely sniffed at dirt as she ran her finger across a sideboard, and the butler occasionally condescended to clean silver. Ivy, as under housemaid, had already grown weary of sooty fireplaces.

She sprinkled a last handful of damp tea leaves on the Persian rug, before reaching for the broom she had left leaning against the dining table. So far that morning she had swept out the hearths in the downstairs rooms, polished the grates with blacking, laid the fires, dusted the furniture and swept the rugs. And all before a morsel of porridge or sip of tea had passed her lips. After breakfast she would trudge up the servants' stairs to repeat the process in the bedrooms during the family breakfast, while on the alert for the jangle of keys that accompanied Mrs Tucker's every move.

She had never imagined there were such endless possibilities for cleaning; floorboards to be scoured with chloride of lime, others to be shined with beeswax soaked in turpentine, furniture polished with linseed boiled in vinegar and water, brass cleaned with lemon and salt, and all this before Gibbons deemed her ready to begin training in the art of maintaining a lady's wardrobe. The only task Gibbons thought her fit for thus far was emptying

Miss Rose's chamber pot. Ivy's hands were pronounced too clumsy for brushing kid gloves or doing up rows of tiny buttons.

Her first two weeks at Luscombe had been the loneliest of her life. She rarely saw Rose, who was still asleep when she crept upstairs to empty her chamber pot, and was held captive in the schoolroom or out riding with Mr Robert when she made the beds and dusted the furniture upstairs. Mostly Gibbons dressed her, or the head housemaid, Muriel. Rose hadn't sought out Ivy once the entire fortnight she had been at Luscombe, and Ivy certainly hadn't approached her. Servants were forbidden to address the family without being spoken to first. She wondered whether she was being punished for going against Rose's will and accepting her brother's offer of employment.

The other servants did little to make her welcome. Gibbons could barely prise her lips apart to wish her good morning, Mrs Tucker made it clear she disapproved of the master hiring a new housemaid without consulting her, and Muriel clearly hated her. She supposed that if she were Muriel she might feel the same way, for the woman had probably assumed that as head house-maid she would be appointed lady's maid to Miss Rose – crabby old spinster that she was – and now Ivy had come along to usurp her place. The only person who was kind to her was the hall boy, and that was because Ivy had taken over blacking Rose's boots.

Only yesterday she had to fight back tears when Mrs Tucker shouted at her for using the wrong linen on Mr Robert's bed. But how was she to know that a blue cross indicated linen reserved for Miss Rose's bedroom? All the sheets looked the same to her – heavy and white and changed far too often for her liking. After Mrs Tucker's last dressing-down she had run as far as the kitchen yard before realising she had nowhere to go. If she ran back home, Da would send her straight back with a stinging face or pack her off to Bristol on the next train. At least at Luscombe the servants got a bit of boiled beef for supper, and roast on Sundays. And she would see her ma and Danny every Sunday at church.

Ivy wondered why her mother hadn't stood up for her, told Da that she was a good, hard-working girl and they needed her at home. Instead, she had cowered like a hound under the lash of her husband's tongue. Despite this, Ivy couldn't help being angry with her. Sometimes there was so much to be angry about that she thought she might explode – but better that than curling into a ball, trying to hold it all in. Then she would think about her da, with his red face and his loud voice, and vow she would never be like him.

Her sweeping had taken her as far as the hall door when she heard the soft swish of silk and turned to find herself face-to-face with the dishevelled lady of the house, hair loose upon her shoulders and a frothy robe the colour of ripe apricots draped around her slight figure. She could almost be mistaken for her daughter except for the lines at the corners of her eyes and a sad, lost look about her. Mrs Luscombe was rarely sighted beyond the confines of her boudoir, and certainly not at seven o'clock in the morning. Ivy started, realising she had just broken at least two of Mrs Tucker's golden rules. There were so many she couldn't be sure, but blocking the path of a family member and being seen with a broom in her hand were definitely on the list. As far as the family was concerned, Jesus was in the kitchen producing the loaves and fishes while the shoemaker's elves appeared each midnight to keep the house sparkling like new. The small army of servants was merely decoration.

She backed up to give her mistress a clear path to wherever she was going but only succeeded in bumping into the sideboard and rattling the crystal decanters.

'Sorry, ma'am, good morning, ma'am,' she stuttered, trying to stow the broom out of sight behind her skirts.

The mistress regarded her like some new species of creature

and blinked in confusion. 'Who are you?' she asked, drawing together the ruffled edges of her dressing gown.

'Ivy, ma'am.'

'Have I seen you before, girl?' She leaned in to inspect Ivy more closely, her pupils like great dark holes in her watery blue eyes. 'You look familiar.'

'I just came the Friday before last, ma'am.'

'Where did you come from?'

'From the parlour, ma'am.'

'No, girl, where do you live?'

'In the attic, ma'am.' Ivy was flustered. She couldn't tell what was required of her. Mrs Tucker didn't have a rule for situations such as early morning interrogations from the mistress in her dressing gown. She hadn't even had a chance to don her smart black afternoon uniform with the starched collar and lace cap; she wore her dull grey work wear and had rolled up the sleeves of her blouse to keep them out of the way.

'Stupid girl! Where did you live before you came to Luscombe?' Mrs Luscombe snapped, rather like a small terrier.

Ivy would have stepped backwards if she weren't already wedged against the sideboard, not because she was afraid of her mistress's anger – life with Da had cured her of that – but because she was shocked that such an insubstantial person could rouse herself this much over the presence of a new housemaid. She would have thought a new housemaid was beneath her notice, rather like a new mangle in the laundry or a pair of fire tongs in the drawing room.

'On the estate, ma'am, at Ashcott, if it please your . . . your . . . yourself,' said Ivy, convinced she was digging herself into a deeper hole with every word she uttered.

Mrs Luscombe clutched her chest, face paling, and Ivy wondered whether she should call for help. It wouldn't do if the mistress dropped dead in the dining room. But she was forbidden to speak in a loud voice – another of Mrs Tucker's rules – and caught between the possibilities of a dead mistress or a tongue-lashing from Mrs Tucker, she held her silence.

'Who is your mother, girl?' Mrs Luscombe demanded, twisting the delicate silk of her gown into rope. Her face was mere inches from Ivy's, so close that she caught the strange, sickly sweet smell of her breath.

'Ethel, ma'am, Ethel Toms,' she croaked. She was frightened now, for Mrs Luscombe didn't seem quite right in her head. She stared at Ivy, eyes almost popping from her head, a trickle of saliva at the corner of her mouth. Perhaps she should risk calling out, after all. She opened her mouth to shout for Mr Greep when a small bundle of white fur skittered into the room, claws scrabbling for purchase on the newly shined floor. The creature fumbled to a halt on the trailing apricot silk and sat back on its haunches, barking frantically at Ivy.

'Tuppy, Tuppy,' Mrs Luscombe crooned, her expression shifting instantly from rabid terrier to adoring mother. 'What's the matter, little man?'

The dog barked again, glaring at Ivy.

'Has the nasty girl scared Tuppy?'

Tuppy took a tentative step towards Ivy and yapped again.

'Does Tuppy want his breakfast?'

In response, the dog lifted one skinny little leg and urinated, leaving a small yellow pool beside Ivy's boots. Mistress and maid both stared down at the puddle in surprise, then Mrs Luscombe bent to scoop up her baby and turned for the door.

'Get out of this house. But first, clean up that mess,' she snarled before tottering from the room, the lace edge of her gown drifting through Tuppy's unwelcome gift.

For several moments Ivy didn't move. She might have imagined the entire scene, if not for the puddle at her feet and the clammy sheen of sweat on her skin. Why had Mrs Luscombe taken against her? And what should she do now? The lady of the house had told her in no uncertain terms to leave Luscombe Park; to pack up her bundle of belongings and trudge back to the cramped, ivy-strangled cottage and her da's anger. She wasn't afraid of Mrs Luscombe; she wasn't truly fearful of Mrs Tucker or Greep either. They could shout at her but they couldn't hurt her, not really. The worst they could do would be to send her home. No, it was the thought of returning home that had made her break out in a cold sweat. She might curl up at night feeling sorry for herself but she knew that, given time, that would change. The other maids would get to know her; Rose would come to depend upon her, and she would become accustomed to Luscombe Park and its ways.

Da would never change. When she was small she kept hoping that if she could make herself silent enough and good enough, he might accept her. If she could calm the angry feelings prickling inside, he might even come to love her. But she realised now that her father would always be offended by her existence. If she were a boy things might have been different – he was proud of Samuel's doings, even when he was naughty. But she wasn't a boy, and Da would never change. So Luscombe had become a haven of sorts. Despite her loneliness she couldn't return to the cottage.

Mrs Luscombe had told her to get out, but the mistress was clearly not in her right mind. Perhaps she would forget about the new housemaid to whom she had taken an instant, unfathomable dislike. Perhaps her aversions were as fleeting as her fancies, and tomorrow she would awake with a new one. Perhaps if Ivy went about her work quiet as a mouse, busy as a bee, Mrs Luscombe wouldn't even notice she was there.

But first she would mop up Tuppy's indignant little gift.

16

'What a delight to be out walking on such a glorious morning, don't you agree, Mother?'

Several paces behind the family, Ivy observed her employer as he strolled, arm in arm, with his mother and his sister. His hair showed a sliver of pale neck between hairline and collar. His jacket fitted his broad shoulders expertly and he walked with the confidence that £5,000 per annum will give a man. With her newly acquired servant's eye, she frowned at the way he kicked up dust in his exuberant stride, setting a film over not only his own shoes and trousers but the ladies' walking shoes and Sunday garments, creating work for everyone from the laundry maid to the valet. She slowed so that she didn't get dust on her own Sunday best, a faded print once worn by Miss Rose.

Ivy was obliged to remain within earshot, should her services be required to retrieve a dropped glove or stray hairpin, which meant she was also obliged to walk alongside Gibbons, whose Sunday best was distinguishable from her uniform only by its fuller sleeves. And since Gibbons never had much to say – particularly not to an interloper – Ivy was forced to entertain herself by eavesdropping on the conversation of her betters.

The first ten minutes of the walk, following the carriage drive through an avenue of oaks leading to the gates of Luscombe Park, were punctuated by Mrs Luscombe's cries of alarm over every pebble she encountered or hapless twig that fell in her path, necessitating Gibbons' constant attendance and reassurance. But as they drew closer to the village, where the tower of St Peter's loomed above the surrounding trees, the clamour of church bells proved too much competition for even that lady. The mistress's complaints faded into morose silence so that her children's loud attempts to amuse her fell on deafened ears. It occurred to Ivy that if Mrs Luscombe had been fifty pounds heavier she might have been Ivy's da, ordering his world with his fists. But since she was barely wider than a broomstick, she had learned to bully everyone with loud complaints, silent reproaches and lashings of guilt. All the servants at the big house commiserated over her 'migraines' and 'spells' but it struck Ivy that her mistress's weakness was in fact her strength – and she used it shamelessly.

'I don't see why I'm required at church when I'm unwell, Robert. If I take a fever and die you'll never forgive yourself!' She emphasised the point with a flutter of her lace-edged handkerchief. 'You know what trouble I have with my legs. We could have taken the motor.'

'I thought it would do us all good to take a little exercise.'

'And why is that girl still here?' she continued querulously.

'What girl?'

'The Toms girl. I thought I made my feelings known about her. It won't do. I won't have her here. An apple never falls far from the tree, you know.'

'What on earth are you talking about, Mother?'

'I am talking of apples. And their antecedents.'

Naturally Ivy became anxious at the mention of her name. Having heard no more from Mrs Luscombe since their peculiar encounter in the dining room three weeks earlier, she had thought herself forgotten.

'Maman, I believe Ivy can hear you,' said Rose with a quick glance behind her.

'Servants hear everything. If you want to keep a secret you had better become poor.'

'Mother, Ivy is quick to learn. She has had a more than adequate education at the village school and she is accustomed to basic sewing and mending. She will suit Rose admirably once she is trained up.'

Ivy's heart skipped a beat at his defence. She hadn't expected it. She hadn't expected that he would make the considerable effort it took to defend her to his mother, and she couldn't help wondering why. Perhaps it was merely his way of irritating the woman. Ivy understood that. Once she realised her father would never love her she had often gone out of her way to irritate him, regardless of the consequences. She knew he would win any battle between them, but there was some small power in riling him up, almost like pulling the strings on a puppet or waving a red rag at a bull. Perhaps Mr Robert had his own battles to fight with the Luscombe family legacy and he had chosen her as one of them. She noticed that Rose hadn't uttered a word in her defence.

'I don't see why Muriel would not do for Rose.'

Robert lowered his voice so that the peeling bells muffled his words, ensuring he couldn't be heard beyond a few yards. Ivy wondered whether this was out of consideration for Muriel's feelings at being passed over or a natural inclination to keep family business private.

'Muriel would never do for Rose. She's all of thirty-five. Rose needs someone nearer her own age, someone who can be a companion. Besides, we needn't pay Ivy as much.'

'We could advertise, if Maman is unhappy. I'm sure something else could be found for Ivy.' Rose glanced over her shoulder with an apologetic smile. 'She has many talents, after all.'

Ivy smiled in return because it was expected of her, but she wasn't fooled. She had already grown accustomed to the idea that Rose was no longer her friend – if she ever had been. A little girl from the big house could have a secret playmate in the village – for it was an adventure to sneak into the garden behind her governess's back and play with the Toms girl – but Miss Rose Luscombe could hardly befriend her maid. What would her friends think? Ivy might one day be Rose's companion, listening to her woes, entertaining her with gossip, protecting her from unpleasantness and keeping her secrets – but the reverse would upset the social order. A lady's maid knew not to overstep the mark, for her place would never be in the pages of *Tatler*.

They had reached the church now, the square battlements of its tower standing guard over the small settlement of Luscombe. St Peter's was so old that its stone was spotted with lichen and crumbling in places, a little like Reverend Nicholls whose hands and face were spotted by age and his molars crumbling. Gravestones leaned higgledy-piggledy in the grass amongst the daffodils and the weathered door stood open to reveal a glimpse of a whitewashed interior and curved oak ceiling with two neat rows of hat pegs along the walls, barely enough for the small congregation.

The family halted at the edge of the laneway that wound through the village, and the household servants – who had been trooping behind, sensing an argument – marched discreetly around them and up the paving stones leading to the church. Mr Robert and Miss Rose turned to face their mother, the three family members each taking up a corner of a triangle with Mr Robert facing Ivy, Rose facing away from St Peters and Mrs Luscombe looking towards the sanctuary of the church. The noise of ringing bells was so loud now that even Ivy and Gibbons, waiting patiently at a short distance, couldn't hear their betters' conversation; they could only see their faces, animated by dis-agreement. In a fit of emotion, Mrs Luscombe flapped her handkerchief with such force that she dropped it on to the dusty lane and Gibbons stepped forward to retrieve it.

It was at this moment, with her employers devoted to their discussion and Gibbons' attention monopolised by the recalcitrant handkerchief, that Ivy noticed a wagon approaching from the direction of the village, its clatter drowned out by the noise of the bells and the argument. There was nothing unusual in this fact – every farmer in the district had his wagon or his pony cart – but there *was* something unusual in the behaviour of the horse. Upon closer inspection Ivy realised that, unbeknownst to the farmer, the shaft of the wagon had broken and was jabbing the horse in its flank. The horse, understandably agitated at being stabbed by the jagged piece of wood, was tossing its head from side to side in an attempt to dislodge the offending object. Ivy thought to call out, warn her employers in some way, since they were too involved in their argument to notice for themselves. But she didn't like to draw any more attention to herself, and perhaps the farmer would realise what had happened, gain control of the animal and step down from the cart. Then she would merely look foolish.

Her hesitation seemed to stretch, as if time had become elastic, so that she was still considering alerting Mr Robert to the situation when the horse's agitation turned to rage and it took off down the road, catching its driver by surprise. She was conscious of several events occurring: the horse bolting, the driver being flung from the cart, her employers continuing to argue, Gibbons breaking into a trot as she chased the wayward handkerchief, and her own wavering indecision. For now that a runaway horse had become fact rather than possibility, she faced the very real prospect that the horse might knock down the slight figure of Mrs Luscombe, who was standing directly in its path. And should it knock her down, it might very well kill her, thereby solving Ivy's problem. She needed to act immediately to prevent disaster.

If she were to think about it later, she would have to admit that her indecision wasn't due to any moral question, because the correct course of action was obvious. No, her indecision lay in weighing up which course of action – or inaction – would be most beneficial to her. And who could blame her? So far in her short life, she had seen little hope of benefit to herself. All the benefit was going to other people.

Rose wondered how a pleasant walk to church on a fine Sunday morning had degenerated into a tedious argument over servants – one servant in particular. She had tried to tell her brother that employing Ivy wasn't a good idea, but would he listen? He was too busy admiring the girl's pretty face and shapely ankles. He wasn't interested in Rose's opinions, not even about her own life. Not that she didn't like Ivy, who had been her childhood playmate, but it was clear that she knew nothing about hair – and even less about the correct way to behave as a maid. She couldn't help putting herself forward at any opportunity. It was most unbecoming, and Mrs Beeton would never have stood for it. And now Maman had worked herself into a paroxysm of nerves, and all because Robert had taken a fancy to the girl. It was really quite annoying.

Rose was diligently nursing her indignation when she heard an urgent shout from behind.

'Mr Robert! Rose! Look out!'

Really, Ivy must remember to address her as *Miss* Rose, she had time to think, before realising from the expression on her brother's face that something was awry. And just as that thought hit, she felt the full impact of her brother's weight slamming into her body, launching her towards the church with such force that they fell into a tangled heap of silk and worsted. Meanwhile, Maman's terror-stricken cries were being muffled by the clamour of bells, the rattle of a wagon and the burden of Ivy sitting atop her, smothering her screams. It was all quite vexing, and Rose's new gown was almost certainly ruined. Her mother was probably in some discomfort too.

Rose levered herself into a sitting position and gazed about her. There was such confusion that she didn't know where to focus first. She could see the rear of a wagon as it travelled away from them at absurd speed, the horse careening out of control. Her mother was lying stunned beneath Ivy; Farmer Wills was running down the street, waving his arms in the air, shouting, 'Stop that horse!' She could see her brother, who had rolled away from her, leaping to their mother's aid. And from the corner of her eye she spied almost the entire congregation of St Peter's rushing towards the three most important personages in Luscombe village: the family of that very name.

'Mother, are you all right?' asked Robert.

'My heart, my heart.'

'Maman!' Rose added her own voice to the cacophony.

'There's a great weight upon my chest. I am dying.'

'It's Ivy. She is lying atop you. Here, let me help you.'

He helped Ivy to her feet, with more solicitude than the situation warranted, considering the maid had knocked their mother to the ground. Then he slipped an arm around Maman's waist and lifted her until she could stand. She made such a picture of suffering, leaning heavily upon Robert in her distress.

'That girl will be the death of me,' she whimpered as Gibbons set to fussing over her with a dusty handkerchief. Rose could appreciate her mother's sentiment, for Ivy was a solid country girl and her mother, though tall, was a frail invalid. Ivy might well be the death of them all, she thought, narrowing her eyes. It occurred to her that her maid might not be as simple as all those childhood games had led her to believe.

'Gibbons, where is my mother's medicine—'

'No, Mother,' Robert interrupted, 'Ivy won't be the death of you. She saved your life. You do realise that wagon was out of control? It would have run you down if she hadn't pushed you from its path. It might have killed us all.'

The three lead actors in this drama now turned to stare at the girl who stood shyly to one side, her head hanging demurely, her great mane of hair escaping carelessly from its pins and framing her face in a halo of curls. Robert's face wore an expression of puzzled admiration. Maman gazed at her in horror, while Rose didn't know what to think. The girl had weaselled her way into Robert's good graces and now it seemed she had set about playing the heroine. Of course, even Rose couldn't blame her for the runaway horse, but was throwing herself upon poor Maman really necessary? There was simply no precedent for such a situation in Lady Colin Campbell's *Etiquette of Good Society* – and Lady Campbell had seen it all.

'She did?' asked Maman.

'Yes. She did.'

'What on earth for?'

'Because she is kind and keen-eyed and just the sort of girl to suit Rose as a lady's maid, don't you agree?' he concluded, turning first to his mother and then to his sister, while Ivy remained staring at the ground.

In the face of such heroism, what could they do but concur? After all, Ivy's quick thinking had saved their lives. Surely that must be worth more than a position paying £20 per annum and Rose's cast-off gowns?

Just how much more, Rose suspected she was going to find out.

17

North Devon

2017

Richard hadn't been exaggerating when he said that the attics were as dusty as the Sahara. Molly's nose intermittently tingled and she was on high alert for spiders amongst the chests and boxes that crowded the room where the Luscombe documents were interred. The single light bulb was too meagre to do any meaningful work, so she positioned herself at a table near the dormer window where she had light enough to read, yet not enough to cause damage to the documents.

The family wasn't prominent enough to warrant clerks or secretaries who would have conserved important documents, so the earliest records were few. Any surviving deeds and royal grants were held at the North Devon Record Office amongst the Estate Records and Personal Papers. It was the later records, from the nineteenth and twentieth centuries, that jostled for her attention. The attics were too susceptible to changes in temperature and humidity to be the ideal home for an archive. She should suggest that once the documents were sorted they would be safer housed on the ground floor, perhaps in the library on the north side of the house. Depending upon what she found, she would also need to order appropriate archival boxes, folders and sleeves – if there were funds to purchase them. In the meantime, she donned a pair of white cotton gloves and made a start on sorting the first of the materials into the broad categories of letters and personal diaries, financial records, legal documents, photographs, newspaper clippings and other memorabilia. Each of these categories would be further subdivided into decades.

It was a start.

Unfortunately, there seemed to be no existing system. Over there was a box containing a collection of Victorian-era visiting cards that had belonged to one Henrietta Luscombe, who may or may not have been Robert and Rose's great-aunt (she would have to ask Richard). While here was a box of household records from the latter part of the nineteenth century to the 1920s, including assorted receipts for clothing and household items. She decided to begin with this box, since it covered the period when her great-grandmother had lived at Luscombe.

She was sorting the various receipts into decades when she came across an invoice from Harrods, dated 7 August 1916, addressed to Miss R. Luscombe for '4 custom-made, blue cotton VAD regulation overalls, 8 white aprons, 8 pr white sleeves, 8 collars, 4 handkerchief caps'.

'Trust the aristocracy to order their uniforms from Harrods.'

'Who's ordering from Harrods?' Lucas popped his head around the corner with a quizzical smile.

'Watch your head over here,' she warned from her table where the ceiling sloped down towards the floor. 'I don't know how the footmen managed sleeping up here. Weren't they chosen for their height?'

'I think so. Anyway, how's it going up here in the servants' quarters?'

'It's daunting. Look at these boxes. It's like wading through quicksand. That's the trouble with history, there's no bottom.'

'What have you got there?'

'Oh, I found an invoice from Harrods for VAD uniforms – four dresses plus accessories. I wonder if that means Rose ordered Ivy's uniform from Harrods too, or whether she ordered several sets for herself.'

'I suspect the latter but will withhold judgement.'

'Given the date of the invoice, she most likely began nursing in August 1916. She would have been eighteen then.' So young to be dealing with the wounds of war, yet some of her patients would have been younger. Molly held the invoice so that Lucas could lean in and read it. 'Best not to touch it without gloves,' she warned, conscious of his breath close to her ear and the light brush of his shoulder against hers. He smelled of wood and grass and a hint of marmalade.

'You look like a ghost with those gloves and the cobwebs in your hair.'

'Ow!' she yelped as she felt a sharp tug of her hair.

'Sorry, I meant to pluck out the cobwebs and must have grabbed a hair by mistake.'

'So long as it isn't grey, I'll forgive you.' She turned her head to find him gazing intently into her eyes. 'What are you looking at?' she asked, trying not to dwell on how gorgeous he was. Not Hollywood good looks; craggier and more lived in, more approachable.

'Checking to see if I can find any family resemblance between you and Rose,' he said, his eyes caressing every inch of her face. 'I suppose it was a long way back.'

'Everyone says I take after the Wilsons rather than the Turners.'

'Do they?' For a moment she thought he might lean in and kiss her but he straightened, shoving his hands in his pockets, and took a step back.

'Ouch!'

'I told you to watch the ceiling,' she said, surprised at the regret she experienced when he backed away. She could almost taste marmalade on her lips.

'I came up to see if you want anything in Barnstaple. I have to go on site today and I usually pick up a few things for Richard while I'm there.'

She shook her head. 'Nothing I can think of right now. I have to return my rental car on Saturday, so I'll pick up anything I need then. I can get a cab back.' The trouble was there was so much she needed, she couldn't begin to remember. And she certainly couldn't be asking this very cute erstwhile plumber.

'All right.' He hesitated for a moment as if considering his options, glancing down at his footprints in the dust and chewing over invisible words. Then he seemed to come to a decision.

'By the way,' he said, 'if you need a break from your labours by Saturday, I could show you some of the local sights. So far, all you've seen is a crumbling old house and dusty boxes.'

She wondered whether Richard had put him up to it, since he didn't seem overly committed to his invitation. More like a little boy forced by his mother to invite girls to his birthday party.

'I wouldn't want to put you to any trouble,' she answered coolly, pushing a lock of hair behind her ear so that she didn't have to look into his eyes. If she looked into his eyes he might see the lie in hers. Of course she wanted to go for a lazy weekend drive with this attractive man – but perhaps he was already taken? She really couldn't afford any further romantic trauma.

'No trouble, I thought you might enjoy seeing some of the scenery.' He jammed his hands into the pockets of his jacket, as if he wanted her to say no. No was always a safe option. She was quite good at saying no, actually.

'The coast around here is very scenic. Quite wild in places.'

For an instant, a picture of another rugged coastline flickered into her mind.

'Molly?'

She had better say something, or he would think her rude. Safe Molly was urging her to make her excuses, except she had come to Britain to get away from Safe Molly. And knowing Daisy, her sister would prise the story from her and tease unrelentingly. After all, what could happen in a couple of hours?

Anything. Anything could happen in a couple of hours. Your whole life could change forever in a couple of hours.

'Thanks, I'd love to.'

He accepted her decision with a nod. 'Great, I'll swing by about ten and follow you into town.'

She couldn't tell whether he was pleased or not. She wasn't even sure if she were pleased. But at least it was a decision. Now she could spend the rest of the week dreading and anticipating Saturday at the same time.

After he left, still rubbing his injured head, she returned to her sorting, trying not to think about Lucas, rugged coastlines or anything beyond the documents in front of her. Receipts seemed to have been kept randomly, mostly for items of clothing and furniture. Thank goodness she didn't have to sort through decades of invoices from butchers, bakers and candlestick makers. Informative though they may be about household costs, they weren't her current priority – and she doubted Richard would be interested to know how much the housekeeper had spent on mutton in the month of May 1912. The papers did indicate that Rose Luscombe and her mother Elsie had very nice wardrobes, thank you very much.

She was about to put aside her work for lunch when the letters 'VAD' peeped out at her from the edge of a yellowing receipt. At first she thought she must have misplaced the earlier Harrods receipt, but when she slid the paper out from the pile she saw that although it was indeed charged to Miss R. Luscombe, this order was from a store called Garrould's of Edgware Road; another order for '4 blue cotton VAD regulation overalls, 8 white aprons, 8 pr white sleeves, 8 collars, 4 handkerchief caps'.

So Rose had ordered Ivy's uniforms. But unlike her own from Harrods, Ivy's weren't custom-made and were significantly cheaper. She should have expected this. Ivy was Rose's maid, not her sister. By tradition she would have accepted her employer's cast-offs as part of her wages. Except Molly couldn't help picturing that image of the two girls, hands entwined in one pocket. There must have been more between those two young women, she was sure of it. The hands symbolised a bond of some kind, and she was determined to unearth it – if she had to don gumboots and wade through an avalanche of papers.

18

North Devon

1916

'I don't see how we're going to manage,' Rose complained as Ivy dressed her hair. 'It was bad enough when Merrell enlisted.'

In fact it had taken Greep several weeks to find a replacement for the chauffeur.

'And Donaldson never looks as smartly turned out as Merrell, with that gammy leg of his.'

'Yes, miss, I remember,' said Ivy. How could she forget? Mrs Luscombe had taken to her bed for two days when her daughter volunteered to drive, announcing to the butler that if the war didn't kill them her daughter would. Gibbons had blamed Ivy for putting 'silly suffragette' ideas into Rose's head. As if anyone could put ideas into Rose's head that she didn't want there. She might be all soft and sweet on the outside but Ivy had learned that inside she was harder than toffee. Gibbons loved finding things to blame her for, she decided, as she gave Rose's hair a final tug with the brush.

'Do be more careful! You're becoming quite clumsy. You stuck me with a hairpin yesterday.'

'Sorry, miss.'

'Anyway, Gibbons still thinks I'm a child. She's been with Maman far too long and can't believe I have ideas of my own.

Well, she'll soon see, and so will Maman . . .' she said, trailing off mysteriously, while studying her face in the mirror as if looking for signs that these 'ideas' might be evident there. But all Ivy could see reflected was a pale, pretty face with a shining crown of blond hair and a vexed expression.

'And you can leave out the "rat" today. I'll wear my hair in a loose bun just here,' she said, indicating the nape of her neck. 'It's more . . . bohemian.'

'Yes, miss.'

Ivy put aside the wad of hair used to pad the chignon. Late morning light streamed through the lead-paned windows of the bedroom in the south-east corner of Luscombe Park, giving her mistress's hair a golden glow. Mr Robert had moved his belong-ings to one of the smaller rear bedrooms when he went off to war, bequeathing his sister the second-best bedroom, looking out over the terrace and the lake. Their mother, of course, had the largest, most elegant room for her boudoir, with a bay window and an adjoining bathroom.

Since Ivy had graduated to lady's maid, she had ventured into Mrs Luscombe's bedroom just once. She had been obliged to make an emergency delivery of misplaced reading glasses to Gibbons and became entranced by the dusky-rose and gold patterned wallpaper, the delicate gilt furniture, the window seat plump with tasselled cushions, and an ebony writing table with legs carved to resemble black bamboo. One day, she vowed, she would have a bedroom with a window seat where she could curl up and do nothing at all. If only she could work out how that might be achieved. She wasn't sure which would be more diffi-cult: having nothing to do, or having a window seat. For a girl like her, both appeared unattainable at the moment.

She forced her attention back to Miss Rose, who was still complaining about petrol shortages and the fuel rationing the Chancellor of the Exchequer had introduced.

'How are we meant to survive on the trickle of petrol they're allowing us? It's barely enough to drive into Barnstaple and back. And Greep says the farm manager insists he needs the farm rations for the tractor.'

'I'm sure we'll manage, miss. We've still got the pony trap, and most of the suppliers deliver.'

'That's all very well for Cook, but how am I supposed to get around? And with Robert arriving home on leave today too.'

'I'm sure I don't know, miss. It's quite vexing, but we all have our crosses to bear,' Ivy agreed, so sympathetically that Rose turned to stare at her through narrowed eyes.

She considered her for a moment, suspiciously, before remarking, 'We do. We *all* have our crosses to bear.'

'Perhaps you could have Donaldson convert the automobile to gas, miss, and install one of those big rubber balloons on the roof to contain it.'

'I saw a picture in the *London Illustrated News* and I don't see how the car wouldn't float away. Oh . . . did you hear that?' Rose leaped up from the dressing table so suddenly that she knocked over a bowl of hairpins that Ivy would have to pick up later.

'What is it, miss?'

'I can hear voices in the hall. It must be Robert come from the station,' she said, flying towards the open door.

For an instant, Ivy felt her chest tighten in anticipation. Mr Robert had been gone such a long time it felt like he would never return. She pictured him with his smooth, handsome face and perfect grooming and wondered whether he would be different. He had been in a war, after all. He had faced death. Surely that must change a man?

Rose halted at the door. 'He's been gone so long. What if I don't know him any more?'

'Of course you'll know him, miss. He's your brother.'

'But they all come back changed, every single one. Even if it doesn't show.'

Ivy didn't know how to answer, for it was true; they all came back changed in some way. Except for the ones who didn't come back at all.

'Robert!' Rose squealed as she launched herself headlong at her brother.

She couldn't believe he was finally home. It might only be for ten days but she promised herself she would make every minute count. She had missed him so, and not just because she was lonely and bored without him to squire her about, despite what *some* people might think. *Some* people who were always judging others. She wasn't so naïve that she didn't realise her brother might never return, nor so selfish that she didn't worry about him over there on French soil, with maggots in his food and worse. And now here he was at last. She felt a burble of something that might once have been happiness but these days she usually put down to indigestion.

Greep relieved him of his duffle bag and peaked cap so that he was free to gather her in his arms, ruffling her hair before standing back from her to declare, 'Chicken, you're all grown up.'

'Of course I'm grown up – I'll be nineteen soon. And I still haven't come out properly because of this silly old war.'

'Well, you look adorable if that's any consolation. It makes me happy just to see you.'

Under her brother's smiling gaze she pirouetted, showing off her new dress, ordered from Maman's dressmaker in London.

'I'm sure all the chaps find you irresistible,' he added, his newly acquired moustaches curving upward with his grin. It would have made him look quite dashing if it weren't for the hollows in his cheeks.

'What chaps? The only chaps around here are old men and boys.'

'We'll have to get you up to London then, before I return to France,' he offered. 'See if I can round up a few fellows for a party. What do you think, Chicken?'

She considered her brother, his khaki tunic hanging loosely on his frame, breeches ballooning over his puttees. 'You've become very thin. And your hair is as bristly as a clothes brush. Are you taking care of yourself?'

'I'm doing my best—' He broke off, staring in the direction of the foyer, where Ivy was loitering outside the great hall.

That girl had a knack for being in the right place at the right time – the right time for Ivy, at any rate. Rose couldn't help noticing the look in her brother's eyes, his lips curving upwards almost involuntarily before he schooled them into a benign expression. His eyes, which had been warily happy to see Rose, were suddenly alight. And Ivy, who a few minutes earlier had been wearing her habitual sulky expression, was smiling with her entire body, her shoulders and hips swaying slightly to an inaudible tune. It was as if they stared at each other across a crowded ballroom, oblivious to all the other attendees. Rose couldn't help finding the display quite nauseating and was glad it was some hours until luncheon.

'Mr Robert, I mean, Captain Luscombe, we're all so pleased to see you home,' Ivy purred, the welcoming smile lighting up her green eyes. 'With the fighting so bad in the Somme, everyone at Luscombe has been worried. We've heard terrible things, sir. We heard as how tens of thousands of our boys have died there. They say you can hear the guns in Dover.'

'That will be all, Ivy. I'm sure the captain knows better than us what is happening at the front.'

'I'm sure she means no harm, Rose.'

'I wondered whether you needed anything further, miss.'

Her words were for Rose but everything else was for Robert. She was wearing her best dress, the fine navy wool skirt and cotton blouse with goffered lace trim that Rose had bequeathed to her only last week. Somehow, the girl had altered the high collar that had constricted Rose's neck so that the blouse now revealed a glimpse of collarbone. She had also tugged and twitched the skirt to mould her hips, the waistband buttoned tightly to emphasise her small waist and womanly chest. Rose's own chest looked more like a ten-year-old boy's, no matter how unforgiving her corset or cleverly cut her blouse.

'You're all grown up too, I see,' Robert was saying, his eyes lingering speculatively on the maid. 'It's good to be home, especially to such a warm welcome.'

Rose didn't know who she was most annoyed with – Ivy or her brother. Between them they were ruining everything. 'You can go now,' she ordered pre-emptively, 'but tell Greep we'd like tea.' She wasn't pleased at the prickle of jealousy she felt over Robert's attentiveness, but that didn't mean she was going to ignore it. She had waited so long to have her brother back; she wasn't about to share him, and certainly not with her maid.

'Yes, miss. Thank you, sir.' Ivy nodded before exiting towards the service rooms with a swish of her skirt.

'Getting Ivy away from that father of hers was the best thing we could have managed for her,' Robert observed, following the girl's departure with his eyes. 'She's done well.'

And she had Rose to thank for it. Not many employers would have been as forbearing. She was inclined to point this out but risked getting into a silly spat about a servant when she finally had him to herself. 'And I'm sure she's very grateful, but enough about Ivy. Let's talk about you. Has it been truly awful in France?'

'It hasn't been a jolly picnic, Chicken, but the lads are brave.'

'It must be a hard life,' she said, unsurprised at her brother's understatement. She knew he wouldn't want to worry her. But he couldn't hide the war's effect on him. She could see it in the tiny lines at the corners of his eyes and the new boniness of his frame.

'They ship us about like livestock in horseboxes labelled "40 *hommes*, 8 *chevaux*". We spend half our day hunting lice from our clothes and the other half chasing rats. The rats are loathsome – huge as otters, and they glow in the dark,' he said in attempt to make her smile.

'How repulsive!' She shivered, wondering if the rumours of rats eating the dead were true. 'Robert . . . I've been thinking about how I could help.'

'Just knowing you're here is a help, Chicken.'

'About how I could help the other soldiers . . . Lady Waring has opened her house as a convalescent hospital for officers, and she needs nurses. I've been studying for the First Aid and Home Nursing examinations.' Rose had already discussed her plans with Lady Waring, who had been most encouraging.

'You're too young to join the VAD.'

'No one's taking any notice of that now, not in the auxiliary hospitals. They're too short staffed.'

'Nursing isn't for a girl like you. You have no idea what you'll be up against.'

'Diana Manners is nursing, and she's everybody's darling, so why shouldn't I?' She would have emphasised her point with hands on hips but knew it wasn't ladylike – as Miss Sarah would have reminded her, if she were still in their employ. Thankfully, she had moved on to educate two lucky sisters in Cornwall.

'As I understand it, Lady Diana is nursing in her own mother's hospital and comes and goes as she pleases.'

'But the world is changing, Robert. *The North Devon Journal* reports on lady clerks and post-women, girls driving bread carts—'

'Not girls like you.'

135

'No, I can't see myself driving a bread cart, but I can see myself as a nurse. I need to *do* something!'

'And what do you imagine you'll be doing? Parading around in fancy dress, mopping fevered brows and reading aloud to smiling officers? It's not just the missing limbs and shrapnel wounds, have you ever seen a man afflicted by mustard gas – his skin peeling off and organs rotting from the inside?'

'No.'

'Or a soldier so infected by trench foot that his feet have swelled to twice their size and gone bulbous with gangrene?'

Rose schooled her face into a polite mask. She wasn't about to let her brother see how the thought repulsed her. And anyway, she could learn to deal with such things if she had to – surely that would be part of the training?

'I've seen men choking for breath, from gas attacks, who are more afraid of living than dying.'

'All the more reason why they need help.'

'I wouldn't want you to see that.'

He probably didn't. He probably thought she was too weak. He didn't know her very well then, did he?

'Besides, once you're married you'll have your husband to help and cherish . . .' Robert paused for breath, running his hands through his hair as if searching for words he couldn't find.

She knew she was seeing the real Robert now, not the young man who had left Luscombe, but the soldier who had endured two years of this horrible war. People didn't want to admit how bad it was over there, but it was impossible to hide the maimed and the wretched, returning home so changed they seemed like different men. And Rose would never become accustomed to that jolt of shock on hearing that a boy she went riding with one summer had died at the bottom of a trench in France.

'There may not be any young men left to marry after the war.'

Everyone believed she didn't have a serious thought in her

head but it wasn't true. She could be selfish but she also knew she could bring comfort to others. She knew she had a way about her – a habit of laughter that was contagious. It was more than men's bodies that returned home wounded, and she knew instinctively that she could nurse their spirits.

'That's why I want to help,' she told her brother solemnly, 'because someone must listen to those fears.'

Ivy waited in the library doorway, only vaguely aware of the pretty garden view from the east-facing window and the musty smell of seldom-read books and old leather. Mr Robert stood looking through the window, his hands clasped behind his back, his khakis replaced by a pair of pre-war flannel trousers and a jacket that dangled from his shoulders as if he were a coat rack. She didn't know why he had summoned her and hoped she wasn't about to lose her position. Miss Rose was always threatening to find a new maid. So far, it was all talk but she had seemed particularly put out in the great hall earlier.

'Ivy, come in, come in.' He turned in response to her soft tap.

There wasn't as much of him as there had once been. She'd heard that the Luscombe hounds ate better than the soldiers, and it certainly showed in Mr Robert's lean face with the lines of weariness bracketing his mouth. In the years she had served at Luscombe, he'd been an intermittent presence. She would pass him on the landing with a bob of the head and a 'good morning' or 'good evening, sir'. Occasionally he would detain her for a moment or two of conversation, or ask after her family on the walk to church, but after his initial burst of benevolence he had largely ignored her. He was the dashing 'lord of the manor', happy to order the world to his liking, and she was a working girl who should be grateful to have a safe place paying a fair wage. But the world had changed since 1914, and he probably found it not so much to his liking. The shininess that had once repelled her had been chiselled away by war, leaving him gnarled and careworn. It was odd, but in a way, the suffering that now showed on his face made him seem more approachable.

More like her.

More like someone she could . . . come to like.

'I didn't have a chance to tell you before I left for France, but your father came to see me.'

Her heart skipped a beat at the mention of her father. She did her best to keep out of his way, seeing Ma and the boys at church. Her da wasn't a church-going man, thank the Lord. It was a silent conspiracy in her family that Ivy would only visit when he was away from the cottage. And by handing over her wages each month she ensured that this particular dog lay sleeping, if not peacefully, then at least unlikely to bite her hand.

'He did, sir?'

'He wanted to know when your wages would be increased to reflect your greater responsibilities as lady's maid.'

'I'm very sorry, sir. I'm sure he meant nothing by it.'

'Well, I won't say he was looking out for your interests because I suspect he was only looking out for his own. However, you did by rights deserve an increase once you began seeing to Miss Rose full time.'

She felt her stomach clench tighter than a corset. She wasn't sure what was coming next but she suspected she wasn't going to like it. She didn't like much that had to do with her father. She hoped he hadn't caused trouble for her here at Luscombe.

'So I felt it prudent to tell Mr Toms that owing to the uncertainties of war there would be no increases for staff. But in fact that was a . . . prevarication.'

'Sir?' Since coming to work for Rose she had observed that people like the Luscombes often disguised their meaning behind words that people like her didn't understand. She often wondered whether they did it to accentuate the distance between them or whether it was merely a way of dealing with awkward conversations – conversations about money, for example – something that people like her only felt awkward about *not* having. Talking about money didn't bother them a bit.

'What I mean to say is that I intended to increase your wages. But I told your father that I didn't, so that I could hold some back. For you,' he said, handing her an envelope, marked with her name.

'This is my wages, sir?'

'This is the increase in your wages that I neglected to pass on to your father.'

Glancing from the envelope to his face twice, Ivy wanted to make sure she understood what he was saying, that he had paid enough attention to her situation to think of doing this. She was glad of the money – any money accumulated despite her da was a sweet pleasure – but having Mr Robert care about her situation was unaccountably sweeter. She wasn't used to having anybody but Ma care much about her at all.

'Thank you, sir.'

'No need to thank me for money you've well and truly earned.'

Sensing that he was about to say more, but uncertain what it might be, she waited. In its stillness, his face remained handsome but the aristocratic glow that came with good food and a regimen of manly pursuits had been dulled by a year in the trenches. She felt a small stirring that she recognised as sympathy and perhaps something else, something she couldn't put a name to. But there was little point following that thought. He was the master and he was going away again soon, back to the battlefields of France. Miss Rose wasn't the only one who worried about Mr Robert. She had thought about him at odd times too, wondering whether he would ever make it home to Luscombe Park. She had never been a carefree girl, not like Rose, not like some of the other girls in the village to whom laughter came easily, but now those same girls were more like her, weighed down with fears that their men might not return, that even if they did they might not be the same.

'Is there anything more, sir?'

'Yes, it concerns Miss Rose.'

She tensed, the old fear that she was about to be reprimanded resurfacing. Rose was always finding fault with her, but Ivy was careful to go about her job well enough so that she wouldn't lose her position. She had known Rose long enough to realise that training a new maid was too much like hard work to be undertaken lightly and as long as she went about her work with reasonable diligence, she would probably keep her position. Unless she did something . . . unforgivable.

'Yes. She's determined to do her part in the war effort and is intent on joining the Volunteer Aid Detachment. She'll be helping Lady Waring with the convalescent home for officers at Oldbridge Manor.'

When she forgot to hide her surprise behind her usual servant's mask, he continued, 'Yes, it's difficult to imagine Miss Rose up to her elbows in blood and soapsuds, but there you have it. She's determined – and when Rose is determined, nothing short of a war will stop her. And we don't need another war.'

She remained silent, for it wasn't her place to comment on her mistress's character defects with her brother. What she said below stairs was another matter.

'Of course, I can't in good conscience let her loose upon the poor unsuspecting officers without a chaperone, so I was hoping that you might volunteer *with* Miss Rose. Keep an eye on her, so to speak.' His smile transformed his face into something approximating the young man he had been.

She didn't know whether he smiled because he believed he was bestowing a trust or because he was embarrassed to be asking her a favour. He had smiled in the hall earlier but Rose shared in it. This was just for her. She wasn't sure what to do with it, so she ignored it. Instead, she concentrated on his words, for these she understood quite clearly. He wanted her to be his sister's keeper, smoothing her way, protecting her from harsh realities. Wasn't that what she did every day? Cosseting her like a child, changing her clothes, bringing her food, listening to her woes? Playing at nurses couldn't be much harder.

'What do you think?'

Mr Robert phrased his request as a favour but she thought she should treat it as a business arrangement, an extra duty on top of those of lady's maid. That was the safer, less personal way. She should make a bargain, come to terms with him. That's what Ma would advise. 'Always hold yourself dear,' she would say. 'Don't give nothing away for free. No one will thank you for it in the end.'

'Would there be . . .' she began, thinking to mention her wages, despite his uneasiness about talk of money. Except as she met his eyes, what she saw in them stalled her. She couldn't explain exactly what it was – a spark of hope, perhaps a hint of tenderness – but it made her think again, and what she thought was . . . she *wanted* this to be personal, no matter what Ma would advise. She wanted to be linked to him by more than a smile. He liked her – she could see that – and it might be nice to have a handsome man to dream about as she mended her mistress's gowns and cleaned her jewellery. It might be nice to have a man to care about, a handsome man with clear skin and fresh collars. So what if it was only dreaming? The world *was* changing, wasn't it? Who knew what might happen once the war ended? It couldn't hurt to have Mr Robert linked to her, even in a small way.

'I've heard that the VADs are made to work like navvies, Captain. Miss Rose won't be used to rolling up her sleeves and scrubbing pots,' she said, once she had caught her breath.

He smiled again. 'Lady Waring is the Commandant and a

family friend, so I doubt she'll make Miss Rose work like a navvy.'

Perhaps not, but the same wouldn't hold true for Ivy. She would be up at six each morning, making Miss Rose beautiful for her work at the hospital, and she wouldn't be finished until she had put her to bed after supper. She was accustomed to hard work but she didn't know if she had the strength for that, five or six days a week. 'And then I'll have my own work looking after Miss.'

'I'll make it a condition with Lady Waring that Rose is only obliged to attend the hospital four days a week,' the Captain suggested with an understanding nod. 'I would appreciate it greatly.' His words were simple but the message in his eyes was far more complicated.

'Well then, I can hardly say no, sir, can I?'

He reached out a hand and for a moment she thought that he might be going to hold her arm. Then she realised that he intended for them to shake hands on the arrangement.

'And Ivy . . .' he added, still holding her hand.

'Yes, Captain.'

'I'd be most obliged if you'd write and let me know how Miss Rose is getting on. If you don't mind,' he added with a bashful smile. 'It would be comforting to hear a voice from home.'

He released her hand and she clasped both hands in front to hold hers still. 'No, sir,' she said, 'I don't mind at all.'

In her head she could hear Ma's voice, warning her, 'Be careful, sweeting, a girl needs to be as strong and determined as ivy to get on in this world.' That day, her mother had spoken as if she knew what a moment of weakness could cost.

But Ivy had been tough for so long. She had been heavy with anger, churning with loneliness. Surely she deserved a little lightness for a change?

19

North Devon

1917

After an hour spent scrubbing basins and disposing of bloody refuse in the sink room, Ivy arrived on the ward to hear Sister Talbot shouting for a nurse from behind screens set up in one corner. Most of the men were dawdling about in their hospital blues, or resting on their beds, studiously ignoring what lay behind the screens, while talking more loudly than usual about the 'shows' across the Channel.

'I need help with these dressings,' Sister called gruffly.

Ivy wasn't inclined to dress wounds after all her scrubbing. She had seen enough blood for one day. Neither was she keen to discover what lay behind the screens. She checked to see whether Miss Rose might respond first, since she had been on the ward all morning. But her employer was sitting at Captain Smith's bedside reading poetry, deaf to Sister's calls now that Ivy had arrived on the scene.

'Nurse Toms,' Sister barked as Ivy ducked around the screens. 'You must learn to be more prompt.'

'Sorry, Sister.' She didn't bother to explain that she had just come on to the ward, for Sister dealt with excuses like vermin, to be eradicated at every opportunity. It didn't do to explain. Ever. And it wouldn't do to complain that Nurse Luscombe had been available, for complaints constituted an even greater menace and were scuttled without mercy.

By keeping her eyes fixed on Sister's face she didn't need to look at the man beneath the sheet. She knew she would need time to condition herself to what she might find. Oldbridge Manor was an auxiliary hospital, a convalescent home for wounded or ill officers. Men were sent here to recover rather than undergo surgery, but that didn't mean they were made whole. Some would return to the war; others would struggle to return to any kind of life at all. Ivy doubted Rose had realised how seriously afflicted the men might be when she determined to become a VAD nurse. She probably thought she would soothe fevered brows and flirt with the handsomest of the officers. Neither of them knew they would be dealing with septic wounds that refused to heal, pain that never quite retreated and nightmares that lurked constantly in the corners of men's eyes. Neither of them understood the loneliness such pain might bring. In time, Ivy had become accustomed to it – but never immune, no matter how much she tried to harden her heart. And there was always the dreadful thought that someone she knew might end up here.

'Lieutenant Turner needs his dressings changed.'

She stood by the patient, supporting his injured right arm as gently as possible while Sister took her forceps to it, prising wads of gauze stiff with dried blood and pus from a long, deep wound. Beneath the blankets she noted that the lieutenant's right leg ended above the knee. And when she risked a glance at his face she had to restrain a shudder, for his right eye and much of his nose was missing, the wound shiny and puckered and pink. His left eye, however, followed her every movement as if waiting for her to look away in disgust.

'Where are you from then, Lieutenant?' she asked, looking him straight in his good eye. He deserved that from her at least. She wasn't sure whether she was trying to distract the patient or herself with her words, for she usually wasn't very talkative.

'Australian First Division, miss,' he replied, breathing tightly through the pain.

'I'm Nurse Toms. You're a long way from home, then.'

'Too right. Too far from home.'

'What's it like then, home?'

'It's beautiful. Wuurnong's the best place on earth. Four thousand head of sheep and three hundred beef.' He sighed. 'I wish I'd never left.'

He closed his eye as Sister inserted the syringe and rubber tubing of Dakin's solution deep into the wound before carefully drying the skin around it. Ivy held his arm and her neutral expression firm.

'What do you reckon is worse, Nurse Toms, wanting to scratch a leg that isn't there or having no arm to scratch it with?' he asked through gritted teeth.

She didn't know what to say to this. Surely it was a trick question, and any answer she gave was bound to be wrong. Then she noticed a slight tug at the corner of his mouth and realised he was making a joke. Ivy was generally a serious girl; she hadn't found much to laugh about in her life so far, but if he could find humour somewhere in this mess then she owed it to him to try too.

She smiled. 'Not having eyes to see where to scratch?'

'Ha! She's a joker, this one, Sister. Not having eyes to see where to scratch! That's a good one.'

'Keep still, Lieutenant, or we'll never get this wound healed,' Sister reminded him sternly.

'You see, I don't have an arm any more. I have a wound!'

'You won't have a wound at all once it heals, just a nice tidy scar,' she ventured cheerfully.

'I've had my arm in a sling for two months now and my wound isn't going anywhere,' he said resignedly.

Once he would have been a fit, lean farm boy, his muscles hard from working in the fields. She could imagine him sitting high and strong on his horse, working his sheep with a dog at his side, or splitting logs for fence posts. His arm might have healed swiftly with the right care but after months or years in the trenches, his worn-out shell of a body couldn't deal with wounds so severe. It had betrayed him. Ivy wished she could fix him, like she wished she could fix all the men, but thinking like that was pointless. Recovery was as uncertain as who was wounded in the first place. The world was nothing if not a random place. It was best to take what you could, when you could, before it was snatched away.

'You must give it time,' Sister admonished. 'Your chart shows you're making progress. Let's see what the doctor has to say when he makes his morning rounds, shall we?'

The lieutenant didn't answer. They all knew that time was in short supply.

'How is Lieutenant Turner doing?' Rose asked Ivy as they came off their shift.

'Not so well, miss, the wound in his arm is slow to heal and Sister is worried that he's struggling with it.'

'You're much braver than me. I don't have the stomach for septic wounds – and facial deformities terrify me,' said Rose, screwing up her nose in distaste. 'When I see men with bad facial wounds, I can't help thinking that it could happen to any one of them. And then their families would have to go on looking at them for the rest of their lives, all the time remembering how they used to be. I don't know what I'd do if that happened to Robert. It just doesn't bear thinking about.'

Miss Rose had very selfish sensibilities at times. But at least she wasn't as useless as some of the VAD ladies who dropped by to hold hands and arrange flowers. Ivy suspected they merely wanted an excuse to don the uniform and parade around looking like they were doing their part for the war effort. Miss Rose avoided helping Sister with the worst wounds whenever she could, but she'd become quite adept at making beds and serving meals, something she had probably never imagined doing before the war.

'You just have to look at the good side of his face and it isn't so bad. And most of the time the bad side is covered with a light bandage.' Sister didn't like to chance the patients seeing their faces reflected in a window or basin. Not when they were still so ill. It might set them back further.

Ivy would never hint that Rose wasn't doing her part, even when she started the day as dog tired as when the previous day had ended. After her years in service, she knew her mistress would keep her up until all hours if she heard even a shadow of criticism in her voice. Rose liked to think that she was a free spirit, but Ivy knew better. She became quite frosty if she thought a servant was getting uppity – and positively nasty, if contradicted. Most of the time they rubbed along quite well . . . as long as Ivy knew her place. Sometimes Rose could be almost friendly. And if Ivy ever thought back to those childhood days when a little girl from the big house had sworn to be friends forever . . . well . . . every girl had to grow up.

'And the lieutenant is a funny one. I don't mind spending time with him,' she added, knowing Rose liked her best when she was chatty but not presumptuous.

'You don't?'

After the first shock, Ivy had realised that she didn't mind nursing Henry Turner at all, despite witnessing his pain and the brutality of his wounds. In fact, she quite liked that in order to help him she had to find the lighter side of herself, a side she had put away long ago. She liked to make him laugh and hear him tease.

'He was telling me about his home in Australia, the property where he farms with his older brother. I liked hearing about it. It sounded different, so far from the war and everything.'

'Australia is about as far away from this war as you could get, isn't it?' Rose mused, a thoughtful look in her eyes.

'I believe Australia is as far away as you could get from anywhere, miss.' Far enough to get away from this life she had been born into. Almost another world, really. She wondered what that would be like – to put away her fears, and bring out her desires instead. To be Ivy, yet not Ivy.

The screens had been removed by the time Rose arrived for duty the following day, but she had no occasion to examine the patient who lay there until a voice called quietly, 'Nurse . . . nurse, have you seen Nurse Toms?'

She felt bad about avoiding the lieutenant yesterday, but Ivy had a stronger stomach and coped better with the nastiest wounds. Rose consoled herself by thinking that no one would appreciate it if she vomited all over the bedclothes, least of all the poor lieutenant. She was better at lifting men's spirits than swabbing wounds. Yet right now she was the only nurse on the ward. Ivy was in the sink room, Nurse Giles was in the kitchen and Sister was consulting with the Medical Officer upstairs. She debated slipping away, but the man's plea pinched at her conscience until she left off dusting and headed reluctantly towards the lieutenant's bed.

'Yes, Lieutenant?' she said, her eyes flitting about the room, searching for anywhere to rest except upon the patient sitting up in bed before her.

'Nurse Toms offered to read this letter from my brother, since my good eye tires easily. I wondered if she was about.' Letter reading was often code for a bit of company to distract the men from their fears, and the lieutenant had every reason to be afraid.

148

From what Rose had heard, he might be lucky to survive his wounds.

She took a deep breath and forced herself to look him in the face.

What she found wasn't nearly as awful as she expected. In fact, if she had happened upon the lieutenant in profile she might never have noticed anything amiss. His left side showed an ordinary young man of fair complexion and sandy blond hair, his body thin like most of the men now, but whole. It was his right side that shocked, with its missing leg, damaged arm and mutilated face. Luckily for Rose, the injured side was veiled in bandages, giving the young man an almost poetic gravity.

'Nurse Toms is busy right now. But I could read your letter, if you like,' she said, compensating for her earlier reluctance with the sweetest smile she could muster. 'I'm Nurse Luscombe.'

'Even with one good eye I can see you're the prettiest girl I've met in a long time, if you don't mind my saying.'

Rose laughed. 'I don't know a single girl who would object to being told she is pretty. Now where's that letter? Your brother must be very worried about you.'

Out of the corner of her eye, she noticed Ivy entering the ward, wiping wet hands upon her apron. She saw the girl look up and register her presence, letter in hand. Her face, which had been unusually cheerful upon entry, registered momentary disappointment before returning to her habitual non-expression as she hurried about some other task. Rose could have relinquished her seat at the lieutenant's bedside and let Ivy take her place, but how could a lady's maid ever take the place of someone like Rose Luscombe? She wasn't being smug in thinking this, for it was a fact, unpalatable as some might find it. She had been graced with beauty and the good fortune of wealth and breeding, whereas Ivy was a simple village girl. Reality could not be helped, after all.

If she felt a slight tug at her conscience, it was easily dismissed.

Ivy had been foisted upon her in the first place. Rationally, she knew it wasn't Ivy's fault, but that didn't make her like it. Sometimes she felt like an exotic bird in an expensive cage; no matter how hard she rattled the bars, she could only see the world from inside her prison. Besides, it might not be very becoming, but she couldn't help enjoying the flash of disappointment on her maid's face.

Sometimes Ivy passed the time by counting the cutlery and crockery she set on each food tray. That's what she did now in the sink room, leaving Miss Rose to take her place at the lieutenant's bedside. Thirteen implements per tray, thirty trays, three times a day, four days a week for . . . how many weeks now? The numbers were becoming hard to calculate, except sometimes it was the only way she could stop thinking. Thinking was wearisome. If you allowed yourself to think too much, you opened yourself to the patients' pain. And they had so much of it. No, it was better to attend to your duties, saving your thinking for when the war ended. That's how she endured the interminable hours making beds with hospital corners and preparing dressings for butcher-shop limbs.

It did no one any good to become attached to a wounded lieutenant's cheeky grin, to his funny stories and unexpected laughter. She was better off in the sink room with the dishes and the bandages. Better to let someone else do the thinking. Better to let Rose do the feeling, even if it meant watching her snatch Ivy's few moments of pleasure away. Let Rose have her ribbons, her pony and her lieutenant.

The world was changing, and one day Ivy would be sure to get what she was owed.

20

North Devon

2017

It was already eleven and Molly hadn't prised her nose from the cartons since before nine. She was due for a break – sitting on the floor with her head bowed over a box of old documents for hours on end couldn't be good for her posture – but she kept finding more treasure. Here were invoices for mechanical work on a Silver Ghost. There were Savile Row tailors' receipts from before the Great War, all muddled in with memorabilia from Eton College. She had obviously come upon a cache of personal documents belonging to Richard's father, Robert Luscombe.

The memorabilia from Eton College was particularly interesting, with receipts from Tom Brown Tailors for a three-piece tail suit, shirts, collars and ties, several tattered copies of *The Eton Chronicle* from 1905 to 1910, and a number of photographs of tail-coated, top-hatted boys in pinstriped trousers and wide collars, looking like they had stepped straight out of a Dickens novel. Her favourite photograph was a group portrait of the rowing eight of 1909.

The boys were posed in front of a brick building with a white door and staircase in the background, while in one corner she thought she distinguished a section of river, a bridge and perhaps boat ramps. The boys stood or sat in three rows, with one boy cross-legged on the ground. All wore white trousers and jackets with white caps and white shoes. They should have looked identical in their outfits, yet each boy was subtly different to the next. They had crossed their arms or folded their hands or placed them on their knees. Perhaps their cap was set at a jauntier angle or they were trying not to smile. She liked the way she could read something of each boy's personality in his posture. And there was Robert, standing in the middle at the back, presumably one of the tallest, looking straight at the camera. She felt that he was looking out at her. That he wanted to tell her something. But what it might be she had no idea.

Putting aside the photograph to show Richard later, she continued sifting through the pile of assorted invoices and receipts, noting each item in the database she was establishing on her laptop. After another thirty minutes of sorting and cataloguing, she came across a 1917 invoice written in French. She had only taken French until Year 11, and even that was rusty, but she recognised the word *bijoux* as meaning jewellery. And given the English word *nacre* meant mother of pearl, she guessed that *sautoir de nacre* meant that she may have found the original receipt for the pearl sautoir they had found amongst Nan's belongings. To think that a hundred years ago one of her ancestors had gone shopping for jewellery in the middle of the war – that he had taken time out from the trenches to choose jewellery. Yet she supposed that these ordinary tasks were a way of keeping up your spirits in the midst of violence, a way of connecting with home.

Since she had found the receipt from a French jeweller amongst Robert Luscombe's documents, it seemed likely that he gave Rose the necklace – not her husband, Jim Turner, as they had assumed. And given that Rose wore it every year on her birthday, perhaps it was a birthday gift. Despite their estrangement, she must still have retained some fondness for the brother she'd left behind.

Richard would like the idea that his father and his aunt weren't completely estranged. In fact, Molly decided that she liked the idea too. The connection between the English and Australian branches of the family wasn't merely a few pencil lines scribbled on a family tree, or a fragment of DNA, but a real attachment.

Unfolding her legs and stretching her creaky back, she wandered over to the window, ducking her head to avoid the sloping ceiling. The windows gave a view northwards over the walled forecourt with its circular gravel drive and grassed edges, towards the road and neighbouring farms. A giant oak grew just outside the wall beside a door that she knew led to Lucas's house. That door stood open. As she watched, Lucas strode across the gravel, heading away from the house. When he reached the door leading towards his place, he turned and looked back towards Luscombe, lifting one arm in farewell. He didn't spare a glance for the attic windows where he knew she was at work; he was waving to someone standing at Luscombe's Gothic arched entryway.

She tried to quell her disappointment that he hadn't popped his head around her workroom door to say hello, that he hadn't stopped by for a chat or a cup of coffee. But why should he? Richard was his friend. She was merely an interloper. He would be polite and pleasant, as he would be for any guest of Richard's, and then soon she would be gone. With a sigh, she returned to her box of goodies. She was on safer ground here, living vicariously through others, tracing their lives, fishing for their secrets, dwelling upon their loves. Her own feelings were far too messy, and better kept under lock and key.

She put aside the French receipt and dived into the carton once more, her hand surfacing with a faded red ledger book marked 'Wages Book 1895–1920'. Lovely, more treasure. She was so happy here, she realised, despite distracting thoughts about Lucas. The work was the main thing, and it was intriguing, rewarding and invariably fascinating. She hadn't been this happy in a long while, probably not since she first met Matt. Each new fact she unearthed was as exciting as a nugget of gold. She was even beginning to think that perhaps she did have the mettle to give up teaching and strike out into research, now that she had a taste of sorting the Luscombe archive. This is what she should have been doing all along – sifting documents, poring over pictures – sieving the facts to find the story. This is what would make her happy.

Except why should she expect happiness?

Luscombe Park may have dwindled but the grounds were still large enough to require the services of three doughty sheep to maintain the lawn. As Richard and Molly stepped from the gravel terrace on to the grass, the small flock lifted their heads to stare at the intruders. They were overdue for shearing by the look of them, with their fleece straggling in long curls. Unlike the Merino crosses and Polwarths of Wuurnong, their ears were high and they had a distinctly Roman cast to their profiles.

'Very distinguished-looking lawnmowers, Richard.'

'Bluefaced Leicesters. They like me because I give them treats,' he said, finding a small shrivelled apple in the pocket of his tweed jacket and offering it on his palm to the bravest of the flock. 'I expect you wouldn't know that we have more breeds of sheep than any other country. Being something of a grazier, I know these things,' he added with a wink.

'No, I can't say I knew that.' She smiled as the other two sheep nosed forward for their share of Richard's largesse, one importunate fellow butting his head against her leg.

They continued their walk towards the boundary of the property, Richard with one arm linked through hers and the other gripping his shooting stick firmly. He pointed out features of the grounds as they walked, describing how the park had once included an ornamental lake and a folly that was lost to sub-division in the 1950s. He had been sorry to see the lake go but his father said it was the only way to keep the estate at all. He had missed, most of all, the little jetty and rowing boat.

'I found a photograph of your father and the 1909 Eton rowing eight this morning. I put it aside for you.'

'Did you? I knew it was a good idea asking you here, Molly. I would never have known it existed.'

'I'm having a great time up there with the dust fairies and spiderwebs.'

'Father loved his years at Eton, you know. Couldn't wait to get away from home, I imagine. I wasn't quite so keen. I loved it here. I spent a lot of time by the lake until I was sent away to school.'

'How old were you?'

'I believe I was eight. Confused Mother with Matron regularly when I returned for the hols.'

They turned to gaze at the house, the sprawling structure reclining on its bed of smooth lawns, roof bristling with chimneys. It looked majestic, with the late afternoon sun gilding the stone, but she knew that in reality the roof leaked, the down-pipes were rusting and the woodwork was in dire need of painting. Richard had told her he was recently quoted £70,000 to repair and repaint the guttering and woodwork.

'You know I also found the wages book from 1895 to 1920. Whoever managed the estate was quite meticulous about keeping the accounts.'

'Father managed the estate after the war, but I believe we employed an estate manager in the years between my grandfather's death and Father's return from France. The estate account books are somewhere in the library. I must look them out for you.'

'I've discovered that until the First World War, Luscombe's average staff included ten indoor and five outdoor workers, not counting the home farm. Of course, the scullery maid and the hall boy were only paid about twelve pounds a year. Even the butler, a Mr Alistair Greep, was only paid sixty, but even so . . .'

'Dev used to say that the dishwasher accounted for a scullery maid, the washing machine for a laundry maid and the vacuum cleaner for one housemaid. But that still leaves us terribly short, doesn't it?'

'Just a bit.'

'I suppose Tesco helps out with the cooking,' he sighed.

'Even so, I don't know how you keep it going with Judy only coming in two days a week.'

'The truth is I don't. That's why I've had to close off most of the upstairs rooms. They say people's lives get smaller as they grow older. Dev and I once roamed the world but now I'm confined to three rooms: the drawing room, the study and the kitchen. Even at 1900 wage rates I'd be pressed to find funds to staff this house.'

'I found Ivy in the wages book from 1913 to the beginning of 1919. She must have been fourteen when she came to work at Luscombe. I also found a Daniel Toms who began work in 1917.'

'That would be Lucas's grandfather. Daniel started at Luscombe as the gardener's lad and went on to become head gardener – the only gardener by the time he retired in the 1960s. Daniel and I were great friends. I used to follow him around like a puppy when I was home, and he was very indulgent of me. Splendid chap, Daniel Toms.'

'Was he Ivy's only sibling?'

'She had a middle brother who died during the war. Lucas would know.'

'Ah, yes, Lucas.' She threw him an enquiring look. 'You didn't suggest that he invite me out for a drive on Saturday, did you?'

'I would never meddle. And I should think a man like Lucas would be eager to escort an attractive young woman on an outing.' Richard shook his head so that the wattles of his neck quivered. If it hadn't been for the wrinkles he might have been a naughty ten year old denying he was the one who let the dog out.

'Hmmm,' she answered with a sidelong glance. He was all indignation but he didn't actually deny prompting Lucas. She was beginning to suspect that Richard Luscombe was much sneakier than he appeared. It was only that twinkle in his eye that gave the game away. 'You'll never guess what else I found.'

'What?'

'A receipt for a mother-of-pearl necklace. The same necklace that my mother and I discovered at Nan's. I think it might have been a birthday gift from Robert to Rose.'

'My father regretted saying goodbye to his sister for the rest of his life. I suppose no one could know then that he would never see her again.'

Twelve-year-old Molly hadn't known she would never see her father again either. It was as unthinkable as the sun not rising. If she had, she would have done so many things differently. But Richard was right, how could anyone predict that last goodbye? It might sneak up like a rip towing you out to sea, so that no matter how hard you struggled you could never go back. All your goodbyes had already been said.

21

North Devon

1917

Although the sun was yet to creep over the cypresses, Ivy was so tired that her bones ached. She sagged against the ladder-back chair in the servants' hall as the hall boy bustled about the scrubbed pine table, setting out porridge and bread and butter for the staff breakfast. Miss Rose hadn't retired until eleven the previous evening, and after helping her undress, Ivy still had to clean a pair of kid gloves, as her mistress couldn't possibly take tea at the Eldridges' on Friday without them. So before she collapsed into bed, she had cleaned the gloves with benzene and tonight, once they were dry, she would rub them with sweet oil, wrap them in flannel and weight them down so Miss Rose would have her shiny blue gloves for Friday.

You wouldn't think there was so much to learn about gloves. There were rules for cleaning them, rules for mending them, even rules for removing them. Gibbons would throw a fit if Ivy forgot to turn the wrist wrong side out before taking off Miss Rose's gloves. She often wondered how anyone could go on caring about gloves when there were men in their thousands who needed mending more.

When she first came to Luscombe, the long days scrubbing, polishing and sweeping had stripped the plumpness from her bones and replaced it with hard edges. But once she took up her duties as lady's maid those curves gradually returned. Men liked a girl with curves, but now hers were once more slipping from her bones like melting butter. What if the war lasted so long that all her youth and prettiness were worn away? What if she missed her chance at life and died an old lady's maid?

If it wasn't for the captain's letters, she didn't think she could continue. She had kept her word about writing to reassure him of his sister's welfare, snatching moments whenever she was alone to pull a flimsy sheet of paper from her pocket and jot down a few more hastily assembled words. But she was surprised when he wrote back. Mr Greep had presented her with an envelope one afternoon at tea, his eyebrows quirked. The envelope was marked 'Passed by Censor' and in place of a stamp the words 'On Active Service' were scrawled at the top. The address was written in a loose, untidy hand and there was no return address on the rear of the envelope. She would discover later that the captain had asked a friend to address the envelope in order to allay any gossip that his handwriting might cause. He hadn't realised that *any* letter to her was bound to arouse curiosity.

'Have you got a sweetheart then, Ivy?' Muriel had teased when the butler handed her the letter.

Put on the spot, she said the first thing that entered her head. 'It's from my brother Samuel, who's gone and joined up.' That at least wasn't a lie. Her brother Samuel, at a bare seventeen, had gone and joined the Somerset Light Infantry. Ma had been red-faced with misery for weeks after he left, and her da took up residence in the pub for three long days. 'My da is right sore about it too,' she added to authenticate the claim.

She had been tempted to rip open the envelope on the spot, but it demanded more reverence than this. It had come from the trenches. And although she only suspected the identity of the writer, something told her that it had come from the captain. Mr Robert Luscombe. Her employer. A fleeting memory of his smile as he requested that she write. A tiny fluttering of her heart as she received the battered envelope from Mr Greep's hands. So that afternoon, when she finally found herself alone in Miss Rose's room, she borrowed the ivory letter opener to slit one edge, sliding free a frail slip of paper.

'*Dear Ivy,*' he had written, '*thank you for your kind letter of last week. I'm embarrassed to admit that its folds have already frayed with constant reading . . .*'

And so the correspondence began, with a letter she had patched together over days, writing whatever nonsense entered her head, and his short but heartfelt reply from the middle of a war. Who would have thought that the captain would find her stories comforting, her gossip entertaining? Certainly not Ivy. And who would have thought that little Ivy Toms would come to live for the days when a letter arrived for her all the way from France?

This morning, having gulped her breakfast, she was about to scrape her tired body from the chair and hurry to the porch, where Donaldson would be waiting to drive them to the hospital, when Mr Greep appeared in the door of the servants' hall, saying, 'Miss Toms, if I might have a word?'

He phrased it as a request but all eyes at the table turned to stare.

'Yes, Mr Greep,' she answered, for what possible other response could there be? But she was nervous. The arrival of a letter did not require conversation.

She followed him through the kitchen, wondering what she had done wrong. Was it Miss Rose's lace handkerchiefs that had gone a sad shade of grey? The pearls she had forgotten to lock away last night, too busy cleaning gloves? Or was it the trailing hem on her own black dress that was yet to be repaired?

Unless he had become suspicious about the identity of her correspondent . . .

The kitchen, which steamed and stirred from dawn until well after dusk, was momentarily quiet while the servants ate breakfast. The enormous table that dominated the centre of the room was neat and ordered, and the giant range lay dormant but for the simmering stockpot as she shuffled across the sawdust-covered floor in Greep's wake. The butler's pantry was situated on the south side of Luscombe Park, overlooking the drive, so that he would receive advance warning of any visitors. It was also conveniently located next to the knife house and the storage room where linen and plate were kept, and adjacent to the cellar stairs. His domain was furnished with a bench, a writing table and a comfortable fireside chair. The walls were decorated with an assortment of firearms, many of them so old only a fool or a madman would attempt to fire them.

'Now, Miss Toms,' the butler began, clearing his throat with a little cough. 'Another letter came for you in yesterday's post but I haven't had a chance to give it to you.' He picked up the letter from a silver salver on his table and handed it to her.

She slipped it into her apron pocket without inspecting the envelope and stood waiting, pretending that the letter wasn't the brightest spot in her day, that its author didn't haunt her dreams. He didn't say anything further for several seconds and she held her breath, waiting. What would happen if he discovered the letter's true author? She would certainly be chastised. Perhaps even dismissed if Miss Rose were to find out – and then what would she do?

'From your brother Samuel?' he asked finally.

'I expect so, sir,' she said, as nonchalantly as possible, when her throat was tight with fear.

'How is he getting on, then?' he added.

She relaxed a fraction but was still wary, since Mr Greep

wasn't known for his pleasantries. 'As well as can be expected, sir.'

In truth, she didn't know. Samuel had never been fond of learning and his letters to her parents, although regular, were brief – a hurriedly scrawled postcard here, a badly spelled note there. Out of duty she had sent him some socks that she'd knitted and a parcel of cocoa and carbolic soap. But since there had never been much love lost between them, she hadn't heard a word in return.

'So I believe you have another brother. A younger boy?'

'Yes, Mr Greep,' she replied, wondering where the conversation was heading. 'Daniel. He's thirteen.'

'You might know that the gardener's lad has left to join up, which leaves Pedrick shorthanded. For obvious reasons there's a dearth of young men to be hired. I thought that your brother might be interested in the position. Pedrick would train him, of course, and if he proved suitable he could make a very respectable career here. You yourself have risen far very quickly,' he said, his mouth working hard to smile. 'We look after our own here at Luscombe.'

She knew she couldn't say no to Mr Greep, and Danny might indeed like the work. He would be learning a trade and getting away from their father at the same time, but she also knew that her da would feel like the war had stolen one son, now Luscombe was taking the second. For a working man like her father, who had a very small voice in the wider world, the one thing he could control was his family. If he felt that was slipping away from him too, well, someone would have to pay. And since she was rarely at home, that someone would probably be her mother. It seemed as if Ma had been paying her whole married life for one thing or another. Ivy had realised young that she couldn't do much to help her mother, but perhaps she could help Danny.

'I'm not sure if my da needs Danny. I can ask.'

'Thank you, Miss Toms, please do.'

Anything to keep in Mr Greep's good books. Anything to deter him from delving into her correspondence. She didn't know what she would do if she lost that.

Rose brought stationery from Luscombe Park to write Lieutenant Turner's letter to his family. She added a few drops of Yardley's April Violets to the stiff white paper. When the envelope was opened the scent of violets and jasmine would linger. She hoped that the creamy paper and the waft of flowers might temper the lieutenant's difficult words to his family. She had spent many hours listening to soldiers spill their darkest fears, things they couldn't or wouldn't say to their mothers or sweethearts. Mostly they feared not being the men they once were. They feared they had lost an essential part of themselves, even if physically they remained whole. A man like Henry Turner, who had lost so much of his physical self, needed to hold fast to his inner self with an unrelenting grip.

She sat at Henry's bedside, pen in hand, waiting expectantly. The clatter of the ward continued around them but as she transcribed his words she found herself drawn into his world, imagining how he must feel, knowing that his life could never be what he had once planned.

'*Dear Mum and Jim,*' he dictated. '*I suppose you've seen the casualty lists some time ago and will be wondering how I'm getting on. Sorry I haven't been able to send more than a cable until now. The truth is my right arm isn't up to much. You'll be relieved to hear that my leg is healing nicely, though. The shrapnel wounds to my face have healed too but I have a mug that will scare little kids now.*'

'Lieutenant, you know that's not true!' she interjected at this point. She was sitting at his left side at his insistence. He said it was so that he could see her better, but she knew he wished her to forget the damaged face beneath the bandages. Still, she was relieved.

'Nurse Luscombe, we both know I've lost me looks.'

'Looks aren't everything,' she said sternly. 'Now let's continue.'

'*I arrived at Southampton six weeks ago (Jim, your letter of 8th March finally caught up, having chased me around Europe) with a company of other Australian wounded. We excited a great deal of curiosity, with children staring and crying out, "Look at them hats, Ma! It's the Australians!" and the girls throwing kisses.*

'*We took the train to Queens Street Station in Exeter, where the boys blinded by gas walked in crocodile file to the hospital. Me they carried on a stretcher. I had more surgery at Exeter before being moved here to Oldbridge Auxiliary Hospital in North Devon. It's very comfortable here. Lady Waring, the Commandant (not as frightening as it sounds), has turned her home into a military hospital and there are about thirty men here. It's a pretty place, surrounded by gardens with spreading oak trees and meadows. You'd like it, Mum. Very grand! The nurses are all kind, the beds are comfy and we eat better than at the front, although the nurses don't smile very much.*'

Rose cleared her throat, raising one eyebrow to remind him of her presence.

'*Except for Nurse Luscombe, of course, who is the kindest of them all and has a smile like an angel.*'

'There's no need to exaggerate.'

'My brother appreciates a pretty face as much as I do, if you don't mind me saying. Now, where were we?'

'*I shall tell you how I came to be in this pickle after getting through two years with not much more than a few scrapes,*' he continued. '*It was a pretty awful show, with a growing pile of dead covered with tarpaulins and the smell of blood and smoke in the air. The Bosch were moving, shell fire covering their advance. Two of my men were down and I didn't need to look closely to know they weren't getting up again, the poor beggars. The sergeant, two other men and I scrambled into a shell hole for cover as shrapnel burst around us, but we knew it was too shallow to protect us for long. The captain was signalling for us to retreat to the trenches, where we could make our stand against Fritz. So it was bellies and elbows back through the wire.*

'*The machine guns on the hill were popping and shells whistling all about us. You can hear the shell coming, Mum, hissing and screaming before it explodes in the air, hurling its great load of bullets to the ground. I guess I knew it was coming my way but there was nothing I could do. I remember curling into a ball, must have been lying on my left side because my right took the hit. Then I don't remember much until I woke up at the Casualty Clearing Station after the first surgery, but they tell me Sergeant Collins dragged me fifty yards to the trenches.*'

'Perhaps that's enough for now,' Rose suggested, noticing that her patient had slumped further down in his bed and the eyelid of his good eye was drooping. Her hand was becoming quite cramped too.

'I'd like to finish, if you don't mind. Mum and Jim have waited two months already. It isn't fair to leave them wondering any longer.

'*Jim, I don't know when I'll be home but it looks like I won't be returning to the front. So please give my bat to old Shadwell at the school. I won't have much use for it, and the kids can always use another bat. And Mum, please pass on my best wishes to Bessie Tait. I hope she finds some nice chap to keep her company.*

'I want to add a little about you, Nurse. Will you tell them that you're writing this for me and how kind you've been?'

'*This letter has been penned by Nurse Rose Luscombe.* How will that do?' she asked.

'Not very informative,' he said, a twitch to his mouth. 'What about adding . . . *who makes my life bearable . . . Will write again soon. Much love, Harry.'*

Rose imagined his mother and brother receiving this letter addressed to them in a strange hand from the place that had swallowed up their wounded son. She couldn't imagine what it would be like to be so far away from your loved ones when they were in need, too far to rush to their side, too far for letters to reach them in time. Would they hesitate in opening the envelope, putting off the moment that might confirm their worst fears? They may not have received the dreaded cable but there were worse things than death for a man like Henry Turner.

She pictured Henry's elder brother, Jim – the man he looked up to, the man who had stayed behind to look after the farm so there would be something to return to after the war. Henry hadn't described the extent of his injuries but Jim would know him well enough to understand what couldn't be put into words. That there would be no more cricket for his little brother, no more droving, and small chance of love.

'*Don't give up hope – Rose*'. She scratched the words at the bottom of the letter.

Don't give up hope. For hope was all they had left.

22

North Devon

2017

'It looks prettier than when I was driving,' Molly remarked as the road narrowed to a single lane, the hedgerows crowding close.

'Too busy concentrating?'

'Too afraid to take my eyes off the white line. Navigating out of London infected me with white-line fever.'

'I drove through Rome once.' Lucas took his eyes off the road for a moment in a conspiratorial smile. 'That was a steep learning curve, even with my personal navigator sitting beside me. Italian drivers are quite expressive.'

'Well, I'm not much use as a navigator in Britain but my friends would vouch for me at home.'

The conversation during the first ten minutes of their drive was rather stilted, as if neither of them quite knew what they were doing there. It was unclear whether they were on a date, a sightseeing tour, or a friendly outing. And for her part, she couldn't quite forget that Lucas hadn't dropped in to say hello when he visited Richard the previous day. She worried that he had only invited her along out of some misplaced sense of duty. She was nervous. And nervous Molly meant lots of inconsequential chatter about the weather and the passing scenery.

He wasn't much better, decidedly formal and overly concerned that her seat was comfortable and she had enough legroom. But after they had been driving for a while they both loosened up. Lucas described points of interest and Molly forgot her nerves and behaved like a normal human being. He was a busy man and there *were* a lot of stairs up to the attics. He could be forgiven for deciding not to climb them. Besides, she liked the way his eyes crinkled when he smiled. He had strong features that gave him a rather careless grace.

'So, no navigator this weekend?' she ventured, trying not to sound as if she were fishing, yet suspecting it was as obvious as if she had a rod and tackle in her hands.

When he kept his eyes fixed on the road, unsmiling, jaw tense, she wished she could retract her question.

'No. My former navigator decided she's really a London girl, after all,' he said quietly after a while.

Molly would have liked to ask who *she* was and what *she* had been to Lucas, but since they had only known each other for a matter of days, probing personal questions were presumptuous. On the other hand, silence was cold and unfriendly. Her sister would have dived right in, questions accompanied by a smile so engaging that no one would take offence. But Molly had never quite mastered this art. She once asked Daisy how she charmed people and was met with a puzzled frown.

'I'm not charming. I'm nosy.'

Perhaps that was it; Daisy was truly curious about other people. She wanted to know how they felt, how they lived their lives. She put herself in their shoes. Without that curiosity she wouldn't have been such a good photographer, for how could you capture people's essence without understanding what made them tick? Molly's curiosity was mostly reserved for dead people.

An oncoming car saved her from her dilemma by appearing around a bend of the single-lane road so that Lucas slowed down, pulling into a lay-by to let the car pass. Once he had completed the manoeuvre the conversation moved on naturally.

'My sister lives in London,' she said. 'She arrived two years ago and hasn't returned. London has swallowed her.'

'It has a habit of doing that.'

'Daisy's a lot more adventurous than me. Mum says she's responsible for at least half the grey hairs on her head.'

'And are you responsible for the other half?'

'Oh, I'm much too sedate. My life is very ordered—' She broke off, unsure how to finish her sentence, how much of herself she was willing to give away.

'Trying to create order out of chaos maybe?'

'Yep, but life has a way of throwing the best-laid plans into disarray, doesn't it?'

'Yep,' he echoed her with a grin. 'I thought I'd be married to the girl of my dreams by now, but it turned out she had a different dream altogether. A Londoner, born and bred, whereas I suppose I prefer a less hectic existence.'

Molly had discovered something similar not so long ago. They talked about broken dreams; about the interior designer girlfriend he met at university, who decided that a practice in North Devon wasn't a big enough stage for her (or the country architect who lived there). Then Molly surprised herself by confiding in him about Matt's abrupt departure and Jordana, the girl who had taken her place in his life.

They told funny stories about their families and talked about their work, about the irony of futures that were so entangled with the past. Lucas proved to be a lively and insightful companion and she wondered why some girl hadn't snapped him up as soon as he became available. If she weren't merely a tourist and a romantic cripple, she would certainly have given it a shot.

'What are you doing here, Molly?' he asked, breaking into her thoughts after she fell silent for a time.

'In Devon?' she said, wondering whether his question meant anything or whether it was merely conversation.

'Mmm. What are you looking for?'

'I don't know, really. Time, I suppose. Time to decide.'

When the car joined a wider, busier road she barely noticed. She didn't think to ask where they were going. All she knew was that as they drove, she felt a loosening in her chest as if something that had been lodged there was coming unstuck.

After an abundance of Devonshire tea, which she learned to call simply 'cream tea', they resumed their journey, leaving the charming village of Lynton behind and venturing on to the edge of Exmoor. Lucas told how the nineteenth-century author R. D. Blackmore had stayed in the area to research his novel *Lorna Doone*, as they emerged from a lightly wooded area into a treeless valley. On the moor to their right loomed a lofty formation of stone, standing sentinel on the cliff top above the sea. It was crowned with a bulwark of weathered rocks that resembled the battlements of an ancient fortress. And rising out of the moor around it were other craggy, grass-encroached mounds that reminded her of a series of ruins that had been buried beneath the accumulated rubble of centuries, their stones slowly but inexorably returning to nature.

'Valley of the Rocks,' he said. 'There's no river now but the Lyn River probably flowed this way once, carving the valley from the rock, while the waves did their work from the seaward side.'

He pulled into a car park at the edge of the road and they got out. Her nose was immediately assaulted.

'Do I smell poo?'

'Probably, there's a—' A chorus of insistent bleating interrupted him.

'Is that a goat?'

Perched on a high crag overlooking the ocean, a shaggy, long-haired goat sat sunning itself, the grey and rust-coloured hair almost camouflaging it amongst the rocks. It was the massive curving horns that caught her attention.

'There's a herd of feral goats living in the valley. And wild ponies on the moor. If we take a walk we might see some of his friends.'

'I don't think we need to walk far.'

When she swung her gaze back to Lucas, she realised that trotting atop a low stone wall on the other side of the road were three of the goat's fellows. After taking a few shots of them on her phone, they walked along the cliff-top path, skirting the foot of the rock formations that seemed ready to tumble into the sea at any moment.

'It's so wild,' she commented as they paused at a point jutting out into the Bristol Channel. 'It reminds me of the Victorian coast. I always think of England as rolling pastures and stately homes. I never imagined it would be so rugged.'

'We can be quite deceptive here. Underneath our cool exterior you never know what you might find.'

She glanced at his face to see if he was laughing at her, but he was looking out to sea. Was he telling her something about himself? For the first time since meeting Matt, she felt that quiver of anticipation, that shiver of recognition that comes when you find someone who could be . . . something more.

It was a frightening thought and she didn't know if she was ready.

'Are you cold?' Lucas asked.

'No. Not cold. Just . . . surprised.'

Their tour continued in the car, past a slate-roofed stone cottage with a sign warning of a toll ahead – the only honour system toll road she had ever seen – then past the candy-turreted Lee Abbey and onward through rolling pastures, sheep grazing placidly on lush grassy slopes. Looking out to sea, she noticed the headlands jutting out into the Bristol Channel, like giant paws clawing a tenuous hold from the sea. Then the road descended through a wooded section before arriving at the small settlement of Lee Bay.

'Do you feel like walking?' Lucas suggested, after parking the car.

They headed down the road to the bay, where the beach waited below a sea wall. The tide was out, a jumble of rocks and pools poking from the sand that stretched invitingly towards the ocean. She felt its lure, the waves whispering their inducements in her ear, but these days she wasn't so easily seduced.

'There's a beach around the point if you're up for a scramble. The tide won't be in for a while yet.'

The sea had seemed blue and glassy from the hill above the village but down here, within its reach, she could see the swell and knew that within minutes it could change, could pull you out and drag you under. Once upon a time, this coast had been the haunt of wreckers who preyed upon unwary ships. She wasn't about to be taken unawares.

'Maybe another day,' she said, gesturing ruefully at her tight jeans. She was glad now that she had opted for jeans rather than a skirt. That morning, a short skirt had seemed too vulnerable, not to mention no proof against changeable weather. It was funny that at home she wouldn't have given it a second thought. At home she was a shorts and singlet girl. Here she wasn't sure who she was; Luscombe Park had immersed her in the past but made her question her future, her certainties shifting beneath her like quicksand.

'We could come back for a swim another time maybe.'

'Actually I don't usually swim in the surf.' She shrugged, keeping her eyes on the ocean. It wasn't safe to turn your back on it.

'I thought you were all bona fide lifesavers. I've seen *Home and Away* – under duress, of course.'

'Not all of us,' she said with a rueful laugh.

Perhaps he realised more lay behind her words than a reluctance to feel the grit of salt on her skin. Yesterday he would probably have let the moment go but today they had ventured into more personal territory.

'Sorry, I didn't mean anything by that . . .'

'No, it's fine. I used to love the ocean but . . . um . . . my father drowned when I was twelve and I've never felt quite the same way about the sea since. You could say the ocean and I have a love-hate relationship.'

'Why don't we return to the car?'

'It's fine, really. It's just . . . I . . . I was there. He was trying to save me.'

And then she told him.

She had been taught that you don't fight a rip; that you let it carry you out, and when it wanes you swim parallel to the beach until you find a safe place to swim to shore. If you fight the rip you will exhaust yourself, get nowhere and possibly drown. But it's one thing to know what to do and another to do it, especially when she could see that the rip was pulling her towards the point of the bay where waves surged on to rocks. Then a tiny figure wearing familiar grey track pants and a yellow T-shirt appeared on the beach waving to her, arms crossing each other in wide sweeps. Perhaps she should have felt anxious that her dad had discovered her swimming alone, without flags or lifesavers, but she was relieved. Her breathing slowed, quieting her stammering heart. Her father was surely a match for the rip dragging her out to sea.

Her dad realised that she was caught in the rip. He was down to his shorts and splashing through the shallows before slowing as the water crept to his waist, then swimming when the water reached chest height. He swam towards her, propelled by the underwater current and his own practised crawl, as her legs weakened and her strokes slowed. Then through the splash of her swimming she glimpsed another person, jogging along the path through the dunes with his surfboard under his arm, the top of his wetsuit flapping loosely over the bottom. She paused for a moment to wave, hoping he would look her way. Surely he must look out to sea to check the break? She opened her mouth to shout for help, swallowing a mouthful of saltwater for her trouble. Then, pushing herself higher in the water and raising her chin, she tried again, fighting the pull of the rip with thrashing legs.

'Help! Help!' she managed to shout, just as her father reached her.

'Dad!' she sobbed as he put one arm around her. Everything would be all right now that her dad was here. Her dad could fix anything.

'Are you all right, sweetheart?'

'I'm really tired.'

'Okay, we're going to let the rip take us out but at the same time we're going to swim away from the rocks. Got it?' he said, nodding encouragement.

Her legs were spent, her arms aching, but she smiled tentatively then more broadly as she realised that the surfer had seen them. 'Dad, the surfer is zipping up his wetsuit. He's seen us . . .'

'Good. Save your breath. Let's go.' He pushed her off with a gentle shove and set out at her right side, putting himself between her and the rocks. And although they fought to keep the rocks at a distance, bit by bit Molly could see that they were being pulled in that direction. She had walked this beach so many times, leaping from rock to rock with her sister, hunting for crabs in the tidal pools. The rocks always seemed mild and friendly from the shore but bobbing through the water, with the rocks at eye level, they were the enemy. Sharp, unforgiving and pounded by breaking waves.

'Keep going, pet,' her dad said, gargling saltwater.

She heard the splash of movement behind her but didn't stop to look. She had to keep going, trusting that her father would see them safe.

'Here, hold on to the board.' The surfer floated alongside, then sliding off his board, he bobbed like a seal in his wetsuit.

'Take my daughter first,' her dad coughed. 'I'll be all right.'

'Can you pull yourself on to the board?'

Using the last of her strength, she dragged her body out of the water, so that she was lying across the board. Then she wriggled sideways, pulling up her legs too.

'Drop your legs into the water either side of the board,' the surfer said from behind, before drawing himself on to the board, lying so that his body was above her, his chest over her thighs.

He didn't waste words – just a brief 'Hang on, mate' for her father – before setting out once more, his arms digging deep into the water, drawing them away from danger. Gripping the edge of the board white-knuckled, she twisted her neck to gaze behind her as the struggling figure of her father receded. He looked so small, one arm raised as if to hail someone. He seemed to be saying something but she couldn't see his face properly, couldn't make out his words. And then they were too far away to hear anything other than the cresting waves.

'Okay, hold on, we're going to ride a wave in,' her surfer instructed, paddling harder as the next swell reached them, carrying them forward in a surge of power. Molly's rescuer steered the board along the face of the wave as it cascaded towards the beach, dwindling to a trickle as it gained the shallows. Then he threw himself from the board and she scrambled to follow so that he could push the board through the water with one hand, while holding her arm and propelling her along with the other.

'Are you okay?' he asked, panting as he put his board down on the sand, saltwater draining from him in rivulets.

Looking at his face for the first time, she realised he was only a boy really, the bridge of his nose sprinkled with freckles, his straggly brown hair bleached by the sun. He was only a few years older than her, a boy with the shoulders and arms of someone who had been surfing all his life. She nodded, already turning back to the ocean, straining to catch sight of her father as the boy raced for the clubhouse and two other young surfers appeared on the beach from the dunes.

'My dad's out there!' she cried, flinging her arm out to sea.

Blinking away the saltwater that ran down her face, she searched the place where the rip had dragged them out to sea, then the glassy swell parallel to the clubhouse and lastly, when she still couldn't spot him, she turned her eyes towards the place where waves battered rocks.

He wasn't anywhere.

Molly's chest was so tight, her breath so strangled that she might as well be gasping for air below the waves. Where was he? He had to be there. He was there only minutes ago.

The surfer was fast. Already she heard the urgent cries of lifesavers and onlookers as the beach churned into action around her. Other surfers paddled out to sea on their boards. And some time later the thump-thump of a helicopter hovered above her. But the one person she was desperate to see didn't reappear.

Not alive, anyway.

She didn't know why she was telling Lucas this. She never talked about her father with anyone but her mother and her sister. Even then, they only talked about the good things: the funny Dad stories all siblings share. She hadn't told Matt about her father's drowning until they had been together a year. That's how long it took to feel safe. All he knew at first was that her father died when she was a child. And now she had told this near stranger. Not only that but once the words escaped, more waited to be unearthed – like a cache of relics dug up by accident. Precious, if you knew what you were looking at; worthless fragments of bone and shards of pottery, if you didn't.

Somehow, while she was talking, Lucas steered them towards a seat on a large, flat rock. She should have felt the cold, salty damp seeping through her jeans but the warmth of his body shut it from her mind. There was only the story and Lucas next to her. And after a long time, when she had finished talking, he didn't say anything. He just moved his hand that had been leaning on the rock and placed it around her shoulders, sheltering her.

'So that's it. That's my story.'

She waited for him to say what others had before him: her mum, her sister, Leo, Matt, her friend Amy. 'It wasn't your fault. Your dad wouldn't want you to blame yourself. You were only a child.'

But he didn't.

'That's a heavy burden you've been carrying,' he said.

If only he knew. She had told him about the day her father drowned but she hadn't told him about what had come before. She hadn't told him the full extent of her guilt. Not even Daisy or her mother knew that. It was her secret shame.

'It was my fault that he died.'

'I suppose you could argue that. You could argue that if you hadn't gone swimming alone your father wouldn't have drowned. But he made the decision to go in after you, Molly. And I'm sure that even if he'd known the result, he would have made the same decision.'

'Maybe.'

'There's no maybe about it. You were twelve. You were doing

what twelve year olds do, taking risks, making mistakes. Are you going to punish yourself for taking one bad risk for the rest of your life?'

'I don't know. Maybe I can't help it.' Maybe some things were forever.

'I hope you can let it go, one day.'

'So do I.'

Her father's drowning had been the defining moment of her life. Everything that had happened since had been shaped by it – her refusal to take risks, her need for order and routine, her lack of faith in herself. Nothing had been able to block it out, not even her feelings for Matt. Maybe it takes a truly powerful emotion to override such a momentous event. But what could be more powerful than guilt?

23

Wye River, Victoria

2000

Salt spray needled Molly's face as she battled the waves on her body board. Daisy struggled to keep up a few metres behind, pausing to complain every few strokes. Their dad had bought the polystyrene boards especially for this holiday and the girls had used them every day so far. Molly was becoming an adept paddler on her blue board while Daisy splashed through the waves like a human windmill on her yellow one.

'Come on, Dais, don't be a chicken,' she shouted, turning her head to see where her sister had got to.

'I'm not a chicken. The wind is really strong. I can't go any fast—' Her sister spluttered, swallowing a mouthful of the salt-water.

'Pwak, pwak, pwak,' Molly goaded before focusing on the swell forming further out in the small bay.

'Dad said not to go out too far.'

'We're not. The waves are really small.'

Molly was disappointed. They had walked their boards out chest deep – the rope straps Velcroed around their wrists – then clambered aboard on their bellies and paddled out level with the more adventurous swimmers who had ventured out beyond their depth. And still the waves were piddling little things. Even the surfers, sitting on their boards far beyond the flags, had been waiting ages for a set big enough to ride.

'Dad said not to go past the swimmers.'

'Don't be a baby.'

Anyway, they weren't beyond the swimmers. There was still that man in the green boardshorts – and he didn't even have flippers, so it couldn't be too dangerous.

'Dad will be mad.'

'Dad's probably asleep under his newspaper.'

After an hour in the surf their father said he was so water-logged he was in danger of sinking and his nose was turning into a beacon. He wanted them all to return to the campsite, but Molly had begged for just another half-hour. Their dad agreed reluctantly, saying he would wait for them on the beach, and ordered them not to go out too far. Except the swell had all but disappeared and she couldn't resist paddling out just a bit further in search of a wave to ride.

She put her hand up to her forehead, shielding her face from the glare of sun on water, then out of the corner of her eye noticed a scramble of activity amongst the surfers.

'Hey, Dais, get ready. The waves are coming.'

The green-boardshorts man had noticed the swell too. He stopped treading water and started swimming, positioning himself to catch the cresting wave before it broke.

'Come on, we need to go a bit further out!' she called. 'Paddle faster!'

She lay flat on her board and plunged her arms deep into the water as if she could drag herself across the expanse of sea between her and the forming wave. Faster and faster she paddled, forgetting her little sister windmilling along behind her, creating more splash than propulsion. Forgetting that Daisy's arms were weaker and shorter. And then, when the man in green stopped swimming and turned to face the shore, she stopped paddling. She too turned shoreward, calling out to her sister, 'Turn around!'

She hadn't realised how big the wave was until it loomed over her, its crest curling over on itself. Setting out with as much speed as she could muster, she caught the wave before it broke, powering down its glassy face with mounting exhilaration, the wave surging behind her, driving her to the shore in a cataract of white water. Once the breaker had slowed to a gentle ripple, she slid from her board to stand thigh deep. Breathing hard with excitement, she looked around for her sister, expecting her to have ridden the wave alongside her. But there was no sign of her. And when she looked out to sea, all she saw was Daisy's yellow board floating riderless on the churning waves.

'Daisy!' she shouted. 'Daisy!' she screamed louder when she received no response.

She swung this way and that, seeking her sister, instead spotting her father splashing through the shallows, calling as frantically as she was.

'Daisy!' he shouted.

He looked as if the world might be about to end. She thought at first that he was heading towards her but realised his eyes were scanning the foaming water to her right. She turned to peer in that direction too, noticing the telltale pink and white stripes of Daisy's swimsuit and her skinny little-girl limbs flailing beneath the water.

'Daisy!' he shouted as he reached her sister, grabbing one of the flailing arms and hauling her above water.

'I got dumped,' Daisy said with a dazed grin as he steadied her on her feet. Then she coughed, blinking away the water streaming from her hair on to her face and down her body back into the sea.

'Honey, are you all right?' her father said, hugging his daughter to him.

'I'm okay, but I lost my board,' she said, holding her bare wrist up to show him. 'The Velcro isn't very good.'

'Take your sister back to the sand. I'll swim out and get her board. And then wait for me,' he said, giving Molly the death stare, the one he reserved for the most serious misdemeanours.

She breathed a sigh of relief. Her sister was safe. But trouble was coming.

Daisy was bundled up in a beach towel and sent to wait on the sand, with instructions to drink plenty of water. Meanwhile, her dad pulled Molly aside, out of earshot of the other beachgoers but still within sight of Daisy. The sand was so hot under her feet that she couldn't help doing a little jig. She could feel flies congregating on her back too and shrugged her shoulders to encourage them to move.

'Stand still when I'm talking to you!' her father growled.

'The sand's hot. And the flies are tickling my back.'

'Well stand on the wet sand, then . . . only stop wriggling about.'

Sidling a few metres closer to the water, she buried her feet in the wet sand so that she sank up to her ankles, water pooling around them. Salt was drying to a fine film all over her skin and an unpleasant wedge of sand had lodged between her legs. But her discomfort was both physical and mental for she knew that she had put her sister's life in jeopardy and she also knew that her father was about to call her out on it. She only hoped he wouldn't confiscate her board; she didn't think she could bear that.

'I don't have to tell you what you've done wrong because you know. But I'm going to anyway, just so there are no misunderstandings.' His face had that same look he got when his footy team played so badly that it let all its fans down.

'Yes, Dad.'

'You were told not to go out too far. You were also told to look out for your sister.'

'I was looking out for her. I kept turning around to check on her.'

'Well, you weren't doing a very good job, were you? I expected better of you. And you certainly disobeyed me about going out too far.'

'We weren't out there by ourselves, there was a man in green boardshorts,' she said, her eyes fixed firmly on the shallow froth of water creeping towards her feet.

'You put your sister's life in danger. She could have drowned,' he said quietly. Then, 'Look at me!' in a harsher voice. 'You knew you weren't supposed to take your sister beyond her depth, not without me there.'

'Sorry.'

'She's only ten. You're bigger and stronger than her,' he said, pushing his hair back from his forehead in a frustrated gesture, then looking towards the ocean as if for inspiration. 'How can I trust you if you take such stupid risks?'

'I'm sorry.'

'Sorry isn't good enough.' Taking her chin in his hand, he forced her to face him, saying, 'I only took my eyes off you for a few minutes. Do you know how I'd feel if I let you or your sister drown? I couldn't live with myself.'

Tears dripped down her face, adding to the salt, and she had to bite her lip to stop it from wobbling.

'You have to promise me. You have to promise me that you will never swim outside the flags or go out beyond the other swimmers again. Not until you're old enough to make your own decisions. Understand?'

She nodded.

'And you will never put yourself or your sister in danger

again.' His eyes bored into hers, daring her to look away. 'Tell me that you promise.'

She couldn't find her voice. She could only nod silently.

'Promise me.'

'Yes, Dad, I promise.'

24

North Devon

2017

Her eyes took a moment to adjust to the dim library after the brilliant light of the drawing room. The only window was shrouded in dark velvet curtains, making the room a place of gloom and shadows, like a room in mourning.

'I haven't ventured in here for a while,' Richard said, sniffing the air, 'smells of mouse. I'll have to ask Judy to set a trap.'

'Shall I?' she asked, indicating the curtains.

'Please do. I feel like a bat in here.'

The curtains had seen better days, the velvet nap worn to thread in places and the hems fraying. She drew them back carefully, trying not to breathe in the dust that floated hazily from their folds, revealing a view over a rose garden rampant with late spring blooms. Richard had skirted the library on his earlier tour of the house so this was her first acquaintance with the bilious green carpet and chairs upholstered in velvet. It was a shame the carpet and chairs were so hideous; they stole attention away from the ornate carved bookcases lining the walls, the magnificent coffered ceiling and another grand Tudor Revival fireplace. A matching desk stood in the centre of the room, its surface obscured by tottering piles of books, an elderly wooden swivel chair sitting forlornly in front of it.

'As you can see, I'm a bit behind with the shelving.'

Each shelf was brimming with books, folios shelved conventionally and smaller tomes stacked horizontally so that every inch of space was used. At a glance the spines told the same story as the rest of Luscombe Park, with the most precious objects sold off to meet day-to-day needs and the remainder old but not particularly valuable. Faded orange Penguins were crammed shoulder to shoulder with crime thrillers. There was an ancient set of *Encyclopaedia Britannica* and what appeared to be a collection of *Boy's Own* annuals from the 1930s or 40s.

Richard noticed Molly peering at them and said, 'Mine, I'm afraid. Couldn't bear to part with them. I spent many happy hours here as a boy, curled up in an armchair by the window.'

'Mum threatened to glue *Lord of the Rings* to my face once.'

'Did she? Dev was a big reader too. Those are his.' He indicated an entire bookcase laden with art and architecture books. 'I used to tease him they were picture books for grown-ups, and he referred to my crime novels as brain candy.'

'Surely more nutritious than candy?'

'This was his favourite room. Whenever he had a break from touring he liked to spend his days in here, feet up in front of the fire in winter or lazing by the window in summer. Something of a cat, my Dev.'

He sniffed and she hoped it was merely dust, not tears. He and Dev had spent thirty years together. She wondered what it would be like to share half a lifetime with someone, and for a moment Lucas's face drifted into her consciousness. It was six days since she had shared her darkest memory with him and he hadn't even called to ask how she was faring. Perhaps he was accustomed to random confidences from women he barely knew. But she wasn't used to offering them.

Oh, stop being so melodramatic, she told herself sternly. Lucas was just doing Richard a favour taking his houseguest out for a drive. He couldn't help it if you drivelled your feelings all over him.

'It's a lovely room,' she said pathetically.

'Well, except for the carpet,' said Richard, and she was relieved at the change of subject. 'Mother had a redecorating fit sometime in the sixties and this was the result. Thank God she ran out of money before she could do the rest of the house.'

'It's . . . ah . . . quite a startling colour scheme.'

'Mmmm. Dev hated the colour but in the end it grew on him. Like moss, I suppose,' he laughed. 'Now, for the estate account books.'

She followed him across the room to a bookcase in the far corner holding a series of red leather-bound ledgers with dates embossed in gold on the spine.

'The ledgers date back to the 1850s, when the house was built, and finish in the 1980s when our accountant moved to computer records. I'm afraid I won't be much help with them. Father managed the estate until his death in 1967, when I took over, but my bookkeeping system consisted of a series of labelled shoeboxes and the accountant did the rest. You're welcome to look through any of them, dear, although what they'll tell you I'm not sure.'

On a shelf above the ledgers she noticed an aged, cloth-bound collection of the landowner's bible, the *Estates Gazette*, and various agricultural titles.

'Ah yes, those shifted over here with the ledgers when Lucas converted the stables,' he noted when he saw her inspecting them. 'The estate manager's office used to be located there. I snuck the wooden swivel chair in here too. Father let me swing around on it when I harassed him in his office.'

'If you don't mind me asking, was Luscombe's income all from the estate?'

'For the most part. There was some property in London. It's

a pity Father didn't get himself a few directorships or invest in the stock market, but I don't think any of us were reading the future very well,' he sighed, 'least of all me when I inherited. I don't suppose I had posterity in mind, back then.'

Without children or grandchildren, she wondered what would happen once Richard was gone. She supposed there must be someone lined up to inherit. But whoever inherited Luscombe Park would acquire both a treasure and a burden.

'The library would be the perfect place for your archive.'

'Are you referring to my squirrel's nest?'

'Hopefully it won't be quite such a muddle once I'm finished. But I'd really like to see the records moved to a more stable environment. And ideally they should be stored in archival-quality boxes and folders.'

'Let me know what we need and I'll see what I can do.'

'You might be able to put some of these books on eBay, if you don't want them. That would free up space for the archive too.'

'Is that a new kind of storage system, dear?'

She laughed. 'No, it's like an Internet auction house. I can help you get started, if you like. It's a good way to get rid of stuff you don't want. The danger is you replace it with stuff you don't need.'

'Well, if you think it might help. I'd like to get my affairs in order.' His free hand fluttered vaguely while the other hand clutched his stick. 'I have a good feeling about your arrival. I think you may help me sort out more than the odd old paper or two.'

'I'm happy to help with the archive, and I've made a start on the cataloguing, but I'm no archivist. And sooner or later I have to go home. I have a job to return to in six months,' she said gently, not wanting to disappoint him but conscious that her time here was limited.

Ignoring her last words, he said, 'I don't need an expert. I'd rather have a friend. When you get to my age, friends can be in rather short supply.'

He left for his morning walk soon after, leaving her to her own devices. She zeroed in on the ledgers for the first two decades of the twentieth century and curled up in one of the armchairs by the window with the account books resting on her knees. Flipping open a ledger at random, she scanned the first few pages of 1919 to familiarise herself with the accounts system, when an entry for two first-class tickets on the SS *Osprey* from Southampton to Melbourne leaped from the page, demanding her attention.

That was the year Rose sailed for Australia, accompanied by Ivy. But if Ivy were Rose's maid, why did they both travel in first class? Wouldn't Ivy be lodged below deck – in second, or even third class? Perhaps there was a reason why Rose needed her close during the night. But if so, what could that reason be?

Molly spent the remainder of the morning puzzling over various scenarios as she flipped through page after page of dry numbers. Sometimes a ledger contained as much mystery as one of Richard's thrillers.

25

Colombo, Ceylon

1919

A ribbon of lanky palms fringed the coastline as the SS *Osprey* steamed towards the harbour, while in the distance a tall peak loomed above the long mountain range standing purple against the dawn sky. Even at that early hour the ship's railings were crowded with second- and third-class passengers milling about, curious for their first sight of the tropics. From her place on the upper deck Rose listened to the chatter of war brides sailing to join newly acquired husbands, emigrants looking to escape the poverty of war, and the last of the wounded returning home to Australia. Their ship was only in Colombo for a day – to take on mail and cargo – and her passengers longed to stretch their sea legs and bring back tales of monkeys and palm trees to enliven the remainder of the voyage.

Not Ivy. She had been in a mood all morning, since before their steamer anchored inside Colombo's great breakwater. She complained that she wanted to stay on the ship and rest where it was cool, while Rose wanted to make the most of the day. She couldn't wait to wander beneath the bent spindles of coconut palms and smell the cinnamon-dusted air. As she bustled Ivy aboard a canopied longboat, her body was alive with pent-up energy like the charged air before a lightning storm. She wanted something to happen, some proof that she was finally leaving the old world behind, that her journey wasn't just another dream conjured in the fog of war. There were still eight days of sailing before they touched Australian shores in Perth – and even longer until they reached Melbourne, where Jim would be waiting. There were too many long, uneventful hours on board ship, too many opportunities for nerves or regret. A day of adventure ashore might act as a tonic to keep her sustained for the remainder of the voyage.

That was her plan. But when they disembarked at the passenger jetty, Mrs Brigham accosted them, garbed for action. She was wearing her best hat on which perched a brace of pheasants, while her bosoms were encased in a double-breasted linen coat, stiff with authority. Close to, Rose noticed that her pores were clogged with too much Coty face powder, which quite ruined her air of formidability. Quite frankly, she found Mrs Brigham tedious and was glad she and the Colonel were disembarking at Colombo. Only her long-drilled habit of politeness made the matron's behaviour bearable.

Mrs Brigham didn't approve of Ivy, either – particularly her presence in Rose's cabin – and had once commented quite pointedly that a good maid knew not to chatter and never offered an opinion unasked. That morning, Rose had deliberately waited until the Brighams were safely ashore before leaving the ship, hoping to avoid that lady's gushed farewells and threats of correspondence. So when she spotted her out of the corner of her eye, marching back along the jetty, she slowed her pace, staring with great interest at the row of bullock drays waiting outside the cargo sheds like a series of enormous baskets on wheels. It did little good, for there was no escaping Mrs Brigham. She wedged herself between Rose and Ivy, expecting Ivy to make way.

'Rose dear,' she squawked, her voice soaring above the cries of seagulls wheeling and diving overhead. 'Rose dear, why don't you join the Colonel and myself for luncheon at our bungalow? We're going to be quite bereft without your company.

'We're just out by the lake, a lovely drive,' she continued, when Rose did not answer immediately. 'You can leave your maid on board. I'm sure your wardrobe needs attention,' she added, glancing pointedly at Ivy.

Ivy returned her look with all the haughtiness she could muster – and she could muster considerable haughtiness. Even her father had not been able to beat that out of her.

'Oh, Mrs Brigham, so kind of you, but I had rather promised myself a day of exploration.'

'I'm sure our driver could take you for a turn about the lake, dear. Our motor will be waiting outside the Customs House.'

'And there are a few necessities I must look for in town.'

'Surely your maid could look for those?'

'Companion,' Ivy corrected, rolling her eyes behind Mrs Brigham's back.

'Oh no, Mrs Brigham, I couldn't trust anyone else with my purchases,' said Rose, stifling a laugh. 'I want to find a gift for my fiancé in Australia. It wouldn't do to entrust that to my maid.'

'Well, yes, I see that. But I'm quite disappointed. We had so hoped to have you to ourselves today.'

'Once again, dear Mrs Brigham, I appreciate your thoughtfulness. I don't know how to thank you.'

'Think nothing of it, and do take my card. You must write. I shall not rest easy until I know you have arrived safely in Australia.'

Mrs Brigham offered her card with a gloved hand, not without a glance of disapproval at Rose's bare fingers, and set off towards the Colonel, who was waiting further up the jetty, her pheasants already drooping a little in the warm morning air.

'Vicious old biddy,' muttered Ivy, as the matron's broad beam sailed away.

'Shhh, she might hear you.'

'Well she is, and I don't care who hears me. And what did you mean, "It wouldn't do to entrust that to my maid"?' Ivy said with a scowl.

'We both know you're much more than my maid, I was only saying that to get rid of her.'

'I'm here as your companion for the journey only. Once we arrive, I shall be my own woman. Yet everywhere I am regarded as your maid. Have you seen the passenger list? *Colonel and Mrs Brigham and valet, Mr and Mrs Marshall, child and nanny, Dr James Alsop, Mr and Mrs Jones, Mrs Hume, three children and governess, Miss Luscombe and maid* . . . It does not even show my name!' she barked, a cough serving as exclamation mark.

'Surely you do not blame me for the passenger list?' Sometimes Rose wished to slap her. It was all Robert's fault.

'Did you give them my name when you purchased our passage?'

Most women would not countenance their maids speaking to them in such a manner, but most people did not share Rose and Ivy's history. Most people would think she had done Ivy a great favour in employing her. But most people did not know how deeply their lives were entwined. Rose hoped they never would.

'That was weeks ago. How should I remember? Let's forget about passenger lists and Mrs Brigham and just enjoy the day. Look at the sky. It's perfect.'

'The sky is the same blue it has been every day for a week.'

26

North Devon

2017

Richard produced an excellent tomato soup for lunch – 'Made by my own two hands, shaky as they are' – and invited Molly to join him on the terrace, since the day was so mild. She put aside her ledgers reluctantly, not that she wasn't happy to lunch with Richard, but she was so immersed in her reading that she had to tear herself away. If you had told fifteen-year-old Molly that one day she would find numbers on a page riveting, she would have erupted into hysterical laughter.

'Richard, I'd like to talk to you about something I found in the ledgers today. Just a little puzzle about the Toms cottage that you might be able to clear up for me.'

'I can try,' he said, taking a sip of his soup.

'The account for Walter Toms . . .'

'That would be Ivy and Daniel's father.'

'On the first of January each year an entry is recorded for "annual rent Ashcott".'

'Yes, the cottage the Toms family inhabited was part of the estate, but Daniel purchased it from us in the 1950s.'

'The ledger credits Walter Toms' account with an annual rent of one shilling . . . that's quite a discount, even by Edwardian standards.'

'Yes, it does seem so. Toms was an irascible character by all accounts. I remember him as a gruff old man who spoke with the most alarmingly broad Devonshire accent. Daniel seemed quite scared of him.' He frowned and placed his spoon neatly in his bowl. 'We must assume that the family felt they owed him. Though why is anyone's guess.'

She was silent for a time, sipping her soup and pondering the reason why the Luscombe family leased a perfectly sound cottage for a shilling a year. There had to be more to it than good will. None of the other estate workers were so lucky. The connection between the Toms and Luscombe families must run deep.

'Lucas called a short while ago,' Richard informed her between mouthfuls of soup. 'Sounded so busy, poor chap, and I wondered whether you might take him a Thermos flask of soup. Probably hasn't had time to do more than heat up one of those dreadful dog dinners of his.'

She raised her eyebrows, saying, 'Surely he can do better than dog food for dinner?'

'I mean those dreadful frozen boxes that one gets from the supermarket. He does love my soup. By the way, have you seen him since your outing last weekend? It sounded like an enjoyable day was had by all . . . ?' He had that gleam in his eyes again.

She fixed her gaze on the sheep grazing placidly on the lawn so that she didn't have to look at him. Richard had a disconcerting habit of staring as if he was reading you like one of his detective novels. Perhaps it was a perquisite of age – being allowed to ask personal questions with impunity.

'No, I haven't spoken to him. He's probably busy.'

Since their day at the beach he hadn't popped in or telephoned to say hi. Not even a text message. There had been nothing but silence. She shouldn't have expected more, she supposed. She had shared too much. She had probably imagined the ease between them, and her revelations had driven him away. He wouldn't be the first man to disappear at a whiff of intimacy. Just as well she had resisted the urge to tell him the rest. She had almost confessed, except she couldn't bring herself to speak her shame aloud.

If she hadn't broken her promise, her father would still be alive. *No one* knew about that promise: not her mother, not even Daisy. She had been too afraid to tell. She might have lost their love – and she wasn't strong enough to survive that loss, as well as her father's death. And although she was rendered almost a zombie for months by his death, she wasn't so far gone that she couldn't recognise her mother's pain. Wendy continued to get up every morning, make their lunches and go to work. She still ferried them to netball and drama and whatever else Daisy was up to that week. But there was a hazy quality to the way she navigated each day. Some loss of crispness to her conversation, and her attention. Part of Wendy was still living with her deceased husband. How could Molly add to her pain by confessing her crime? No, she had to live with the secret drilling away at her.

Anyway, if Lucas was backing off before they had so much as kissed, so be it. The last thing she needed was another floundering romance. She knew better than to trust her heart. Clearly, Lucas wasn't interested, and she would do better to accept that. Still, she would have liked to be friends.

'Would you mind terribly, dear?' Richard interrupted her thoughts.

'What?' she asked with a shake of her head.

'Taking a flask of my soup over to Lucas? He's probably quite peckish about now,' he added with that wide-eyed stare that didn't fool anyone, at least not a second time. 'No time like the present and all that.'

No time like the present, except when you're stuck in the past. She could think of nothing she would like less, given the man's obvious disinterest, but in the face of Richard's generosity she could hardly decline.

'Of course,' she said with an attempt at a delighted smile.

'Excellent,' he said, and she could have sworn he was rubbing his hands in glee beneath the tablecloth.

Ten minutes later, Molly set out for the stables armed with a Thermos of soup and a determination to be friendly but reserved.

She was curious about Lucas's home, but if Richard hadn't intervened she wouldn't have ventured anywhere near without an invitation. Somehow, the weekend drive that might have brought them closer had erected a barrier. He was probably in fear of what might follow: outpourings of emotion with the usual trappings of neediness. Well, Molly was determined to prove him wrong. She would be cool but polite. Poised but friendly. Not much like herself at all, really.

Stepping purposefully through the arched gateway that separated Richard's imposing manor from Lucas's more modest abode, she traversed the gravel path towards the stables two hundred metres distant, the soup swishing carelessly in its steel container, her thoughts swishing somewhat more cautiously. She was only delivering soup.

What could possibly go wrong?

27

Loud barking greeted her arrival as a shaggy dog of indeterminate origin came bounding out to meet her from the stable yard. The stables were laid out in a U-shape with a central two-storey dwelling and single-storey wings that were presumably used for storage and garaging. The walls, constructed of the same golden-hued dressed stone as Luscombe Park, enclosed a gravel courtyard with a small lawn and vegetable garden in the centre. The dog's arrival was followed by the sliding of a glass door and the appearance of Lucas on the doorstep, shouting, 'Stop barking, Nelson! Where are your manners?'

Nelson tossed him an indulgent look, quit barking long enough to comply with the command, then immediately started up again, prancing around Molly in an excited dance of welcome.

'Hello there.' She bent to caress the dog's ears, giving him a scratch under the chin, which he lifted obligingly. 'I've brought soup,' she added for Lucas's benefit, holding up the Thermos as if to prove her mission.

'I've never had a woman bring me soup before,' he said with a lift of one eyebrow. 'Wine, yes. Flowers, occasionally. But soup . . .'

'From Richard, he's worried about you eating out of boxes.'

'Well, he's not wrong there. What with clients making last-minute changes, planning authorities demanding more detail, and builders not showing up, I've been snowed under,' he said, rubbing the back of his neck. 'Come in.'

'I don't want to interrupt.'

'Believe me, I need it.'

She stepped over the threshold and into his home, startled for a moment by the light filtering through full-height windows opposite. She hadn't expected a wall of windows. They seemed incongruous; they didn't fit with her historical idea of a stable, a place of cobbles and stone, rough beams and wooden horse-boxes. A mixture of stark contemporary furniture and rustic antiques furnished the space and light flooded in from all directions. Lucas had converted the building to form one vast open space with an industrial metal staircase leading to a mezzanine level above. The original massive beams were exposed, like ancient trees spanning the entire room, and a wide-planked oak floor shone with wax. Most of the interior walls were plastered and painted an off-white shade, but she noticed a section of wall where the plaster was pared back to reveal bare masonry. Unlike the exterior of the stables, this masonry was comprised of smaller, irregularly shaped stones that looked like they had been purloined from a much earlier building.

'Is that stonework medieval?'

'We discovered it during the refurbishment. Fourteenth-century, according to the archaeologist. It would have been incorporated into the new walls when the stables were built. Presumably part of an earlier hall.'

According to the Domesday Book, Lucas explained, there had been a manor on the site since the eleventh century, so there were probably bits and pieces from the last thousand years buried in the vicinity.

'I'm glad you made it into a feature. Your house is so

contemporary, yet ancient at the same time. It's beautiful.'
Layered with the past, she thought, like everything about this
place and this family.

'Come on, I'll give you the grand tour. Not that you can't see
it all from where you're standing.'

Surprising her by taking her hand, he led the way towards
what was obviously his studio. Her hand felt warm and comfortable in his and she allowed herself to look up into his face to
see what she might discover there. She found him looking back
at her intently, studying her as if she were a puzzle he hadn't
quite worked out.

'Have you solved me yet?'

'Hmm?'

'You're looking at me as if I'm a puzzle.'

'Not yet, I think I need more time.' Had he meant his reply
in the same joking fashion as her question? Or was he flirting
with her? She wasn't sure whether she wanted his answer to be
serious or not.

He halted beside a long bench with a large computer monitor
at one end and sheaves of folders stacked neatly at the other. She
noticed a series of plans and elevations stuck to the wall above
the bench that looked oddly familiar.

'So this is where I work. Mostly a range of new build, refurbishment and restoration. Dovetailing the new with the old, to
borrow a carpentry metaphor.'

'It must be rewarding.'

'Uh-huh, but frustrating too.'

'Are those drawings of Luscombe Park?' she asked, indicating
the drawings on the wall with a nod of her head.

'Yes. Last year Richard asked me to look at subdividing it
into apartments. He thought selling them off might pay for the
restoration and maintenance. He only lives in three rooms most
of the time.'

'I've noticed. But you didn't take it further?'

'No. It's complex and drawn-out. I doubt he has the stamina. I wouldn't want to put him through it,' he sighed. 'And finding the capital would be difficult. Better to leave it to whoever inherits. I just do what I can to help him keep it together. Which is a monumental struggle, since the house sucks up money like a vacuum cleaner.'

He hesitated for a moment, then added, 'Richard means a lot to my family. We try to look out for him.'

'He's lucky to have you.'

'He has a way of drawing people to him. It's partly charm and partly that little-old-man act of his,' he laughed.

'He's very trusting. A bit sneaky too.'

'You've noticed?'

'Uh-huh. He usually gets his way,' she said, reminded of the soup errand.

Lucas still hadn't let go of her hand and she didn't like to take it from him now that he had it, but she did wonder what he was going to do with it. It was only her hand, yet every nerve in her body was focused on that one point. She could feel the rough skin where their palms pressed together, the potential power of knuckles where her fingers curled around his. And there was the hint that this smouldering warmth threatened to ignite something in her that she wasn't sure she was ready for. She made to pull her hand away but he gripped it more firmly.

'I should probably go.'

He drew her towards him so that there was less than a hand's width between them, so close that all she had to do was breathe in and they would touch. He looked at her thoughtfully but didn't breach those last few millimetres.

'Are you sure? I can offer you coffee.'

She wasn't sure, not at all. That was the problem.

She breathed in.

'I don't think I need coffee.'

'What do you need?'

He leaned in, so close that the gap between their bodies disappeared. So close that the tension could only be relieved by shifting closer. He bent his head and her lips met his automatically, drawn by an almost gravitational pull into his orbit. His lips were rough – and tasted faintly of the salty Devon air – but they touched hers with gentle force, buffeting and caressing at the same time. When his arms encircled her waist, pressing her body hard against his, she felt her legs turn to jelly and was glad he held her tight or she might have crumpled.

After a while he released her, saying, 'That was unexpected.'

'Totally,' she lied.

'Or opportunistic, depending how you look at it,' he grinned and kissed her again, briefly this time. 'I've been thinking about you a lot since last Saturday.'

And I you, she thought, but was too timid to say it. Daisy would have been more honest – but her sister wouldn't have let five days go by without some contact. She would have assumed that he wanted to hear from her, and called. Molly would rather hug the idea of Saturday to herself, ponder its mystery and possibility before someone spoiled it. That was the true difference between them, she supposed. She expected things to be spoiled.

'I didn't call you or come by, because . . .' Lucas continued tentatively.

'That's okay, you don't have to explain yourself—' She really didn't want to hear excuses, but he put his fingers to her lips and she had to restrain herself from biting them.

'I didn't want to scare you off. You do seem a bit . . . skittish,' he finished with a shrug. That was one way of describing her hesitancy, she supposed. 'You said you'd come to Devon looking for time. I wanted to give you time to . . .'

'To what?'

'I don't know, maybe to adjust to the idea that we could be . . . friends.'

Maybe her confidences hadn't scared him away, after all.

'Just friends?'

'Special friends. I suppose when we met I wasn't prepared for the . . . connection I sensed,' he said, searching the ceiling as if for the right words. 'You did arrive out of nowhere.'

So he had felt it too. Perhaps he wanted to give himself time to adjust as well. Having recovered from those years with his previous girlfriend, he probably wouldn't be in a hurry to hook up with a girl who was going to pick up and leave – a girl who belonged on the other side of the world.

'I thought it was better not to rush anything. But now you're here, I'm reluctant to let you go.'

Very reluctant if the shape of him moulded against her was anything to go by.

'Don't worry, I'm not going to bolt.' Not this time.

'We could finish the tour upstairs. That is, if you'd like to see more,' he said, pressing her even closer and raising his eyebrows suggestively.

'Do you give this tour often?'

'Only special people get the VIP tour.'

She was still uncertain, still terrified of all the bad things that could happen. Had happened.

Rejection. Loss. Pain. That nasty old bag of tricks.

But really, what can a girl do when beset by planetary forces? Nothing but go along for the ride.

Afterwards, she wondered whether she looked as if a gale force wind had bowled her over or if she only felt that way. Her hair was tangled where he had wound his hands through it, her clothes had disappeared and her heart was hammering. Her flesh felt battered, not with pain, but with pleasure. And there he was, sprawled beside her with his face buried in the pillow, one arm flung over her body – she wasn't sure whether in a possessive or protective gesture – breathing deeply. It was such a cliché but she really didn't know what had hit her. She felt trampled, pummelled, knocked out. Sex had never been like this with Matt. Never had this awkward, jarring, ungainly . . . urgency.

Lucas groaned and she swallowed her confusion. She really didn't want him to turn over, because she had absolutely no idea what to say to him.

'What was that?' he muttered into the pillow before turning to face her with another groan.

'I don't know,' was all she could think to say.

'Maybe we should try to find out.'

'Maybe we should. I could always bring you more soup.'

'Tomorrow?'

'Pumpkin, next time?'

Somehow, their bodies manoeuvred into an embrace so that she was snuggled up against him, breathing in the salty, musky tang of him. And despite the whispers from Safe Molly, urging her to duck for cover, she decided she didn't mind it at all.

Later, as she circled the room in her underwear to retrieve the rest of her clothes, she noticed an arrangement of framed photographs on the wall opposite the bed and paused to inspect them. The four photographs were arranged in a quadrangle, each bordered by a wide cream mount and slim black frame. They had been enlarged from old prints and featured local buildings by the look of them. One photograph showed a boy with a wheelbarrow standing in front of a garden folly in the style of a Roman temple. Another she recognised as the church in the nearby hamlet of Luscombe. There was a shot of an old stone bridge, and the final photograph pictured a thatched cob cottage besieged by creeping tendrils of ivy. Standing outside the front door, their faces as sombre as their plain garments, were a large ruddy man, a small thin woman with her hair parted severely, two rangy boys and a forlorn girl verging on womanhood.

Her clothes forgotten now, she stepped closer for a better look. 'Is that Ivy?' she asked, pointing to the small, sad figure of the girl.

'I'd rather look at you than an old picture,' Lucas answered from the bed where he gazed at her appreciatively.

'It looks like a younger version of the girl in the photo I found of Rose and Ivy.'

'Yes, those are my great-grandparents, Walter and Ethel Toms, with their children: Ivy, Samuel and my grandfather, Daniel.'

'Did the house have a name?'

'Ashcott. I grew up there.'

'Is that the same cottage your grandfather bought from the estate?'

'Uh-huh. This photo was taken in 1913, probably about the time Ivy came to work at Luscombe Park. And that's Granddad with the wheelbarrow in front of the Roman temple, a folly that used to be part of the estate. You remember, he worked here as a gardener.'

They were so young, children really, yet already hard at work for the Luscombe family. She wondered how their parents felt, sending their children out to work so young. But then, what choice did they have? The school leaving age in the early 1900s was twelve, and many children attended sporadically even before that age, especially at harvest time.

'It must have been hard seeing your children work for someone else and for so little reward. I wonder if they resented it,' she said, pulling her T-shirt over her head.

'Granddad used to say that his father, Walter, never had a good word to say about the Luscombes. As far as he was concerned, he had lost one son to the war and they'd stolen the other.'

'I suppose he was right in a way.'

'Apparently he was especially eloquent on the subject when he'd had a few, which was regularly. He used to complain bitterly that Granddad had given his loyalty to the enemy.'

'The enemy? As in a class war?'

'Granddad seemed to think it was more personal than that, but he never discovered why.' Lucas wandered over to slip his arms beneath her T-shirt and nuzzle her neck. 'Walter wasn't exactly an easy-going character, by all accounts.'

'And what about Ivy, did he blame the Luscombes for losing her as well?' She turned to face Lucas. He really was gorgeous.

'You know you're like a terrier. Here I am, ready to ravish you, and all you want to do is talk about dead people.'

She couldn't tell from his voice whether he really was annoyed or merely playing with her. She didn't know him well enough yet. But then she had thought she knew Matt and it turned out she didn't know him at all. Perhaps you could never learn someone completely – and the fun was in the finding out.

'It's the historian in me. Once I'm on a scent I can't let a fact go.'

'Well, I'm not sure about Walter but I know my grandfather blamed himself for Ivy's death. He used to say that he'd let her down. That he hadn't stood by her.'

'But surely he was just a boy when she died?'

'Sometimes people feel the losses of childhood more strongly than they do as adults. They haven't learned yet to forgive themselves for their failures or their mistakes.' He moved his hands to her shoulders, staring at her thoughtfully. 'Have they, Molly?'

'You know, I discovered something quite odd about Ashcott in Richard's archives,' she said, sliding her hands up his back to distract him from this line of questioning. She didn't want to talk about loss now. She only wanted to . . .

'Mmm?'

'The Luscombes leased Ashcott to Walter for the vast sum of one shilling per annum,' she said, enjoying the feel of smooth, hard muscle beneath her hands.

'A shilling? Are you sure?'

'Yep, I found the ledger entries.'

'Maybe that's why he was so bitter. He was beholden to them. A proud man like Walter wouldn't like that at all.'

'Either that, or they were beholden to him.'

She turned in Lucas's arms to look again at the photograph of the Toms family, arranged so formally in front of their cottage; of the boy frozen in time with his wheelbarrow next to a folly far from Rome. And she wondered what other secrets linked them with the aristocratic Luscombes. The more she learned, the more she became convinced that Rose's disappearance was linked to Ivy and the Luscombes. The Turners, the Luscombes and the Toms were all connected in ways she was only just beginning to discover.

And Ivy was the key.

28

North Devon

1917

Helping Henry Turner from his bed to a chair that morning was a torturous business, every tiny movement driving spikes into his arm. He didn't complain but Rose noticed that his forehead was dotted with perspiration and his breathing laboured. Sister had warned her that he was running a slight fever the previous night and clearly it hadn't abated that morning.

'You Australians are a hit with the ladies,' she declared as she finished making up his bed. 'It must be the riding breeches and shiny leggings.'

Sometimes when she sat at his left side, with his poor damaged body obscured, she could imagine him mounted on his horse, rounding up sheep or chopping wood with his sleeves rolled to the elbow, the sweat shining on his bare skin. She wondered then what it would be like to be Henry Turner's friend instead of his nurse. What would it be like to take his arm at country dances, or gallop at his side across wide-open paddocks? What would it be like to be young and free?

'Or the feathers in our caps,' he joked, gritting his teeth in something resembling a smile as she helped him back into the tidied bed. 'The Light Horse, at any rate. They're the glamorous chaps.'

'The nurses on the other ward are throwing themselves at their Australians. And one of Lady Waring's housemaids has become engaged to a boy from Western Australia. She was boasting to Nurse Toms that he owns two outback stations with a million sheep,' she chattered, trying to distract him from his pain.

'I hope the silly girl didn't believe him.'

'Do you have many admirers then, Lieutenant?' She arranged his pillow more comfortably, setting a copy of the *North Devon Journal* within reach.

'I wouldn't be much use to a girl like this. Have to be a saint, I'd say.'

'Don't underestimate the uniform. It does wonders for a man. Besides, I've heard there's a doctor at Queen Mary's in Sidcup who is working miracles on men's faces. Patching them up almost like new.'

Rose had only meant to cheer him up and was disconcerted at the turn the conversation had taken. The worst part was he was right – what future would there be for a man who had lost so much of himself? Come to that, what future would there be for any of them if the war didn't end soon? There would be no able-bodied men left, and women would be driving the tractors and bread vans for the next twenty years. She felt cheated. She viewed the war as a personal affront. It had stolen all the joy that should have been hers; all the youthful fun that her parents had enjoyed was gone from the world. And she wasn't allowed to complain, because men like Henry Turner had it so much worse.

'What girl would go dancing with a one-armed, one-legged, one-eyed man?' he laughed without a shred of humour in his voice.

'Is that a riddle?' she said, trying to coax him back into a more cheerful mood. One thing she had learned in the months she'd been scrubbing and polishing at Oldbridge was that a positive disposition was as essential to healing as good hygiene and vigilant nursing. 'Your arm will heal. We have to give it time. And after the war you'll find your place with your family again, they'll help you . . . adjust.'

The words babbled off her tongue but she could see that he didn't believe any of it; he neatly changed the subject not to burden her with his woes. Most of the men were like that – you could see they were suffering but for the most part they kept their pain to themselves. It was only in their nightmares that they screamed aloud.

'Have I showed you a picture of my family? In my locker there, inside my Bible.'

She opened the locker at his bedside to reveal a small blue Bible, its butterfly-thin pages edged in gold. Flipping through, she discovered a postcard-sized photograph slipped between the cover and the flyleaf, slightly creased and smeared a rusty brown in the bottom right corner.

'It's been through a lot. I had it taken on my first leave, before we shipped out, and it's been with me ever since. That's Mum and my brother, Jim.'

The photograph showed three people, with Henry Turner standing between an older woman and a man of perhaps twenty-five or thirty years of age. Henry stood at ease in his uniform, legs slightly apart, hands behind his back. He looked a little older than Rose – perhaps twenty or twenty-one – and she could see the bravado on his face as if he were about to embark upon a great adventure. His mother was a plump woman with the same open, ready-for-anything countenance as her son. She wore a white cotton blouse with a scalloped collar, tucked into a long dark skirt. Her hands hung at her sides, twisting the fabric of her skirt as if she were surprised not to find an apron there. On his right side stood a taller, slightly older version of Henry with broader shoulders, wider chest and a face where all the features were bigger – larger nose, heavier brows, higher cheekbones and stronger chin. She could see the family resemblance. But in his brother Jim, Henry's boyish good looks had graduated to a darker, more rugged Turner male.

'Your brother isn't married?' she asked, curious about the serious-looking man in the photograph.

'Jim says he's got too much to do on the farm. Hasn't the time to go gallivanting after a woman. One will have to come to him.'

His laugh turned to a cough that emerged like a bark. She handed him a glass of water and made to prop him up a little higher, but he waved her away.

'I'm surprised someone hasn't done that already,' she said with a decidedly unladylike wink. 'He's a well-set-up fellow with a prosperous homestead.'

'By Jove, he's had his chances. But he says he's not about to get hitched just to oblige some girl with marriage on her mind. It will take a special kind of girl to coax my brother into giving up his bachelor ways.'

'Well, I think that's an eminently sensible attitude. You and your brother both have plenty of time to find exactly the right kind of girl.'

She wondered what kind of girl that might be. Would she be quiet and unassuming, with a talent for looking pretty? Would she be sturdy and hard-working, an asset to the farm? Or would she have opinions and objections and demand to make her own choices? That was the thing . . . someone was always making Rose's choices for her, so she had to speak up when she could. Her brother loved her but essentially he didn't know her. He knew Miss Rose Luscombe, daughter of Edward Luscombe, sister of Robert Luscombe and, one day, wife to . . .

She wondered what Jim Turner would make of a girl like her. He didn't know anything about her family or her situation. To him, she would be his brother's friend, Rose . . . Nurse Luscombe.

And she could make of that whatever she chose. But Jim Turner was so far away that she was unlikely to ever find out what he might think.

Ivy couldn't wait to be out the door of Oldbridge Manor and down the oak-lined drive. She was tired of aching feet, blood-soaked bandages, and visiting sweethearts who stirred up the patients with their sobbing. And she was most tired of arriving on the ward to find an officer she had laughed with only yesterday gone, back to the front, back home or just . . . gone. It didn't do to get too friendly for, one way or another, the men would take your hearts with them. Look at Miss Rose and Lieutenant Turner. Anyone could see he wouldn't be around much longer. He would be shipped back to a surgical unit for amputation or carried out beneath a flag. And then Rose would pay the price of friendship in tears.

Ivy was a practical girl. Her patients needed kindness and careful nursing; much better to hoard her tears and save her friendship for someone who might still be alive when the war was over. She felt like a rag that has been wrung out and worn thin until it is no use even for washing floors. She hoped that Donaldson had brought the Rolls, for the trip back home in the pony trap would shake the little remaining meat from her bones.

When they finally stepped off the porch, the day had turned dark and a heavy shower greeted them. The hedges were glossy and the lawns spongy from the rain. Luckily, the car was waiting and Donaldson trotted towards them, raising a huge black umbrella. Except that the man's legs were clad in khaki, not grey. The face shadowed by the umbrella didn't belong to the dour-faced chauffeur but to Mr Robert himself. Mr Robert was home. He was in one piece and he was walking towards her, his eyes drifting to her face rather than his sister's, his body leaning slightly as if being reeled towards her. He was still thin, his uniform bagging about his waist, but he walked with purpose, his gait agile despite the ungainly umbrella and the puddles underfoot. Even from ten yards' distance she could see that his eyes were less sad. He had got some of his youthful sheen back.

Her heart began a little polka and she had to take a deep breath to quiet it. How was she to behave like a proper servant now there were all those words between them? Letters that had begun as simple exchanges of news had gradually developed into something more, an exchange of impressions, opinions, fears and uncertainties. Despite herself, she had let him into her world. Ivy had never been a girl to share secrets. She had never giggled over boys with the other village girls or housemaids. Growing up at Ashcott had taught her to rely upon herself. Yet somehow, the act of writing had freed her to share her thoughts as if the words were writing themselves.

'What are you grinning about, Ivy?' Miss Rose asked with a puzzled frown.

'It's the captain, miss. Captain Luscombe's home.'

'Robert!' shouted Rose, launching herself into her brother's arms so that he dropped the umbrella in surprise. 'You didn't tell us you had leave!'

'I didn't get much warning and decided to surprise you.'

'Well, you succeeded. Oh, how lovely!'

Ivy bent to retrieve the umbrella, giving herself a moment to pull her face into some semblance of order. Despite those letters, and the captain's glance in her direction, she wasn't silly enough to believe their confidences could mean anything. She hadn't confided in anyone since she was a foolish child and thought she could be a friend to his sister. She had been mistaken then; she wasn't about to make the same mistake twice. Captain Luscombe wasn't interested in a girl like Ivy. He was just lonely and afraid, like all the others.

'Thank you, Ivy,' he said casually as she handed him the

umbrella, but his eyes were anything but casual, trapping hers for a moment and holding them as if he didn't want to let go.

She looked away. All well and good for a man with £5,000 per annum. 'Wait on the porch and I'll come back for you,' he said.

'Ivy will be fine. She's accustomed to a little rain, I'm sure.'

'Here, Rose, take my arm,' he commanded.

Ivy returned obediently to the porch, watching as her employer ushered his sister into the back of the Rolls, checking on her comfort before turning back to the house. She stepped out to meet him, ducking under the umbrella to stand at his side, so close that their shoulders touched. So close that she noticed the drops of rain glistening on his woollen sleeve, the hairs bristling on his chin. She realised that she had never stood so near to a man. It was an odd feeling, prickly as a thistle lodged in her stocking, yet as delicious as Cook's bread and butter pudding melting in her mouth. She wished that she could stay here sheltering from the rain, hiding in this small world where there was no war and it didn't matter that he was the master and she was the maid. It only mattered that they were together.

Her head told her that if she abandoned herself to this feeling she would come away empty-handed and broken-hearted. The captain was a kind man, and clearly he liked her, but he was a Luscombe. People like the Luscombes, who had so much, only valued what they paid for dearly. Anything handed to them on a platter they took as their due. Ivy couldn't afford to be primped and prepped and set before them on that platter.

Yet why shouldn't she have something sparkly all for herself? Why shouldn't she have a kind and handsome man who loved her, a house with a window seat and time to do as she pleased? It wasn't so much to ask. Why should she content herself with somebody else's cast-offs? But if ever she were to satisfy that yearning, she would need to become so desirable that the captain would pay whatever it cost him. So unattainable that he would do whatever it took, no matter what anyone might say. No matter who might look down her nose at his choice.

How this might be achieved, Ivy hadn't a clue.

'It's good to come home,' he said, his eyes adding the silent words, 'to you.'

She felt a sharp pain in her chest and had to take a deep breath. Suddenly her head and heart were at war and all she could think to do was put herself in his path and wait to see what happened. Surely a girl could take a small risk?

'It's good to have you home . . .' She looked up at him, standing so tall and solid beside her, and smiled. 'Sir.'

As he ushered her into the car, Rose considered her through narrowed eyes. 'It won't do to get any silly ideas,' she said as her brother walked around the outside of the car to the driver's door.

'Excuse me, miss?'

'You know what I mean. Besides, I'm quite sure Donaldson is sweet on you. Now that would be just the ticket, wouldn't it?'

29

The rain had cleared and late afternoon sun filtered through the trees of Luscombe Park. Raindrops trembled like pearls from leaf and bough. Ivy decided she had time for a short walk before dressing Rose for dinner. She would swing around the western end of the house and trip across the lawn towards the lake. And if she happened to pass within sight of the study where the captain relaxed after his long journey from France, well she would just be taking the air. Rose could hardly begrudge a hard-working nurse that. And if she did, Ivy no longer cared.

It had been years since Ivy strolled by the lake – not since before the war. At first she wondered whether a lack of rain had affected it, for it seemed smaller than she remembered, as if someone had let out a plug to drain it. But the water lapped at the foot of the jetty, just as it always had, and she realised that the lake looked smaller because she was larger and her world had grown with her. Once her world had comprised the cottage, the school, the village and the fringes of Luscombe Park. Now she went wherever her mistress went. She had been to Barnstaple and Bristol; she had ridden in a motor more times than she could count; she had even travelled to London twice. And she had seen men die.

Meanwhile, the magical lake of her memory dwindled to a neglected pond. An ageing punt was moored at the jetty, the tiny island in the middle of the lake floundered under a thicket of overgrown vegetation, while half the lake was clogged with water lilies. Once Luscombe Park had boasted three gardeners and a boy. Now there was only old Pedrick and her brother Daniel, who was barely out of short pants.

A single circuit of the lake was all it took before she heard footsteps crunching on the gravel path. She willed herself not to turn around – to pretend that she hadn't heard – while continuing her amble by the shore as if she was merely a tired lady's maid taking the air after a long day.

'Ivy,' his voice beckoned, a heartbeat behind her.

Even then, she didn't turn but waited for him to catch up and fall into step beside her, a mere hand's breadth away. And yet there was a chasm a mile wide between them.

'I wanted to thank you . . .' he began hesitantly.

She wondered that a man like him could be unsure about anything. 'Thank me, sir?'

'For writing. For keeping me informed of things here at Luscombe.'

'It was no trouble, sir. I'm only sorry for my poor handwriting.'

'Your writing is like you, friendly and sensible. My sister's letters are . . . quite brief and mostly concern parties, or lack thereof, and new clothes. And Mother is too ill to write.'

'Miss Rose is probably trying to cheer you up.'

'Perhaps.'

She had always pictured him as having a bevy of young ladies clamouring for his attention, all penning him their *billets-doux*. But perhaps their attention didn't have the stamina for this war.

'I understand, sir. It was my pleasure.'

She kept walking, her eyes fixed on the surrounding park, anywhere but on the man at her side. He strode along silently, all his concentration seemingly focused on avoiding puddles. Was this the same man who had nearly run her down in his shiny motor, four years ago? That man had words to spare; easy, confident words that tripped off his tongue and knew no contradiction. This man's whole world had been contradicted.

'I wanted to thank you too for giving me hope.'

'Hope?' she said with a frown, while hugging his words for when he was gone. Risking a fleeting glance at his face, she was disconcerted to find that he had abandoned his study of puddles to stare at her. She thought of Rose's words such a short time ago and shunted them aside. Why shouldn't this sad, lonely man enjoy her company? Why shouldn't an honest, hard-working girl enjoy a young man's gaze? Miss Rose wanted to hoard all the attention.

She smiled and looked away. How strange, that she was acting the way she had seen other girls do a hundred times – drawing-room girls like Miss Rose, VADs like Nurse Giles – fluttering with shyness, nervous with emotion. How had that happened? She had thought she was immune to all that.

'Before you wrote to me, I was afraid I was running out of hope. You see, every man's death took a little more of my hope with it. I thought if I did, somehow, manage to shuffle home from the war I would have nothing left but despair.'

'You'll come home, sir, I know it. Luscombe needs you. We all need you. And you have so much to live for,' she said, risking another glance at his face. He was still facing her but his eyes had that unfocused look, as if he were *seeing* something else.

'Perhaps I do, Ivy. Perhaps I do. But I'd forgotten that. I'd forgotten what I was over there fighting for – the fighting had become an end in itself. And it seemed so pointless. At night I'd dream of waking to find myself covered by a tarpaulin, thinking,

"Oh, so this is death," as if it were no matter at all.'

She wasn't a tearful girl, for tears were useless in her world, yet she felt them welling now. For Robert Luscombe, who had forgotten the point in being alive. 'You're fighting for us, sir,' she ventured, 'for your mother and your sister and all the folk here at home.' It was something.

'I needed someone to remind me of that. I needed someone to come home to.'

His eyes returned to hers. She still wasn't sure exactly what their message was. No one had ever needed *her* before. Her da needed a wage. Her ma needed an extra pair of hands. Miss Rose needed a maid. But no one needed *her*. Despite her earlier resolve to keep her distance, to make him reach for her, she stretched her hand across the gap to brush his fingertips. Before she could retrieve it his fingers curled around hers, cradling her palm so that she felt hard calluses pressing into her flesh.

'Tomorrow I'm going to drive you and Rose into Ilfracombe to sit for a portrait at Catford's studio. I'll be stronger, knowing that you're both with me when I return to France,' he said with a sheepish grin. She had never thought to see the master looking sheepish. 'Perhaps I can persuade you to keep me close to your heart too.'

Should she agree that his portrait would keep her strong? That she needed him close to her heart? Except it would be a lie, for she was already strong, she knew this in her bones. She had learned to fend for herself a long time ago. But feeling her hand snuggled in his, she knew that although she might not need him, she wanted him.

'I have something for you. I saw it in a shop in Paris on a two-day leave.' Reaching his free hand into his inside coat pocket, he withdrew a dazzling chain of pearly light and offered it to her. 'They're not real pearls but they caught my eye. I thought you might like them.'

The long, dangling necklace glittered like a prize in his hand, all shining silver and mother of pearl. She imagined it resting cool against her skin. Even if it wasn't real, it was beautiful. A pity she would only be able to wear it in her imagination. She could hardly tend to Miss Rose's toilette ornamented like a Christmas tree. How could she expect him to know this? He had thought of her, after all. And no one else had done that before, either.

'It's very beautiful. Thank you.' She raised her face to his, fidgety with a smile. As he lowered his head to press his lips against hers their noses bumped. But that didn't matter, for somehow she felt the mere touch of his lips the entire length of her body, so that she was leaning into him without realising how she got there.

'Ivy,' he breathed between parted lips. 'I need you.'

He pressed against her, reeling her in with his need. Her arms snaked around him, crushing the brass buttons of his uniform against her chest. His hands roamed the length of her, settling on the cheeks of her buttocks, pulling her even closer if that were possible. She felt that he was holding her erect, that if he released her she would slip to the ground in a puddle. Perhaps this is what he meant when he said he needed her – this urgent, aching emptiness that only he could fill.

Her hands fumbled under his jacket, small enough to slip between shirt buttons, dexterous enough to untuck his vest, sliding against skin.

'Ivy, I want . . .'

Out of the corner of her eye she spotted movement. Wrenching herself from Robert's embrace, she saw a man – no, a boy – wheeling a barrow on the far side of the lake. He paused to stare in their direction, halting mid-stride like a rabbit sniffing the wind for danger. It was her brother Daniel, and even with a lake between them she could tell that he had a look of surprise on his face, as if he had spied a thing he never thought to see.

Rose was annoyed. She had rung for Ivy three times and was finally delivered an out-of-breath Muriel in her place. Rose needed her embroidery scissors and they were nowhere to be found, not in her sewing basket or on her writing desk or the whatnot by the fireplace. How was she expected to embroider a monogrammed handkerchief for her brother without her scissors? Muriel ransacked her drawers but they weren't to be found anywhere. Ivy had probably hidden them. It would be just like that girl, always putting things away where Rose couldn't find them. She sometimes suspected Ivy did it deliberately. There was something decidedly sneaky about her expression when she thought Rose wasn't watching. Her lips would quirk in a half-smile, as if she was oh-so-pleased with herself, like a cat licking cream from its paws. No, like a cat with a mouse clamped in its jaws.

'I'm sorry, miss,' Muriel said. 'I can't find the scissors anywhere. And Ivy has disappeared.'

'Never mind. You may go.'

Ivy had disappeared, had she? Working alongside her betters at Oldbridge had gone to the girl's head. She had discovered initiative – a very dangerous quality in a maid – and worse than that, she had discovered self-will. Look at the way she had responded when Rose simply pointed out the ridiculousness of a maid setting her cap at a gentleman. She would have to do something about that or Ivy would have to go, never mind what Robert might say about loyalty and such like. What if Ivy hadn't noticed the runaway horse that day at church? Then Rose wouldn't have to owe her anything and could send her packing without a qualm.

Yet if Ivy hadn't been there to push Maman out of the way of that runaway horse, Maman might be dead. Well, perhaps it was better not to think about that.

She could see now why Maman and Miss Sarah had warned her not to make a friend of the Toms girl, all those years ago. She had been too young and headstrong to understand. Playing with Ivy had been an adventure. Their differences had been the point of the friendship, after all. But that friendship had encouraged Ivy to be too familiar, and now there was no going back. It would be easier to employ a maid who knew nothing about her – that way she could be friendly, without encouraging intimacy. With Ivy she had to set herself apart to have any measure of authority at all. She could never quite be herself, and it wasn't fair to either of them. Yes, if she let Ivy go, the girl would be free to find a more suitable employer, one who could appreciate her skills without dwelling upon her faults. Ivy would be much happier, and out of Robert's – and harm's – way. And Rose would be free to find her Odette.

She wandered out on to the upstairs gallery that connected the main bedrooms of Luscombe Park. Her mother's boudoir was situated three doors from hers, opening on to the landing at the top of the stairs. Perhaps Gibbons had seen her scissors . . . or her maid . . . either would do. Gibbons was usually floating about somewhere on the first floor, chasing after Maman or that frightful dog.

'Gibbons!' she called. Striding the length of the gallery, she turned the corner towards her mother's room to discover Maman's door gaping a few inches.

'Gibbons,' she repeated, unsure whether to enter. It wouldn't do to come upon Maman unawares, as you could never be sure in what state you might find her. It could be quite embarrassing, for example, if she had fallen asleep under the dressing table.

'Yes, miss,' Gibbons called softly, from somewhere inside, but she didn't appear at the door to admit her. It was decidedly odd.

She gave the door a gentle shove and stepped into the boudoir to find Gibbons standing at the window overlooking the park, with the curtains open to reveal the last tentative rays of sunlight. Maman was reclining on the chaise in a silk peignoir, her eyes closed and mouth ajar, snuffling a little in her sleep.

'Gibbons, have you seen Ivy? I can't imagine where she has got to.'

'Yes, miss,' replied her mother's maid, still standing sentinel at the window. 'I know exactly where she is.'

'Where?'

'She's walking in the park. By the lake.'

'In the park? Whatever for? And what has she done with my scissors?'

'I'm sure I don't know. You'll have to ask Miss Toms. Or the captain,' said Gibbons, and Rose detected a smug note of self-congratulation in the woman's tone.

'What does my brother have to do with my scissors?'

Rose crossed the room to peer out of the window, following the direction of Gibbon's gaze. What she saw made a pretty, rural tableau: the verdant lakeside, the majestic trees trickling with rain, the gardener's boy trudging towards the stables with his loaded wheelbarrow, and a man and a woman silhouetted against the setting sun.

Well, it would have been pretty if it wasn't her brother she saw, locked in an embrace with her ungrateful, unworthy, untruthful maid.

'Your mother's not going to like this, miss,' sniffed Gibbons. 'Not one little bit.'

'My mother isn't the only one. But best not to worry Maman with this. You know how . . . anxious . . . she can become. I'll take care of this situation. Understand?'

'Yes, miss, I understand.'

Gibbons might understand. But for the life of her, Rose didn't understand Robert at all.

30

'Come along, Chicken,' Robert said cheerily. 'You and Ivy are comrades-in-arms. Keeping the home fires burning and so forth.'

'You make us sound like a couple of parlour maids,' answered Rose, but unless she wished to cause an embarrassing scene in front of Mr Catford, the photographer, she had to go along with her brother's plan and have her portrait taken with her maid. Robert insisted they be photographed together – as if they were friends. The outing to Ilfracombe to have their portraits taken in uniform was bad enough, but now he had sprung this delightful surprise upon her.

'That's it, Ivy,' he urged. 'Don't be shy.'

'You could never accuse Ivy of being shy, Robert.' Sly would be more apt. Since spotting her in the garden with Robert, Rose had been quite frosty, yet the girl didn't appear to have noticed. Usually she could be counted upon for pertness verging on insolence, but since that evening she had been the model of affability. And Rose made it her business to be particularly demanding. She couldn't bring herself to chastise her maid openly but she hoped Ivy would take the hint.

Apparently not. Apparently Ivy wasn't about to give her the

tiniest excuse for dismissal. It was really too vexing, so tawdry and demeaning. And now Robert was urging them to link arms.

She shoved her hands in her pockets in protest, remaining determinedly unsmiling, despite Robert's imprecations to smile. But then she felt a hand slide into her apron pocket and nestle against her own like a small furtive creature, and she could hardly believe the gall of the girl. Glancing at Ivy out of the corner of her eye, she saw her lips curving in that sneaky half-smile, before turning her head in Robert's direction to find him watching the proceedings with a moony, addle-headed expression on his face. She could hardly believe what was happening, and would have pinched the girl if it weren't so unladylike. And there would be more photographs to come. Robert had arranged for Mr Catford to come to Luscombe the following afternoon and make a record of the entire household.

'That's it,' said Mr Catford, raising his head from under his photographer's hood. 'Lovely, ladies, thank you.'

Lovely for some. But not for long, if she had anything to do with it. Her brother clearly needed protecting. Ivy had already entwined herself about him. If Rose didn't do something soon, she would get her rootlets into him too, and then nothing would pry them loose. She would speak to her brother tonight, and he would be gone – back to the front – in a couple of days. She would never have thought she would wish that on anyone.

After yesterday's tedious proceedings in Ilfracombe, Rose had never been so glad to arrive at Oldbridge Manor. She didn't wait for Donaldson to escort her from the Rolls but threw open the door and marched for the entrance, her skirts flapping about her like a call to arms, hoping Ivy would bury herself in the sink room with her bandages and bedpans and stay out of her way. Rose would give the men their tea and read to Lieutenant Turner, coaxing a laugh or two from the poor suffering boy.

Surely joy was a more useful commodity than bandages?

But when she arrived on the ward it was cloaked in gloom. Sister usually had the curtains pulled back at the crack of dawn, yet this morning it was already gone eight and nobody had bothered. An orderly was removing screens from around Henry Turner's bed, and the other men sat about strangely silent. The young Australian lieutenant – so hearty and brave in his fight for survival – was nowhere to be seen. Stripped of sheets and blankets, his naked mattress confronted her in silent reproach.

'Where's Lieutenant Turner?' she asked one of the men, who answered her with a silent shake of his head.

'Oh, Henry,' she chided softly, 'you went without saying goodbye to me.'

He was gone, and she hadn't been there to hold his hand and ease his passage on his final journey. While she had been fussing over a sordid affair between her brother and her maid, Henry had come to the end of his struggle.

She thought of the photograph he had shown her of his mother and brother, and imagined them receiving the cable with news of his death. They seemed so far removed from the chaos of war, thousands of miles away on their farm in Australia, yet they were all casualties, weren't they? Flotsam and jetsam tossed upon unpredictable seas. She was fooling herself if she thought anyone could bring order out of this chaos. It didn't matter how hard she tried to help the men find their way home. The best they could hope for was a temporary safe haven, a brief respite from thinking about death.

Henry's stories of Wuurnong had offered her a glimpse of another life, one where there was purpose to each day. She had imagined herself standing on a porch looking out at nothing but pasture and sheep in any direction, a strong man at her side. She had wondered what it would be like to rule her own kitchen, the warm smell of bread greeting her menfolk as they came in from a long day in the fields. Would it be better or worse than drifting through the days with little to fill her hours but looking decorative? The hospital had given her purpose but once the war was over she would be expected to resume her role as a charming ornament. Clearly, that was what her brother expected, that was what convention demanded. But Rose didn't think she could do it. She didn't think she could live with that hollow, brittle feeling any more. There were only so many parties to attend, so many dresses to purchase. What if she ended up like Maman?

There had to be something more. There had to be some way to set her own course in life.

Well, there was one thing she could do. She would write to Jim Turner. She could let him know that someone else mourned his brother's death. And she would keep alive the dream that there were other lives possible for a girl like her, lives that might be more challenging but also more purposeful than staying here and marrying someone suitable. That is, if anyone suitable were to be found after this war was over.

She didn't have to live the life that was expected of her. She could live an unexpected life. If she chose to. If she dared to reach out and make it so.

31

In a place as large as Luscombe Park, with its sprawling grounds and endless parade of rooms, it was surprisingly difficult to find somewhere private. Even for a maid who had cleaned every nook and cranny at one time or another. There were always prying eyes on the lookout for wrongdoing, ears alert for trouble; Ivy could think of no place sure to evade them. It was the captain who thought of the folly. And it was Ivy who lied and schemed to escape her duties and meet him there. Ivy who contrived to avoid her mistress's shrewd gaze and sharp tongue.

She hurried across the lawn and around the lake, fearful that the captain may have given up waiting for her and returned to the house. The last frail light of dusk flickered through the trees, so that she must keep her eyes to the ground to avoid danger. It would be so easy to trip in this part of the garden, where Pedrick and her brother devoted hours to maintaining its natural state. When she took a moment to glance ahead, the folly loomed out of the trees, a temple to the gods of olden days, according to Miss Rose. Round, and built upon a platform of rough stone blocks, it was encircled by stately columns, yet gaping open to the encroaching night above. And there, standing between two pillars, his eyes searching the shadowy park, stood the captain.

Her captain.

The thought left her breathless with daring.

'Ivy.' Her name drifted to her in a whisper on the breeze.

She quickened her pace, almost leaping up the uneven stairs, so that she might have tripped if he hadn't grasped both her arms, pulling her to safety. Safety or danger? She wasn't sure. She still heard her mother's voice warning her to be careful. To beware of men with smooth hands and linen whiter than Miss Rose's fine sheets, marked with their blue crosses. Ma had told her as much, so many times, once she came to work at Luscombe Park.

But Mr Robert wasn't like that any more. His hands had grown hard from the business of war. And no amount of laundering could make his linens white now that they were smeared with the mud of France. He was the captain now, not the smiling, carefree young man who had rescued her that day in his Silver Ghost. She knew instinctively that he was the one who needed rescuing now. And he had chosen her as his saviour.

He drew her behind the sheltering wall of the folly. 'You came. I thought you might change your mind,' he said, looking at her as if he didn't quite believe she was real.

'I'm sorry, sir. Miss Rose kept me. I'm sorry I'm late.'

'No. I'm sorry we have to meet in secret.'

'It's for the best, sir.'

No need to say more than this. They both knew what they faced.

'Not *sir*. Not here. Can't we be Robert and Ivy?'

'It's a temple. If the gods smile upon us, we can be whoever we like,' she said, lifting her head to the sky with a smile for whichever gods might be glancing their way. The first star glistened faintly overhead. 'Although if it rains, we'll know they're displeased,' she added, laughing at her own daring in the face of gods and men . . . and Miss Rose.

'Ahh. I believe one of my ancestors was of a philosophical bent. The unfinished roof is meant to suggest that mankind's knowledge will never be complete,' he said, brushing a wisp of hair from her cheek.

'Sometimes a roof is more help than knowledge,' she said with a shrug.

'You're such a practical girl, Ivy.'

'I wouldn't be much use to your family if I weren't.'

'You would to me.' He cupped her chin with one hand and tilted her face so that she must look into his eyes.

She frowned. Would she, though? Wasn't it her practical nature that had charmed him? Her worldly concerns? Her earthy good sense? Her guarding of his precious Rose. Her wild hair that she kept bound by ribbons. Wasn't it her sturdy frame and strong arms that he admired? And what would he do if she demanded he announce their friendship to his family?

'How can I make you believe me?' he asked, when she didn't respond.

With his other hand he traced the contours of her neck so that she shivered despite her shawl. And when he bent his head to capture her lips, as if he might breathe his truth into her mouth, she almost believed him. The certainty of his arm sliding around her waist and the warm pressure of his mouth on hers almost convinced her. That and the shudder of desire that trembled through her. She could put a name to it now.

'If you say so,' she said, adding the 'sir' in her head. 'If you say so, I believe you.'

He wrapped both arms about her, pulling her close so that she felt the pressure of his body through the layers of her clothing. She felt the long contours of his legs, the jutting bones of his hips, the hard strength of his hands. His nearness flooded her with warmth, floating up like a bubble, making her feel so light that she could believe anything he told her, every word of longing he whispered into her ear as he devoured her with his kisses.

He wanted her. He needed her. What difference did it make why? She might not need him in the same way, but she wanted him. She wanted every part of him. And once she had him, she would find a way to keep him. For no doubt once Rose learned of it she would do everything in her power to destroy their love before it could take root. She wouldn't take kindly to her handsome brother wasting himself upon her maid. All the more reason to give this fragile bond time to grow in secret, shrouded by folly, etched in pale ink on thin paper leaves.

To give her at least a little time to enjoy the feeling, whatever it turned out to be.

Oh yes, Ivy was nothing if not a practical girl.

32

North Devon

2017

Molly woke to an unexpected lightness of being as if the day might hold untold pleasures, something she hadn't felt since she was a child. She yawned and sat up stretching, letting the luxurious feeling wash over her. Then she noticed the faded floral curtains draping stone mullioned windows and remembered she wasn't lying in her apartment in Elwood, with the glimpse of plane trees lining the street. She wasn't in her childhood bedroom in Black Rock, looking out over the tree house her dad had built in the old Pittosporum. She was lying in Rose Luscombe's bedroom at Luscombe Park, her belongings stowed neatly in a homely chest of drawers, her laptop resting on a worn Persian rug atop scattered sheets of paper. The paper footprints left by one hundred and fifty years of Luscombe family history. Her great-grandmother's family history.

Later today she would see Lucas – had seen him, in fact, most days for the past three weeks. She would join him for a simple dinner at his house. Then perhaps they would stroll through the garden or down by the little creek Richard called a brook. She would tell him what new piece of Luscombe trivia she had unearthed and he would talk about his latest project. They wouldn't worry about the next day or the next week or the next year. They would just exist in the moment.

Richard would pop up at odd moments during her day, appearing like a gleeful sprite to tell her of his latest eBay triumph. Since her introduction to his library, he had taken to twenty-first-century trading as avidly as one of his merchant ancestors had traded cotton or coal. She now made regular trips to Barnstaple in his ancient Land Rover to organise shipping, and the mounting proceeds in his account allowed them to order archive boxes and folders to store the most important documents from the attic. Over the years, Luscombe's most valuable items of furniture and art had been appraised and disposed of; what remained were merely the candle-ends of a dynasty, relics that past dealers had deemed unworthy of more than a passing glance or a job lot. Sentiment valued them more highly. But the Internet had opened up a global market of enthusiasts, collectors and shopaholics, and suddenly sentiment was being outbid. Richard didn't seem at all fazed to be selling off the last possessions of centuries. In fact, he felt that he was throwing off a burden he had been yoked to his entire life.

Molly didn't want to think about what she would do when the last carton was sorted and catalogued. She would worry about that when the time came. If she allowed herself to dwell on it, her feelings of happiness would be punctured. For now, she wanted to enjoy the sensation of buoyancy, as if she might finally relinquish her burden of grief and guilt.

Her phone buzzed softly on the bentwood chair she was using as a bedside table and Lucas's name lit up the screen.

She answered, a smile chiming in her voice. 'Hey, what's up?'

'Didn't want to start the day without hearing your voice.'

'You know, you might make good boyfriend material. I can't believe you're still single. Or is it all an act?'

'Totally. Once you get to know the real Lucas Toms you'll discover a complete arsehole in the trappings of Mr Nice Guy.'

Could someone disguise himself so completely? It didn't seem possible that there wouldn't be clues. Some hint that he wasn't quite who he purported to be.

'I think you'd better do something dreadful, then,' she said, 'so I don't think you're too good to be true.'

'How about forgetting a date?'

'Not that dreadful.'

'Not returning a call?'

'I can live with that, I guess.'

Lucas wasn't perfect: she had already discovered that he could become quite deaf when he was preoccupied; he was fussy about his house and his office, and grew quite put out if things weren't returned to the same spot. He was a lot like her, actually. That's probably why they were drawn to each other. She and Matt had been so different that she found it difficult to believe being with Lucas could be so easy. *Was* it too good to be true?

'So will I be seeing your lovely face today?'

'Uh-huh.'

'About seven?'

'Can't wait.'

She rang off, deciding that she wasn't going to over-think this. She wasn't going to make any plans further ahead than tomorrow. She was just going to set out without any navigation aids and enjoy the journey. How hard could that be? Throwing back the covers, she sprang out of bed, humming a particularly silly tune about a girl wearing her boyfriend's underwear. It seemed apt, given her apparel of choice lately, prancing about Lucas's bedroom in nothing but a pair of boxers. She would shower and dress and wait to see what surprises the day had in store.

Molly stood at the large trestle table she used for sorting, surrounded by reams of paper and neatly stacked boxes. It was difficult to believe that when she first entered this room, six weeks ago, the jumble of boxes had represented uncharted territory. There were so many possible routes through the material that setting out was daunting. Now, although there were still several boxes waiting to be discovered – and those she had opened were only partially archived – she felt that the 'squirrel's nest' was no longer *terra incognita*. She had mapped the perimeter, if not the interior, of the collection. Her computer held the beginnings of a catalogue; items she had already sorted were allocated an accession number and given a title and brief description. If she had more time, she could begin the job of tracing sources, dates, authors and other information that should be included in the database. Ideally, she would scan or photograph each object so that the collection could be digitised for ease of use.

The first of the archive boxes and folders she had ordered would arrive soon and she could begin storing items more systematically, especially now that Richard had made room in the library by selling unwanted books. If only she had more time – there was so much more that she could do, so much more she could discover. These six weeks had confirmed for her that teaching was no longer enough. One way or another, she intended to work as a historian. Perhaps she would never be the kind of person who thrilled to the adrenalin rush of wave or wind, but in her own way she relished the chase for that next clue, following a whiff of fact to its source. It was just a different kind of adventure, that's all.

'Molly, there you are,' Richard panted, appearing in the attic doorway, out of breath and very red in the face.

'What on earth are you doing up here?' she gasped, helping him to a seat. 'There are far too many stairs. You should have called me and I would have come down.'

'I know, but I was so excited that I started upstairs without thinking and then realised I'd left my phone in the study.'

'Here. Don't talk for a moment while I get you a glass of water.'

She poured him a drink from the pitcher she kept on a side table away from the precious documents, all the while watching him worriedly. Why on earth had he tackled all those stairs? It was sheer lunacy. Handing him the water, she put a finger to her lips in silent admonition, indicating that he was to drink before he uttered another word. He sipped at the water, glancing up at her so like a naughty boy who has been caught out that she could see the lonely schoolboy still lurking behind the nest of wrinkles. She wondered if others could spot her terrified twelve-year-old self, hiding behind the facade of a competent adult.

'May I speak now, please, miss?' he asked, handing her the empty glass.

'I guess so, if you're sure you're all right.'

'I've had the most marvellous idea.'

'Mmmm,' she replied, scared now of what else he was inspired to sell. He had become so enamoured of online trading that he would be selling the roof tiles if they weren't careful. In introducing him to eBay she feared she had created a monster.

'I've discovered that you can sell old postcards. You can sell them individually and there are people who buy entire collections.'

'People have listed air guitars on eBay. It doesn't mean they sell.'

'What would an air guitar be?'

'It doesn't matter,' she said, shaking her head.

'Now, I know there are boxes of the things up here. Dev sent them to me from all over the world, and Mother's friends travelled everywhere and sent her postcards too. There was also a spinster great-great-aunt last century – no, the century before – who was a very intrepid traveller. I did tell you it was a squirrel's nest.'

'I'm surprised a dealer wasn't interested in a collection like that. Are you sure they're still here?'

'I never let the dealers up here with all the old records. Just as well,' he said, rubbing his hands together, 'because this is so much more fun. I expect we can get at least seven or eight pounds for the oldest ones, and there are hundreds of the things.'

She couldn't help smiling. His enthusiasm was infectious but she hoped he wouldn't sell off family treasures, all those stories yet to be told – the adventurous Victorian spinster, the opera singer and his lover . . . Who knew what secrets lay cached in these innocuous-seeming cartons? Selling historical documents went against all her instincts. But she had to remember that much as she was drawn to the Luscombe story, it was Richard's home, his family. If he wanted to sell the postcards, then that was his prerogative. And he was so happy about it.

'There are boxes of postcards and old photographs here, and a large trunk as well. I'm not quite sure where. Have you come across them yet?'

She nodded. 'I've been dealing with the written documents first, saving the pictures for later.' Like chocolates, saving her favourite flavours until last.

'Marvellous. Well, what do you think? Shall we sell them?'

'Of course. But can I look through them first? To make sure we don't sell anything important.'

'Excellent idea.'

'Actually, would you mind if I asked my sister Daisy down to help? You know she's a photographer. She might be able to help us identify any postcards by well-known photographers.' And she could ask her to bring her scanner so they could begin making digital images of everything.

'I wouldn't want to inconvenience her. I've already monopolised so much of your time.'

'She's been hinting for weeks that she'd like to visit. She's dying to meet you and see Luscombe, so it won't be an inconvenience.' Daisy had been more than hinting. She had practically threatened to arrive unannounced. And she wanted to meet the handsome architect too.

'Well then, it's settled. I'll ask Judy to make up my old room, overlooking the drive,' he said, his wide grin making him appear suddenly youthful. 'I shall be the lucky host to two beautiful young women. Won't Lucas be jealous?'

She sighed. She hadn't told Daisy the entire truth about Lucas, despite her sister's threats of torture by tickling if she didn't confess. Her sister always sensed more was going on than Molly admitted. She suspected Richard knew, for one name did happen to crop up in conversation with monotonous regularity, but she didn't want to explain to anyone. She wanted to hug her secret to herself just a little longer. Whatever existed between herself and Lucas, it belonged to the two of them alone.

Besides, that way it would hurt a lot less if it all went pear-shaped.

33

North Devon

1917

The bells of St Peters trailed Ivy as she set out at a brisk pace towards Ashcott. Her mother and Daniel hadn't appeared at church again that morning, nor had she ventured home for weeks. She had taken to spending her half-day covertly in her room, hiding out from Miss Rose – who stalked her mercilessly – like a fox gone to ground. Rose had tackled her again on the walk to church that morning, asking her to search for some mislaid pearls. The pearls should have been safely stowed in their velvet box, locked in Miss Rose's top drawer, but apparently they had walked. Or perhaps the pixies had got to them? Ivy's old Grammer used to swear there were pixies on Exmoor. She had seen them dancing around a rock one night while walking home. But Ivy thought that this particular pixie was closer to home and bore a startling resemblance to her employer.

Arriving at her parents' cottage, she was surprised by the subtle signs of decay. The gate hung crookedly on its hinges, creeping tendrils of ivy poked and scratched at the cob walls, while the lime-washed render above the downstairs windows was flaking. It wasn't like Da to neglect the cottage, and she wondered whether his drinking had got out of hand. She always assumed that her father was afraid of nothing, but perhaps his worry over Samuel had sapped some of his courage.

'Ma! Danny!' she called, eyeing uneasily the heavy oak door with its overhanging porch and the dormer windows with their glowering thatch eyebrows. She was hoping her father was out.

After a few moments, her mother appeared at the door wiping her hands on an old blue pinafore. Her face was flushed, and even from several feet away Ivy spotted dark circles under her eyes.

'Ivy!' Ma rushed forward to greet her, wrapping her arms about Ivy's shoulders and crushing her to a thin chest. She remembered her mother's chest as soft and pillowy. But she couldn't recall Ma embracing her like this since she had first tied her bundle and left for Luscombe, so perhaps she had forgotten.

'Hello, Ma,' she said as her mother released her, 'you weren't in church so I thought I'd come for a visit.'

'It's good to see you, love.' Ma stood at arm's length to survey her daughter with a frown. 'You look tired.'

'It's the work at the hospital. All the VADs are tired.'

'But all the VADs aren't toiling after two masters,' Ma said with a shake of her head. 'It isn't right.'

'Is Daniel here?'

'He's digging another vegetable patch for me. The short-ages . . . and –' glancing over her shoulder towards the house – 'your da isn't bringing in as much coin as he once did. I don't know what we'd do without yours and Danny's wages.'

She wondered again whether Da's coin was being redirected at the pub.

'Is he here?'

'Inside. He's not himself. We haven't heard a word from your brother for weeks. You know Sammy's the apple of his eye.'

They all knew Sammy was the apple of Walter Toms' eye.

She stepped over the high stone threshold and followed her mother into the cottage, taking a few moments for her eyes to adjust to the dim interior. The earthen walls were thick and the roof low after the vast spaces of Luscombe. Rugged oak beams supported the ceiling, and the interior walls were plastered with a rough mixture of lime and clay. Winding stone stairs led to two tiny attic chambers above. A fire burned in the rubble fireplace, where the cat lay curled before it upon a rush mat. The cottage smelled of earth, damp and animal hair – like a den, or lair.

Her father dozed in the only good chair, his mouth hanging open and emitting a rumble of soft grunts. His features had coarsened in the months since she had seen him last, the ruddy hardness turned puffy and bloated, with grey bristles stubbling his cheeks and chin. He twitched as she watched, immersed in some troubling dream or other. Then, as her mother beckoned silently towards the kitchen, she left him to sleep.

They sat at the familiar table, scratched and scrubbed from decades of use, as her mother poured her a cup of well-stewed tea. She thought about her brother's whereabouts. He wasn't much of a correspondent but he dutifully kept his parents in postcards. Sometimes Ivy forgot that her soldier brother was still a boy, a boy whose father loved and missed him.

'Are they treating you well at the big house, then?'

She shrugged. 'You know Miss Rose, nothing is ever good enough.'

'And Mr Robert?' her mother asked. 'We heard he was home on leave not long ago,' she said, staring speculatively over the rim of her earthenware mug.

'The captain is kind enough.'

'You be careful. Men like that, they're used to getting their way.'

'He's my employer, that's all.'

'Just you be careful, love. You keep to your own kind.'

'He's been good to me,' she answered, not meeting her mother's eyes. She didn't want to see the warning there. Despite Robert's words, his hand cradling hers, his kisses, she knew that she walked a dangerous path. What if he woke one day to find that he no longer needed her in his life? That he needed a different kind of girl. A girl more like his sister . . . A flash of memory jolted her, a scene from her childhood. Robert Luscombe and his fancy London friends thundering across the countryside on their massive hunters, a pack of yelping dogs bounding before them. All those hounds and horses chasing one lone, terrified fox.

Sometimes she felt she was that fox, doing whatever was needed to survive.

She heard the sound of a heavy tread behind her and turned to see her father thundering into the kitchen, his face bloated with rage.

'He's been good to you? And why's that?' he boomed.

She leaped from her chair, backing towards the tall oak cabinet that served as larder and dresser, where her mother's few bits of wedding china were displayed. She sensed the fine hairs on her arms standing on end and her breathing quickened.

'What you be doing, maid? Your brother saw you . . .' her father sneered. 'The master is sweet-talking our Ivy, he says.'

She tried to calm her breathing, to forget that a frightened girl cowered inside. Her father fed on the fear of others, she knew that, had known it for years.

'Nothing, Da, I've been doing nothing. Mr Robert asked me to write and tell him how Miss Rose was getting on, that's all. They don't write him much, Miss Rose and the mistress. He's homesick.'

'You be a lying baggage just like your mother,' he shouted, his hand twitching and his arm drawing back so that she knew what was coming, knew to take cover. He was slower than he had been once and she had time to duck aside before he brought his fist crunching towards her face, only to connect with the oaken board of the dresser. Ivy heard the threatening sound of a loud thump. Her mother's precious cups and saucers teetered there for a split second before toppling from the shelf and falling to the stone-flagged floor in a tinkle of broken china.

Her mother gasped. Her father cursed. And Ivy sidled away as he recovered, nursing his injured fist and lumbering for her again. She searched for the clearest path to the back door, noting obstacles small and large – the heavy table, a twig basket, a wooden bucket, a broom leaning in the corner – while realising for the first time that her brother Danny stood in the doorway. He was silhouetted against the light, his arms rigid at his sides, clenching and unclenching his hands, with an expression of fear and outrage on his face. She skirted the table, catching her heel in her trailing hem, momentarily tripping herself up. She would have fallen except that Danny broke her fall, shoving her out into the garden and barring the door with his wiry thirteen-year-old body.

'I'm sorry,' he said, 'but you have to go now. It's not safe for you here.'

She hesitated, standing on the outside and watching the domestic turmoil raging within, her mother's china shattered on the floor, her panting father being restrained by her mother and brother. Had it always been like this? Had she and her brothers spent their childhoods hiding from their father's rage? Is that where this blackness inside her originated, welling up from deep within and threatening to choke her? Sometimes she worried what would happen if she gave in to it.

'Ma and me will be all right,' said Danny. 'He'll calm down once you're gone. He's worried about our Sammy.'

'You're a good brother, Danny,' she said, backing away from the cottage, knowing there was no haven here, if there ever had been.

'Not good at all. I should have known to keep me mouth shut.'

*

All morning Rose was conscious of the letter buried deep in her apron pocket. A mere wisp of paper, it felt heavier than it should, sharp where its edges were worn soft from the long journey. Sister had handed it to her, shaking her head in disapproval.

'There was one for the young lieutenant too. I shall have to send it back, I suppose,' she said gruffly. 'But I can't think why the family would be writing to you, Nurse.'

'I expect Lieutenant Turner may have mentioned me in his letters, Sister. His family must have sent this before the cable arrived telling them of Henry . . . I mean the lieutenant's . . . death.'

The letter called to her, speaking of Henry and all the other lost boys. She wasn't sure if she wanted to know what it said, whether it was a good idea to be reminded, but curiosity got the better of her. Slipping through a side door during her break, she found a secluded spot beneath a rose bower in the walled garden. The seat was damp from a brief morning shower but she barely noticed, so intent was she on sliding a fingernail under the seal of the envelope and tearing it open.

Inside was a single sheet of paper covered on one side with the same loose, looping writing as the envelope. *Dear Miss Luscombe*, she read, *please forgive me writing to you. I don't want to presume upon your kindness but your care for our Harry encourages me to hope that you will take pity on his brother.*

Rose found she didn't mind Jim Turner's presumption at all. In fact, she rather liked the idea that he would presume upon her. She pictured the strong, brooding figure in Henry's photograph and imagined him sitting by a fire in a rustic study on his picturesque farm, writing these few words to her.

I fear there's more to Harry's wounds than he lets on and wonder if you might be willing to write and tell his mum and me honestly of his condition. He went on to thank her profusely for her time, apologise once more, and hope that she might find it in her heart to write as soon as she had a spare moment.

Their letters had crossed at sea. His, imploring Rose for honesty, hers written in a futile attempt to soften the blow dealt by the dreaded cablegram. She had hoped her letter might prove some consolation. But the Turners were already trudging through the days, burdened by grief. Only time or love could distract them from their loss. She should have known this from the frantic dance she witnessed around her, the speed with which girls snatched up any loose soldier, the eagerness of men to claim a sweetheart for their arm. They were all trying to make up for what had been taken.

That's all her brother was doing, she supposed, snatching the nearest pretty girl. He didn't love Ivy; he was merely looking for distraction. He had told her as much when she tackled him about toying with the help after she witnessed that scene in the garden. Nothing could come of it. Deep in his heart Robert knew that. Just as Rose knew that her words couldn't console Jim Turner for the loss of his brother. There was an ocean between them. But perhaps her attention might distract him from the pain, if only for a moment. Everyone deserved a little distraction.

34

North Devon

2017

'How long have you lived in London, Daisy?' Lucas asked as the four of them sat down to lunch on the terrace.

Richard had brought out the last of the good china for the occasion, a Royal Worcester service in a square Japanese-influenced design, setting it upon a snowy damask cloth. He and Molly had prepared a simple ploughman's lunch with delicious local cheddar and homemade pickles.

'Not long enough!' Daisy laughed. 'I've decided to apply for the ancestry visa so I can stay longer.'

'You didn't tell me that!' said Molly. 'You said you were coming home soon.'

'Can't a girl change her mind?'

Molly thought it more likely that the mystery man her sister was seeing had changed her mind. Love chemicals had infiltrated her brain, clouding her judgement. She had never mentioned applying for the ancestry visa before. She always implied that London was temporary, a gap year grown into two. Maybe that was just her way of avoiding the issue – because they both knew that it would be an issue when Wendy found out. But their grandfather on their father's side had been British and their father had lived in the UK for several years as a young man, so

246

strictly speaking she was eligible. She might be able to swing it if she was prepared to do the legwork.

'You're going to be bogged down in paperwork.' Dealing with bureaucracy was not her sister's forte. 'I hope it's worth it.'

'Oh . . . it will be worth it.'

'Mum won't be happy. Thanks for that.' If Daisy didn't come home Molly would bear the brunt of motherly attention. Wendy would be even more on her case, all the while pretending that she trusted her daughters to choose their own paths in life. *Who . . . me? Interfere?* was her refrain every time Molly rebuked her for checking that she had remembered to renew her car insurance and wasn't eating too much junk food.

'She'll come round. She and Leo will visit me. Oh, I've just had a great idea,' she gasped, turning to Richard, her eyes alight. 'We can have a family reunion here at Luscombe Park. Mum will adore you. And she'll be begging you for the recipe to that beef stew thingy you made last night.'

'It's a long way to come for stew, dear, but I'd love to meet your mother and her husband. It's been so long since I had family around, and now . . .' Richard paused, looking from Molly to Daisy with a tear welling in his eye. 'I've acquired an entire family tree.'

'A veritable forest, it seems,' Lucas quipped cryptically, and Molly turned to stare at him. She supposed any normal person might find her sister overwhelming. She came with so much enthusiasm.

'A eucalypt forest,' said Daisy. 'You'll have to come of course, Lucas, since you're family. Plus I shall take far too many photos and they will definitely need some eye candy.'

'Daisy!'

'You are so PC, Molly. Lucas isn't offended, are you?'

'What man could take offence at being described as eye candy by a beautiful woman?' he said with such a straight face that Molly wasn't sure how to take it.

'There, you see. Now, Lucas, why don't you and Richard show me the gardens, since it was dark when I arrived last night, while Molly clears lunch? Then she and I can start on the attic,' ordered Daisy.

Molly glared but her sister merely gave her a merry smile. She had, after all, solved the problem of clearing up while also managing to monopolise both men at the same time. Who could be offended by such ingenuity? It was clear that Richard was charmed; Daisy had a way about her, as if she were ready for anything that life threw at her. Sometimes her enthusiasm and spontaneity got her into trouble but, one way or another, she always scrambled to safety. She could be exasperating, yet endearing, and Molly had learned a long time ago not to resent it. What was the point? She wouldn't want her sister to be any different. She loved her, even though she sometimes wanted to throttle her.

Of course, that didn't mean she was ready to relinquish *all* her conquests to her sister.

'I'll help you clear up,' Lucas volunteered as Daisy busied herself with Richard, linking an arm through his and helping him to his feet. Lucas took the opportunity to let his hand stray into the back pocket of Molly's jeans and brush against her. She inhaled his woodsy, soapy scent, with undertones of pickle, and resisted the urge to press closer.

'It doesn't matter. It won't take long. Once you get to know her, you'll realise that my sister can be very enthusiastic,' she said, breaking away reluctantly.

'She's certainly . . . um . . . irrepressible. I imagine she might be quite exhausting in large doses.'

'You could say that. Anyway, best not to leave Richard alone with her or they might both get into trouble.'

'Kindred spirits?'

'Must be in the blood.'

'What was all the flirting with Lucas about?' she asked later as she and Daisy tackled the first cardboard box, its sides bulging with photographs and postcards. Daisy had set up her scanner on the trestle table, connected it to Molly's laptop and was busy scanning images of postcards deemed suitable for Richard's entrepreneurial activities.

'What flirting?'

'You know what I mean.'

'I wasn't flirting, I was just being polite.'

'So I suppose when Cleopatra seduced Julius Caesar *and* Mark Anthony, that was just good manners?'

'She probably thought so. Anyway, why would it matter if I flirted with Lucas? You're not interested in him – at least that's what you said.' Daisy looked up from the scanner to consider her sister speculatively. 'Or are you?'

Molly avoided her eyes, suddenly finding the jumble of photographs cascading from a brown manila envelope riveting. Despite this, she felt a rush of embarrassment suffusing her cheeks.

'You are! Come on, out with it. I knew you liked him. I knew I could flush it out.'

'There's nothing to tell. We're just friends.'

'You lying hussy! And don't tell me you're not sleeping with him – the tips of your ears go all red when you're lying. And you blink.'

'I've got dust in my eye.'

'Bulldust.'

'You know me; I don't want to jinx it. I don't want to say anything in case . . . in case . . . I'm only a fling.'

'You a fling? What about him being a fling? But then, you don't fling, do you?'

'No. I have yet to acquire that skill. I need to take lessons from someone,' Molly fired back.

'Very funny. Anyway, I'm impressed. It's good to see you back in the fray.'

'Love isn't a battlefield.'

'No?'

'Let's just concentrate on the postcards for a while, hmm?' Molly said firmly. On the one hand, she would have liked to explore her feelings with her sister; it would take her back to those days when they had lain awake until all hours, trying on boys like sweaters. On the other hand, she was afraid talking about Lucas would make it more real. And real things were so easily crushed.

They worked in silence for a time, Molly sorting through decades of postcards, putting aside those she felt important to the story of Luscombe while handing Daisy those that were mere traveller's tales from long-dead friends and acquaintances. In turn, Daisy put aside for further research any images taken by photographers whose names she recognised. Amongst the postcards Molly found various photographs of family and friends that she carefully placed in another box for archiving and cataloguing.

'Oh my *God*!' She inhaled sharply, in shock at what she was reading.

'What is it?'

She had discovered the postcard amongst a bundle of correspondence tied with a length of greying black lace. Most of the letters were addressed to Mrs Elsie Luscombe, Rose's mother, who died before Richard was born. The postcards had been sent by acquaintances from various corners of the globe in the last decade of the nineteenth century and the early decades of the twentieth. Most featured cruise ships, hotels on the French Riviera or summer homes in Scotland, but this one was different.

Molly scanned the few words on the postcard swiftly before turning it over to stare at the photograph. She had recognised the man in uniform the moment she picked up the card. She was familiar with the First World War tradition of personal postcards. Itinerant photographers and local studios captured images of soldiers in army camps and made the photographs into postcards for the men to send home to loved ones. This particular card was a *Carte Postale* produced in France, featuring a photograph of Richard's father, Captain Robert Luscombe, with a pet terrier perched on his knee. Unsurprising in itself, the words on the back of the card turned everything she knew about Robert and Rose Luscombe on its head.

'It's a postcard from Robert Luscombe, sent from France.'

'To his sister?'

'No . . . to Ivy. Here, read it.'

Daisy took the card from her sister's white-gloved hand, glancing at the image of Robert with his dog. 'I can see the resemblance with Richard,' she mused before turning it over. When she finished reading, the two sisters stared at each other in silent awe.

'I know,' nodded Molly. 'This changes everything.'

'*Until then, my darling, keep me safe in your heart. I remain yours always, Robert,*' Daisy read aloud. 'But if Robert and Ivy were in love, why did she board a ship for Australia?'

Why indeed did Ivy board a ship for Australia? What had happened to tear them apart?

'They could have fallen out of love, I suppose.'

'Or maybe Ivy was only chaperoning Rose and intended to return,' suggested Daisy.

'*Or* Robert may have been a real cad,' said Molly. Noticing her romantic sister's face fall, she added, 'I know you don't like to think so but it happens all the time. Or someone might have prevented them marrying.' There were so many possible reasons.

'I wish we had some way to find out what really happened.'

'You're the history sleuth. Maybe we'll find another clue amongst all this other stuff, if we look hard enough,' said Daisy, throwing up her hands ineffectually.

Molly sighed. 'It's like sifting through sand. Maybe Richard will have a clue.'

She had begun her pilgrimage intent on researching the truth behind her great-grandmother's disappearance, a quest bequeathed to her by her grandmother. Nan had been convinced that Rose ran away. While Molly, in her heart of hearts, suspected that, for whatever reason, she had committed suicide. Now with each clue she unearthed, her connection to her great-grandmother was becoming more real. In a way, she felt she was searching for her own lost self in Rose's journey from young English debutante to a lost soul on a lonely beach, half a world away.

Ivy Toms was part of that puzzle. But she had never been part of the love story. That belonged to Rose and Jim alone. Now it appeared that Ivy had her own love story. And that story was as much a part of the Luscombe legacy as Rose's.

She caught her breath, thinking about those two young girls, hands clasped inside an apron pocket. 'Forever' had not lasted, and neither had togetherness. She wondered if they had shared their secrets, or hidden them from one another. Or perhaps, like she and Daisy, a bit of both. Sharing was a risk, like any other.

Molly needed to know. And she also needed to know why Rose and Ivy's love stories had ended tragically. If nothing else, the knowledge might offer her some guidance. You could learn from the past, even if you couldn't rewrite it.

They found Richard in the downstairs study that had become his bedroom, living room and shrine. He told Molly once that he envied people their mobile homes and bedsits, their cosy one-roomed cottages and beach shacks. There was something comforting about living in a den where he could stretch out his arms and have his entire life within reach. At Luscombe there were so many rooms full of other people's memories that he was in danger of losing himself. Then he apologised for his ingratitude. Life had bestowed so much on him, with very little effort on his part, he said. He didn't mean to sound ungrateful but it sucked getting old, as the young would say.

She understood his feelings. She could inhale the past at Luscombe Park.

She tapped on the doorframe – for he rarely closed his door – and the two sisters entered to his breezy, 'Come in.'

She wasn't certain how to broach the subject of Ivy and Robert, but Daisy solved that conundrum by launching straight in.

'Richard, guess what we found up in your squirrel's nest?'

'Dare I ask? Should we set more traps?'

'No,' she laughed, 'nothing like that, though I think something has nibbled through the corner of one box. No, this secret has nothing to do with vermin.'

'A secret? How intriguing. I do love gossip. Don't get out enough these days to hear any, but Dev and I entertained for years on opera gossip.'

'I love gossip too. Molly teases me for reading trashy celebrity magazines but I find them riveting.'

'I'm sure I'd read them too if I knew who any of the people were. Unfortunately, there's no market for gossip about dead people, is there?' he observed.

'I think they call it a biopic,' said Molly. 'Gossip dressed up as history.'

'So, what gossip have you found at Luscombe of which I am unaware?'

They looked at each other, deciding silently who would tell.

'Molly found a postcard your father sent from France during

the First World War, a picture of Robert with a fox terrier on his lap.

At her words, his face crinkled. 'Ah, that would be Charlie. Dead and buried in the rose garden long before I was born, but Father used to reminisce about that little ratter.'

'Yes, well, the postcard was addressed to Ivy, not Rose,' Molly elaborated. 'And it suggested that . . . they were fond of each other.'

'I believe Father was fond of Ivy. Even decades later, he would mention her. I think he blamed himself in some way for her getting the Spanish flu. He was the one who encouraged her to accompany Aunt Rose to Australia, you see.'

Did he? Now that was strange, given his words on the postcard.

'He was more than fond of her. It sounded like they were in love,' said Daisy.

Richard didn't say anything for a moment. Molly wondered whether he had heard her words. Then he gave his head a small shake, saying, 'That would explain it, why Father felt her loss so keenly. Why he waited more than ten years to marry after the war. It might also explain why he and Aunt Rose had their falling out.'

He turned away and shuffled over to a tall dresser near his bed. The dresser was crowded with a veritable gallery of photo frames, a shrine to his long, full life. He picked up one of the larger photographs in a dark wood frame and handed it to Daisy.

'It's a photograph of the family and staff taken on the front terrace in 1917. My father and Aunt Rose are standing behind my grandmother, who is seated. Greep, the butler, stands next to Aunt Rose, and Ivy stands beside Father. Mrs Tucker, the housekeeper, and Miss Gibbons, Grandmother's maid, are next in line and so on down through the ranks of servants to the scullery maid and the hall boy,' he explained. 'I always thought it was strange.'

'What?' asked Molly, peering at the photograph with sleuth-like intensity.

'Well firstly, because I would have expected the housekeeper, as the senior female member of staff, to stand next to my father, not his sister's maid. And secondly, I wondered why he kept a photograph of the servants close at hand. I always assumed it was because it represented a time before the house and family were in decline. But perhaps I was mistaken. Perhaps it's the only photograph he possessed where he and Ivy stand shoulder to shoulder.'

He had that faraway look again, and Molly could see that the photograph had taken him back to a place where he could wander freely amongst his memories. Perhaps he was thinking about Dev, his father and mother, and all the other people he had lost along the way. Or perhaps he was reliving some happier event. Often the past was so pervasive that it touched every aspect of your life. And perhaps as you grew older it became ever more comfortable than the present.

She returned her gaze to the photograph in Daisy's hands, considering the main characters in the story: Rose, Robert and Ivy. They stood shoulder to shoulder behind the matriarch of the house, Rose and Robert of a similar height, looking like they belonged, with Ivy in her simple dark dress looking out of place beside them. She realised there was something wrong with the picture that she couldn't put her finger on. Something out of kilter that she couldn't quite decipher. But she would.

She was as determined as that little girl standing on a chair refusing to eat her peas.

35

North Devon

1918

Rose was in the library when Greep entered with the letter that would change her life. She was deep in *Lord Tony's Wife*, the latest instalment of Baroness Orczy's Pimpernel series, and had just read the page where the peasant Pierre threatens to kiss Yvonne on the lips as punishment for being the daughter of the brutal tyrant Duc de Kernogan, when Greep entered bearing that morning's post. The butler seemed weighed down by the letters, his spindly frame almost creaking as he bent to offer Rose the salver. It occurred to her that he was getting old, that he should have been settled in a cottage somewhere to live out his days pottering in his vegetable patch. The war was a thief, stealing Greep's retirement as surely as it had stolen Henry Turner's life.

'The post, miss.'

'Thank you, Greep.' She was barely able to refrain from ripping open the top envelope when she recognised the writing. She and Jim had been writing for a year, yet her excitement grew with each delivery of post. His words were the one thing in her life that couldn't be rationed or wounded or stolen from her.

'Will there be anything else, miss?'

She looked up to find the trace of a smile in his eyes. He knew. He knew letters from Australia had been arriving with remarkable

256

regularity. He would be as familiar with the bold looping strokes on the envelope as she. Did he wonder about the correspondent? Ponder the nature of their relationship? Rose found herself resenting his knowledge. Jim was *her* secret. She didn't know where it might lead but she could dream. She could imagine a different life where there was no war, no army of servants anticipating her needs before she knew them herself, making her choices before she voiced them. A life that would be what *she* made it, not what the weight of her family's history made it.

While her friendship with Jim remained a secret, it could be anything she wanted it to be.

'That will be all, thank you, Greep.'

Still he hovered, straightening a stack of books, repositioning a lamp with obsessive care.

'Is there something else?'

'No, Miss Rose. That is, I observed that you have *several* letters, this morning.'

She had eyes for one letter only. She hadn't bothered flipping through the others. However, he was clearly waiting for something. Tearing her attention from the precious envelope, she sifted through the others while he watched. There was a communication from her dressmaker, a postcard from Cissy who was holidaying in Scotland, and a letter addressed to Ivy, bearing the familiar phrase 'Passed by Censor' in lieu of a stamp.

'There seems to be a mistake. This letter is addressed to Ivy.'

'I'm sorry, miss,' he croaked. 'That would be from Miss Toms' *regular* correspondent. I must have placed it with your post in error.'

Ivy had a regular correspondent, did she? Who would be writing to her maid regularly? The girl never went anywhere. And the missive was from the western front by the look of the envelope. Rose might have suspected the conniving baggage of corresponding with Robert, except this wasn't his handwriting.

She made to return the letter to Greep but he didn't extend the salver to receive it, nor did he hold out his hand.

She frowned, suggesting tentatively, 'Perhaps I should . . . ah . . . give Ivy the letter myself?'

'Excellent suggestion, miss,' he nodded approvingly. She had the distinct impression that, if he dared, he might have winked. 'I shall leave it safely in your hands then.'

When Greep departed, Rose was torn between opening the letter from Jim or discovering what her maid was up to. Despite her desire to curl up with her letter, snooping won out. Ivy's envelope was scrawled in an unfamiliar hand, the script sloping backwards and forwards in an untidy fashion, and it felt stiff, as if it contained a postcard rather than the frail leaves of a letter. Why would someone enclose a postcard in an envelope, she wondered . . . unless they were trying to conceal something?

She felt no compunction about slitting the envelope with her ivory letter opener. After all, Ivy would never know, for she had no intention of passing it on. She withdrew the rectangle of card and perused the photograph on the front. It showed a seated soldier, a captain, with a fox terrier on his knee, both dog and man smiling. A sign propped by the man's feet read 'Somewhere in France' and tendrils of rose climbed a wall in the background. But this wasn't just any soldier. This was her brother.

Flipping over the card, she read the printed words *Carte Postale* and beneath these, in her brother's handwriting, she read aloud the words, 'My darling Ivy . . .'

She gasped, her breath catching on the words like barbs hooking her throat. *My darling Ivy.* Three small words causing a world of consternation. All this time she had thought the incident she observed in the park a year ago was an aberration, a moment of indiscretion that would go no further. That's what Robert had told her when she confronted him, the night before he left Luscombe after that last leave.

'It was nothing, Chicken. Ivy is a pretty girl, what man could resist a stolen kiss? She's a sensible lass, she knows there can be nothing further,' he had said, throwing a casual arm about her waist as if she were still a little girl whose worries could be placated with a peck on the cheek. And Rose had believed him. Believed Ivy's air of unconcern, the unctuous words that belied her sneakiness. And all the time . . .

Meet Charlie, the newest member of our unit – a most excellent ratter – and the darling of the regiment. One day I shall bring him home to you. Word is that it won't be long now. Until then, my darling, keep me safe in your heart. I remain yours always, Robert.

She shouldn't have minded, she supposed. The war had thrown all notions of the world up in the air to land willy-nilly. Men died with alarming regularity, women drove delivery vans and duchesses swabbed wounds. The rules had changed. Why should the rules of love be any different? Yet they were. The idea that her brother should love her maid was unthinkable. The image of that foxy face adorned with the Luscombe pearls brought bile to her throat. It wasn't the realisation that her brother loved a servant that incensed Rose; it was that he loved *Ivy*, the girl who had inveigled her way into her life and stolen her brother. The girl who would steal Luscombe and all its history if she could get her hands on it, steal it away from the kind of girl who *should* become Robert's wife, a girl who understood him, a girl who would love him for himself and not what he could give her. A girl much like Rose.

She knew she should have compassion for Ivy – and she would, if the dreadful girl had stayed out of her life. But somehow, in her dull stoic way, Ivy was getting what she wanted whereas Rose was stuck here at Luscombe Park, with no foreseeable way forward. Robert was deluded if he thought Ivy loved him, for clearly she had eyes on his fortune. Well, if her brother was too love-addled to look out for his own interests, Rose would have to do it for him. She could never, ever allow him to marry Ivy. The mere idea was preposterous.

'Maman?' Rose tapped on Elsie's door.

The servants were at tea, so Gibbons wouldn't appear to dress her mistress for a while. Gibbons made the pretence of dressing her mother every evening, but increasingly Rose ate alone at the small breakfast table in the drawing room while her mother ate from a tray in her room.

She half expected her mother to be asleep but after several moments a breathy voice answered, 'Rose? Is that you?'

'Yes, Maman, may I come in?'

'Certainly, *chérie*.'

Schooling her face into the bland expression she habitually wore when visiting her mother, Rose entered, but for once Elsie was vertical rather than horizontal. She was standing in her dressing room in the middle of a heap of discarded clothes. Silks, taffetas, velvets and voiles lay in a muddle of padded clothes hangers and evening shoes.

'I can't find anything to wear this evening. What do you think of this?' Her mother pirouetted, the effect losing some of its elegance as her foot tangled in an evening coat lying in a puddle of velvet on the floor. Maman might not be lucid much of the time, and she rarely ventured outside the house, but that didn't prevent her from ordering new clothes.

'It's lovely.'

It was lovely, if a trifle short for a woman of almost fifty years. But the French had decreed less material must be used, so what could one do? Any fashionable woman followed the French. The gown was a loose, ivory silk kimono with flowing black cuffs and trailing black hem, beautifully simple and elegant. Adorning her mother's neck was the double choker of lustrous pearls that had been in the family for at least a century. Rose thought that both the gown and the pearls would look exquisite on her.

'I had it copied from a design by the Callot Soeurs. I'll be so glad when this dreadful war ends. Perhaps we may go shopping in Paris.'

'Maman, there's something I must tell you.'

'Are you going out this evening?'

'It's about Ivy.'

'Oh, that abominable girl, is she still here?' Elsie hadn't taken an interest in the running of the household for years. Mrs Tucker and Greep managed everything between them. 'I don't know why your brother insisted we employ her.'

'She saved you from being run down by a horse. Don't you remember?'

Her mother blinked before sighing heavily. 'Your father should have let me dismiss her and none of this would have happened.'

None of what, Rose wondered. Did her mother know about Robert and Ivy already? Or was she dwelling in the past again? She had a habit of talking about Rose's father as if he were still alive. She also liked to twitter on about the postcards she received from various acquaintances as if she had seen her correspondents only last week, when in reality Rose could count on one hand the visits her mother had made since the war began.

'No, it was Robert, Robert wouldn't let you dismiss her.'

'Robert? That's right.'

'Robert is in love with Ivy. He's been writing to her,' she said, handing her mother the postcard. 'I think he means to marry her after the war.'

She closed her eyes to block out the image of Robert and Ivy holding hands. When she opened them she realised that her mother had turned white. Rose thought she might be about to faint or even worse . . . vomit. But Elsie managed to steady herself by grasping the edge of a sturdy chest of drawers.

'I would dismiss her but, knowing the cunning little sneak, she will write to tell him. Then he'll become even more protective and we will never be rid of her.' Rose knew her brother, knew how loyal he was. She could dismiss Ivy but he would find another place for her, one that might be more insufferable. 'We have to find some way of persuading her to leave of her own volition. Perhaps we could pay her off . . . Maman?'

Her mother had become so vague that Rose wasn't sure that she could count on her. She feared that Elsie no longer had the strength to fight Ivy. The maid had got her claws into her brother and without help Rose didn't know how she could prise them loose. However, the faraway look in Elsie's eyes vanished, to be replaced by a gleam of determination. Perhaps her mother was stronger than she imagined.

'What do you think? Should we pay her off?' Or perhaps they should let nature take its course and wait for Robert to tire of her. Except the consequences might be catastrophic if he didn't.

'No. No,' whispered Elsie, grabbing her daughter's hand and pulling her close so that Rose caught the sweet fruity scent of her breath. 'No, it can't be. Don't worry,' she said, nodding several times, her eyes wild. 'It won't happen. When Robert returns, I'll put a stop to it, you'll see.

'He will never marry her.'

36

North Devon

2017

Molly woke in the middle of the night, her head buzzing with thoughts of Robert, Rose and Ivy. They had pursued her all evening and now wouldn't leave her alone in sleep. Even Lucas's compelling company late last night had only silenced them for a while. She sat up in bed, then wandered over to the window overlooking the south lawn where the photograph of the Luscombe family and staff had been taken. There was little to be seen in the wan moonlight other than shadowy trees and midnight-blue sky. For some reason, she couldn't shake the staff portrait from her head. She kept imagining Robert, Rose and Ivy as an isosceles triangle: two equal sides with a third, unequal side; the rich, aristocratic Luscombes and the lady's maid forming their own peculiar triumvirate.

Rose and Ivy are friends. Robert and Ivy are lovers. Rose and Ivy set out for Australia. Ivy dies en route, in Colombo. Forty years later, Rose disappears a few days before her brother visits. Sister and brother never meet again.

It just didn't make sense – of Jim's letters, or Robert's postcard, or the photographs. What had broken the triangle apart? She couldn't shake the bleakness of it from her head. Ivy loses Robert. Rose loses Ivy. Then despite their blood tie, Rose and Robert lose each other. And why did she keep seeing that photograph of the family and staff when she closed her eyes? It was as if her subconscious was telling her something. A photograph of the tall, elegant Luscombe siblings, their pretty little maid standing between them – an isosceles triangle.

Two equal sides and a . . . and a . . .

Of course, why hadn't she seen it before? How could she have missed it? Something Uncle Ted had said so many months ago now, something that hadn't registered at the time. But now . . .

Groping towards the chair by her bed, she scrabbled for her phone in the dark. She hit a button and the phone lit up to show the glowing time. Four o'clock. That meant it would be two o'clock in the afternoon at home. Brian and Joan would be finishing lunch in the kitchen at Wuurnong, the perfect time to catch Uncle Ted awake. Then, if her theory was correct, her great-grandmother's story might assume a completely different complexion.

The next morning, a bleary-eyed Molly found her sister and Richard sitting at the large oak table, shuffling postcards over tea and toast.

'I couldn't find the white gloves,' Daisy said, dropping the postcards to surreptitiously wipe jammy crumbs from her hands.

'What?'

'To sort the postcards.'

'Daisy and I are deciding the best way to sell the postcards,' Richard said happily.

'You know a lot of the cards upstairs are actually real photo cards or hand-tinted lithographs,' Daisy said, flashing a picture of a sepia-toned street scene in front of her face. 'There are so many of them that Richard might do better to sell them through an auction house. An enthusiast might purchase the entire collection at a premium. I could take them to London with me for an appraisal.'

'That's a great idea, if Richard thinks it best.'

'And you've put aside the ones you think we should keep in the Luscombe archive?' Richard asked.

'Uh-huh. You know, Richard, there's something I need to talk to you about, you and Lucas, something important. So I wondered if we could all get together this afternoon before Daisy returns to London.'

'That sounds ominous, dear. You're not leaving us, are you?' he asked with a frown.

'Well, I have to leave eventually. But no, not quite yet. This is about the Luscombes. I think I've discovered something unexpected.'

'Well, spill,' said Daisy, rolling her eyes.

'When Lucas gets here. I sent him a message as soon as I woke up. He's coming over after lunch.'

'You can't tell us you have big news and then say we have to wait,' Daisy complained.

'Yes, I can. They do it all the time on TV.'

Robert and Ivy had been waiting so long for their story to be told, they could wait a little longer. Molly felt the excitement of discovery fizzing inside her, like a bottle of champagne waiting to be popped. And then, maybe, they could all celebrate. Or drown their sorrows. It depended on which way you looked at it, really.

Molly and Lucas sat side by side on a worn Art Deco sofa in the drawing room, the sagging springs a good excuse to lean closer together. The drawing room was her favourite – and the only room, other than the study and kitchen, that Richard regularly used. It was long, with an east-facing bay window and French doors opening on to the terrace, and a further door leading to the adjoining library. The walls were lined with honey-hued timber panelling and although the floors were scuffed from decades of traffic, they still bore a warm glow. Richard sat opposite them in his favourite armchair, while Daisy was curled up on the other sofa. All eyes were focused on Molly, the little tableau rather like a theatre set, where the main characters await a dénouement from the protagonist.

She risked a fleeting glance at Lucas. His profile looked different from this side, she realised, the nose slightly more hooked, the eyebrow thicker. How had she so quickly grown accustomed to waking up next to him that she could discern a tiny difference in profile? He sat with his legs slightly apart so that one thigh rested against hers, making her conscious of his every shift of position. If they had been alone, she would have leaned into him.

'Okay,' said Daisy, 'what gives?'

Molly cleared her throat, looked from Richard to Lucas. She wondered how Richard was going to take her announcement. It was all so long ago now, perhaps it wouldn't mean much to anyone other than her. She was the one who had embarked on her grandmother's quest. She was the one who had chosen to entwine her life with the lives of two young women born more than a century ago. Until she arrived at Luscombe Park, no one had thought to question the women's stories. They had each been part of their own family histories. The Luscombes and the Toms. No one had thought to link them. Now, in fate's ironic fashion, she found herself linked to both families. She had found the hidden link between Rose and Ivy, a link that the writer of those words 'Together forever' must have known.

'Okay. This may sound a bit far-fetched but here goes. I guess I must have started thinking about this subconsciously after you showed us that photograph of the staff and family,' she began, turning to address Richard. 'And then I woke up in the middle of the night and decided to call Mum's cousin Brian and her Uncle Ted.'

'Why would you call Great-Uncle Ted?' asked Daisy, a puzzled frown creasing her forehead.

'Because he should remember his mother. And if he couldn't recall her clearly, I thought Brian might. I wanted to ask how tall Rose was.'

Lucas turned to look at her, his shoulder brushing hers. While Richard tapped unconsciously at the arm of his chair.

'Richard, how tall are you?'

'I believe I was six foot one in my prime but I daresay I've shrunk. Time has a way of reducing everyone.'

'And your father?'

'A fraction shorter.'

'That's what I thought. If you study the staff photograph, you'll see that Richard and Rose tower over everyone in the photo except for the footman. Rose must be touching five foot nine or ten, since I doubt she was wearing six-inch heels in 1917, whereas Ivy barely reaches Robert's shoulder. She would be no taller than five foot one, or two, at the most.'

She turned to find Lucas staring at her, his lips parted in realisation. He had already worked out where this was going.

'And how tall did your Uncle Ted say his mother was?' he asked.

'He couldn't recall exactly but he thought she couldn't have been very tall. He remembered her scolding him for using her shoulder as an arm rest.'

'What have Rose and Ivy's height got to do with anything?' asked Daisy.

'The thing about Ivy is I don't think she died in Colombo,' Molly said, gazing around her circle of avid listeners.

Daisy blinked in confusion and ran a hand through her mop of curls. 'What are you saying exactly? I'm not following.'

'I think Rose was the one who died of Spanish flu in Colombo on the way to Australia and that for whatever reason . . . Ivy took her place.'

For a momentary breath no one spoke. Molly's revelation had swallowed all sound, even the rustle of leaves against the windows. Each of them seemed to be testing her words to see if they had heard true. She had been wrestling with this idea since the early hours of the morning, so small wonder it should come as a surprise to the others. They needed time to absorb it. It was Richard who concerned her most. Rose was his aunt, and although he had never met her, it might come as a shock to think that she died long before he was born. If he had thought about her at all, he would have imagined her living a different life with her family in Australia. She was like an echo of the Luscombe family, faint and far away, and when she died the echo slowly faded through the following generations. Molly's revelation meant there wasn't even an echo. The real Rose had never welcomed children and grandchildren into the world. She had died, ill and childless, in Sri Lanka.

Molly wasn't sure what her theory meant for Lucas. Would it mean anything for him to think that his great-aunt might not have died of Spanish flu in Colombo nearly a century ago? That she had appropriated another woman's life? Would it matter to him that she went on to have children and grandchildren and then drowned, forty years later, on a wild ocean beach half a world away? It had been a momentous discovery for Molly. It shifted her entire understanding of her family's story. But she wasn't sure how it would affect Richard or Lucas.

'But in the portrait of Rose and Ivy that you showed me, I don't recall them looking greatly different in height,' Richard said croakily.

'Apple boxes,' Daisy answered for her, 'or something like them. Photographers often use boxes to stand people or props

268

on, or if they want to make someone appear taller. They're standard equipment for the grip on a movie set. They come in full apple, half apple, quarter apple and pancake.'

'Apple boxes . . .' he murmured, his face crumpling like a paper bag so that it was all creases. 'But if Aunt Rose died in Colombo and Ivy took her place . . . that means we're not related.'

Molly had been so intent on her discovery, so taken with finding another piece of the puzzle, that she hadn't truly thought through this aspect of her epiphany. She had been concerned about how Richard would take rearranging his perception of the past; she hadn't considered how he might have to rearrange his present. She hadn't taken into account how quickly he had become attached to her and the idea of family, however distant. She hadn't realised that he might feel he was losing that one small thread of family he had rediscovered.

'You're right, it does,' she answered. 'I'm sorry . . .'

The last thing she wanted to do was hurt Richard, but she wasn't sure how she could fix this. Ivy had set these events in motion a century ago. She had merely found the puzzle pieces and put them together.

'Richard, family is what you make it,' Daisy said quietly. 'Lucas is more family to you than we are. You've known him since he was born. We like you and we would love to visit you. But we don't have to be connected by blood to be friends.'

Richard frowned, his mouth turning down at the sides. 'Before I met you, Molly, I had never thought to look into Aunt Rose's descendants. My father returned from his trip to Australia very despondent and died not long after. He refused to talk about the trip, other than to say Rose was dead. And I was too busy enjoying life at the time to pay much attention.'

'You never met her, so she probably didn't mean much to you.'

'No. And I was still relatively young and selfish, and having enough adventures of my own not to be upset about her death. But after you showed up, the connection became real. I rather liked the idea of having all those cousins out in Australia. I didn't need to meet them, just knowing they were there . . .' he trailed off.

She could understand that. For a man without children, without descendants of any kind, it would be comforting to know there was a thin tendril of the Luscombe family reaching out into the world somewhere.

Lucas had been silent this whole while and she wondered what he was thinking. His face was very still, the same way it got when he was struggling with a design problem. She knew him well enough now to realise that he was wrestling with something.

'Lucas? What do you think?'

He picked up the hand that was resting on her leg and cradled it in his. Then he took a deep breath and looked down at his feet.

'Ivy couldn't have taken Rose's place, because you're almost certainly related to Rose,' he said, speaking to his shoes.

'What do you mean? How can you know that?'

'Because I had your DNA tested. I had your DNA compared with Richard's.'

'What!'

'The results came back last week. There's a greater than ninety per cent probability of accurate genetic matching between third cousins and closer. And the results suggest that you and Richard have a predicted relationship range of second to fourth cousins – most likely third – which would be correct if Rose was your great-grandmother.'

All the attention in the room now centred on Lucas, Daisy staring at him with a disbelieving expression as if she had suddenly found herself in one of those television dramas where actors make improbable announcements against the background of a portentous musical score. Richard leaned forward, his hands sliding to the front of the chair's arms to prop himself up. Molly felt as if her expression was frozen in place. Lucas raised his eyes to hers.

'I don't understand,' she murmured.

'I plucked a hair from your head that first day in the attic. And sorry, Richard, but I stole your toothbrush,' he explained. 'You're supposed to take mouth swabs but . . .'

'Mouth swabs,' she repeated, as if the concept was so alien that only repetition could make it intelligible.

'I'm sorry. I wish I could take it back. Now that I know you.'

'Why would you do that?'

He gazed out of the window as if searching for an answer. But what possible answer could he find for such betrayal?

'You arrived out of nowhere with a story of being long-lost family, and Richard invited you into his home, into his life. He didn't know you from a bar of soap . . .' He looked to her for reassurance of some kind, but she remained silent, unwilling to give him anything. 'He's my friend. I was trying to protect him.'

'Protect him from me?' Why would Richard need protection from her? They were friends.

'But what about the difference in height?' Daisy asked. 'Did Rose shrink?'

'Your Uncle Ted must have been mistaken. A tall young man hugging his old mum . . . you know. Rose has been dead for fifty years so . . .' Lucas trailed off.

Molly slipped her hand from Lucas's, trying to keep her voice steady as she said, 'Do you think I'm a gold digger? That I'm going to worm my way into an old man's heart, marry him and take all his money? Well, that is so wrong on so many counts.'

'Not least being that you're a woman,' said Richard, 'but charming, of course.'

'How could you think that of me?'

'I didn't want to, but it was before I knew you. It was a kind of insurance, just in case,' said Lucas. 'There are so many con artists out there who prey on older, vulnerable people.'

'Now hold on, old man, I think I'm quite capable of looking after myself. Though I appreciate the sentiment,' said Richard, shaking his head indignantly.

Had Lucas been protecting Richard's interests or his own interests, since Richard had no heirs? It was a nasty thought – but of course, if that were true, Lucas wouldn't be speaking up now. He would let Richard believe that Molly and Daisy and their whole tribe were no relations at all. No, Lucas may have betrayed her trust but he hadn't betrayed Richard's.

She coughed. She could feel something jagged catching in her throat and hot tears of rage welling in her eyes. 'You know me now,' she said.

Daisy looked across the room at her sister and the man next to her and shook her head sadly. 'You shouldn't have told her. Honesty isn't always the best policy. That's just an old wives' tale.'

'It means so much to Richard. Having family. I could see that, and I couldn't take it away from him. Despite everyone being mad with me.' Lucas heaved a great sigh, bowing his head.

'But you could take my trust away from me,' Molly said.

'I didn't know what was going to happen between us. I tried to keep a certain distance, but who can fight fate?' he said, raising his hands in a gesture of surrender.

'I can.'

Summoning all her strength, she forced her traitorous legs to stand, walk across the room and out the door. She didn't let herself look back. If she looked back and saw him sitting there with that empty place beside him on the sofa, that place that should belong to her, she might weaken. She might allow herself to be persuaded. She had taken a risk in letting him into her life, and look what had happened. He had betrayed her trust. More than that, she had betrayed her own quest to rediscover her strength. She had let Lucas fill the void, instead of figuring it out herself. If she turned back and listened to his excuses, she might never rediscover her own power, her own strength.

No matter how painful – or how much she might miss them – she realised that in order to find herself she would have to let Lucas and all the Luscombes go.

37

The attic was besieged by a whirlwind of activity. Molly was immersed in a maelstrom of paper. She had boxes, folders and sheaves of all sizes stacked about the room and was sorting them with a wild-eyed urgency.

'What are you doing?' asked Daisy, leaning against the door jamb with her arms crossed.

'I'm getting this finished. Well, at least getting as much as possible into some semblance of order. Then I'm going to transfer all the boxes to the library. And then I'm going home.'

'Lucas is downstairs. Again.'

'Is he?' He had turned up at least twice that she knew of since the scene in the drawing room yesterday afternoon. 'I thought you were returning to London last night,' she remarked, knowing her sister would realise that she really meant, 'Go away and leave me alone.'

'I decided to stay a bit longer and see if I could talk some sense into you.'

'You needn't bother. Because A: after deluding myself for the past six weeks, I have finally come to my senses. And B: no matter how long you stay, I won't change my mind.'

'But what about Richard, he's counting on you to complete the archive.'

'Well, he shouldn't count on me. I can't be counted on. I let people down. Besides, I told him from the start that I didn't know how long I could stay,' Molly said, trying not to let her voice grow shrill but not making a very good job of it.

'You're one of the most reliable people I know. I'm the one who's unreliable – ask Mum.'

'Huh, just goes to show you don't know me as well as you think you do. Anyway, Richard will be okay. I'll Skype him. He's pretty savvy with a computer when you show him how. And we can email. Maybe I'll get him started on Facebook. Then he can befriend the whole Turner clan. He'd like that.'

'Yes, but he'll miss *you*.'

'I know,' sighed Molly, 'and I'll miss him. But you'll come and visit him every now and then. Mum and Leo can make the trip to Devon when they fly to London to see you. And I'll come back . . . one day.' She couldn't help the slight quiver in her voice as she added, 'And then, of course, he has all the Toms.'

'I see. You have it all worked out. And what about you and Lucas?'

'There is no me and Lucas.'

She didn't want to think about Lucas. It wasn't only that he had betrayed her trust; more importantly, it was that she had deceived herself. She had actually begun to believe that she could shrug off the past, that she could redeem herself. But this was mere sleight of hand. Why should she be allowed to find someone who complemented and understood her? Why should she be gifted a career that challenged and intrigued her? It was all too easy.

When she first met Matt she thought she had found a safe harbour. And indeed she had been safe for a time. But she now realised it had come at a cost to both of them. Neither of them had found a partner who understood their dreams or fears. They had both compromised too much: Molly, because she was afraid to cut herself loose; and Matt, because it was convenient. She couldn't afford to fall into that trap again. Safety wasn't everything. She had learned that at least.

'He'll be okay. It was only a few weeks, after all.'

'Weeks, schmeeks. You know as well as I do that time is meaningless when it comes to love.'

'Who said anything about love? It was only sex.'

'Say it often enough and you might believe it. You know what your problem is?'

'No, but clearly you're about to tell me.'

'You're afraid to risk your heart . . . and don't give me the drivel that you risked your heart with Matt and look what happened,' she added when she saw Molly about to open her mouth in protest, 'because we both know that you didn't really love Matt, not deeply and truly, with your whole heart. But you did feel safe with him.'

'I did so love him,' said Molly, falling back into their old childhood pattern of argument. If you can't convince, deny, deny, deny.

She could picture Matt now as clearly as if he stood at Daisy's side: the long straggly hair bleached by the sun, the freckles scattered across his nose, the patches of skin peeling from his shoulders, the strength in his arms . . . She *had* wanted him to save her, she realised, just like that young surfer who had saved her so long ago. Jake. His name had been Jake. She remembered Jake covering her body with his and setting out for the shore. She remembered her dad in the distance, a lone figure with his hand raised. Was he beckoning, or waving, or hailing someone on the beach? The image was there, flickering on the periphery of her memory, if she could just catch it in her mind's eye. And then Jake was paddling harder, catching the wave that would carry her to safety, leaving her father to the mercy of the rip that would claim his life.

Yes, she had wanted Matt to save her. She had wanted him to fill the emptiness inside her. Except she was a woman now, and this was her life. No one else could save her. She had to save herself.

'You still believe that you don't deserve love,' said Daisy, her arms swiping at the air in frustration.

'Phwah!'

'That was articulate.'

'It's not true.' Her sister didn't understand.

'Yes, it is. Mum can't convince you otherwise. I can't convince you. Only you can convince yourself. So what if your heart takes a beating in the process? It won't break. Hearts are tougher than that. You're tougher than that.'

'It's not about love! Don't you understand? Not everything is about love.'

'What's it about, then? Why are you running away from Lucas?' asked Daisy, shaking her head. 'I don't believe it's because of the DNA test.'

'I'm not running away from him. I'm running away from myself.' Or to be precise, she was running away from the self who always took the easy way out, the self who was tempted to remain in this warm, comfortable environment, sorting Richard's fascinating archive and allowing herself to fall for a warm, albeit fallible man. It wasn't that she didn't deserve a happy life; it was that she hadn't earned it yet. If she grasped the first safe proposition that came along, she would just end up back where she started.

Daisy blinked at her in confusion. She looked so like her younger self, perplexed at her big sister not wanting to go on the fastest ride at the Royal Show, too cautious to ride a dirt bike on their cousin's farm. How could she understand Molly's constant battle with fear and self-loathing when she was so easy in her own skin?

'You're right, I don't understand.'

'You're happy with yourself. You like yourself. No matter what happens, you manage to get on with life. You don't beat yourself up over mistakes; you don't second-guess your decisions. I'm still trying to work all that out,' she said, delving into the nearest box as if the answers to her life could be found there amongst the postcards.

But Daisy wasn't about to let her get away with that grand pronouncement. They were sisters, after all. She covered the distance between them so quickly she might have been a cat pouncing, squatting so that they were eye to eye, whisker to whisker.

'You think I don't struggle with self-belief? You think it's easy for me? I've wanted to come home to Melbourne so many times – when I'm broke, when I don't know where my next job is coming from, when I think my work is crap – but I haven't. And do you know why?'

Molly hadn't seen her sister this worked up for a long time. Usually, even when they were fighting, Daisy had a gleam of amusement in her eye. But not now. In answer to her sister's question she could only shake her head.

'I could invoke some psychobabble about losing my father young and trying to fill that void with experiences, but the truth is I haven't come home because I knew I had to prove myself. At home I could skate by, knowing you and Mum and Leo were always there to pick up the pieces. At home I was the baby, but here I have to survive alone. I've had to learn to be strong, to be organised, to make better decisions.'

'I thought you stayed because you were having fun.'

'Just goes to show you don't know me as well as you think you do,' said Daisy, echoing her sister. 'You don't have a monopoly on loss.'

'I know you lost Dad too, but it wasn't your fault.' No matter how much time passed, it would always be Molly's fault.

Daisy didn't have to live with the knowledge that she had caused her father's death. She was allowed to wake up the morning after he drowned and ask her mother, 'But who's going to take me to netball on Saturday?' as if life could continue normally.

'You didn't lose yourself too,' Molly added, staring into those eyes, so like their father's.

'Why do you think I spent my growing-up years changing my boyfriend more often than my toothbrush? Did you really think I was that shallow?' Daisy stood up, brushed the dust from her jeans and turned for the door without a backward glance, as if she was wiping her metaphorical hands of her sister.

Molly listened to her footsteps as she stomped down the attic stairs. Daisy had never walked out on her before. She had thrown hairbrushes and punched her once or twice when she was too young to do much damage, but until now she hadn't turned her back. Molly knew she should go after her and make amends, but she couldn't find the strength in her legs to stand, let alone run. Daisy was right to abandon her.

She was also right in thinking that if Molly forgave Lucas, stayed and continued cataloguing the Luscombe archive, she would make Richard happy, she would probably make Lucas happy, she might even make herself happy. But for how long . . . sooner or later, Lucas would find her out.

Daisy thought that Molly was running away from love; that she believed she didn't deserve love. Yet that was only partly true. She wasn't running away. She was lurching towards something – some vague, shadowy version of herself, even if she wasn't sure yet who she might be, even if she had setbacks along the way. And she could only do this by going home, facing her fears, finding her place in the world and becoming the woman she was capable of being.

Becoming the daughter to make her father proud.

Becoming the woman to make herself proud.

38

North Devon

1918

The house held its breath, waiting for its master to arrive. Although it was only ten o'clock, the staff had already changed into their afternoon uniforms. Donaldson had departed earlier to pick her brother up from Braunton Station, and the entire household now gathered in the hall waiting for the crunch of tyres on gravel that would herald his homecoming. For the first time in as long as Rose could remember, Luscombe wore a festive air. Greep had ordered the hall to be decorated with red, white and blue bunting, and several occasional tables had been draped in flags. Even her mother had made an appearance, propped upright in a tapestry-covered chair with carved wooden arms. Usually Elsie drifted about in a half-dazed fog of confusion but today her eyes were clearer than Rose had seen them for months. Her hard-eyed gaze kept returning to Ivy, who stood straight and silent, as close to the door as she could manage without pushing Rose or Greep out of the way.

The girl had thrown off her habitual surly expression, her mouth curving in that self-satisfied half-smile of hers. Her hair shone like burnished chestnut in the light of the electric lamps, for it was a grey autumn morning outside, and her skin glowed as if from some internal heat – Rose could guess what kind –

whereas anger and resentment simmered just below Rose's surface calm. Why should Ivy act as if Robert was coming home to her? He was Rose's brother and Elsie Luscombe's son. He was returning to them. Yet Ivy seemed poised on the edge of a barely suppressed excitement, her weight leaning slightly forward on her toes. And as they heard the soft growl of an approaching engine, Rose saw her lips part softly in expectation.

'Ivy, I forgot my handkerchief. Run upstairs and fetch it for me, please,' she said, but the girl was so focused on the door that she didn't respond.

'Miss Toms!' snapped Greep.

Ivy's head quivered a few times as if shaking loose whatever thoughts had lodged there and she turned to face Greep. 'Yes, Mr Greep?'

'Miss Rose asked you to fetch her handkerchief. Please do so.'

'But Captain Luscombe is home.'

Greep rarely showed any emotion other than a grudging satisfaction, but Rose detected a flash of anger as he declared, 'Do as you are asked, Miss Toms!'

'I'm sorry to be a bother. But I may need my handkerchief,' sniffed Rose. She wasn't acting; she really could feel tears stinging her eyes. She had missed and feared for her brother dreadfully during the four long years of the war. And now, against all odds, he was safely back, and Rose was about to turn their world on its head with her news. Luscombe might never be the same. Why should she share the occasion with her maid?

'Certainly, Mr Greep, I'm sorry, miss,' Ivy said woodenly and turned for the stairs, but not before she had taken one last look towards the front door.

'Thank you, Ivy. We're all happy to have the captain home again, aren't we?' Rose felt a moment of compassion for her, but only a moment.

*

Rose threw her body upon the bed, exhausted by the excitement of Robert's homecoming and the effort of keeping Ivy away from him. The girl positively stalked him, appearing around corners, ready to pounce at any moment. Rose and her mother had remained glued to his side all day, to pre-empt any unfortunate declarations. Robert appeared not to understand the danger. In fact, he appeared to be colluding with the girl. Happening upon her just coming from the kitchen, popping his head around Rose's door to ask if she would care for a stroll just as Ivy was dressing her for dinner.

With a sigh she reached for the mahogany box she kept by her bedside, unlocking it with a small key she wore on a chain around her neck. There were too many people fond of snooping in this house. Opening the box, she withdrew a well-handled photograph showing Jim Turner standing by a tall, dappled grey horse, a black and white sheep dog sitting at his feet. He wore a tightly buttoned waistcoat over a white shirt, with sleeves rolled to the elbows and a broad-brimmed hat shading his face. The horse had turned to crop at a clump of grass while Jim and the dog stared straight at the camera almost angrily, as if daring the photographer to waste their time.

Each night, her fingers traced the wide mouth framed by a moustache, the long lean lines of his body, until his features had become as familiar as her own. She imagined standing on the veranda at Wuurnong with his arm about her waist, one large knuckled hand resting on her hip. As her fingers roamed his image, she imagined his fingers roaming hers and she wondered if he took as much delight in her portrait as she took in his, whether her face was the last thing he saw each night before he dimmed the light.

Her life had changed dramatically in these years of war, and her body had altered with it. She was still fine-boned and slender, but the thin limbs of girlhood had grown firm with muscle and her hands were no longer merely decorative. She had learned what it was to work. She had learned that idle hands might be soft-skinned and delicate but that working hands rarely were. She had learned the ways of men's bodies: of pain and fear and loss. And she had learned that she intended to choose her own path in life, no matter what her brother or her mother had to say. Sometimes, when she thought about that other girl, the one she had been, she didn't recognise her. The war had honed Rose into the woman she was: stronger, less compromising but more compassionate. And Jim Turner loved that woman, not the silly young girl that her brother knew.

And now his marriage proposal had arrived and the Armistice had been celebrated. That was a sign, wasn't it? The war had ended and there was jubilation in the streets. There was jubilation in her heart too, for the end of war marked the beginning of her new life. Fate was showing her the way forward. Jim had asked her to be his wife and she had cabled him her answer. Other people might think she was weak, incapable of existing without servants, but she would show them. It couldn't be so hard to get by with only a cook and a maid of all work could it? And there was bound to be a gardener, surely?

She would leave this ailing continent and her sad, lost mother behind. There was nothing she could do for Elsie now; Robert would have to look out for her. Now that her brother had been repatriated, she was free to book her passage to Australia and say her goodbyes. She would forget about Luscombe and the old ways.

Yes. Forgetting might be best. Letting go of the past and all it represented. She could even let Ivy have Luscombe Park, she decided . . . if the girl could wrest it from Elsie. Let Robert look out for himself, she decided; she was exhausted by it. And soon she would be rid of her childhood friend and the last fragments of that childhood forever.

'It won't be long now. I'll be with you soon,' she whispered, pressing her lips to the precious photograph. And if a tiny corner of her brain whispered in silent warning, she refused to listen.

39

Ivy checked for lurking staff before ducking into the library. Reassured that she hadn't been seen, she leaned against the heavy oak door between the drawing room and the library, clutching a copy of *The Getting of Wisdom*. She had found it amongst Miss Rose's books upstairs and wondered why she was reading a book written by an unknown Australian man. Ivy had dipped into it, as she often did with Rose's discarded novels, but the protagonist, Laura, annoyed her so much that she didn't finish it. She couldn't understand why Laura cared what the other girls at the boarding school thought of her. They were just spoiled rich girls who didn't know what life was about. Laura should have ignored them.

Now, however, the book served as a pretext, should the butler discover her lurking in the library. She leaned against the door between library and drawing room, endeavouring to calm her breathing, and listened. Surely her heart hammered so loudly they must hear her?

The Luscombe women had monopolised Robert from the moment the Rolls drew up to the front door that morning. Ivy had to content herself with a fleeting glimpse as she handed over the offending handkerchief to Rose. Then the servants were bustled from the hall, and Rose and her mother had forestalled every attempt to find a moment alone with the captain. But that momentary glance held a world of meaning for Ivy. She had read in Robert's weary eyes a torment of longing, as if he had been waiting to find safe harbour.

Luscombe Park had become a tomb where she was buried amongst the shards of other people's loss. They all knew someone who would never return. Muriel had lost every male in her family and wandered the halls like a ghoul. Nobody was immune. When she wasn't at the hospital, Miss Rose buried herself in her room with her books and her letters; Robert was mired in the mud of France; and his mother was immured in her boudoir with her bottles and her regrets.

Sometimes Ivy suspected that Rose knew about her and Robert, and she wondered why she didn't dismiss her and be done with it. Instead, she did her best to make her maid's life miserable. Ivy could have walked away, but where would she go? She dared not show her face at Ashcott, with Sam missing. It was as if the ivy that twined about the cottage had become a shroud, entombing her father and mother with her lost brother. Besides, she needed to be here for Robert's return. He had made her promises. Not of marriage exactly, but what else could he mean when he vowed to take care of her always? Despite Ivy's caution, despite her reservations, her employer had wormed his way into her heart with his letters. She had intended to hold herself dear. Instead, she had bequeathed him her heart. Now all she had left was faith.

All those words had to mean something.

Well, dinner was finally over. The moment the family retreated to the drawing room, she had abandoned Rose's list of urgent tasks and hurried towards the adjoining library. There was small likelihood that any of the other servants would venture here that evening. They had business elsewhere, restoring order after the homecoming dinner. Ivy's business lay behind the door to the drawing room, whether she was invited or not. She needed to know what was so important that the Luscombe women couldn't relinquish Robert for even a moment. She suspected that Rose would do everything in her power to destroy her relationship with Robert. How she had discovered it, Ivy wasn't certain – perhaps she had intercepted one of his letters? – but her behaviour suggested she knew.

Above the sound of blood drumming in her ears, she heard Rose's raised voice. Something had got her goat.

'He knows me better than anyone. Sometimes I think he is the only one who knows anything about me!'

'But Australia is so far away. How can you propose to travel ten thousand miles to marry someone you've never met? The idea is ludicrous!' Robert scoffed.

'You forget that I'm a grown woman, and if I want to travel to Australia I will. You can't stop me.'

'In that case, you'd better save some of the income from your trust, for I won't be paying for your ticket. Or your return ticket when you realise you've made a mistake!' Robert snapped. 'A thousand pounds per annum won't be enough to live on – not even for love in a cottage. And what do you actually know about him?'

'I know he's a good man. I know he loves me. What more do I need to know?'

Ivy was confused. She had expected to hear Robert announcing his intentions towards her; instead, she was listening to Rose announce her intentions towards someone else. Someone she suspected might be related to their former patient, Henry Turner, hence the sudden interest in Australia. She knew, of course, that Rose was receiving regular letters, since it was difficult to keep matters hidden from a lady's maid. But Rose had kept the letters locked away in a box, the key hidden.

'I should say you need to know a great deal more than that,' said Robert. 'You're accustomed to a certain way of life, a privileged way of life. A gentleman wouldn't expect you to give that up.'

'I won't be giving up anything. Jim is a sheep farmer and owns a large property with a substantial homestead. He's a well-respected man.'

'A well-respected man in Australia is quite different to the kind of man you might look for in a husband, don't you agree, Mother?'

'I don't know what to think. My nerves are quite shattered,' Mrs Luscombe moaned. 'Your sister never listens to me, in any case. She may as well not have a mother.'

'And I don't know how you can stand here and lecture me on Jim's suitability when you have been carrying on with a servant behind Maman's back!' Rose shrilled. 'It's so demeaning.'

There was silence behind the door for a few moments, and Ivy willed Robert to rise to her defence. She had known for a long time that Rose had only played at being her friend when they were children. Then she had played at being a nurse and now she wanted to play at being a farmer's wife. Yet Ivy put her faith in Robert's sincerity.

'You can't deny it,' Rose continued. 'I've seen your letters. You can't seriously mean to marry her.'

'My intentions towards Ivy are none of your business,' he said in a calm voice.

'You are such a hypocrite.'

'My situation is different to yours. Luscombe is mine and I can marry where I please. You, on the other hand, have only a modest trust fund. You need a husband to pay your Harrods' account and your staff salaries.'

Elsie Luscombe bestirred herself enough to venture, 'It's true that you have Luscombe. Except Ivy . . .'

Ivy heard her name and waited for the threats and pleas that would follow. She knew that Elsie Luscombe hated her, although she did not quite understand why.

'Ivy and I love each other, Mother. And I intend to marry her, if she'll have me. Though why she would want to take on a family like ours, I don't know.'

Ivy felt the great tangle of dread inside her chest loosen. He did love her. He could be counted upon to fight for her. Now, no matter what Elsie Luscombe said, no matter what Rose did, they couldn't steal Robert away from her.

He was hers and she was free to love him without fear. The thought enveloped her like a gentle breeze. But Mrs Luscombe was still talking.

'You will never marry Ivy. Because Ivy is your sister.'

She heard the wispy sound of Mrs Luscombe's voice, supposing at first that she must have misheard. The solid oak door had muffled her words, for surely, she must have said something else? Something like 'Ivy is your servant' or 'Ivy is in your service'? Not Ivy is your sister.

Rose was Robert's sister. Not Ivy. She was his love.

She waited for him to correct his mother, for Rose to protest this nonsense. But Elsie's words had silenced all the actors in the drama being played out in the drawing room. It was as if one of them had missed a line and they all waited for the prompt to remind them of the correct script, while Ivy waited anxiously in the wings for her cue to enter.

'Maman, is that true?'

'What are you saying, Mother?'

'I am saying that your esteemed father – my beloved husband, Edward – seduced Ivy's mother, who was then a servant in my house. A scullery maid at that. And when it became apparent the slut was with child, he paid off Walter Toms to marry her. Now where is my glass, Rose?' added Mrs Luscombe, slurring over the last words, now that the damage was done. Now that the killing blow had been delivered.

Ivy still couldn't believe what she was hearing. It had to be another weapon the Luscombe women were using to shut her out. The rich had so many weapons in their arsenal.

'If you don't believe me, check the estate accounts. Ask Toms. He knows. He knows whose bastard he has raised.'

Sick to the very pit of her stomach, Ivy didn't want to believe her. Yet in a strange way the words made sense. They made sense of nineteen years of hatred from her da. They made sense of his dislike of her from the moment she could toddle around the cottage. He didn't hate her because she was Ivy. He didn't hate her because she was a girl. He hated her because she was another man's bastard.

But Elsie hadn't finished. There was another slurry of words to deliver, to bury Ivy's dreams beneath the weight of other people's sin. More words to destroy her hope that there could be a different life for a girl like her – a life that was built upon love and friendship instead of toil and obedience.

'I think it best under the circumstances that the girl be sent away, as far away from Luscombe as possible. Don't you. Robert?'

'Send her away?' he murmured, so softly that she barely caught his words through the door.

'Yes. I'm sure she can be made to agree, if the suggestion comes from you. It would be best for us all. Not to see her. Not to risk her discovering the truth.'

'You call that truth? It has to be a lie, a dirty rotten lie.'

'Yes. The truth. We could offer her a stipend. And since Rose is determined upon leaving, perhaps Ivy could accompany her to Australia. As her maid and companion. Australia is about as far from here as you could go, isn't it?'

'With me?'

'She is your sister, after all.'

'Ivy can't be my sister.'

'Your sister. Robert's sister. Your father's little by-blow.'

Without realising she was about to act, Ivy reached for the door handle. She didn't know what she would say, she only knew that it was her life they were discussing, her past they maligned, her future they mapped, as bleak as both now appeared to be. So she pushed open the door, and three heads turned in her direction.

One face, the dearest face, was a picture of loss, with all the broken pieces put back together askew. Another face was frozen white in shock. And the third face smiled serenely, as if a great wrong had finally been righted.

Rose thought she might faint. Surely that's what any sensible young woman would do, given her situation? Close her eyes and pretend this wasn't happening. Except her mother had tottered from the drawing room, leaving devastation in her wake, and now somebody had to pick up the pieces. Judging by the look on her brother's face, it wouldn't be him. He sat like a statue, his arms rigid at his sides, his face frozen in horror. Ivy was collapsed in a heap at his feet, like a hollowed-out version of herself, sobbing his name over and over.

That left Rose.

She lowered herself to the sofa and tried to think. It couldn't be true. Perhaps it was only another of Maman's delusions. She didn't want to believe her mother's dirty revelation, but there was something . . . if she squinted her eyes, blurring the outline of the girl's face, she could almost see herself in Ivy's features.

It could be true. Ivy acted as if it were true.

Rose had always thought of her maid as implacable. Most of the time, she showed so little emotion that she may as well have constructed a great wall around herself, piled up stone upon stone of defences. Only once had Rose seen her brought to tears, that one day when they discovered her walking alone down a country lane. Since then, all Rose's taunts and tasks had rebounded like arrows hitting a castle wall. Ivy was impervious to the demands and reprimands of Mrs Tucker and Sister. Yet now she crumpled like a doll with the stuffing leaking out of her, sunk to her knees and staring sightlessly at the Persian carpet, her tears washing over Robert's boots. And still her brother didn't move.

'Robert,' Rose began, 'I think you need to help Ivy.'

'What are we going to do?' he said.

'I don't know yet.'

He bent and lifted Ivy her to her feet. As she tried to wrap him in her arms, he prised her loose. Then with one hand grasping her elbow, he steered her towards a chair by the fire.

'You need to sit down.'

As he released her arm, she grasped his hand with both hers and looked up into his face imploringly. 'You said you'd take care of me. You said you loved me.'

'I know.'

'You said I gave you hope.'

'My mother has just stolen that hope from both of us,' he said, removing his hand from hers. 'You have to let me go now.'

'Our father stole it, you mean,' Rose said, with a rather unladylike snort. But there wasn't much point being delicate now that she had discovered her maid was her bastard sister. There was nothing ladylike about that. Surely even Lady Colin Campbell wouldn't know the etiquette for that.

'But I . . . I let myself love you. I didn't listen. I should have listened.' Ivy hiccupped the words through her tears.

'As I see it,' Rose said, shutting out the sobs, 'we have to find a place for her. Somewhere she can start again.' Somewhere away from Luscombe Park, away from Robert, and preferably as far away from herself as could be managed.

'You can't send me away,' Ivy hissed. 'I won't go.'

Rose tried to harden her heart. If the girl hadn't skulked into their lives with her foxy half-smile and her cunning ways, none of this would have happened. Except even she had to admit that Ivy was as much a victim as herself and Robert.

'Ivy, you can't stay here,' Robert said, running a hand through his hair. 'It will tear us all apart.'

'But I'm one of you now. I'm a Luscombe.'

'Then you won't wish to destroy us.'

Yes, they were all Luscombes now. Rose wished she could throw off her name, and with it the weight of her entire history, to start anew. In her new life there would be no Ivy, a burden bestowed upon her by someone else. There would be no rules, no expectations. She could just be herself . . . whoever that might turn out to be.

40

North Devon

1919

The scent of cigar smoke told her that her brother was cloistered in his study. In the weeks since her mother had hurled her terrible secret into their midst, he had spent a good part of each day hiding out there. Doing what, she couldn't say. 'Going over the accounts,' he would reply if queried. And when he wasn't going over the accounts, he was taking himself off to Bristol or London, anywhere to get away from Luscombe Park. Once or twice she had asked to accompany him and been met with a series of transparent excuses. Sometimes she thought he would rather return to the western front than face her. On his darkest days she suspected he would have thrown himself off a steep cliff, if that were his only escape.

She tapped at the door so softly that he wouldn't hear, for if he didn't hear he couldn't tell her to go away. Then she ventured in a few yards, her slippers padding silently across the Persian carpet. He sat at his desk, his back to the door, facing out over the terrace to the park. Despite the newly tailored suit ordered from Mr Poole's establishment, his shoulders seemed bonier than ever, if that were possible. His clothes hung on him like an adolescent boy whose mother had ordered his jacket be made too large. It was almost as if their mother had stolen something more than Ivy from him that evening in the library. Robert seemed to have lost a part of himself.

Well, he wasn't about to sulk himself into oblivion if she had anything to do with it. He had inherited the Luscombe name and fortune and he had a duty to live up to it, whether he wanted to or not. That was the thing with men. They wanted everything but weren't prepared to pay the cost. They would rather leave that to someone else.

She took a few more steps towards the desk. So rapt was he in whatever he was staring at that he didn't notice her presence, even when she stood at his shoulder. She saw that in his hands he held a portrait, one of Mr Catford's photographs taken that fateful day in Ilfracombe, when Ivy had still been a sneaky baggage intent on snagging her brother. Before she became Rose's secret half-sister. If only she hadn't listened to her brother's protests that day. If only she had given Ivy her notice, then and there, and to hell with the consequences. Yet she had taken him at his word, believing that the maid meant nothing to him, and look where his word had taken them.

Ivy stared out from the photograph with that cunning half-smile, already smug in the knowledge of Robert's love while Rose, unsuspecting, tried valiantly to evade the girl's hand in her pocket. Little did she know how insistent her grasp might be, how much she would come to destroy.

'Robert.'

'What?' He turned sharply, seeing her, but momentarily so deep in reverie that he appeared not to recognise her.

'Robert, it has to stop. You're doing none of us any good.'

'I don't know what you're talking about,' he said, shifting his attention back to the photograph.

'This,' she said, snatching it from his hands, 'I'm talking about this.'

'That's mine,' he said, reaching for it, 'you have a copy, as does Ivy.'

'I understand, truly I do,' she said with a sympathetic sigh. 'You needed her love to give you hope during the war. I understand that. We can all forgive that. But the war is over now . . . and Ivy is over too.'

'You understand nothing.'

'I understand more than you think. I didn't spend two years nursing wounded soldiers with my eyes closed.'

'This has nothing to do with the war,' he said, sounding more and more like a petulant child.

Their father had betrayed them all, yet Robert acted as if he were the only one who had been betrayed. What of her? What of Ivy? What of their mother? Well, Edward Luscombe was long dead and Rose didn't intend walling herself up at Luscombe Park with his tawdry secrets. Robert would just have to pull himself together and get on with things.

'Dwelling on it isn't fair to you – and it's torturing Ivy. So if you won't help yourself then I am going to have to do it for you. Beginning now.' With that, she pulled the photograph beyond his reach. Holding one corner in each hand, she ripped the image in two. Stripping the smile from her maid's face. Obliterating Ivy to save them all. Then, as he lurched towards her, she backed away. Saving her brother. As the pieces fluttered to the floor he stood, watching helplessly, before looking up at her with an expression of pure venom.

'You always hated her.'

'No. Once I loved her. But that was a long time ago. Before any one of us knew the truth about the world,' she said, wishing she could be rid of Ivy as easily as she was rid of her portrait. 'There's no place for her at Luscombe now.'

*

Ivy had heard tell of spiritualists; famous mediums like Mrs Gladys Leonard who spoke in trances or penned messages in shaky handwriting sent from beyond the grave. It was said that some could travel without leaving their bodies, although how much fun it would be floating around without your feet on your ground, she couldn't imagine. The head housemaid, Muriel, had attended a meeting once at the Spiritualist Society in Exeter, hoping to speak to her dead brothers. Ivy doubted that Muriel's brothers were going to turn up at the Market Hall in Exeter when they were probably rotting in a field in Flanders. Nevertheless, that is exactly how she felt on the day she and Rose were to depart Luscombe Park. As if her body was standing on the gravelled drive, bidding the household goodbye, while her mind was off travelling somewhere else altogether.

Robert stood at the bottom of the stairs, the entire staff lined up alongside him. At the last moment Gibbons announced that Mrs Luscombe was too ill to leave her room. Somewhere behind Ivy, Donaldson was loading Miss Rose's trunk and her own wicker case into the Silver Ghost. She was aware of a light breeze ruffling Rose's hair as her mistress extended her gloved hand to each of the staff before pausing in front of her brother, arms outstretched. After a moment, he leaned forward and encircled her stiffly in his arms, whispering in her ear so that when she turned away tears welled in her eyes.

'Goodbye, Robert. I'm sorry.'

'We're all sorry, Rose.'

'Don't forget me,' she murmured.

'Never.'

And then it was Ivy's turn to be bidden farewell. Her hand shaken by Greep, hugged by Muriel, nodded at by Gibbons. She could see it happening. She was aware of words issuing from her mouth, yet her mind had escaped to another plane altogether, one where Robert encircled *her* in his arms, whispering words of love into her ear. She escaped to a place where they could be together. A world where he told *her* he would never forget her.

'Goodbye, Ivy. You will be missed.'

She saw him speak the words by rote, extending his hand like an automaton. She was aware of staring as if she didn't know what to do with it, as if she wasn't intimate with the sprinkle of golden hairs on the back of his hand, the inch of white cuff or the carefully buffed nails. Her own hands hung limply at her sides. But her mind cleaved to him – pressing her lips to his, crushing her body to his chest – while she stood there, motionless, so that Greep had to step forward and lead her to the car where Rose waited. He ushered her on to the front seat, next to Donaldson, a carpet bag at her feet, as the engine coughed into life and she and her sister lurched into the future.

A future far from Luscombe Park. Far from the only man she could ever imagine loving. Leaving the old Ivy standing on the gravel drive, longing for a man and a world that could never be hers.

41

Melbourne, Victoria

2017

When she hadn't seen her daughter for five days after picking her up at Melbourne Airport, Wendy descended upon the Elwood flat armed with a box set of *Poldark* and a pot of homemade minestrone. Molly didn't want to talk to anyone – was more inclined to curl up on the couch and wallow – but her mother didn't give her the opportunity to demur. She arrived, banged on the door and demanded entry. Then she put the soup on to heat, cut a few slices of sourdough bread and set the table with two yellow rosebuds cut from her garden. Molly had to admit that a bowl of soup and a generous slab of bread did wonders for her constitution – much better for the soul than Weet-Bix smeared with Vegemite, or cornflakes straight from the carton, which had been her diet for the previous few days.

She had spent a lot of time thinking in the week since she'd left Luscombe Park. In travelling to England to discover Rose's story she had hoped to find out more about herself, yet she had failed in both quests. Certainly, she had uncovered some truths about Rose and Ivy. But there were so many questions she would probably never be able to answer. For a few hours she had been convinced she had figured it out, then Lucas and his DNA test squashed that. One girl succumbed to fever in a tropical port far from home and the other lived out her life on an Australian sheep farm. Again, which one? Each time she thought about her great-grandmother and her unlucky maid, she returned to the same theory – despite the DNA, with its twisted strands like a necklace of atoms linking the generations. Did it always tell the whole truth?

And now, not only did she feel a disconnection with Ivy; she also felt that she had lost Rose. She had lost her grip on the past, and for the moment she had nothing to replace it. In her present life, she was more conflicted than ever. She had abandoned Richard, sent Lucas packing and alienated her sister. Great job, Molly!

Somewhere she had misplaced her optimism – the same day she lost her father – and ever since, she had been waiting for him to return and tell her that things would be all right. Except he was never going to return, and he could never tell her things would be all right. She had to do that for herself.

'Mum. There's something I never told you about Dad's death.'

Setting down the spoon that had been midway to her mouth, Wendy gazed at her with mingled curiosity and concern. 'There are lots of things you've never told me about Dad's death, sweetheart. You've kept it all in here,' she said, tapping her left breast.

'Actually, it's about the day before he died.'

Wendy remained silent.

'You'd gone back to the campsite to get out of the sun, and Daisy and I persuaded Dad to let us stay in the surf for a bit longer.'

Wendy nodded encouragement.

'Well, I talked Daisy into going out further than she wanted to, and then . . . then a bigger set of waves came through and she . . . well, she got dumped. For a few moments, I thought she was gone altogether . . . and then Dad came running into the surf and found her and hauled her to the surface.'

'You must have been very frightened.'

'I was. So was Dad. Daisy wasn't, though.'

'Mmm. She's never been very conscious of danger.'

'Afterwards, Dad gave me a big lecture. And he made me promise . . . he made me promise that I would never go out too far in the surf, that I would never swim outside the flags and that I would never put myself or Daisy in danger again.'

Pushing back her chair, Wendy came to stand beside her, arms sliding around her shoulders and hugging her.

'I broke my promise,' Molly whispered into her mother's embrace. 'And Dad died.'

'I know. Your father told me that same night after you and Daisy were asleep.'

'You knew? But you never said anything. Not then . . . not ever.' It wasn't like her mother to be so forbearing.

'At first I was waiting for you to tell me. Then, later, I came to understand that you probably couldn't tell me. That with all that had happened it was just too painful.' She frowned, then continued, 'I've often wondered whether I made a mistake in not pushing you to tell me. Whether it would have helped you to confess.' She looked at Molly, her eyes filmed with tears, as if waiting for her own absolution.

Was that how it was? Were they all looking for absolution of one kind or another?

'If I hadn't broken my promise, he would still be with us.'

Wendy sighed and hugged her tighter. 'Maybe. But maybe something else would have taken him from us, we can't know. He blamed himself for Daisy getting into trouble that day. He told me she was too young to be out in that surf without an adult by her side.'

'But I was supposed to be looking after her.'

'No, that was your father's job, sweetheart. He never blamed you. Neither did I. You were simply a little girl who made a mistake.'

After Wendy had left, Molly propped herself on the sofa with her computer on her knee and opened her browser. She typed in her father's name and the single word 'drowning', then watched as the page filled with text, each ribbon of blue leading to the past. For years she had resisted this search, all those ghosts lying in wait at the click of her mouse, but perhaps it was time. Perhaps she was ready to excavate her past.

Scanning the lines of text, she selected a reputable news source, closed her eyes and clicked. In the split second it took her to blink, the page loaded and she found herself staring into her father's eyes. It was a photograph of him and her mum taken on that same beach holiday – before Wendy's face grew its little crop of lines and her jaw lost its razor edge – with her dad appearing as he did framed in Molly's memory, a man in his prime, his eyes laughing, unaware that the next day would be his last. He looked happy with his arm slung about his wife's shoulders, sunglasses perched on his forehead, and a big grin splitting his face.

Above the photograph the headline read: HERO DAD DIES SAVING DAUGHTER IN RIP.

He had always been a hero to her but she hadn't realised that others recognised it too, that in the eyes of the world he would *always* be a hero; immortalised by the ephemeral monument of cyberspace.

A distraught wife and mother has told how her husband drowned while rescuing their twelve-year-old daughter from the dangerous waters of popular Victorian surf beach, Wye River.

She didn't remember her mother being distraught. She remembered her mother being an island of calm in the churning wake of tragedy, the only person who could be relied upon to behave in the same way she always had, continuing to smile when Daisy said something silly, frowning when Molly argued. And if she sobbed alone in her bedroom at night, Molly hadn't heard her. Hadn't wanted to hear her.

Andrew Wilson, a Melbourne teacher, was holidaying with his wife Wendy and their daughters Molly, 12, and Daisy, 10, at a busy camping ground on Victoria's south-west coast when his eldest daughter got into trouble early yesterday morning in a rip current close to shore.

Local residents explained that the beach isn't patrolled at the early hour of 6.30 a.m. when Molly Wilson ventured into the surf alone.

'The daughter has found herself in difficulty, the father has discovered her in trouble and gone into the water to help,' Victoria Police Superintendent Gerald Dugan said.

Jake Green, 16, a local surfer, arrived on the beach to see father and daughter being pulled towards the rocks by the rip. He paddled out to aid them but was only able to save the daughter. By the time other rescuers were roused there was no sign of Mr Wilson.

Surf rescue operations were put into action and a helicopter joined the search but Mr Wilson was not found until several hours later. Attempts to revive him were unsuccessful. Paramedics treated Molly Wilson for shock at the scene.

She didn't remember being in shock, either. She remembered the paramedics draping a blanket around her shoulders and fussing about her, but she hadn't realised she was in shock. She only knew that her world was ending.

Local resident, Todd Weston, recalled that the swell would have appeared quite small that morning but the rip was unpredictable. 'People are always getting into trouble out there. They need to stay inside the flags.'

Camping ground manager, Sophie Konstantinidis, said of

Mr Wilson, 'He's a lovely man, always says good morning, and the family camp here every summer. Those poor little girls.'

Those poor little girls.

Reading the newspaper account, she could hardly believe it was the same event that she had experienced almost seventeen years ago. The participants were the same and the location was correct but the account was missing the most salient details. For years she had resisted searching her father's name, afraid she would learn something so painful that all her hard-won armour would be revealed for what it was – eggshell thin. But the newspaper report gave the barest outline. It couldn't tell her what her father had called to her as Jake Green paddled her to shore. It couldn't show her his face as he was towed out to sea. It couldn't tell her what she needed to know.

She heard the sea as soon as she crossed the busy road and plunged into the ti-tree plantation. Stray branches brushed her coat as she emerged on to the broad grassy foreshore above the sand. Usually the sand stretched in a wide expanse from the bluestone retaining wall to the lapping waters of Port Phillip Bay, but today the bay had turned wild, churned into a frenzy of dark grey waves crashing past the high-tide mark and dowsing the path in a threatening spray. Despite the howling wind and flurry of salt and sand, she wasn't alone. A man walked a solid-looking Staffy down past the lifesaving club, and two kite surfers sailed high above the water nearer to Point Ormond. She considered which way to walk: left towards the expensive houses and yachts of Brighton, or right towards the marina and Luna Park in St Kilda. Coming or going, one way or another, she would have to fight the wind. She turned right.

Head down, she battled the wind, wondering what on earth she was doing out here on this God-awful winter's day. She should be hibernating in her flat, eating chocolate and bingeing on *Poldark*. She didn't even like the sea. Hated the way it hounded her, always reminding her of what she had lost. But since she had returned from the UK the sound of the sea had changed. It had begun sounding more like a nagging friend than an enemy waiting to take her down.

Except not today. Today it was wild and unpredictable and had to be confronted head on.

She reached the breakwater at the foot of Point Ormond's green mound and continued around the point where waves pounded the sea wall. Even the angry roar of the waves wouldn't deter her today. A cyclist passed her on the bike path, chased by the gusting tailwind. Spray was needling her face now, flushing her eyes and nose with salt-water. For a moment her heart battered at her chest in the old, familiar reflex. But she had its number now. She knew when to fight, when to flee and when to hold to her true course.

'Molly?'

The voice ripped her from her reverie. She looked up to find the owner bearing towards her, mere metres away. His hoodie was pulled low over his forehead but she would have known that voice anywhere. His long legs were encased in black tights, running shorts over the top and black Nikes on his feet. Tendrils of wet hair stuck to his face and his lips had parted in a broad smile.

'Matt.'

'You look great.'

'I look like a drowned rat.'

'A cute one.'

He jogged on the spot as they exchanged greetings, and she wondered fleetingly why he hadn't run right past her. He could have pulled his hoodie down even lower and she mightn't have noticed who he was. She wrapped her arms around her body and drew in a deep breath, tasting the seawater in the air.

'Nice weather for a run.'

'You know me – I go stir-crazy cooped up inside.'

'Yeah, I had to get out too.'

'How have you been, anyway? I ran into Amy the other day and she said you'd been to the UK.'

'Yep. Finally found the courage to go further than Hobart.'

'That's good. I'm happy for you,' he grinned.

Molly realised that he *was* happy for her. That he had always been happy for her. She was the one who hadn't been happy for her. She wondered then if he had even noticed that she had finally unfollowed him on Instagram.

'Thanks. How's Jordana? I saw your posts.' For an aching moment she imagined him saying that they had broken up and she wasn't really the girl for him, after all – that the girl for him was someone calm and steady and not adventurous at all. Just for a moment.

'She's great,' he said with a rueful grin. 'But even she's not stupid enough to go running in a storm!'

She laughed, then said, 'Well, better get going before we both drown.'

'Yeah. Yeah. It was good seeing you. We should catch up. Properly.'

'Sure. That would be great,' she said automatically, before realising that she meant it.

42

Colombo, Ceylon

1919

Out by the lake, men bathed wearing scraps of cloth tied at their loins. They had drawn their bullock drays and rickshaws into the water, dotting the lake with palm-thatched carts and the little bullocks called zebus. The zebus were enjoying this respite from the heat; dipping their humped necks into the lake, water streaming down the long dewlaps dangling beneath their chins. Some of the men washed long glossy black hair, or sat on rocks to comb it dry, while further along the lakeshore there were small groups of bathing women. Rose had never seen so much naked flesh. She supposed she should avert her eyes or affect not to notice. Instead, she was conscious of an almost scientific interest in the way muscles shifted and flowed underneath skin polished by sun and sweat, the mechanics of joints lifting and pulling.

Back in Devon, she had seen her share of bare limbs and torsos in the course of her nursing, but those poor souls' skin was bleeding and jagged, torn by shrapnel, or peeling away to leave raw, red flesh where mustard gas had seeped through uniforms. But here in Colombo, the port jostled with workers loading boxes of tea on to barges, wearing only a long, skirt-like garment fastened at the waist. In the main street, bare-chested men carrying umbrellas mingled with men and women wearing skirts topped with neat white jackets and blouses, their feet bare on the hot streets. Even the policeman, formal as a London bobby in his brass-buttoned uniform, wore no boots on his dusty feet.

Their rickshaws bounced along the wide carriage road that wound around the lake, passing yet another bungalow set in a luxuriant garden. The wide veranda was rampant with flowering bougainvillea and hanging baskets. Bamboo rustled in the warm breeze and the massive leaves of what she assumed to be a plantain tree hailed her as she passed. Rose beat at the humid air with a fan she had purchased from a Sinhalese trader earlier that day. The delicate blades were carved from sandalwood so that a pleasant scent accompanied each wave of her hand, but it did little to cool her for the air was hot and wet as steaming tea.

Something about the heat and the exuberant scents of flowers, spices and coconut-oiled hair pricked her awareness of her own body. She was conscious of moisture seeping through the cloth of her high-necked blouse, wetness creeping beneath her armpits. She wished she too could walk about wrapped in a length of cloth and a thin white blouse instead of layers of petticoats and long drawers clinging to her legs like bandages.

That morning Ivy had wanted to stay in the cool lounge, reclining in a tub chair, resisting the headache she could feel coming on, but Rose overruled her, bustling them aboard a canopied longboat to be escorted ashore by a flock of seagulls wheeling and diving overhead. And once ashore, they had been accosted by Mrs Brigham before Rose herded them into rickshaws for a scenic tour of Colombo, rattling past the waiting bullock drays like rows of enormous baskets on wheels, and on towards the fort and the beachfront.

Ivy tried to rouse herself as the rickshaw pullers carried them past a lake where men bathed wearing scraps of cloth tied at their loins. She had never seen such a sight before, and was unlikely to again, but she was so tired that she could hardly keep her eyes open. It was all new and strange, yet she could barely find the strength to lean forward in her rickshaw. Ever since that day in the library at Luscombe Park she had been plagued by a creeping blackness of spirit that threatened to overwhelm her, an anger so powerful that she could feel it eating away at her soul. Sometimes she thought that if she could only release it she might find some semblance of peace, but now the malaise had become tangible, weighing down her limbs and pounding at her head so that she could barely hold it erect.

She lay back in the rickshaw, eyelids fluttering, head lolling, with Rose's rickshaw bouncing along the wide carriage road alongside. They passed small groups of women bathing waist deep, lengths of wet fabric tied tightly over their breasts, leaving arms and shoulders bare. Their abundant hair was roped into thick plaits hanging almost to their waists, and she watched as one girl tipped a pitcher of water over her head. Ivy imagined the water pouring down her own arms and back in a cooling stream.

Despite the light awning she felt the sun stinging the back of her neck, leaving tendrils of wet hair stuck to her skin. Rivulets of moisture trickled down her forehead but she didn't bother to wipe them away; that would require too much energy. A sticky warmth invaded her entire body, filling her head with a dull thud and her limbs with such heavy languor that it was too much trouble to respond to Rose's chatter about the scenery, her fiancé Jim and the arrogant old biddies aboard the *Osprey* who looked down their noses at Ivy. And if she tried to think of home, of rain and snow and chill autumn mornings, she was overcome with thoughts of what she had lost.

'You're not still sulking about Mrs Brigham, are you? She probably counts the eggs and shouts at her scullery maid,' Rose laughed from her rickshaw, but Ivy could only respond with a sigh and a languid wave of her hand.

Through the slits beneath her eyelids she was aware of the scenery changing. Gone were the lake and the luxuriant bungalows in their lush jungle gardens. Their route now passed alongside the railway line, and a clock tower appeared in the distance as they joined other traffic heading into town. She became aware of a light two-wheeled bullock hackery being driven alongside them, the driver setting a cracking pace, and several heavier carts drawn by pairs of large, dark-red cattle, drivers striding alongside. The noise of the vehicles only made her head thump louder.

'See, we'll be back in port before you know it,' said Rose, but it was becoming increasingly difficult to concentrate on her words. Perhaps if she closed her eyes the noises might go away. If she could only cool off a little . . . she imagined joining the women bathing in the lake, cooling streams of water running down her back, pooling around her waist . . . if she could just get out of this heat . . . if her head would cease its incessant hammering.

She could almost feel the cool waters of the lake now, like an icy shiver that trembled in her limbs . . .

In the rickshaw beside Rose, Ivy barely stirred. Her face had turned a livid pink and hair hung in lank strands on her cheeks. Rose wondered if it would be this hot when they reached Australia. Jim had written often of the dusty heat of summer, when ponds became craters of cracked mud and streams disappeared into the parched earth. She thought she might be able to bear the heat with him by her side, but the hot climate of the tropics certainly didn't please Ivy. She had kept up a string of complaints from the moment the *Osprey* entered the Suez Canal, almost as if the further they sailed, the stronger the lifeline she needed to connect herself to home, to Robert. She was still clinging to her Cinderella story, despite all evidence to the contrary. But Rose knew she had to make her own way in the world, setting sail towards Jim and his farm.

'We agreed I'm to make a new life,' Ivy complained whenever Rose asked her to perform a simple task such as hanging her gown or finding her gloves. Did she think Rose could wave a magic wand and transform her into a princess?

'That's the only reason I agreed to come. Perhaps I shall marry or take a position as a housekeeper. They need professional women in Australia.'

Ivy assumed Mrs Tucker was the power behind the throne at Luscombe Park. Rose rather thought it was money that controlled the ropes, and Robert who controlled the money. But who was she to argue with Ivy's plans when her own involved a man she was yet to meet, a man she knew solely through a bundle of letters at the bottom of her steamer trunk?

'I know, and I shall help you. So will Jim,' she replied whenever Ivy launched into her familiar refrain.

'Do you think I would travel across the world in order to remain a maid? Spend the rest of my life mending other people's undergarments and washing the sixpences from their pockets?'

Actually, Ivy would probably spit on Rose's sixpences if instructed to wash them. Even now, she suspected the real reason the girl had decided to accompany her was out of spite. She could have gone to Bristol, or even London, and made a life for herself, but she had decided to follow Rose. Or perhaps she wasn't as brave as she liked to pretend.

'Once we arrive in Melbourne, I'm to be my own woman.'

'Of course you shall.'

'I shall be a woman of means with the stipend allowed me from the estate.'

Rose could not help but wince each time she heard Ivy utter

the word 'estate'. As if Luscombe were her birthright too. In reality, it was blood money, paid to keep her silent. Although no amount of money could repay either of them for their suffering. Through no fault of their own they had been forced to take responsibility for all the Luscombe sins, all her father and brother's indiscretions. The men dallied and the women paid the price. For in the end, Rose had given in to her mother's directive that Ivy accompany her to Australia. How could she not? Especially with that taunting voice whispering in her head, 'What if it was you growing up in the cottage and Ivy in the big house? What if it was you feeling the sting of Walter Toms' willow stick?'

As they ventured once more into the hubbub of Colombo's wide tree-shaded streets, Ivy seemed to have run out of complaints. She lay back in the rickshaw, silently absorbing each bump in the road, while Rose observed the mud and bamboo houses, open to catch stray breezes, the stalls selling all manner of foods laid out on banana leaves – mangoes, melons, pineapples, limes, small spiky red globes, and a bulbous green giant larger than any fruit she had ever seen. The fruity scent made her mouth water. But even the pungent aroma of fish couldn't wake Ivy from her torpor.

Sometimes Rose wondered what her life might have been like without Ivy. But they were bound together by blood now. And she would never be free of her. For as well as cunning, Ivy had added guilt and the threat of exposure to her arsenal.

Presently they were back in busy Chatham Street, dodging tramcars as they headed towards the port, before rolling over the bridge to draw up outside the passenger terminal. Her rickshaw puller let the shafts down and straightened, arching and stretching his back before turning to help her down.

'Thank you, Chandra,' she said, sliding from her seat.

In the rickshaw beside her Ivy ignored her driver.

'Miss, miss!' he hissed, probably unsure what to do about the young Englishwoman asleep in his rickshaw. Clearly she couldn't stay there.

'I'll wake her,' she said, crossing to the other rickshaw. Already several other passengers were looking their way. 'Ivy, wake up.' She touched a hand to the girl's shoulder. Close to, she could see her lace-trimmed blouse rising and falling rapidly. Ragged little breaths gusted from her mouth.

'I'm so cold,' Ivy murmured, her eyelids fluttering open to reveal a slit of red-rimmed white.

Rose looked up at the rickshaw puller, standing several feet away now, not bothering to hide his frown, no doubt wishing the young woman far away. And beyond the rickshaw a curious band of fellow travellers from the *Osprey* had gathered. No one ventured closer to render aid. They watched, unsmiling, as she placed her hand on Ivy's forehead.

'You had better fetch the ship's doctor,' she said, looking up at the rickshaw puller.

Ivy's skin burned to the touch.

Dr Sullivan was rather a good-looking young man, with an air of capability that he had probably acquired somewhere in Flanders, leading Rose to expect reassurance and a speedy remedy when he reached the wharf. But instead of reassurance, he arrived toting his black leather bag, a stern mask, and accompanied by Mr Pettigrew, the ship's purser.

Standing several feet distant from Ivy, he frowned, saying, 'Miss Toms has a fever.'

Why was he being so perfunctory when he had always been so charming previously? He had even flirted with her a little after their brief expedition in Port Said, despite her engagement.

'Perhaps if you examined her more closely?' she suggested.

'Miss Luscombe, I do not need to poke and prod the poor girl to see that she has contracted the flu, the Spanish flu no doubt . . .'

Surely not? They had been at sea. She noticed Dr Sullivan glancing meaningfully at Pettigrew, just as Ivy's body shook with a paroxysm of coughing so violent she fancied she heard the rattle of her lungs. Or perhaps, after all, it was merely the clatter of the imitation pearls at her neck.

'But how can you be sure that she has the Spanish flu?'

'I've seen it often enough,' the doctor sighed. 'You'll note her weakness, a result of aching muscles. There's a high fever and a severe cough. As her illness progresses, her skin will turn a vivid purple, the fever will climb higher and her lungs may haemorrhage a thick scarlet jelly.'

Rose found herself holding her breath, waiting for his next words.

'And I'm afraid death may follow within days, even hours.'

Surely he couldn't be speaking of Ivy? The girl was too tough to let a little influenza take her.

'No, it's just a reaction to the change of climate. She doesn't have the Spanish flu. We must warm her, perhaps a mustard plaster or . . .'

But neither the doctor nor the purser would meet her eyes, the purser consulting a brown leather folder he had previously been tapping against his thigh.

'We have to consider the other passengers,' he said. 'You will find, if you consult your Contract Ticket, that it is issued subject to a number of conditions. Specifically,' he read from the folder, '*if the Steamer shall be prevented by any cause from sailing or proceeding or it is deemed that the Passenger cannot be conveyed by the Steamer, the Passenger may at the Shipowner's expense be transshipped to any other Steamer bound for the port of destination.* In addition you will note the clause, *The Owners will not be liable for loss of life or injury or delay suffered by any Passenger, whether caused by the perils of the sea, negligence in navigation, or otherwise howsoever.*'

'What do you mean by "otherwise howsoever"?' How could he be so concerned about words when Ivy's life was clearly in danger?

'Aside from the risk to passengers,' explained the doctor, 'the Australian authorities have a quarantine order in place. The entire ship will be quarantined at Woodman's Point if we arrive with Spanish flu aboard. Anyone found to be infected may be deported—'

'What I mean, Miss Luscombe,' the purser interrupted, 'is that *you* may board the ship but Miss Toms may not. If she recovers, she will be offered passage on the first available ship of our line . . . at the Shipowner's expense, of course.'

She considered the girl, stranded on her rickshaw island. Although her eyes were closed, her eyeballs moved restlessly beneath the lids, her limbs quivered, her breath raced. Her curls stuck to her cheeks in lank misery. This girl who had become an inescapable fact of her life might very well die. She should feel overcome with sadness.

'But if I leave she might die,' she breathed the words.

She lifted her face in mute appeal to first one man and then the other, but neither seemed to care whether Ivy lived or died.

Perhaps they had grown so accustomed to death that one more made little difference.

43

Western District, Victoria

2017

Molly and Joan watched the dogs playing with a soccer ball that was devoid of air and coated in slobber. Sukie worried it with her teeth while Bob pranced around barking encouragement. Molly was rugged up in an old cable-knit jumper, for it was chilly this time of year, especially with a cold south-westerly blowing in from the Southern Ocean. The lawn was wet from an earlier shower but the late afternoon sun streamed through the bunya pines, warming the veranda where the two women sat companionably in fraying rattan armchairs, a pot of tea and two mugs resting on a table between them.

'It's a pity Richard's travelling days are over. He would love it here,' Molly mused, sipping at her tea. 'He'd like to see where his aunt made her home.' The Luscombe roots were ancient but the Turners appeared to be the only living branch.

'I'm sure he could identify with the perils of nursing an old house in serious need of resuscitation,' Joan chuckled. 'Are you sure his travelling days are over? It sounds like he was a bit of a gypsy when he was younger.'

'The flight's so long, I think it would be too much. Maybe if someone came with him . . . business class,' she shrugged. 'Unlikely.'

'We'd love to have him stay.'

Molly pictured Richard roaming the paddocks of Wuurnong with his shooting stick, comparing notes on breeding sheep with Joan, lamenting the finer points of ancient plumbing with Brian, picking the bones of dead relatives with Uncle Ted. He *would* love it here.

Joan offered her a scone from a rather wonky ceramic plate. 'Connor's handiwork, he made it for Brian and me for Christmas.' Connor was another grandchild.

'It's very . . . individual.'

'I'm sure we have a budding artist on our hands.'

They devoted a minute or two to scooping homemade plum jam and a dollop of cream on to their scones before Joan ventured, 'And what about you, do we have a historian on our hands? Your mum said you were thinking of returning to study.'

Molly sighed and closed her eyes, gathering her thoughts before answering. 'I took six months' unpaid leave from the department so I'll go back to teaching in July for third term. But next year I'm applying to start a PhD at Monash. Hopefully, I can get a scholarship or some tutoring to help out. Plus I still have some money from Nan.'

Joan smiled, putting down her jammy scone to place her hand over Molly's. 'I'm so pleased, love. And if you ever need somewhere quiet to stay, out of the rat race, well, you know where we are.'

'Thanks, you and Brian and Uncle Ted have been great, helping me with all the questions about Rose, having me to stay.' She doubted she would have found the courage to go back to studying if she hadn't embarked upon Nan's quest to trace Rose's story. And then spending those weeks at Luscombe, getting Richard's family archive into some semblance of order, had forced her to admit that she had turned her back on her true passion when she went into teaching.

'Because you don't believe you deserve to realise your dreams,' she imagined her sister saying. Was that the truth? She stared into the dregs of tea left in her mug. She wished she could read the future there, could see whether she had made a terrible mistake. She left Devon not only because she felt betrayed by Lucas but also because she knew instinctively that staying would have meant taking the easy way. Again. She would have slipped back into another cosy bunker like the one she had inhabited in Australia, with teaching and Matt. She did deserve to achieve her dreams, she believed that now, but she would need to work for them.

So many times since she returned home she had reached for her mobile, her finger poised above the delete button next to Lucas's name. In making love to her, hadn't he made an implicit promise to be honest? Yet she didn't quite have the courage to delete him from her life entirely. Of course, Daisy said that he didn't really betray *her*; he betrayed a girl from Australia he had only just met, a girl who had barged into Richard's life and only later found a place in his heart. Perhaps, in his shoes, she might have done the same. Anyway, she hadn't deleted him – but she wasn't ready to forgive him, either. She would let him remain, like a ghost haunting her, for how can you delete someone from your heart?

'How do you stay married for thirty years?' she mused out loud.

Joan's forehead lifted in surprise. 'Are you planning to embark on that journey?'

'No, not me, just . . . research,' she laughed. If anyone could tell her, it would be Joan. She and Brian seemed so easy together, like tennis doubles moving in synchronised harmony.

'Well, some people will tell you the secret of a long marriage is compromise. Others will say that it's communication. But as for me,' she said, looking at Molly with a wry smile, 'I say it's

319

having a bad memory that holds a couple together. Forgetting the small slights *and* the big betrayals. Of course, having said that, if Bri ever cheated on me he'd be a dead man.'

'Who's a dead man?' the man himself asked, appearing around the side of the house with his working gloves in one hand and a shovel in the other.

'No one you know, Brian love.'

The dogs interrupted any further discussion by bounding over and dropping the soccer ball at his feet. He kicked it obligingly before turning back to the two women, saying, 'That rosebush wants moving.'

'Mmm, I don't think it's getting enough sun around the side there. Have a cuppa first, there's plenty of tea left in the pot.'

'Don't mind if I do.'

Brian joined them, propping his shovel against the house and pulling up a chair from the other end of the veranda while Joan fetched another mug from the kitchen. He gave Molly a wink and helped himself to Joan's pre-jammed scone.

She was glad she had driven down to Wuurnong for a couple of days. Those first weeks after she returned from England she had drifted about the flat aimlessly, taking endless walks by the beach, trying not to think about Luscombe. Except she was fooling herself. She missed those long, rambling conversations with Richard; the engrossing work of sorting through the archive; and her yearning for Lucas was like a hunger that gnawed through every waking hour.

God, she was stupid.

'Your mother told us about your theory,' Brian said, licking his fingers, 'that Rose was really Ivy.'

'Yep. It was a good theory. It fitted all the pieces, but I suppose DNA can't be argued with, can it?' She kept coming back to something Uncle Ted had said, about he and Uncle Harry and their dad towering over Rose. Plus there was the puzzle over why

Rose disappeared, just days before Robert was due to arrive to see her, after forty-four years apart. The timing was so perfect, as if she had planned it. Yet if Rose was really Ivy then she couldn't risk meeting Robert again. He would have exposed her. After all, she was his sister . . . and Ivy had been his lover. He would certainly know the difference between the two women.

'I was ten when Granny Rose disappeared and I remember her pretty well. She wasn't the sort of woman to commit suicide. Too tough, too bossy,' offered Brian.

'You think she drowned accidentally?'

'She must have.'

'And you remember her as a small woman too?'

'Yes, but size can be distorted by memory. For example, I'm sure Tim Tams were a lot bigger when I was a kid. Now I can eat half a packet in one sitting,' he said, patting his stomach affectionately.

They heard Joan's tread on the old planks of the veranda and her voice saying, 'Well, my memory is certainly lying to me. I could have sworn I'm the same size as when we got married, but for the life of me I can't fit into my wedding dress.'

She set the mug down in front of Brian and poured the tea in a dark stream. Brian picked up the mug but halfway to his mouth he stopped and looked at Molly, his face resembling a light that had just been turned on. 'Of course! The wedding dress! We've got Rose's wedding dress in an old trunk in the back bedroom. Like Joanie said, memories can lie. But wedding dresses tell the truth, every time.'

There were six bedrooms at Wuurnong, the back bedroom being up a few extra stairs from the main landing. It was built under the roofline, with a sloping plank ceiling and a view over the cobbled yard. It was also the room where they stored junk, a living museum of old suitcases: from heavy leather models with brass corners and clasps to scuffed cardboard imitations, fraying nylon, scratched plastic and even a large wicker basket. But the object of Brian's search was an enormous travel trunk resting atop a wooden crate in the corner of the room furthest from the window. The trunk was varnished canvas, with light wood strapping and brass fittings, several luggage labels adhering to it. Molly had a similar one under her bed that she used to store winter clothes.

'There it is,' he announced with a satisfied grin. 'I knew it was up here somewhere. Go ahead, it isn't locked. I tell the grandkids this room is haunted or else they'd be in here playing dress-ups with all Joanie's finery.'

The trunk was about a metre wide and thirty centimetres deep, early twentieth-century probably. It was made for taking long journeys by sea, not rolling on to aeroplanes or throwing in the boot of a car.

'I'm not sure where it came from,' he said, scratching his thatch of grey hair, 'it may even have come from England with your great-grandmother.'

'One of the luggage labels is for a shipping line, so it's quite likely. They operated steamers on the London to Australia route.' The second luggage label featured a line drawing of a colonial-style hotel with a bold red typeface on a yellow background. 'And look, here's another label for the Galle Face Hotel, in Colombo.'

She knew that most steamers had called at Colombo after the Suez Canal opened, so perhaps the trunk really did belong to Rose. Using tissues she carried in her jeans pocket, she wiped the dust from the trunk, before snapping open the fastenings one by one and lifting the lid with a mixture of expectation and trepidation. Did she want to find a tiny wedding dress that would prove her theory, or did she want to remain a Luscombe descendant, whatever that might entail? She wasn't sure, but she did know that once she was on the track of a mystery she couldn't let go until she followed the clues to the very end.

The trunk opened to reveal a lining of red, checked fabric, a protective layer of crisp white tissue paper and the distinctive smell of naphthalene. She removed the first layer of tissue paper to reveal a wedding dress of white satin with puffy sleeves folded behind and a scooped neckline, a refugee from the 1980s. Lifting it carefully from the trunk, she placed it beside her on the rag rug. Then she removed the accompanying veil, a confection of tulle and fabric roses.

'Joanie's,' Brian said. 'You've seen our wedding photo downstairs?'

'Uh-huh, Joan looked gorgeous and you were a real hottie.'

'Didn't think I had a chance with her when we met. But I grew on her.'

The garment beneath was older, 1950s cream lace with a heart-shaped neck, fitted sleeves and pearl buttons. Molly removed it too, thinking that her wedding gown of choice would also be cream lace, with long elegant sleeves and a slim silhouette.

'My mother's. This is the burial ground of wedding gowns past.'

There was one last wedding dress left, shrouded below the next layer of tissue paper. Molly took a deep breath before lifting it reverentially from the trunk and removing it from its nest of tissue, to drape over both of her arms. The fabric had probably begun as white but had yellowed in the century since it was made. Of creamy chiffon with a silk lining, the dress had short, lace sleeves with a loose bandeau-style bodice, flounces at the hips and, judging by the proportions, a draped calf-length skirt. She stood and held it against her own body. She was five foot seven, and a size ten. The dress was way too small for her. In Australian sizes it was probably a six. The woman who had worn this dress couldn't have been much more than five foot tall.

'I think you have your answer,' Brian observed.

'If this was Rose's wedding dress then she must have been a good eight inches shorter and a handspan narrower than she was in the photograph taken in front of Luscombe Park. Either that or whoever wore this dress wasn't Rose Luscombe at all.'

'But if Ivy was the one who married Jim, why did the DNA test show that you and Richard are distant cousins?' He frowned at the dress as if it was the culprit.

'I'm not sure. But Luscombe is a tiny hamlet, and both the Luscombe and Toms families have lived there for generations. Maybe there was more funny business going on than people let on. Or maybe those tests aren't very reliable,' she suggested, aware that something else lurked at the back of her mind, if she could just reach it.

Brian dipped his arms into the trunk to lift out the accompanying veil. It was a silk, mob-cap style that fitted over the hair with a single layer of tulle floating from it. He placed the cap on his head and arranged the veil around his shoulders.

'What do you think?'

'Very stylish, but quite impractical around the farm,' she laughed.

'One thing I'd like to know,' he began with a puzzled shake of his tulle-clad head, 'if Rose was really Ivy, what happened to the real Rose?'

'*If* my theory is correct then I expect Rose died of Spanish flu in Colombo – and, for whatever reason, Ivy took her place.'

44

Colombo, Ceylon

1919

If someone asked her later why she stayed, Rose wouldn't have been able to answer. At the time there seemed no other option, for how could she leave Ivy alone and ill so far from home? She was a nurse, after all. Dr Sullivan assured her that Ivy would be cared for at the General Hospital, imploring her to consider her own future and the fiancé waiting in Australia. Except she had seen the results of the Spanish grippe that had infiltrated every town and village in England the previous year. She had even heard children skipping rope to the plaintive chant:

> *I had a little bird*
> *And its name was Enza,*
> *I opened up the window*
> *And IN-FLU-ENZA.*

If she abandoned Ivy, the girl might die.

England was long gone, and Port Said – their last port of call – had been eight days ago. Too long for Ivy to have picked it up there. So she must have caught the flu on board ship. No wonder the doctor had appeared on the wharf with the purser in tow: they already knew. They already knew there was infection aboard and Ivy might not be the only person put ashore in Colombo.

So here Rose was, back in her rickshaw, with Ivy lolling restlessly in the vehicle alongside. She was almost certain the rickshaw pullers would have abandoned them if not for the purser's threats. But the kerfuffle at the wharf meant that news had already travelled and the nearest suitable hotel suddenly found it was fully booked. She had no alternative but to risk the four-mile journey out to the elegant Galle Face Hotel.

She wasn't sure why she felt responsible, since she sensed that Ivy, in her own sly way, despised her. Once Maman had sprung her secret, the girl no longer needed to hide behind her usual servant's mask. Rather, she assumed that Rose and the Luscombes owed her for stealing away her birthright. They owed her because they had stolen her chance at happiness. Now she had entwined her life around Rose's and nothing could pry her loose. Besides, if she abandoned Ivy, her brother might never forgive her. Plus Jim knew Rose as the compassionate young woman who had nursed his wounded brother. She didn't want her fiancé to believe she was just another silly debutante. Once, she might have been intent only on amusement but the war had honed them all into better or worse versions of themselves. Either that or it broke them.

The road stretched ahead in an interminable line of red gravel, jostling with rickshaws, bicycles and strolling pedestrians, the last rays of early evening sunshine bathing them in a pale light. A wide sward of green ran the length of the road on their left, with the ocean to their right. Rose was conscious that the sea, which had glittered like green crystal that morning, now crashed angrily on to a thin strip of sand. If it weren't for the retaining wall, she felt sure they would have all been swept away.

In the distance the hotel beckoned, surrounded by the bent spindles of coconut palms waving their mop of fronds – in welcome, she hoped, for if the hotel refused to accommodate them she didn't know what she would do. Three storeys tall, crowned by a red roof and extending across several veranda-lined wings, the Galle Face Hotel was the epitome of colonial splendour. The rickshaws pulled up outside the hotel portico and she girded herself for the task of coaxing Ivy into the foyer. The white-jacketed doorman was already hurrying to her side and exclaiming over the young lady, seemingly asleep in the rickshaw.

'Can I be of service, miss?'

'I think my friend has had too much sun. If you could ask the clerk to arrange a room, I will help her into the hotel,' she announced in her most authoritative voice. 'Miss Rose Luscombe and Miss Ivy Toms, our luggage will be following from the *Osprey*.'

'Certainly, miss.'

The doorman clicked his fingers and a porter appeared at his side to usher them into the foyer after being given whispered instructions.

Leaning over Ivy's still form, she whispered into her ear, 'Ivy, you must get up. If you don't get up I shall have to leave you.' An agitated flutter of lashes answered her threat and Ivy opened her eyes a slit, the whites showing an irritated red.

'I know you are sick but you must make the effort or I won't be able to help you.'

Her breath emerged from her lungs with a harsh rattle, and Rose felt a whisper of hot stale air on her face. Two dark angry spots coloured Ivy's cheeks and her lips were parched and cracked.

'I'm going to place your arm around my shoulders but you must help, for I cannot carry you. And no one else will.' She slid her arm behind Ivy, feeling the wet heat of fever. 'And whatever you do, don't cough.'

'Miss is unwell?' the doorman enquired with a frown.

'So foolish of us to have left the awning down, Miss Toms isn't accustomed to the heat.' She smiled as she gave Ivy an encouraging butt with her shoulder.

Thankfully, Ivy responded by leaning forward, sliding her body from the rickshaw to stand shakily on two feet.

'Come along, let's get you into the hotel,' she said cheerily. 'Such a lovely hotel.'

'May I help, miss?' the porter asked uncertainly.

She could see that he was unconvinced about the sunstroke. He was welcome to believe Ivy was inebriated for all she cared, so long as he got them to a room.

'Miss Toms and I will manage. But if you could lead us straight to a room I will register as soon as I have made her comfortable.'

'Of course, please follow me to the lift,' he said, holding open the door and then leading them into the foyer.

She was relieved that the hotel had all the modern conveniences of electric light and a lift, for Ivy could not manage stairs. They followed the doorman across an airy foyer cooled by overhead fans. The porter reappeared at their side with a key, watched by the curious faces of both desk clerks.

'This way, miss,' said the porter, indicating the lift, as the doorman relinquished them into his care.

Ivy leaned heavily upon Rose and she thanked her stars that, like them all, she was lighter than she had been before the war. Really, how could such a tiny person bear so much malice?

'Miss has a room overlooking the ocean on the second floor,' the porter explained as the lift clanked into action. 'Breakfast is served in the dining room, high tea on the veranda, very good high tea. Must not be missed. Miss may also enjoy the view from the rooftop garden.'

She very much doubted she would be enjoying the view from the roof garden. She would be glad of a view of a bed. The lift stopped and the porter gestured for them to step out into the corridor. She hoped their room wasn't far, for she could feel Ivy sliding from her grasp. They passed two more doors before stopping outside a dark timber door that the porter proceeded to unlock.

'Very nice room,' he said. 'Very beautiful view.'

'Thank you, and please tell the desk clerk I shall be down momentarily to register,' she said, turning her back on him decisively and leading Ivy over to one of the carved wooden beds. 'Do arrange for our luggage to be brought up when it arrives.'

He stood irresolute for a few seconds then, leaving the key on a table, he departed. Meanwhile, Ivy collapsed on to the bed, her eyes rolling in her head. She was shivering now and Rose didn't bother to undress her, merely removed her shoes and somehow manoeuvred her beneath the light cotton blanket. They would need more than this if she were to nurse a fever.

'So cold.'

'I'll get more blankets.'

There was a tall wardrobe against one wall of the room, as well as two rattan armchairs and the low table where the porter had left the key. A jug of water and two glass tumblers sat atop a chest of drawers, and she presumed that a second door led to a private bathroom. She crossed to the wardrobe and was rewarded with the sight of two woollen blankets folded within. Perhaps the nights could be chilly here, after all. Spreading both blankets over Ivy, she lifted her upper body and tried to coax her into taking a few sips of water. Then she placed the tumbler on the side table next to the bed, saying, 'I must go down and register, but I'll return soon,' before scooping up the key and heading for the door.

She drew a deep breath, looking back at the sick girl sweating under her load of blankets. The small oval face with its lurid cheeks resembled a porcelain doll, except for the hacking cough that shook her entire body. She was sorely tempted to have that obliging doorman call another rickshaw and take her back to the wharf. With luck, the *Osprey* wouldn't have weighed anchor and she could pay her sixpence to a boatman and be delivered to the gangway. Her hand on the doorknob quivered. Ivy was her childhood friend, her girlhood companion. She should be reminiscing about the escapades of two little girls playing in the grounds of Luscombe Park and despairing that it had come to this. Two little girls separated by wealth and class yet closer than either could ever have imagined. And now one of them was deathly ill and the other must try to save her.

But she wasn't despairing; she was angry. What choice did she have? Robert had foisted Ivy upon her. Then Maman had coerced them into travelling together. Ivy's very existence had turned her life into a thing of secrets and shame. And now this illness might destroy Rose's future altogether. Ivy wouldn't cry for her if their positions were reversed – Rose rather thought she might be inclined to gloat.

She took a last look at the room, considering the French doors leading on to a balcony, the gleaming teak floors and the whir of the ceiling fan. She wasn't sure how long she would be stranded in this room. If Dr Sullivan was correct, Ivy could be gone by morning. She might recover quickly. Or she might linger for days or weeks. Rose hadn't been a VAD without learning something. She knew that she might also succumb to infection herself. But if she returned to the ship she might infect others. Better to stay in this room until they were both recovered.

Clearly, only one of these foreseeable futures was encouraging.

As she closed the door behind her, she found herself dreading the forthcoming days of mopping up vomit and bathing feverish limbs. Of dealing with all the unpleasant bodily functions of this girl whose reluctant keeper she had become. It was enough to give her a very bad headache.

'Ma? Is that you?' Ivy felt a great weight filling her chest and she was cold . . . so cold. She seemed to be fading in and out of the light.

'Robert?'

If only Robert were here, he would put things to rights. He would look after her. He had promised.

'Rose?' Rose had been here, she felt sure. She remembered a voice urging her to stand. Ordering her to walk. Leading her down a dark corridor, a white-garbed figure at her side. She remembered a drift of air from above and a feeling of falling.

'Rose?' she murmured again. There was no answer – and no white figure, either. But Rose had been here, she knew. And Robert had been left behind at Luscombe Park. He couldn't be her husband because he was her brother. She let herself love him and he sent her away.

But where was here? And where was Rose?

She shivered so hard that her teeth clashed together. Her limbs ached, her throat was rasped with pumice stone and she could feel the crackle of her chest at each breath. She was dying. Drowning from the inside out. Her nurse's instincts told her that she needed to find the will to save herself. But she was so very tired, too tired to fight. Too tired even to love any more. What was the point? Her father betrayed her long ago. Her mother was too weak to protect her. And Robert abandoned her, his love not strong enough to withstand his mother, his sister and their world.

The tiny flame remaining to Ivy was fuelled by anger rather than love.

If she died, Rose and her mother would win. Rose was already possessed of the Luscombe name and heritage. If she died, Rose could take back her happiness and freedom too. Rose would have everything and Ivy's life would have counted for nothing.

She felt the flame of her anger rising, fuelling her fever. She couldn't die. Someone had to pay for the Luscombe legacy. Someone had to pay for stealing Ivy's birthright, and the only person left was Rose. If she couldn't have Robert then Rose owed her a future.

45

Western District, Victoria

2017

As Molly drove east towards home, flat-topped Mount Leura and the green cone of Mount Sugarloaf rose above the surrounding farmland. Salt lakes shimmered in the distance and drystone walls snaked across pastures. The early settlers had built these walls, collecting the honeycombed rocks shot from volcanoes thousands of years earlier, levering them from the ground with crowbars and moving them into place using makeshift sleds. Professional wallers, who had learned the skill from their forebears in Britain, sculpted the walls, laying two rows of stones three feet apart and filling the interior with rubble. To Molly, the walls were merely one episode in the long history of the region: from the giant wombat-like megafauna that roamed here 50,000 years ago, to the Djargurd Wurrung people who used the stones to build fish traps and weirs, and the European settlers who later cleared the land of stones and people to build their walls.

As she drew nearer to the Stony Rises where craggy, cone-shaped outcrops erupted from the volcanic plain, she was reminded of the drive with Lucas through the Valley of the Rocks. She had opened her heart to him that day without realising the danger. She had allowed herself to dream of *some* kind of future with him. She was fooling herself to think that she hadn't, futilely guarding her heart.

And that wasn't the only lie. Her connection with the Luscombe family was a lie too. Rose was her great-grandmother in name only. Her real great-grandmother was Ivy Toms. She was sure of it now, despite Lucas and his toothbrushes. The conundrum was *why* hadn't Robert and Ivy married? She thought of the photograph of those two young nurses, faces subtly alike yet in other ways vastly different – a bit like herself and Daisy, really. You could see the resemblance, once you knew they were sisters, but most people didn't pick it up immediately.

Oh my God . . . the pieces rearranged themselves in her head, clicking silently into place.

Checking her rear-view vision, she steered on to the verge, coming to a standstill with the Stony Rises dominating her mirrors. She cut the engine, hardly daring to believe the thought that had occurred to her. Reaching over to the rear seat, she grabbed her computer, propping it on her lap and opening it. With shaky hands she clicked on the database cataloguing the Luscombe archive.

She opened the Documents category, then the Legal Documents subcategory, searching for the object she knew was there, listed amongst other similar documents from the last one hundred and sixty years that she had found amongst the dust fairies in Richard's attic. She entered the key words 'lease' and 'Toms' and waited while the program sifted the records to find what she wanted. And there it was, the very object that she remembered puzzling over with Richard and Lucas. She clicked on the listing and the program opened to a page showing the details she had entered about that object.

The lease was for Ashcott, a cottage that formed part of the Luscombe estate, a cottage leased to Walter Toms. She read the object title: 'Lease of Ashcott dated 3 March 1899'. And then the description she had written: 'five-roomed cottage leased to Walter Toms for 21 years for annual rent of one shilling and signed by Edward Luscombe'. She had known this, of course, but until now she hadn't put two and two together and made four. Apparently, the Luscombes were beholden to Walter Toms.

Yet why would Robert and Rose's father lease a significant cottage to an agricultural worker on his estate for the peppercorn rent of one shilling? And what a coincidence that the lease was dated a few months before Ivy was born and concluded when she became an adult. Could it be that the lease had been a payment? And if it were payment, could it have been payment to Walter Toms for taking on another man's child? For if Ivy was actually Edward Luscombe's illegitimate daughter, that would explain everything. It would explain why Robert couldn't marry her. It would explain how Molly could have a genetic connection to the Luscombes even though Ivy was certainly her great-grandmother. It might explain why Rose/Ivy had cut off all contact with the Luscombes. And it would go some way towards explaining why Ivy had taken Rose's place, for if she had discovered the secret of her birth, she may have taken Rose's death as an opportunity to grasp a small part of the birthright she had been denied.

Molly's great-grandfather Jim Turner hadn't met Rose before he proposed marriage, and she knew from the photograph that there was a resemblance between the two women. Rose was clearly prettier, but they could have been – and, she believed, indeed were – sisters. Apart from the height difference, it would have been a simple matter for Ivy to take Rose's place. If she managed to solve the apparent height disparity on the passport, then all she needed to do was cut all contact with her home, and ensure that no photographs of her existed. And Jim Turner would never know the difference.

The words 'together forever' made perfect sense now. In a way Rose was Ivy. Ivy was Rose.

And if Ivy had the strength of will to live a lie for more than forty years, wasn't it also possible that she was strong enough and vigilant enough to live a further lie until she died?

Wherever and whenever that may have been . . .

Maybe Nan was right all along.

46

Melbourne, Victoria

1919

As the *Oracle* steamed through the heads of Port Phillip Bay she selected the most inappropriate gown in her trunk. It was a dress a debutante might wear for afternoon tea rather than a long journey with a strange man through unknown country. Made of delicate blush-coloured linen, the dress was cut simply with a high round neck and elbow-length sleeves. It had been hand-embroidered with a geometric design in pink and rose, edged at hem and sleeve with intricate dark pink lace, the waist cinched with a wide band of black silk. Today she didn't want to look sturdy and appropriate. She wanted to look pretty. Pretty had always been one of Rose's strengths.

She draped the pearl sautoir about her shoulders. Yet as she was fastening the clasp she noticed that the sheen had flaked from several of the pearls, exposing the glass beneath. There was another necklace in her luggage, a string of true pearls, but on such a hot and humid day her perspiration might damage their lustre. So she put away all thoughts of pearls and left her neck bare.

Her trunk was almost ready, only a few last items to pack before the steward arrived. There was the portrait of two young nurses linked forever by a photographer's art, a bundle of letters and a handful of crumpled paper covered in the words 'Rose Luscombe', written over and over. She scrawled two words on the rear of the photograph and slipped it amongst the bundle of letters before depositing them in the trunk. She had reread those letters a hundred times, savouring the words, as if she could learn Jim Turner from the lean of his 'l's and the curve of his 'c's. She had studied his photograph, wondering what kind of man lurked behind that devil-may-care moustache. It was a different kind of confidence to Robert's. Robert Luscombe's self-assurance came with the knowledge that he could handle himself in any drawing room in the Empire. Somehow, she couldn't picture Jim Turner sipping tea in the Duke of Devonshire's salon.

Well, he would suit her. She had had enough of drawing rooms to last a lifetime. She had had enough of ribbons that constrained more tightly than chains. Perhaps in the wide-open spaces of Australia she would find freedom.

Time had slowed to a trickle since the feverish fortnight in Colombo, as she waited uncertainly for the next steamer while dealing with the Colombo authorities, the hastily summoned doctor and distressed hotel staff. Dealing with the officialdom of death. Sometimes she thought she was living a dream, a nightmarish version of her real life, and that any minute she would wake to hear Greep announcing dinner or Mrs Tucker jangling her keys. But there was no Greep and no Mrs Tucker. She had made a decision in a moment of great duress and it was too late to retreat. She had wanted the power to choose her future . . . well, now she must live with that choice.

The journey from Colombo had been tedious, lost in a babble of excited war brides and rowdy returning soldiers. Even the novelty of seeing flying fish couldn't stir her from her malaise. She was exhausted from the constant vigilance necessary in the first-class dining saloon with its timber panelling and lofty stained-glass ceiling. And when the customs official in Fremantle gave her passport only a cursory glance, not even remarking upon the stain that partially obscured the recorded height – a blot that turned a statuesque five foot ten into a modest five foot one – she could breathe for the first time in weeks.

At least the journey had given her time to recover her strength and prepare for her meeting with Jim Turner. She cabled ahead so that he knew of the flu outbreak and Ivy's death. Knew to expect her changed by her illness, a little haggard, less lustrous of hair and skin. Not quite Rose. The Spanish flu had taken its toll on both mistress and maid.

The pier was bustling with well-wishers as the SS *Oracle* moored alongside New Railway Pier in the Port of Melbourne, many people wearing white muslin masks covering their mouths and noses. Futile protection against this flu, she could have told them. She didn't know how she would find Jim in this excited crowd. There were almost a thousand passengers aboard the *Oracle*, and many of them would have someone waiting expectantly on the pier. So she shuffled along the gangway, caught up in the pressing crowd, until finally she stepped on to the pier that stretched five hundred yards towards the shore. She felt the warning sting of the hot day to come. Settling her hat, she tucked a stray curl behind her ear and moved a few feet from the gangway, hoping to find a space large enough to be visible to anyone looking for a young woman waiting alone.

Gradually the crowds cleared so that only scattered pockets of people remained. Standing with a small carpet bag at her feet, she gazed nonchalantly about her, for a Luscombe would never look forlorn. And then she spotted him. Standing a dozen yards distant, slightly taller than the men around him, his hat a little more battered, his suit a little more wrinkled, his face more tanned. He was staring in her direction, a frown creasing his forehead, a question in his eyes. Raising one gloved hand, she smiled tentatively.

'Rose?' he asked, coming to stand next to her. She hadn't realised he was so tall, taller than his brother Henry. She had to tilt her head to look up into his face, checking for a welcoming smile.

From his letters, she had sensed there were chinks in his armour that he hoped Rose might mend. He had lost something when his brother died, lost something by staying on the farm rather than dying in a stinking trench in France or on a blood-drenched beach in the Dardanelles. She supposed she would find out sooner or later exactly what that loss was. That's what wives did, wasn't it? Supported their husbands in sickness and in health.

'Jim?' She extended a silk-clad hand, which he held firmly for a few moments as he studied her.

'I was sorry to hear about your troubles. That poor girl.'

That poor girl who had died struggling for each exhausted breath. But she didn't want to think about that. She had put it behind her with the last sight of the brown and red buildings of Colombo retreating into the distance. She was a new woman in a new land.

'Yes. Those last days were difficult, and I'm afraid the flu has taken its toll on me too. Taken its toll on my looks, I mean,' she said, looking down modestly.

She wasn't sure how she expected him to answer – that she was prettier than her picture, or some other nonsense. But Jim Turner was nothing if not a practical man.

'Not to worry,' he said. 'Mum will feed you up. We'll soon have you looking as good as new.' He picked up her bag and placed his other arm against her back to steer her towards the waiting baggage truck. Then he paused, turned to consider her once more, before adding, 'I'm glad you're here. They've been hauling the dead away in carts in Sydney and shutting down schools all over the place. Closed state borders, even turned the Exhibition Buildings into a hospital. I'm glad you made it, Rose.'

'I'm glad too.'

'So here you are, then. And we'd best be moving if we want to reach Wuurnong. We've a long way to go.'

Jim had described his home in his letters but she hadn't known what to expect. Words could only tell you so much. She wasn't prepared for the empty miles of brown paddocks and stony fields they passed on their journey, the alien cones of extinct volcanoes in a sea of dead grass. She felt ambushed by this topsy-turvy world, where swans were black and lakes full of salt. Dusty, yellow streets were lined by timber storefronts with tin awnings, ugly red-brick buildings unsoftened by time, lumbering wagons piled high with wool bales. Only the occasional handsome stone homestead or town hall had any grace to it.

She had risked everything to reach this place. She had relinquished an entire life for this one. The Rover, its paint dulled to a dirty brown by years of bouncing over cart tracks, protested at every bump in the road. She couldn't help thinking of Robert's shiny silver Rolls Royce and his mesmerising blue eyes, so different to Jim's serious green ones, the washed-out colour of a eucalypt leaf. But there was no going back now, no place for her at Luscombe Park.

She tied her hat down with a gauzy scarf but there wasn't much she could do about the dust that trailed them implacably for a hundred miles. The man behind the steering wheel of the battered Rover wasn't what she expected, either. He didn't say much. From the outpourings in his letters, she had expected a talker. Instead, she discovered a man who let silence do his talking.

'Mum's real pleased about the wedding,' he finally ventured, after the first hour of a long motor journey without the smallest of talk. 'It's quiet on the farm without Harry around.'

She imagined evenings sitting beside a fire in Wuurnong's kitchen, Jim's mother quietly mending while he read or did the accounts by the light of a kerosene lamp, for there was no electricity at the homestead, this much she knew from his letters. She could imagine his mother's loneliness. Jim had his dog and his horse for company, after all.

'Mum's taken Harry's death hard, it will do her good to have you with us.' He turned his head from the road to consider her profile, adding, 'Do me good too,' in case she should think otherwise.

'Henry was brave to the end.' She knew it wasn't much but perhaps it would be enough. 'Your brother was a fine man.'

'He was a crack shot, our Harry. He would've accounted for a few Bosch. I should have been there with him.'

She wasn't sure what she was supposed to say to that. He was still looking her way, searching her face as if for a sign. But she wasn't good at making people feel better. She could tend wounded bodies, yet when it came to wounded souls she was at a loss.

'You were here on the farm. Someone had to stay on the farm.'

'Harry needed me in France.'

'And then you would both be dead,' she said bluntly. Like so many other boys; specks of blood and bone puddled in the French mud. Years from now, someone might come upon those splinters of bone and wonder what, or who, they had found. 'You have to make the best of things,' she said. 'Take what life offers. That's what Henry would want.'

'Do you think so, Rose?'

Is that what Rose thought? Is that what Rose would do? Make the best of things? She didn't answer him immediately. She looked beyond him to the scene they were passing, a plain timber cottage squatting in a brown field, the house yard bordered by the beginnings of a cypress hedge struggling to stay alive through the dry summer. She thought how hot it must be underneath that tin roof with no trees to shade the house from the sun, just a narrow awning stretching futilely above the veranda. Painting a roof green didn't fool anyone, it was still tin. She didn't want to spend her life in a cramped wooden house with a tin roof. Or live her life at the beck and call of a woman with privilege running through her veins. And she didn't want to die in a damp earth cottage on someone else's grand estate.

She had taken what life offered, since it rarely offered much. And now she must make the most of it. She turned away from the little tin-roofed house and the sad brown fields and looked her fiancé in the eyes. He was her future now and they must both make the best of it.

'Yes, Jim. I do.' She placed her work-worn hand upon his arm. Taking his eyes from the empty road to search her face, he nodded in silence and kept driving.

47

Tasmania

2017

The flight was devoid of incident. The rental car was waiting at the airport. And Hobart was too small to make satnav lady cranky. Yet Molly couldn't help feeling that something was about to go wrong. She felt edgy, as if she were standing on the brink of chaos with her bare toes scrabbling at the earth. Heading out of town along the A3, she tried to quell her jitters by telling herself that she was merely locating the last piece of the puzzle. When she did, she could finally let Rose and Ivy go. What did it matter that she would no longer be related to the Luscombes, with no compelling reason to return to Luscombe Park and no believable excuse to bump into Lucas Toms?

It was probably pointless making the flight to Tasmania, except she wasn't the kind of woman who dealt in maybes and could-have-beens. She needed to confirm her hunches with cold, hard facts. She told herself that she owed it to Nan, but the truth was she owed it to herself. The fact that she was having as much trouble putting Lucas Toms from her mind as the story of Rose and Ivy was irrelevant. Sooner or later, she would. She was stronger now. She hadn't had the drowning dream since she left Devon. Next week, she would start back at school for one last term but she had already handed in her resignation. She had even given her grandfather's footy jumper to her young cousin. She would get over Lucas too.

Sometimes she wondered whether she had made a terrible mistake. She was tempted to call him, saying that she hadn't meant all those things about betrayal and trust and blah-de-blah-blah. But how could he believe she was a woman of her word if she took them back so easily? And how could she rewrite the past and remain true to herself? Of course, if he had called she might have been persuaded. But she hadn't heard a peep out of him since before she left Devon, and at that point she had been too furious to speak to him.

She still had that last message saved on her voicemail. If someone had asked her why, she would have answered that it was merely lazy electronic housekeeping, except it went deeper than that. If she deleted the message, she might never hear his voice again.

'Hi Molly, it's Lucas.' She had his words by heart now. 'Just checking to see if you've relented . . . but I guess not. Well, you know where to reach me . . .' Then a longish pause before his last words were cut off by the message service, 'I w—'

I what? I want . . . I was . . . I wish . . . She was hung up on the technological suspense of it. The missing words were like an apparition. I . . . what . . . what had he meant to say? One thing was clear. She was too much trouble, a woman toting too much baggage – a woman who needed a porter not a lover.

Even Daisy had given up on her. Molly hadn't heard a word from her sister since that day at Luscombe Park when she stormed out of the attic room. Normally her days pinged with messages from her sister, now there was only silence. She knew she was in the wrong, that she had been so self-absorbed that she had ignored Daisy's pain, thinking it less than her own because her sister had been an innocent bystander. Except innocent bystanders often suffer the greatest wounds, don't they? She knew that she had to make amends, but she wasn't sure how.

The Hyundai toiled up hill after hill – Black Charley's Opening, Bust-Me-Gall and Break-Me-Neck – the names testimony to the bullock drays that had hauled their loads up and over this same road two hundred years earlier. The original highway had been built by convicts, some of its stone bridges still lying concealed beneath modern asphalt. The past was always knocking at the door, demanding to be let in.

She passed the town of Buckland, then drove through the Prosser River Gorge to Orford. When the landscape opened out to a panorama of Great Oyster Bay, she pulled over to the first lookout point she came to, cut the engine, opened the door and got out to stretch her legs. Taking a dozen steps, she stood by the rail that guarded the edge of a steep drop.

The waters of the bay lay before her like a sheet of turquoise glass ornamented by the emerald jewel of the Freycinet Peninsular and long white ribbons of sand. Molly drew in lungs full of salt-tinged air and waited while her breathing slowed. She realised this is what she had been waiting for – the reassurance of the ocean in all its unpredictable grandeur. Had Ivy felt the same? Is that why she chose Cape Bridgewater for Rose's ending? Molly closed her eyes, trying to shut out the picture that flashed into her mind at that moment. But the blackness only served to illuminate the image – of a man sinking into the ocean as a little girl drew further and further away. She imagined his raised arm as the last part of his body to disappear beneath the waves.

A helicopter thumped overhead and she looked up, torn from her reverie by the sound. Tourists, probably, enjoying the beauty of the ocean from high aloft. All her life she had turned to the sea, even as she feared it – ever since she was twelve and had first discovered the ocean's unruly power. She had been lugging the guilt of her father's death around with her every day. She had become so accustomed to the burden that she was afraid to let it go, afraid that without it she might not know who she was.

She had made of the ocean a personal memorial, each cresting wave whispering 'lest we forget' in her ears. She could never escape her past . . . but perhaps she was finally coming to terms with it.

48

Cape Bridgewater, Victoria

1963

Ivy often came to this quiet backwater to walk along the beach and think. It was somewhere to go to get away from her life . . . Rose's life. In winter, the long curving beach of Bridgewater Bay was deserted, hers was the only car parked at the water's edge. There was only the occasional dolphin, or a fur seal that had ventured away from the colony at Seal Point. Twice, she had seen a southern right whale breaching out in the bay. And once, the majestic form of a giant humpback making its annual migration.

Now she was about to join them in the ocean's briny embrace.

For forty-four years, she had inhabited Rose Luscombe's life. In most respects she had made it her own. Harry, Ted and Queenie were her own beloved children, stamped in her mould with a determined spirit and a no-nonsense approach to life. She had made the homestead at Wuurnong her domain, intimate with the quirks of the huge black wood-burning stove, warring with the wasps that nested under the eaves outside the kitchen window. She was a prominent figure in the community, with several stints as president of the Country Women's Association. Except that a part of her always felt like a fraud, as if at any moment she might be exposed for the simple maid she had once been. And for all her efforts, after forty-four years, Jim Turner remained a stranger. How was it possible to share a bed with someone for four decades and still not know his secret self?

Of course they had married. A solid, decent chap would never bring a woman ten thousand miles and then renege on his promise. But from those earliest days she had sensed her new husband's puzzlement, his disappointment with his bride and his marriage. Even on their wedding day, with Ivy at her prettiest in a dress made just for her, Jim had the air of a man walking in someone else's shoes.

'Well, it's done now,' he had said by way of congratulations once his ring circled her finger. 'We're husband and wife.'

Did it count, though, when you signed your wedding vows with another woman's name? When you assumed another woman's life?

'Yes,' she had answered, waiting to see that glint of home-coming in his eyes. 'Now we have to make the best of it, don't we?' He nodded then, never one to waste words, and pecked her lips. And she knew that this was her punishment and always would be.

Jim Turner thought he had been sold a pup, not only for her not-quite beauty, and her missing air of fragility – although Ivy could have told him the real Rose was as fragile as a glittering diamond – but also for the cold heart at her core. The cinders that remained when the fire of her anger had finally burned itself out in that tropical paradise of Ceylon.

In those first months of marriage, she would catch him glancing at her out of the corner of his eye in bewilderment, as if he didn't know who she was. Jim Turner had expected a sweet English rose and instead he received tough, resilient ivy. He knew their marriage was a mistake, the hasty decision of a grieving, heartbroken man, but he would never admit it. A Turner took his mistakes on the chin like a man.

And while he endured the long years of their marriage in silent longing, she held the emptiness at bay with activity. For more than four decades they had rubbed along well enough, producing three children and seven grandchildren. They were familiar with each other's habits, yet their souls remained foreign territory. She was fond of him but she couldn't say she was disappointed when he moved his belongings to the back bedroom, two years ago now. They had always been roommates rather than lovers, and now they weren't even that. Sometimes she wondered whether he might have grown to love her if she had been more open with him – he was a kind man at heart – but there was an essential falseness at the heart of their marriage which could never be washed away, no matter how much truth came later.

She reached into her pocket for Robert's letter, unfolding the stiff cream stationery to peer once again at that familiar handwriting, the paper still bearing the faint smell of cigar smoke. Funny how her heart still rankled with jealousy over a dead woman. When she was a young maid, trailing in Rose's perfumed wake, she had thought it was resentment she felt for Rose, righteous anger that someone who had so much cared so little for others. Now she knew it for what it was . . . green-eyed jealousy. Well, Rose had been dead for more than half a lifetime. Yet now, after all these years, her brother . . . their brother . . . had decided to visit.

> *My dearest Rose,*
>
> *I shall not begin with a pointless preamble asking after your health but go straight to the heart of a matter that has shadowed me these forty-four years. One of the greatest disappointments of my life has been our estrangement, an estrangement that I do not feel I have done enough to bridge. In my defence, may I say that at first my grief and guilt over Ivy's death numbed me. There*

was no room in my heart for my only sister. It seemed to me then that the world had deprived me of every comfort a man might enjoy – my comrades, my faith in my father, my self-respect and the girl I loved. Later, the occasional telegrams we exchanged built like a wall between us, each brief missive a cold stone of regret.

Yet I should have done more to knock down that wall. I know that when we parted you were hurt and confused, angry with our mother, humiliated by our father and, dare I say it . . . bitter about your brother. I'm ashamed to say that in my despair I blamed both you and Mother, yet you were blameless in every sense, dear Rose. It was up to me to find a way back to you and I didn't. I'm sorry for that neglect.

So here we are, four decades after you departed for your new home. I trust that Australia and Jim have been good to you and that the life you made together has been satisfying. I can't complain about mine, for I've been lucky in my wife and my son, yet I have regrets. And if I don't make the journey now it will be too late. To that end, I am embarking on the long flight to Australia. You may expect me on the 17th of July. I'm not asking your permission, for I suspect it will not be given. I hope I won't be too late to make amends.

Your loving brother
Robert Luscombe

Her loving brother, her once-upon-a-time lover, handsome, aristocratic Robert Luscombe who had fallen in love with his sister's maid. She didn't blame him for being disillusioned and finding comfort in her arms. They were a disillusioned generation. But looking back, she realised that she should have known that Cinderella only ever married the prince in fairy tales.

It was so long ago, yet she was still wounded by Elsie Luscombe's secret. Still struggled for breath when she thought of the events it had set in motion. All these years later, Robert finally decided his conscience must be salved. Why shouldn't he go on living with it? After all, she had lived with hers for more than forty years. A decision made in desperation, paid for with a lifetime of regret.

She had only ever wanted to feel safe. But in the end, instead of a refuge she had made a prison.

She scrunched the letter into a ball and stuffed it into the small canvas holdall on the seat beside her. Checking that the handbrake was engaged, she pulled the key from the ignition, grabbed the bag and opened the door. Then she stepped out of the car and patted the bonnet of the EJ Holden Special fondly. The pale green paintwork was already covered in a film of dust from the road out to Bridgewater Bay. Such a shame, she had driven it less than a year and was about to abandon it miles from the nearest town. She hoped it would find its way back home to Wuurnong, safe and sound.

The sculpted green headland of Cape Bridgewater curved to the west with Cape Nelson to the east, like two giant paws stretching into the ocean. Once this crescent-shaped bay had been the crater of a volcano, now the towering cliffs enclosed a broad expanse of sand and deep blue sea. The bay was deceptively calm, breakers rolling in long lines towards the shore. But she had swum these waters before, though never alone, and knew that beneath the foaming crests strong rips waited to tow the unwary out to sea. The western beach sheltering in the lee of Cape Bridgewater was safest.

She set out towards the east and Cape Nelson, her feet kicking up puffs of sand and shell grit, then squelching through the wetter sand as she followed the shore's edge. Her legs had to work harder the further she walked, her muscles unused to the hard slog of wading through sand and skipping out of the way of encroaching waves, her brown loafers drowning in sand and salt and sea. The cold wind blasted her, whipping up sand that stung her cheeks and tormented her eyes.

After half an hour, she stopped to catch her breath. The high promontory of Cape Nelson loomed ahead, with a dense coastal scrub covering the high dunes to her left. Here was as good a place as any to relinquish Rose forever. She trudged up the beach to the high-tide line, with its garland of drying seaweed and silvery driftwood, before setting down her bag upon the sand, and preparing herself for the shock to come. She took a moment to survey the ocean, trying to judge where the rips lurked along the inner sandbar. Further out, beyond the outer bar, she knew yet more rips swirled.

Then, with a last deep breath, she walked into the sea. The water frothed around her knees, heedless of her stockings, weighing down her shoes with sand and wet leather so that she had to drag her feet through the water. As she waded deeper, the sea engulfed her, her pleated woollen skirt floating around her waist, icy water creeping up her torso, so that her twinset clung to her skin. As the first set of breakers hit, she braced herself as they washed around her, foaming to her chin, so that her chest felt like it was being pierced with icicles.

Her shoes slipped from her feet as she began to swim, weighed down by more than her wet clothes. She remembered a long-ago summer at the beach in Portland when Jim had first taught her to swim. She remembered the heavy swimming costume that had stretched from her neck to her knees. At first she had been embarrassed by the way the wet wool clung to her body, the way Jim couldn't help noticing, but soon she abandoned all self-consciousness for the pure joy of the waves and the water.

Not today.

She felt sorry to be leaving her children. She would be missed, but they had their own families now and would survive without her. After all, she had raised them. She could have waited for Robert, accepted the consequences of her deceit. But she suspected he would have forgiven his only living sister, the woman he once loved. Her children would certainly have forgiven her.

Except Ivy didn't deserve forgiveness.

She kept swimming, each breath becoming harder than the last as she swallowed more and more water. Her clothes grew heavier with each stroke, as she felt the rip pulling towards the open sea.

Not long now.

49

Western District, Victoria

1919

'What do you say to a ride this morning, Rose?' asked Jim as he came into breakfast the morning after her arrival at Wuurnong. He was dressed in his working clothes; moleskin trousers held up by a plaited leather belt; a light blue shirt of cotton drill; tan riding boots and a broad-brimmed rabbit felt hat. Despite the hat, his face and neck were tanned a deep brown. Close to, she could see the fan of tiny white lines that webbed his eyes from squinting habitually against the bright sun.

Riding was the last thing she felt like doing after the long journey of the previous day. Besides, it would take at least a day to learn the ways of his mother's kitchen. Her kitchen soon.

'Perhaps tomorrow? When I've found my feet?'

'Why find your feet when a horse will do the walking for you?' he said, slapping his hat against his thigh to be rid of a fly that had hitched a ride into the kitchen on his back and was buzzing about him. 'Give you an idea what sort of country you'll be in for, if you take me on.'

She guessed that 'taking him on' was his way of describing their proposed marriage. He was looking at her expectantly. She hailed from Luscombe Park. Surely she rode? When she did not answer immediately he scratched his chin, saying, 'I suppose being a gentlewoman you're accustomed to a side-saddle.'

She nodded, although some bold Devon ladies had been shocking the neighbours by riding to hounds in breeches for a good twenty years. Rose was a modern young woman and a pair of riding breeches lay at the bottom of her trunk, stashed beneath a certain red and white dress.

'The ladies in these parts ride astride these days. I can fix you up with a pair of trousers and you'll get the hang of it in no time.' The hat still slapped against his thigh, although the fly now lay dead upon the floor. She realised that Jim Turner was not a patient man.

'I have breeches with my habit. I'll leave off the skirt,' she said, blushing.

'Goodo. Half an hour then. Out by the stables. I've got just the little filly for you.'

A stump served as a mounting block in the dirt yard outside the stables. She stepped up, one foot upon the stump, and stopped, daunted by the distance to the saddle. The little filly did not look so little up close, her nose rounding inquisitively to sniff at the newcomer's hat. Meanwhile, Jim looked on in silence as she stepped her other leg on to the mounting block and stood facing the saddle. She had dressed as quickly as a half-hour allowed, pulling on Rose's dark blue wool riding breeches that buttoned below the knee, her high black boots, cream blouse, matching knee-length jacket with leather trim at the collar, and topping it all with a black bowler hat. She looked as elegant as possible under the circumstances.

'I didn't realise how badly the influenza and the long journey have weakened me,' she said, staring forlornly at the saddle, her knees already quaking at the thought of the ride ahead.

'I should have thought,' he said. 'Let me give you a leg up.' Standing behind her, he cupped her left foot in both hands, and

355

hoisted her skywards, saying, 'Grab the pommel and swing your leg over, nice and easy, and I'll adjust the stirrups.'

She had wanted to play the graceful lady of the manor and instead here she was, awkward and unsteady, the saddle refusing to conform to her contours as she landed like a sack of potatoes upon the filly's back.

'Do you still have the same mount? You wrote of a mare named . . .' Jim said as he walked the filly away from the mounting block, all the while watching Rose, uncertainty creeping like a shadow across his eyes.

'Daffodil. And before that there was my dear old Buttons.'

'Daffodil, eh?' he said, standing at the horse's near side to adjust the stirrup. 'How's that?'

'About right, I think. We won't be jumping, will we?' As long as she did not have to jump, she swore she would stay seated even if the flesh were jarred from her bones.

'There's a bit of rough country but we should be right. And you hunted?'

'Not since the war began,' she said, stroking the filly's neck tentatively as Jim walked around to the off side to adjust the other stirrup. 'I haven't ridden much of late. No doubt Robert will sell Daffodil now that I'm gone.'

'We'll take it easy, then. Let you get your seat back. Your body will remember once your mind allows it.'

But what if her body had no memory of riding? What if her body wasn't her body at all? She could adjust a riding habit – nip it in here, shorten it there – but it took time to retrain a body. It could take a lifetime. Would she have another lifetime?

Walking at a slow pace, he led them out into a paddock of dry yellowing grass, to follow a faint track across flat country towards a distant hill topped with a blue-green crown of gum trees.

'Mount Eccles,' he said, pointing towards the hill. 'She's an old volcano. There are lots of them in these parts. Its crater is filled by a lake. They reckon lava flowed all the way to the sea, once upon a time, leaving behind caves and tunnels and fields of stone. I'll take you there one day . . . when you're feeling up to it.'

He looked across at her as she rode at his side, hanging on to the reins with a death grip, and in his eyes she saw that the shadow of uncertainty was becoming a cloud of doubt. The horse too seemed to doubt her competence, tossing its head in complaint and whinnying in protest.

'You might want to loosen your reins,' he said with a frown.

'Of course, I'm sorry. Everything is so strange and new. I'm ashamed to admit I'm a little frightened.'

Riding with the reins in his left hand, Jim steered his horse so close that his knee bumped hers. Then reaching out with his right hand, he took hold of her left. She thought that he intended to prise loose her grip, that he was concerned for the horse's comfort and welfare. But then he squeezed her hand gently, saying, 'I'm the one who should be sorry, Rose. You've sailed across the world to a strange land. You've lost your friend and companion. Of course you won't be feeling like yourself.

'I'm a thoughtless fool. Please forgive me.' His hand on hers was large and scarred with old wounds, but he cradled her hand tenderly.

'There's nothing to forgive, Jim. We're both trying to find our way.'

'Don't you worry, Rose. She'll be right. You'll see.'

Would she ever be right, though? For she had done so great a wrong.

50

Tasmania

2017

Arriving in the small town of Swansea, Molly took the road out to Waterloo Point and the shearwater rookery. But instead of driving all the way to the waterfront and then following the walking track out to the rookery, she made a left turn. She had begun this journey almost a year ago in her grandmother's house, a short walk from Port Fairy's shearwater rookery. She had come so far since then, both figuratively and literally. Yet her quest was about to end in another small coastal town, next to another shearwater nesting place. Synchronicity.

After passing several houses, she slowed when she spotted what she was looking for. There were no signposts but the scattered headstones were indication enough. A drystone wall bordered the cemetery, although not the honeycombed volcanic rock of Stony Rises; these sharp-sided rocks appeared to be sandstone. Trees shaded the boundary, she oaks drooping beside the entry gate, with a line of eucalypts along the northern wall and a row of ragged cypresses fronting the ocean. Molly parked on the wide grass verge and stepped out of the car. She stood by the open gates, considering a narrow dirt track leading into the small graveyard. The blue waters of Great

Oyster Bay beckoned beyond. The headstones were a hotchpotch of pioneer and twentieth-century graves scattered across the grass in no discernible order. She decided she might as well begin with the perimeter, since there was no telling where she might end up.

Turning left, she struck out, her shoes crunching through dry leaves and twigs. There were several older graves but one in particular caught her attention. She paused to read the inscription on a simple white headstone commemorating the death by drowning of the six Large children on 5 November 1850. Elizabeth aged twelve, Edmund aged ten, William aged eight, Hannah aged six, George aged four and little Frances aged two years. The children were swept away by the ocean when the cutter *Resolution* was wrecked off the coast in the days when the village was still known as Great Swanport. She couldn't imagine how the children's parents, Thomas and Mary Ann Large, had endured such unbearable grief. Mary Ann had born her six children with such regularity, one babe every two years, and lost them all in the blink of an eye. Did they blame themselves?

Didn't all survivors blame themselves?

Molly's eyes welled with tears for the Large family. Sooner or later, you had to let go of blame.

She wandered, directionless, amongst the headstones, searching and blinking back tears. It must be somewhere: not a crumbling stone marker with chiselled words blurred by wind and rain, but something more recent, perhaps a plaque in the unmown grass or a simple cross. She was so certain. Nan had searched all those years and she had come so far to find it.

And then finally, unobtrusively, in a far corner, she spotted it – a neat, unassuming marker of square granite barely protruding from the long grass.

Julie Brooks

In memory of
Ivy Toms
Loving mother of Harry, Ted and Queenie
Passed away 11 May 1977
Aged 78 years
Forgive me

Molly breathed out one long, whistling sigh, unaware she had been holding her breath. As expected, her great-grandmother hadn't drowned in the wild waters of Cape Bridgewater. Somehow, she had found her way here to the east coast of Tasmania, to be buried in a small patch of ground overlooking Great Oyster Bay. Why she had chosen this town Molly couldn't be sure. Perhaps it reminded her of Devon and was far enough from Wuurnong for her to go safely unrecognised. But it was clear that she had lived a further fourteen years as a different person.

A different person, or the person she had always been?

Molly had followed a hunch that, in disappearing, her great-grandmother would resume the life she abandoned in Colombo in 1919. So she searched for Ivy's real name in Australian death registrations, discovering that an Ivy Toms died in Tasmania in 1977. That's why she was standing over this grave, looking at solid proof that the woman who masqueraded as Rose Luscombe for over forty years died bearing her true name. All that deceit had ended in a semblance of truth.

Kneeling amongst the dry leaf litter and grass, she crossed her arms over her chest as a shiver rippled through her. She felt as if someone were walking over her grave. The past was always there, waiting to ambush you when you least expected it. You didn't need to believe in ghosts to get the shivers in a cemetery.

Loving mother of Harry, Ted and Queenie.

She supposed Ivy had been a loving mother in her own way, despite allowing her family to believe she had drowned – or

360

worse, that her death was a tragic suicide. She couldn't know that Nan wouldn't be able to let her go. Her children had led long and productive lives and remembered their mother fondly. She had done her job well enough. Perhaps that's the most that can be asked of anyone.

Forgive me 🌹

Ivy had died carrying her burden of guilt.

Forgive me, Rose.

Not 'rest in peace' or 'into God's embrace'. Ivy had sought a more earthly forgiveness. Not from her children, her grand-children, her husband or Robert Luscombe. Her greatest guilt wasn't that she abandoned her family or lived a lie. Her greatest guilt was reserved for Rose, her mistress, her sister . . . the woman whose life she had taken.

Reaching forward, Molly traced the gold-limned words chiselled into the granite. Had Ivy wronged Rose so badly that she felt compelled to etch her guilt in stone for eternity? She had assumed Rose's identity, but a dead woman no longer needs a life. Unless she had done more than take over Rose's life . . . unless . . .

Molly couldn't quite believe the stray thought. What if Ivy had taken Rose's life in actual fact? But why would she? Rose was her sister.

Two sisters: separated by birth and subterfuge, yet growing to womanhood in as close proximity as Molly and Daisy. Knowing each other intimately, yet not knowing each other at all. Could Ivy have been driven to commit such a desperate act?

Molly ran her tongue over her lips, tasting tears, feeling a sudden ache for her own sister. She missed her nagging messages that buzzed about her like verbal mosquitoes. She missed her sweet face popping into life on her screen. How had she let a rift develop between them? How had she become so wrapped up in her own pain that she forgot to be a proper sister?

Things had to change.

Taking her phone from her pocket, she pressed her finger to her favourites and there was Daisy's face staring out at her from its tiny box. She touched her sister's image, and listened into the silence before the phone cycled through the long melody of chimes that would connect her to the other side of the world.

'It's me . . .'

There was the usual time lapse, then a yawning, 'Me, who?'

'Me, Molly. Your sister.'

'Ah, so now you remember.'

'I'm sorry, babe. I've been a selfish pig.'

'What was that? The line crackled.'

'I'VE BEEN A SELFISH PIG!'

'Uh-huh. You know it's one a.m. here. You're lucky I'm a night owl.'

Molly smiled to herself. Talking to Daisy was the same as always. She needn't have worried. They would never be like Rose and Ivy.

'Dais, I never thought you were shallow. I envied you.'

'You did?'

'Yeah, I wished I had the courage to test myself like you do.'

'I am a bit shallow, I suppose. But mostly I'm disappointed.'

Molly imagined her sister shrugging her shoulders and flicking hair from her eyes.

'I keep falling into love without really seeing the person I'm in love with, and then I blame them for disappointing me. I break a lot of hearts, Moll.'

'At least I'm not the only one feeling guilty,' said Molly, remembering the late-night phone calls from Daisy's rejected lovers pleading with her to tell them where they'd gone wrong and how they could fix things with her sister. She never knew what to say to them.

'Well, we all have to grow up, I suppose. Some of us are just a bit slower than others,' said Daisy, and Molly wondered which of them she was referring to.

'You know, I think Rose and Ivy were sisters. I think that's why the DNA test came back positive. Someone in Luscombe land hatched a little cuckoo,' she said.

'Mum told me. She's been giving me updates.'

She was on the verge of telling Daisy of her other suspicion, that Ivy might have killed her own sister, but thought better of it. It was only a hunch. No need to burden her sister with such a silly idea.

'I'm glad I have you for my sister,' she said instead. 'What would I do without you?'

'What would we do without each other?'

51

Cape Bridgewater, Victoria

1963

Beyond the breakers Ivy trod water, bobbing in the current that was slowly towing her east towards the rocky promontory of Cape Nelson. With numb fingers, she fumbled at her waistband, glad that she had thought to wear the grey skirt with elasticated waist. She didn't think she could have managed a zipper with frozen hands. She fought the wet wool that swirled around her, eventually extricating her legs and letting the garment float free. She didn't bother removing her stockings, knowing that the clips on her step-ins would defeat her. Kicking strongly to stay afloat, she struggled out of her cardigan and short-sleeved jumper in one awkward movement, prising her arms from the tight wet sleeves. Then she shivered out of her slip, watching her discarded clothes bobbing on the water and wondering where they would end up. Would they sink to the bottom of the ocean or be washed up somewhere along the coast to be discovered by a fisherman?

Rose's pearl necklace was a featherweight around her neck and a millstone around her soul. She knew that undoing the clasp would be an impossible task so she grasped the pearls with her right hand and wrenched hard. The string snapped, raining pearls into the ocean. Sending them home.

Her entire body shaking with cold, her fingertips blue, she turned back to shore, striking out in a diagonal line to ease her way free of the current. When a wave swelled behind her she swam strongly to catch it, as Jim had taught her, riding the wave like an arrow. She hadn't experienced that surge since the children were small and they spent family holidays swimming and digging in the sand at Port Fairy. The body didn't forget, no matter how old.

She emerged from the water, shaking and hungry for air. How strange that fever and cold should both make the body tremble, both leave it fighting for breath. She had seen many a fever in her sixty-four years; babies churlish with a first cold, children burning up with chicken pox, old ladies sweating and trembling through pneumonia, but never another such as that of 1919. That terrible fever was so long ago now, yet she remembered it like yesterday, the awful hacking cough, lungs frothing with bloody fluid. For some of its victims, the hazy days of the great flu pandemic were lost in a fug of delirium, but not Ivy. Those days she had endured, closeted in the moist, feverish air of a hotel room in Colombo, were engraved forever in her memory. Etched into her soul.

It was twelve miles to Portland by road but Ivy wasn't sure how far it was across country. She had already covered the first couple of miles along the beach, before setting off into the dunes. Slinging the canvas bag she had left on the beach over her shoulder – lighter now that she had donned its burden of warm trousers, pullover, woolly hat and pea coat – she tackled the long sandy hummocks lining the coast. She had her bank passbook stowed in her bag, the one she had opened all those years ago in the name of Ivy Toms – her emergency fund – slowly siphoned from Rose's trust fund and deposited in Ivy's name. Enough money for a ticket to a new life, such as it might be. Tasmania perhaps. Cool and green, like her first life on that other green isle, and far enough away that she was unlikely to meet anyone she knew.

It was hard going, with her feet sinking into the sand, tripping over the tangle of coastal heath, correa and sedge. She could go only a few hundred feet before stopping to rest. As the sound of the ocean retreated beyond the dunes, the vegetation grew thicker. Thickets of coastal wattle barred her way, the low-growing shrubs catching in her hair and the clusters of long yellow flower spikes issuing a cloying scent that trailed her slow footsteps.

She couldn't be sure how long she had been walking. Her watch had stalled at ten o'clock; drowned in the surf of Bridgewater Bay. Her breathing was laboured, her legs aching with the effort of climbing the dunes. She was no longer a young woman. Luckily, the going eventually became easier, heath giving way to pasture, sand giving way to loam. When she came within sight of the road she had to keep her ears tuned for the sound of an approaching engine. She had to be ready to duck behind tree or rock or even lie flat in the grass, something she hadn't done since she and Rose played the whirling game when they were girls. Holding hands, leaning back and twirling around until one of them became too dizzy, then letting go, they both collapsed in delighted giggles on the lawn.

Rose and Ivy, two little girls defying their parents to be together. How had they come to dislike each other so? Even stronger than her bitterness at losing Robert and being denied her real father, her resentment of Rose had defined her life. Long after the other woman was dead, her shade stalked Ivy, hovering over her marriage, lurking in the place where she kept her love for her children, making her into a colder, harder person. Turning her into someone who wasn't Rose or Ivy, but less than either. She had lost an essential part of herself when

Rose died, and she never managed to find it again. She was a hollow woman.

Rose's life had become her prison. The only way she could escape was by tearing down the walls.

52

Colombo, Ceylon

1919

The room had the smell of something dead. Ivy put her hand up to her face and wiped at her nose, bringing her hand away wet. She tried opening her eyes but her eyelashes were crusted together. Blinking them open, she stared at her hand to discover that the entire length of her thumb and hand was smeared with clotted blood that smelled like a decomposing rat. She pushed the covers back feebly, intending to get up and find a ewer of water to wash her hands and face – indeed, her entire body felt clammy and sour as if she had lain in a bath of sweat for days – yet she could barely turn on to her side. Her head pounded faintly, like the aftershock of gunfire.

Faint stripes of light filtered through timber shutters that blocked French doors to her right. She wasn't sure where the doors led. Raising her gaze to the ceiling, she saw a timber-bladed fan whirring slowly. Turning her head to the left, she made out another bed with someone lying under a thick pile of blankets. She would have stayed where she was, gathering her strength, but the terrible smell and her fetid, parched mouth drove her to try again. She slid her body closer to the edge of the bed, then slowly dropped one leg to the floor followed by the other. She was afraid that if she let her legs take all her weight they might buckle beneath her, so she twisted, levering her body with her arms, coming to a half-crouch and bending over the bed.

'Maman,' a thin voice issued from beneath the blankets. 'Where are you?'

Hearing that name, she realised that wherever she was, she must be with Rose, although what good it did to call for her mother, Ivy didn't know. Elsie Luscombe had done nothing more than birth Rose, before leaving her to the servants. Greep had more care for her than her mother. For a moment an image of Ivy's ma flickered before her eyes and she felt her throat knot for all that she had lost, all that she had never known. She coughed, bringing up more of the putrid phlegm that filled her throat, then wiped it on her damp, stale petticoat. The smell was intolerable.

She wasn't in the cabin on the *Osprey*, she could see that, the windows were too large for a steamer. She straightened gingerly, conscious that her balance was awry, almost as if she *were* still at sea. Her legs barely held as she placed one foot in front of the other, heading for the ewer and washbasin she could see on the other side of the room.

'Maman ... I want Maman ...' groaned Rose, the throaty plea breaking into a barking cough.

Perhaps Rose was ill. Perhaps she too had been ill. She certainly felt as tired and weak as a baby bird. She vaguely remembered voices and there had been a rickshaw, she felt sure of that. That was it. She remembered now. They were in the port of Colombo and there was something about not boarding the *Osprey*. Rose had taken her to a hotel. She remembered men in white jackets ... and she was sick with the Spanish grippe, according to the doctor. Rose bringing her water and tea. Trying to sip the tea and being cold ... so cold ... not having enough air.

Clasping the dresser with one hand to keep upright, she poured water into the washbasin and dribbled a little into a glass tumbler. When had a jug of water become so heavy? Raising the glass to her lips, she gulped the water in one long swallow, then setting it aside, she wet a small towel and dabbed at her face. The blood had crusted under her nose and she rubbed until the towel came away clean.

'Maman . . .'

There was little point in Rose calling for her mother, because her mother was thousands of miles distant, and no use to anyone.

'Maman isn't here,' she answered, trying to inject a sympathetic note into her voice. She didn't have the strength.

'Maman . . .' Rose breathed weakly, before erupting into another bout of coughing.

The water having restored her a little, Ivy considered the humped form quivering beneath the mountain of blankets. She should probably take a look.

'I'm cold . . .'

Rose's fever must be very high for her to be cold in this hot room buried under all those blankets. She teetered over to Rose's bed and peeled the coverings back from the other girl's face. Her fine creamy skin was marred with brownish purple splotches and beads of perspiration mottled her forehead. Ivy fancied she could hear a faint rattle issuing from her chest. The nurse in her knew that it was imperative to bring the fever down, applying cold compresses and sponging the body with cooling water. And there was a vial of laudanum in the luggage that could be administered to ease her discomfort.

She stood staring down at the shivering figure of her mistress and once-upon-a-time playmate. Even with her ruined complexion and lank hair she was beautiful, like a broken doll. Anyone would feel sorry for her, wouldn't they? Ivy searched her heart for sympathy, trawling her memories. She remembered Rose, laughing and twirling her butterfly net. She remembered her, proud and sure, upon her pony. She remembered her talking softly to soldiers who spoke of home with a longing so strong you could almost see it dragging them from their beds. She remembered her scowling, smiling, chastising. She remembered her that day in the library when their world was ripped to shreds. That face had mirrored all the most significant moments of her life.

And yes, she found a few scraps of sympathy, a few ragged threads of love. But even deeper, twined around her guts so tightly that she could barely breathe, she discovered anger and despair. That she had been brought to this godforsaken place so far from Robert. Despair that she would never have the life she longed for with the man she loved.

'Robert . . .' Rose breathed the name that rarely left Ivy's thoughts.

'Robert isn't here,' she said, her voice catching on a sob.

'Robert, you must let her go . . .' wheezed Rose.

'Let who go?' she asked, sidling closer to the ill girl and whispering in her ear. But she already knew the answer.

'Ivy. Tell her to go. She doesn't belong h—' The words rasped from her throat, erupting into another hacking cough.

It was Rose who had forced her to leave, who had stolen her love. She had known it all along. Left to his own devices, Robert would never have made her go. He would have condemned Elsie's words as the ravings of a bitter, drunken old woman who couldn't countenance a maid as mistress of Luscombe Park. He would have treated her revelation with the contempt it deserved. Only Rose could have convinced him that it was true. Only Rose could have convinced him to abandon his love.

Rose had betrayed her brother.

Rose had destroyed their love.

Ivy grasped one thin, bony shoulder and shook it forcefully, feeling the bones as fragile as a bird's wing beneath her fingers. Seeming so brittle that she could break them with her bare hands.

'Why? Why should Ivy go, Rose? Isn't she your sister?'

'Not my sister, never my sister . . .'

Never a Luscombe. Not by birth, nor by marriage. Rose had stolen that possibility and exiled her to the other side of the world.

You could have gone elsewhere, a feeble voice whispered in her head. You could have found another position, where you could make a different life. But she refused to listen to it. She had bound herself so tightly to the Luscombes that it was too late to let go. Even with Robert stolen from her, she was loath to make her own way, free of them and their concerns. She was of them, yet a creature apart. Rose was sailing towards love and she was sailing away from it. Rose was beginning a new life, while she would dine on scraps. Edward Luscombe had fathered them both, and yet Rose was the princess and she was the handmaiden.

'My head hurts . . .' Rose croaked plaintively, her head tossing on the damp pillow.

'Never mind. You'll feel better soon,' she murmured, realising that her hand still gripped the other girl's shoulder.

Her head hurt too, she thought. And her heart ached for everything that had been stolen from her. What she needed was to escape this dreadful room with its dead-mouse smell. She needed fresh air and blue sky and a nice cup of tea to settle her nerves. This was a hotel, wasn't it? She must be able to procure a cup of tea. She could order one for Rose too. A cup of tea would revive her poor dear sister in no time.

Rose's trunk was placed on the floor at the end of one bed, Ivy's wicker case at the foot of the other. Releasing her sister's shoulder, she crossed the floor to the trunk and bent to open it, releasing a waft of clean fresh lavender. How carefully she had folded and primped the garments within, how lovingly she had stroked the fine fabrics as she cleaned and mended them. By rights, they were hers as much as Rose's. Why shouldn't she wear something to take tea in this fine hotel? Especially since Rose wasn't in any fit state to forbid it. And she knew exactly the right ensemble for the occasion.

Kneeling by the trunk, she selected a dress in a waterfall of lemon silk chiffon, its elbow-length sleeves and hem embellished with a froth of ruffles, the waist cinched with a wide sash of satin in the same shade of pale yellow. One of Rose's filmy silk petticoats and cream patent pumps followed. She threw off her nightgown and slipped the petticoat over her head, pausing for a moment to still her dizziness. Then she shimmied into the loose dress that floated over her shoulders and down her body. It was far too large for Ivy, for she had been raised on bread and dripping, while Rose had breakfasted on poached haddock. But she gathered the excess fabric at the waist and secured it with the sash. Only a knowing eye would notice the difference. The shoes were a greater problem, but she stuffed the toes with handkerchiefs and hoped for the best.

In the private bathroom, she splashed her face with water from the ewer, and brushed her teeth with some of Rose's tooth powder, trying not to look at the haggard face with dark circles staring out at her from the mirror. Then twisting her lank curls into a knot at the nape of her neck, she hid them beneath a broad-brimmed, cream straw hat bedecked in yellow satin ribbon.

'How do you do?' she whispered to no one in particular, enunciating each word in the fashion of her former mistress.

Pushing open the door, she took note of the room number before walking hesitantly along the corridor in search of a lift or stairs. She didn't have to go far, discovering the shiny copper doors of the lift a dozen yards away. She pressed the call button and waited, wavering on her feet a little in the heat and the aftermath of her illness.

'To the lobby, miss?' asked the young man at the controls.

'Yes, please. I would like tea.'

'Very good high tea on the veranda, miss.'

'To the veranda . . . then.'

When the lift stopped at the ground floor, the operator directed her towards the veranda restaurant, where he assured her the scones were excellent. She followed his instructions, finding herself at a timber-floored veranda running the length of the hotel where clusters of ladies and gentlemen clad in cool summer costumes sipped tea and cocktails. A cool breeze fluttered through tall arched windows opening on to a grassy terrace overlooking the vast blue mirror of the Indian Ocean. The rich scent of salt and cinnamon and wealthy ease suffused the air.

'May I know your room number, please, miss?' asked a white-garbed maître d', clipboard in hand.

'Room 203,' she managed, stifling a cough.

'Ahh . . . Miss Luscombe,' he said, 'will anyone be joining you this afternoon?'

'No. No, I am all alone.'

53

Tasmania

2017

He was standing in the far corner of the cemetery where the Large children rested, hands deep in his coat pockets, waiting for Molly to finish her phone call. Sensing her attention, he looked up from studying his shoes and began walking towards her. She suddenly wished she had done more than brush on a lick of mascara that morning and pull her hair into a loose ponytail. As he made his way through the graves of old pioneers she tried to school her expression into the right degree of anger, except she couldn't get the muscles to work properly. Despite her intentions, her mouth insisted on pulling up at the corners.

'Fancy meeting you here,' he said with a shrug, stopping a couple of metres away from her. As if she might bite.

'What are you doing here?' she asked lamely.

'I took a couple of weeks off. I've never been to Tasmania before.'

'B-but . . . h-h . . . w-w . . .' The only words she could assemble were a horrible confusion of random Scrabble letters. What did you say to a man who had flown ten thousand miles to see you, a man you had said you never wanted to see again?

'Richard forwarded your travel plans to me. He said he meant to email me a link to a very nice irrigation system he was considering installing. But I have my suspicions.'

Wouldn't it have been easier to pick up the telephone and call me? she wanted to ask. But all that came out of her mouth was, 'Uh-huh.'

'I did try calling before you left Devon, but you didn't pick up. So I decided to wait,' he said, running a hand through that floppy front bit of his hair that had been blown about by the wind. 'To give you time.'

'Uh-huh,' she said, crossing her arms in front of her chest in a protective gesture. Okay, a defensive gesture.

'You bolted, Molly. I knew you were skittish but you took off like a jittery mare frightened by a plastic bag. I had to wait it out, let you calm down.'

She wasn't sure how she felt about being compared to a horse. But he had come such a long way, so she supposed she should make allowances. He had flown all the way to Melbourne or Sydney, then another plane to Hobart, and then probably driven to Swansea . . . and waited for her. She didn't know how long he had been sitting in a car nearby, watching. He had done all that for her.

'You went behind my back,' she snapped.

'I know. I felt bad about that. But that was before I knew you. And once I got to know you, it was already *fait accompli*.'

'You mean when you started fucking me.'

'No, when I started loving you.'

'You shouldn't have told me about the testing,' she said, before registering his last words. What had he said?

'Maybe not, except the genetic test was like a wall – for me, anyway – I couldn't get past it. Every time I kissed you, it was there between us. When we made love, I felt like I was lying to you. I didn't want to have secrets from you.'

But she was still stuck on his earlier words. 'You started loving me?'

There were only a few steps between them but at that moment the distance felt like ten thousand miles. If she closed that gap, it would be so hard to go back. And if she gave in to her feelings, how could she be sure that it was Lucas Toms she loved, with all his faults, and not another surfer boy who might save her from herself?

'Yep.' He looked so gormless standing there with his hands in his pockets, making a somewhat untidy declaration of love in the middle of a graveyard in a small town at the bottom of the world. Surely she must have imagined those three small words . . . ?

'I think I have earwax.'

'Oh, Molly, Molly, Molly, you are such a—'

'Trial? Fool? Bother?'

'Delight. You are such a delight. A troublesome one, of course, who makes a man fly halfway around the world in order to get her attention.'

'I think you've got my attention,' she sighed.

'I want more than your attention.'

She took another deep breath. 'I don't know how much more I have to give. I'm still finding my way.'

He combed his hand through his hair as if he could straighten her out too. 'You're worried about the end of the journey before we've done more than hop aboard.'

Was that true? Was she too wound up in thoughts of the destination? Too worried about taking the easy way, on the one hand, and too afraid of taking a risk, on the other, so that she was immobilised? Lucas had once lost a girl who thought Devon was too far from London, yet he was ready to gamble on a girl who lived half a world away. Was she really such a coward?

'Just relax and see what happens,' he said, with a shrug of his eyebrows.

She looked at him, standing there in his overcoat and plaid scarf, and said, 'Do you surf?'

'Who, me? No. But I could give it a go if it was important,' he said with a puzzled expression. 'Is it important?'

'No. Not any more.'

Taking a step towards him, she slipped her hands inside his overcoat to encircle his body. Perhaps it wasn't so difficult, to take that first step, you just had to be firm with your legs. You had to trust yourself not to fall. You had to let yourself be happy.

Lucas took his hands from his pockets and enfolded her in his arms, pressing against her. It was warmer now. They were generating their own heat like a radiator. He felt so good that she was afraid it might be difficult to let go. No matter how much practice she got at letting go, she feared she would never be very good at it.

'But we live so far apart,' she said, arching back to look up at him. She couldn't help worrying.

'Sometimes you have to take a leap of faith. If we want to be together, we'll find a way to do what we need to do. You might decide I'm a pain in the arse once you get to know me better.'

What if Lucas decided she was a pain in the arse? What then? She supposed she would learn to live with that too.

'And at least we'll be racking up decent frequent flyer miles,' he said, already awake to her foibles.

So he thought he knew her that well already, did he? Well, maybe she needed practice at surprising him. She thought she might enjoy that. She reached up to kiss him. His lips were cold and dry from the wind but she would soon warm them up. They stood locked together for a few minutes, trying to get as close as possible, until she suddenly had a thought.

'We're cousins. I wonder what number. Third, fourth . . . fifth?'

'Kissing cousins.'

'Mmm, definitely,' she agreed, locking lips with him to prove it. 'I wonder how Ivy did it?' she said a little while later. 'Disappeared.'

'She probably had a plan. She would have been living with her deceit for forty years, knowing she could be discovered at any time. When she realised she would be unmasked if Robert arrived, she must have put that plan into motion.'

Men were so practical, she thought – always with the plan, the strategy – but that wasn't what she meant. What she couldn't understand is how Ivy could have left her children and grandchildren, how she could have gone away with no hope of seeing them again. Surely it would have been easier to face the consequences of her deception? It may still have been the end for her and Jim, but she would have kept her children and grandchildren.

She must have been so lonely, exiled here in Tasmania for fourteen long years. Like a convict of long ago. But perhaps she couldn't face seeing Robert again, her lost love, her brother. Perhaps she couldn't face those two worlds colliding. Or perhaps exile was her final act of contrition.

'Why here I wonder?' Lucas asked.

It must be strange for him, standing over the grave of a great-aunt he had thought dead almost a century ago, with his arms wrapped around this neurotic Aussie girl.

'Poor Ivy.' Had she ever managed to forgive herself?

54

Colombo, Ceylon

1919

Each breath was a struggle, loud and rapid, the sound filling the room with hoarse gasps. She was tired of listening to it. She was tired of watching the other girl's chest rise and fall, her limbs thrashing, her head tossing in delirium. She lost track of the hours she had spent sitting at this bedside, watching her struggle with death. She was so tired. All she wanted was to relinquish her vigil, and lay down her head. Why didn't it end? How long could the other girl suffer? Surely, it would be easier if she just let go. And always the niggling thought, what if it didn't end, what if she conquered the infection that was overwhelming her body and found the strength to resume her life?

But Ivy couldn't bear that to happen. Not now, not after she had sat through endless hours of this torturous breathing . . . Her eyes were so heavy, her head bobbing on her chest. All she wanted to do was sleep.

But she couldn't. Not yet. Not until the other girl was gone. And then she could finally get on with her new life in Australia.

Except it didn't have to be like that. She didn't have to inherit her mother's life. She could have her own turn at being the princess. She was Edward Luscombe's daughter too, wasn't she?

No one at the hotel knew them. Two sick young British

women languishing in a hotel room. If one slipped into oblivion and died, who could be certain which one? Both were fair, with light-coloured eyes and similar features. And if a porter had noticed that one was tall and one was short, how could he be certain which of them was which? She could alter Rose's gowns to fit, and the garments would attest to her identity. What maid wore silk, velvet and pearls? She was familiar enough with Rose's signature to attempt a fair copy, and the sisters looked similar enough for the passport photograph to pass a cursory inspection. If anyone thought to question her, she could blame a change in her looks upon the terrible flu she had suffered.

If Rose should die, Ivy could assume her identity and her life. And maybe it would go some way towards making up for all she had lost. Maybe it would fill the blackness that had dogged Ivy her entire life.

But if Rose recovered, she would return to her role of handmaiden.

And still Rose fought the sickness like a wraith, eyes sunken in her head, livid brown patches spotting her cheeks, arms and legs twitching. She hadn't called for her mother for hours – only wordless cries and the endless, tortured gasping for breath. How could she claw her way back to the living, to Jim Turner and Wuurnong, now? She was too far gone. Poor thing.

Someone should ease her pain.

Robert wouldn't want to see his sister suffer, for he had clasped Rose to him in the end, not Ivy. He had taken Rose in his arms while his eyes refused to acknowledge Ivy at all. Rose had poisoned their love as surely as Elsie, and now she was suffering horribly for her crime.

Someone should put her out of her misery, shouldn't they? No one deserved to die like this. Not even Rose. Robert wouldn't like it.

Almost as if sleepwalking, Ivy stood up from the chair she had placed at the bedside and crossed to the other bed to retrieve a pillow. She didn't want to disturb the sick girl by snatching the one from beneath her head. Returning, she held the pillow poised in the air for a moment then quickly, before she could change her mind, before Rose woke, she brought it down upon that once-perfect face, smothering that dreadful rasping sound once and for all.

If she stopped to consider, she would have expected Rose to drift from restless slumber into effortless peace. Except even the dying possess the instinct to survive, the will to thrash and kick and buck the pillow from their face. For days, each breath had been a struggle; Rose wasn't about to surrender to death without a last stand. Yet she was weakened by illness and the long weeks at sea, weaker even than a girl who retained some vestige of her wiry maid's strength, a girl who had wrestled for her place in the world with her brother, sparred with her mistress, resisted her father.

So Ivy held firm, the weight of all her enmity, all her fear, all her longing pressing down upon her childhood playmate. All her conflicted feelings of love and hate, jealousy and sorrow weighing upon her soul, until gradually the other girl stopped thrashing, stopped fighting.

Stopped.

It was done.

And Ivy's second life hung shimmering before her, if she chose to reach out and grasp it.

'Goodbye, Rose. I loved you once.'

55

Gold Coast, Queensland

2018

She wasn't certain why she was here on the Gold Coast, but Lucas had convinced her that a week in the sun, away from computer screens, would be a great break for both of them. She could see his reasoning – for who wouldn't want to take a break from an English winter in Australia's holiday playground? – except the decision was more complicated for her.

'I'll have to buy a new bikini,' she protested when he suggested it. 'I haven't been swimming for ages.'

'Can I come with you? I'm quite handy in a dressing room.'

'I'll bet you are.'

So here they were, on their first morning at Broadbeach, brilliant white sand and glistening towers stretching to the horizon in either direction. Eight o'clock with the sun already biting, the beach bustling with runners, walkers, and toddlers digging at the water's edge. Lifeguards had set up flags at intervals along the beach and were watching the swimmers from raised platforms atop the dunes, as the breakers rolled in, blue and foaming white. Postcard perfect.

'I think I'll take a dip,' Lucas said, after they had spread their towels above the waterline. 'Coming?' He tilted his head to one side and raised his eyebrows questioningly.

'In a minute,' she answered, fishing around in her bag for sunglasses. 'You go ahead, I'll join you once I've warmed up a bit.'

'Don't be long. You need to test out the new bikini.'

He jogged towards the water, splashing through the shallows in his red swimming trunks and winter-white skin. He wouldn't last thirty minutes before he started turning pink, even slathered in sunscreen. She removed her light cotton shirt and sat on her towel, leaning back on her elbows so that she could sun herself as she watched him. He looked so out of place amongst the tanned, retired couples and pink-zinced kids, the girls in bikinis and surfers in summer-weight wetsuits. But it didn't seem to bother him, moored waist deep, with the waves washing around him.

The water beckoned. The sun warmed her face. Maybe she could join him.

She stood up and strode towards the water before she changed her mind, kicking up sand as her feet squeaked across the beach, then as she drew closer to the water, toes squelching through the sludge. She let the foam trickle over her feet and tickle her ankles as she ventured into the shallows. Lucas hadn't seen her yet; he was looking out to sea. She waded knee deep, then thigh deep, as the waves splashed for the shore. He was up to his chest now, bobbing over each swell. His feet would be touching the bottom, then springing up to buoy him above the waves. She remembered that feeling, of being borne aloft by the ocean. She took another step and then hesitated as the waters swished around her waist.

At that moment he turned and saw her heading his way. He raised an arm and even from twenty metres she could tell that his face had broken into a delighted smile. She glanced at his upraised hand to see him gesturing to her – not waving, not beckoning, but a thumbs up. Everything was okay. And then he opened his mouth and she caught his words faintly, above the sound of swirling waves, 'I love you, Molly.'

And that was it, she realised. *That's* what her father had been saying as he drifted away from her. That's what she had locked in her memory, what shock had concealed – her father's last goodbye.

'I love you, Molly.'

'I love you, Dad,' she whispered as she propelled her body through the waves.

56

Tasmania

1963

Ivy didn't recall how long she had been walking, following the banks of the Mersey River to its mouth before she reached the coast. It was enough that she had reached this triangular island, her place of exile. Last night her heart had danced a quickstep, all through the long hours of the crossing, reminiscent of that other longer journey many years ago. Once upon a time, she had kept to her cabin for fear of exposure as an imposter; now she was afraid she would be recognised for herself.

Pebbles crunched underfoot as she trudged through drifts of pale wood washed up along the shore. Behind her *The Princess of Tasmania* lay at her moorings, preparing to make the return journey across the water to Port Phillip Bay. On a grassy bluff to her right, a lighthouse stood watch over Bass Strait, with hundreds of miles of meandering coastline stretching both west and east. Perhaps, no matter which direction she took, she would end up back where she began. Wasn't that the story of her life? Of both her lives? Travelling far, seeking safe haven, yet always an exile.

That was her reparation.

She thought of Robert, arriving at Wuurnong to find her gone. She imagined him clattering over cattle grids in a smooth shiny car, waiting expectantly in the front parlour, only to be told that Rose was dead and gone. Would he mourn her, his estranged sister . . . his Rose? Or had he mourned enough? And what of Jim? Would he mourn Rose, or had their marriage died long since?

The wind blustered around her, picking up spray and tossing it in her face. She licked her lips, tasting salt and with it the ever-present bitterness that had tainted even the sweetest moments of her life. Sometimes she wondered if grief and bitterness were one and the same thing. Surely to grieve was to be bitter with loss? Resentful that something precious had been stolen from you. In her own fashion, she too had mourned Rose, her grief tainted with bitterness. For despite her guilt, she couldn't forgive them. The Luscombes, who had stolen her past and her future.

She wondered if there was still time to reclaim that lost self, here on this verdant isle, oceans distant from the one where she was born. She might have years remaining to her. Years to find a place to settle; discover something useful to do, mark time. Perhaps one day she might even have a window seat where she could curl up and do nothing at all if she pleased. And if her heart ached for her children, well, that was the price she must pay. For Rose's second life. Her third life.

What could she do but go on?

Turning away from the lapping waves, she began the walk back along the river to the bus station.

At the ticket window she asked the attendant, 'If I travel west, can I go all the way around?'

He scratched his thinning hair, looking at her in amusement. 'You won't get far with that plan, love. Only lost in the wilderness.'

But she had been lost for too long already.

'East then, I'll go east.'

Perhaps in the east she would find what she was looking for.

Acknowledgements

This book has had a lengthy gestation, and I would like to thank my partner Vincent Kwok, my daughter Ru Kwok and son Kit Kwok for their continued patience and encouragement with this writer's doubts and torments. I would also like to thank my agent Judith Murdoch, for her continued support and championing, and my editor Kate Byrne and the team at Headline, for their enthusiasm for this story.

Much of this novel takes place in the south-west of Victoria, Australia, where the characters' family settled. I lived in this region for a short time as a young woman and have travelled and holidayed there many times in the decades since. I would like to acknowledge the traditional owners of these regions, the Gunditjmara, Girai Wurrung, and Djargurd Wurrung peoples, who have made this area their home for tens of thousands of years. It's a wonderful place to visit.